PRAIRIE

PRAIRIE

Greg Tobin

BOOK-OF-THE-MONTH CLUB • NEW YORK

Produced by Book Creations Inc.
George S. Engel, Executive Producer

Map copyright © 1997 by Book Creations Inc.

http://www.randomhouse.com

Library of Congress Catalog Card Number: 97-93220

ISBN 0-345-38946-8

Manufactured in the United States of America

This hardcover edition was especially created for Book-of-the-Month Club
by arrangement with Ballantine Books.

Author's Note

It is important to credit the source of the creation myth that comprises a large part of the first chapters of this book. I adapted ideas, themes, and narrative sections from a book that provided much valuable background material for *Prairie*. The source is a classic ethnographic text, *The Omaha Tribe* by Alice C. Fletcher and Francis La Flesche (University of Nebraska Press); mine is a well-thumbed 1992 Bison Books edition.

In a very real and practical sense, this novel was a collaboration: from the original idea and outline, in the research and writing, and, of course, through the editing process and publication.

Paul Block of Book Creations, Inc., offered me the opportunity to develop the story from his powerful concept. Pamela Strickler of Ballantine Books acquired the book based on a less-than-detailed outline and guided me through an intensely valuable revision process early on. Doug Grad took on the project for Ballantine at a later stage and saw it smoothly into print.

Pamela Lappies and Elizabeth Tinsley, BCI editors, wrestled with hundreds of pages of sometimes unwieldy prose and many days of author tardiness—and I am grateful they did. Behind the scenes in Canaan, New York, Sally Smith and George Engel, the president of BCI, worked hard on my behalf and were always there when I needed them.

My thanks to Linda Grey, the president of Ballantine Books, who strongly supported the editorial, marketing, and sales efforts for the book. Also, I appreciate the enthusiastic contribution of Bob Crofut, the cover artist.

I relied most heavily on James Reasoner, a treasured friend in a time of need, and a fellow author, for support in the research and writing of the first draft. His experience and counsel got me to the other side when I was certain I would not get there.

Finally, I am grateful to my wife, Maureen, and to my sons, Patrick and Bryan, who gave me the time and space necessary to work on this book over the last five years.

G.T.

March 30, 1997

This novel is dedicated to the memory of Greg Stephens,
coach and teacher, of William Chrisman High School
in Independence, Missouri.
From him I learned that history is *alive*.

I have made a footprint, a sacred one.
I have made a footprint; through it the blades push
      upward.
I have made a footprint; over it the blades move in
      the wind.
I have made a footprint; over it the ears lean
      toward one another.
I have made a footprint; over it I bend the stalk
      to pluck the ears.
I have made a footprint; over it the blossoms lie
      gray.
I have made a footprint; smoke arises from my
      house.
I have made a footprint; there is cheer in my
      house.
I have made a footprint; I live in the light of
      day.

                —"The Planting Song," Osage

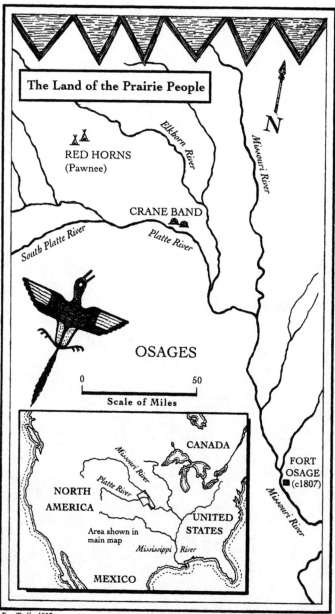

The Land of the Prairie People

RED HORNS
(Pawnee)

Elkhorn River

Missouri River

N

CRANE BAND

South Platte River

Platte River

OSAGES

0   50
Scale of Miles

CANADA

Missouri River

Platte River

NORTH
AMERICA

UNITED
STATES

Area shown in
main map

Mississippi River

MEXICO

FORT
OSAGE
(c1807)

Missouri River

Ron Toelke 1997

©Book Creations Inc., 1997

PART I

The Storm Seeker

Chapter One

Circa 1400 C.E.

In the Moon of the Deer Pawing the Earth, Moon Hawk Sister, one of the older unmarried girls of the Crane band, gathered the children by a large fire in the center of the village.

It was the night before the Crane band was to depart, eventually to join the other bands of the Prairie People on the spring buffalo hunt. A few infirm and old people would stay behind in the town. The able men, women, and children would be away for fifty sleeps, and their earthen lodges would stand empty until their return.

Tonight the men sat in council, singing, smoking, and planning the hunt under the leadership of the Master of the Hunt, who held the ceremonial staff. The women packed supplies, talking quietly about the journey that lay ahead. Grandmothers helped younger women in their labors, following the example of their own grandmothers.

The hunt was anticipated prayerfully and with great excitement among the people.

Darkness had long since fallen, and a chill breeze teased the smoke as the children, tired from packing and playing—the boys having "hunted" with sticks all day—heeded Moon Hawk Sister and sat quietly by the fire.

The young woman said, "It is good that you rest this night, for there will be much hard work and many long days of travel ahead."

"Where are our mothers?" one of the male children asked. It was a ritual the night before the hunt.

"They pack the lodge skins and poles so we will not be without a home when we travel."

"Where are our fathers?"

3

"They sit near the Sacred Pole and ask Wakon-tah, the Creator, to strengthen their hearts and guide their arrows into the heart of Brother Buffalo."

Moon Hawk Sister was a tall girl of seventeen summers with shimmering raven hair that fell past the soft white shoulders of her deerskin dress. In the firelight her eyes seemed even wider to the twoscore boys and girls in her charge. They looked up to her as a leader at such times.

A boy said, "Sing us the story-song of the creation."

"Yes, the story-song has been sung many times for the children of our people. For the grandfathers of our grandfathers it was sung, and for their grandfathers." Moon Hawk Sister breathed in the pungent smoke of the burning cottonwood limbs before she began. "Way beyond, in a time before the memory, the ancestors of our people lived in the sky among the stars, and their life there was good. But they were curious, like children." The storysinger glanced around at the upturned faces illuminated in the firelight.

" 'Where did we come from?' they asked each other. Of course, no one among them knew their true origin. They asked their brothers the stars, but the stars did not know. The stars said, 'Ask our father the sun.'

"So the people traveled a long way to the sun. When they found him, they asked him, 'Are you our father? Will you tell us where we come from?' The sun was silent and did not answer. Our ancestors spent many seasons with the sun and always asked him these questions—but he would not answer them. Then one day he became angry at their asking and told them to go away. He said, 'You are my most bothersome children, and I am tired of you.'

"They knew now that the sun was indeed their father, and they made another long journey, this time to see the moon and to ask her their questions about where they came from. The moon said, 'I birthed you, and the sun is your father. He told me that one day you would come to me like this to find out who bore you. He told me that on the day you receive the answer to your question you must leave your home and go down to the earth and dwell there.'

"The people asked the moon, 'Why must we now go away when we have just learned the truth about our birth?' The moon said, 'This is your father's way, and we must obey him in all things. Go, children, and remember your father, the sun, and your mother, the moon, who love you.'

"And so, in that long-ago time, way beyond, our ancestors journeyed to the earth, and their sorrows as the First People began.

"The earth was covered with water. They plunged from the sky into the water. Some of them drowned, but others swam to the surface and looked around and saw nothing but water everywhere. They wept and cried out for help. No one answered their plea, neither the sun nor the moon nor the gods. They despaired, fearing that all would drown and the race would perish forever. Still they cried out, and at last help came to them.

"The elk, who is the finest and most stately animal, came down from the sky and dove into the water. The elk's bravery inspired hope in the people. The muskrat also was inspired and came down into the water that covered the earth. Next the beaver came down. Next the loon came down. Next, the crane. Then the crawfish came down. Many animals followed the brave elk and came down to the earth to help the people.

"Most importantly, the elk's prayer was heard by the four winds. The winds came from everywhere: the east, the north, the west, and the south. They met at the place where the people and the animals were together in the water. The winds with their strength carried much of the water upward into the sky.

"At first the people could see only rocks, and they clung for life to these. The people and the animals traveled on the rocky places looking for something to eat, but no plants grew there. Then, after many days, as the waters dried and went down, the soft earth was seen by the people. They were glad. And the great elk in his happiness rolled over and over on the rich earth, and all his loose hair clung to the soil. These hairs came to life in the earth, and from them grew beans, potatoes, and wild turnips, and from them grew all the trees and grasses that cover our lands like a soft green-and-yellow blanket.

"Other creatures lived under the earth, and they came up out of the ground: the cougar, the bear, the deer, and the buffalo. Fishes, who had lived in the water, now swam in the rivers and lakes formed when the water was taken from the higher lands.

"The First People were amazed and thanked the elk for the gift of his prayer to the winds—which is why we revere the elk as our elder brother today. They ate beans and potatoes and turnips until their bellies were achingly full. The people were naked and they had no shame, but when many more days passed and the winds returned to the earth, they desired covering.

"So they took the fiber of plants and grasses and wove coverings for their bodies. Now they became stronger and needed more food, and they felt poor and hungry and without good shelter from the winds, who were friends of the people but difficult to live with.

"The people thought, What shall we do to help ourselves? And one man took up a stick to use as a club and killed a deer. He brought it to the people and said, 'Here is food that will give us strength, for the deer has blood like ours and flesh like ours.' The people ate the deer, then asked, 'What else shall we do to help ourselves?'

"One of the men began chipping stones. He found a blue stone that flaked easily and could be made sharp—so he made a knife, then a lance point, which he fixed to a long stick. And the people now had knives and lances to hunt with, but the season grew colder and they thought, What shall we do to be warm?

"A man found an elm root that was very dry and dug a hole and put a stick in it. When he rubbed the stick, smoke rose from the elm root. He smelled it, and others smelled it and came to him and helped him to rub. At last a spark came. They blew on the spark until it flamed. In this way fire came to the people, and they began to cook their deer meat, and it was delicious.

"After this, the First People used the shoulder blade of the deer to cut grasses and built lodges with the grass, just as they had made clothing to cover themselves. Now the cold of the first winter came, and the clothing was not enough to protect them. The people were unhappy, and they thought, What can we do to have something better to wear?

"One woman picked up a deer hide and took a stone knife and scraped down the hide to make it thin. Then she rubbed the hide with grass and with her hands to make it soft. She said, 'We will use the hide for clothing.' Now the people had warm coverings.

"They were always trying to better themselves. When the

winds whistled through their grass-thatch lodges, they said, 'How shall we make our houses better?' Then they took bark and covered their dwellings with it. And so the people had warm lodges, clothing, food, and fire—and they survived their first winter upon the earth."

Moon Hawk Sister paused to ask the children to put some more wood on the fire. The night wind carried the blue-white smoke southward, and the dry wood flamed brightly. The children felt the heat on their cheeks and the coolness of the night on their backs. They loved this time of year: the hungry nights of winter were only a memory; the first of two corn, bean, and melon crops had been planted; the most important event of the year was nigh; and when it was finished, the lazy days of summer would be upon them.

Dogs roamed the village this night. They, too, were a part of the hunt, for they carried the lodgepoles, lodge skins, food supplies, cooking utensils, clothing, and parfleches of ceremonial gear upon travois lashed to their sturdy, narrow backs. How the first dogs were found was part of the story Moon Hawk Sister told.

When the fire was rebuilt and the children settled again, she continued.

"In the spring, during the time of the Little Frog Moon, the people emerged from their bark houses and began to explore the lands around them. One man wandered to the south, where he found some kernels that were blue, red, and white. He thought these were things of great value, so he concealed them in a mound and went back to his people.

"Many days later he remembered his treasures and went back to see if they were safe. When he came to the mound, he saw it was covered with green stalks bearing ears with kernels of these colors. He brought an ear of each kind back to his people, and they tasted it and found it good.

"This is how corn came to them. They took the shoulder blade of a deer and made mounds, as had the man who first found the kernels, and they cultivated corn, which became abundant. Corn has been food for our people ever since."

The girl continued, "Another man wandered to the east, where tall forests grew and there were great lakes that no one could see across all the way. He made a boat from the bark of a birch tree and traveled along the shores, where he fished. Another First Man, who went north, discovered two young animals that were smaller than bears but larger than beavers. These he brought home and fed, and they grew strong but were not wild. He found they would carry burdens, so he fixed a harness on them and fastened pine poles to them, and they became bearers of burden for the people. This saved much labor for the people, so they bred dogs for this purpose.

"Always the people tried to improve themselves, and they never lost their curiosity. In this way they discovered how to make stone axes and lodge skins and how to use sinew to sew skins together and how to use animal bones for tools as well."

A black-eyed boy of seven summers, Muskrat, who always felt pride to hear of his namesake's role in the creation tale, said: "Tell us of the first buffalo hunt. Why did the people ever kill such a great animal who has such powerful medicine?"

Moon Hawk Sister said, "You are just like the First People—always asking questions. Sometimes it got them into trouble, remember? But it is good to ask. In that way you learn." She laughed, as did all the other children except Muskrat, who was a serious young holy-man-in-waiting. He crossed his arms over his chest and scowled.

"Many generations passed, and the people still dwelled near the First Place. It was in the forest country to the east, many sleeps from here." The tall girl pointed in the direction of the sunrise. A hush fell over her listeners. "The people learned many things and formed our bands and societies, and the men and women worked together to keep their children safe and well fed and happy. There were times of war with other tribes, and hungry times among the people. Some of them were worried and prayed to be shown what they must do to keep our bands united and prosperous. It was in this time that the ancient cedar pole came to us and became our Sacred Pole."

The sky was a black blanket upon which the stars shone with cold brilliance. The moon was like a bright shell hanging over the village, and the smoke rose to touch it and cover its face. All eyes, however, were fixed on Moon Hawk Sister as she reached the part of the legend that told of a critical turning point for the people.

"In the wooded country near the big lakes, the people lived in a village that was well known to other tribes. And our people were respected for their skills in war and in council. The men were thought handsome, and the women were considered pretty and very clever in their ways. So when tribes of the region wished to have a council, they sent their peace chiefs to the village to agree on terms of peace and rules of hunting and warfare, and to adopt a peace ceremony.

"A young man, the son of a chief of our people, was away hunting during the many-day council of his elders. On his way home through the forest he lost his way. Night came, and he was exhausted. He looked for signs and looked to the stars for direction, but he was confused and began to be afraid—even though he was one of the bravest of the hunters. He stopped to rest and suddenly noticed a light nearby.

"He thought it was probably a lodge, so he went toward it. But the young hunter was amazed when he saw that the light came from a tall tree that burned with intense brightness. A Thunder Bird atop the tree flapped its wings. The trunk and every branch and every leaf were afire, yet the tree was not consumed. He approached the tree. No heat came from the fire, and no other tree burned, nor the grass around the great tree. The hunter touched the burning tree, but his hand was not burned. He knelt by the tree all night and watched it burn.

"As the sun rose the Thunder Bird flew away, the fiery vision died, and the tree resumed its natural appearance. Mystified by this strange vision, the hunter stayed another night and saw the same thing. When the Thunder Bird alit, the tree burst into flame. The next morning he found the trail home, and when he got back to his village, he went straight to his father, one of the elders who sat in council. He told the old man of the vision, but the old man was silent, for the chiefs were still in council.

"When finally everything was decided and agreed upon among the tribes, the old man stood in council and said, 'My son has seen a wonderful tree that is afire at night when the Thunder Bird comes, but does not burn during the day.'

"When the chiefs heard the tale of the spirit tree, they sent scouts to investigate, and the scouts returned to say it was true: they saw the tree burning, yet not consumed by the flames. Another council was called, and the chiefs sat together again to consider what this vision meant. They prayed and talked and sang. Then the chiefs said, 'Let our young warriors conquer this great tree.' So the warriors prepared as if for battle, stripping off their clothing and putting on their paint and their ornaments of war. In the morning they ran from the village and raced each other, men from many tribes, as if into battle against a great enemy.

"The first to reach his goal was one of the warriors of our people, and he stood before the magnificent tree in awe of its beauty. Then he struck the tree and counted coup as our own warriors do today. The others came behind him, and all struck or touched the spirit tree, and they cut it down. It took six men at a time to carry the tree back to the village.

"Once there, the chiefs and holy men sang their songs and performed new ceremonies to honor the tree and the brave men who had captured it. A big lodge was constructed in the center of the village, and there the tree was kept. The chiefs and holy men worked upon the tree, trimmed its branches, and called it a human being. They painted it and decorated it with grasses, feathers, and animal skins. One of the chiefs said, 'It has no hair!' So a war chief brought a very large scalp lock and fixed it to the top of the pole. Then the chiefs called together all the people.

"Before the lodge the Sacred Pole stood, leaning upon a strong crotched stick. The men, women, and children came to see it and to hear the story of the tree. When they were gathered, just as the chiefs began to speak, a Thunder Bird flew into the village and circled the Sacred Pole four times, then flew away to the west.

"A chief said, 'Here is a great mystery, the fire tree that now lives among the people; we shall bring our questions and troubles to this Sacred Pole with gifts and prayers, and the Pole will be protected and anointed by Keepers from the clan of the First People for all time yet to come; the Keepers shall have a voice in council, in deciding who are the chiefs and when there will be a war, and in all matters of government.' "

Moon Hawk Sister continued, "This, then, was the first anointing ceremony, which we now have in the Moon of the Bellowing Buffalo."

Muskrat, who had been shifting restlessly through the telling of the legend, could no longer contain his impatience. "Moon Hawk Sister, you promised to sing of our brother the buffalo and the first hunt."

She said, "You know that a story must be told in its proper way. I am getting to that part of it, little friend."

Raising her hands, palms turned skyward, Moon Hawk Sister looked up at the cloud-veiled moon. The cadence of her recitation slowed now. She prayed to Eagle, chief of all sky spirits, to carry her words into the hearts of her young listeners.

"On this night before the hunt, when our leader fasts and seeks visions of Brother Buffalo, let the Creator guide his sight and embolden his heart. And may all of us be given strength to perform our tasks for the welfare of the people."

Her gaze shifted to Muskrat again. "It was a time of great trouble and grief for the people. The Sacred Pole had brought order and ceremony to the people who desired to live in peace. But a jealous tribe, who had not attended the great council, made war against the people and killed many—and nearly captured the Sacred Pole. Our people abandoned their village and, with deep sadness for the loss of many warriors as well as women and children, moved to the west. They crossed the wide Father of Waters and traveled many days—always to the west.

"The people came into contact with other tribes during this journey, and some of the smaller bands joined up with them. With so many new members among them, they needed to form a government to keep order, so they appointed seven wise men to a council. The First People and the new people agreed to this way of government.

"They crossed the River of Raccoons and came to the Wild Waters, where they lived for a time in bark lodges on the east bank.

"Across the river was a people who lived in earthen lodges and cultivated corn. At first our people raided these villages across the river, but the earth-lodge people wanted only peace. A ceremony was held, and our people forded the Wild Waters to live ever after on the west side of the river and adopt the ways of the earth lodge.

"The women laid out the circles for these lodges. Men cut the lodgepoles and placed one in each of the four directions and tied frames for doors and smoke holes. Women fixed willow branches and sections of sod to finish the lodge.

So, this is how our villages came to be in the land between two rivers—the Wild Waters and the Flat River. Here the people first saw the vast herds of buffalo that lived in the greatest numbers beyond their forest homeland. And here the people began to hunt Brother Buffalo for his meat, his bone, his skin.

"From the other tribes of the region our people learned the way of the hunt. The Sacred Pole became an ally by giving the people strength and cunning in the hunt. Along with farming ways, earth lodges, and the hunting of the buffalo, the people learned new arts of warfare and became skilled traders. They became known for their wisdom in council and their ability to see spirits."

A large log split and fell into the fire with a crash and a sudden updraft of sparks. The young listeners started. Moon Hawk Sister said, "That is the end of the story-song of the First People, for we are their children who live on this prairie. Tomorrow we leave for the spring buffalo hunt. Go now to your houses, to your mothers. Sleep and dream of the great deeds of our people. When Father Sun rises, we shall put him at our backs and begin our journey."

When the children had gone, she stirred the glowing red logs, the heat enveloping her face. Her heart was good.

Chapter Two

The village came to life with the rising of the sun. The flaps of hide that hung over the entrances of the lodges were thrust back as the people of the prairie emerged. Though this was one of the most important days of the year, the first day of the great hunt, there was no sense of urgency. The buffalo were out on the plains today, and they would be there tomorrow and the day after that and all the days to come. They were one of the gifts of Wakon-tah, come up out of their hole in the ground to live out their allotted time and then die so that the people could live.

Black Snake stepped out of his lodge and breathed deeply of the morning air, still crisp and cool with the season. Behind him, he could hear River Wind preparing the morning meal and their children, Little Rib and Feather, squabbling like a pair of jays. He smiled, the expression relieving somewhat the grim cast of his face.

He was a warrior, one of the leaders of the Crane band without holding a formal position as such. There had been talk among the men that he should aspire to the role of *wathon*—the Master of the Hunt, the one who would guide the people to the buffalo and direct their actions. It was a position of great honor, but Black Snake had declined the suggestion. The Master of the Hunt was required to hold himself aloof from his friends and relatives, even from his wife, during the duration of the hunt and for a time before it began, and Black Snake was not certain he could endure being separated from River Wind even for a few days. She was his light, illuminating his life as surely as the flaming orb above lit the day.

One of the unmarried women, the tall, comely girl called Moon Hawk Sister, hurried past him, bent on some task. Black Snake did not smile at her; a married man was not supposed to take too much interest in the virgins of the band. But in his eyes was approval. She would make some man a fine wife.

All around the village, the women were dismantling the tipis. They fastened the poles to the dogs for travois and placed the rolled-up skins of the walls between the poles, along with pouches containing food and supplies for the coming journey. The earthen lodges remained standing so that the people could return to them when the hunt was concluded.

In a tipi erected with solitude in mind, the Master of the Hunt fasted alone, as he had for the past four days. When everyone else had departed, he would follow, carrying his moccasins, still praying to the spirits to guide him and grant the people success in the hunt. The general direction of the trek had already been decided by the council of chiefs, and the Master of the Hunt would rejoin the band that night, after the first camp had been made. From then on, he would be in absolute control of everything that happened on the hunt. He would bear some of the credit for its success, if the spirits were favorable and the hunt was a good one, and he would bear *all* the blame if the hunt was poor. That was more responsibility than Black Snake desired.

"Come and eat," River Wind said from the entrance of the tipi. "Soon it will be time to leave."

Black Snake looked a moment longer at the rising sun, then said, "Yes. Soon."

Moon Hawk Sister's heart pounded heavily in her breast. She had been told only this morning that she would carry the *washa'be*, the ceremonial staff of the Master of the Hunt. It was always carried by a virgin during the journey of the people as they sought out the buffalo. She would walk near the keeper of an even more sacred artifact, the White Buffalo Hide. The Sacred Pipes were brought along by their keeper, as well, and with all three revered objects accompanying the people, there was no doubt in Moon Hawk Sister's mind that the spirits would bless them with abundant buffalo.

As she hurried toward the lodge of old One Horn, who would place the staff of the Master of the Hunt in her care, she passed Muskrat, who looked up at her with interest.

"Why are you in such a hurry this morning, Moon Hawk Sister?" he asked.

"I have been given an important task," she said. "I will carry the staff of the Master of the Hunt."

Muskrat's eyes widened as his usually solemn demeanor gave way to an expression of surprise. Then he managed to recover his composure. "This is good," he said. "This is an honorable task, and you will discharge it well."

Moon Hawk Sister smiled briefly, then went on. Muskrat was so serious sometimes—but this *was* a serious task.

Over the next hour the people ate their morning meal and concluded their preparations for leaving. Black Snake and River Wind, along with their children, were among the first to depart.

The rest of the people fell in behind them, forming a long, ragged line across the prairie as they walked toward the northwest. Many dogs accompanied the band, pulling burdens on travois. Near the front of the group were the Keeper of the White Buffalo Hide, the Keeper of the Sacred Pipes, and Moon Hawk Sister, struggling a little with the long, awkward staff of the Master of the Hunt.

Finally, when everyone had left the village except those who were too young, too old, or too sick to travel, along with a few warriors to protect them, the Master of the Hunt departed as well. He trailed the others by a considerable distance, trudging along in bare feet, his head lifted toward the heavens, his lips moving with prayers to Wakon-tah.

All day the people walked. It was late afternoon when they came to a halt and set up camp for the night. Later, when the Master of the Hunt caught up to them, he went directly to a tipi that had been prepared for him and entered it. No one approached him or spoke to him. He would continue his fast until the next morning, standing a lonely vigil as he chanted the final prayers. When the sun rose again, he would emerge and take his place as the leader of the expedition.

As night fell the glow of cooking fires shone through the hide walls of the tipis. Other than the absence of permanent lodges, this gathering of the band looked much like their regular village. But come morning, the people would take the tipis down and be on the move once more.

Inside the tipi of Black Snake, River Wind had prepared a pot of thin stew. She dipped it into wooden bowls and handed them to her husband and children. Black Snake brought the bowl to his mouth and drank some of the hot broth, his lips and tongue burning from the heat of it. He lowered the bowl and nodded in appreciation and approval to his wife. He had been very lucky to find a mate like River Wind following the death of his first wife, and he knew it.

The children were tired from the day's walk, and soon after they finished eating, Little Rib and Feather were rolled in their robes and sleeping soundly. Black Snake smoked his pipe for a time, then went to the robe of River Wind. Though her soft warmth in his arms made him long for her, he did not make love to her. Instead, he simply held her until she had gone to sleep, waiting for slumber to claim him as well.

It was a restless sleep that gripped him. He perspired profusely, despite the coolness of the night, and moaned softly as his head jerked from side to side. River Wind, sleeping soundly beside him, stirred briefly at the sound but did not awaken. Neither did Black Snake.

He rolled away from his wife and out of their sleeping robes. Shudders gripped his body for long moments. Finally, Black Snake's eyes snapped open, and he drew a deep, gasping breath into his body and sat up sharply, his hand going instinctively to the knife lying on the ground beside him.

But there was no foe here to fight. The dim glow of the embers showed him that much. The camp was quiet; no dogs barked, and no men cried out. The people of the Crane band were asleep, save those who had been given the job of standing watch. The people were not without enemies—but it seemed that none were about on the prairie tonight.

Black Snake passed a trembling hand across his face, wiping away the beads of sweat that had turned his skin cold. He looked at his wife and children and muttered a short prayer to Wakontah that they sleep safely and peacefully.

The details of his dream danced maddeningly inside his head, and though weariness gripped him, Black Snake was reluctant to lie down again. Those who knew him well knew that he and fear were strangers much of the time, but tonight was different.

Black Snake was afraid to go to sleep again, lest the dream rise up and claim him once more.

Finally, however, exhaustion overwhelmed him. He stretched out again, telling himself that he would not sleep. He would only rest for a short time. His eyes closed.

When he opened them again, dawn was fast approaching, and the camp was waking. Black Snake sat up and saw that River Wind was already bustling around the tipi, getting ready for the new day, the second day of the great hunt. Today the Master of the Hunt would send out runners, the fleetest-footed of the band's young men, to seek the buffalo. With luck, they would locate a suitable herd within the next day or two. Black Snake remembered his own youth and the times he had served as a

runner. He was thankful those days were gone, though he sometimes missed the feeling of his body being able to do without
complaint whatever he called upon it to do.

He was thankful as well that the dream had not returned to
him. He would say nothing of it to River Wind for the present,
he decided. Before he spoke of it to anyone, he would have to
consider it and try to understand what it had meant. The details
were vague now, but the feelings of dread it had provoked were
still strong within Black Snake.

The Master of the Hunt took command that day, and the
people of the Crane band did his bidding, continuing to the
northwest across the seemingly endless, unchanging prairie.
The sameness of the landscape was broken by a few rolling
hills and an occasional stream lined with small trees. For the
most part, however, this was grassland, as flat as the Flat River.

The runners went out full of enthusiasm but returned late in
the day with no news of the buffalo. The young men tried
mightily not to give in to despair. The Master of the Hunt
addressed them, Moon Hawk Sister standing by his side and
holding his staff.

"It is rare indeed to find a herd on the first day of the hunt, my
young friends," the Master told the runners. "You know this, so
do not worry. Go out again tomorrow, and perhaps then Wakon-
tah will guide your steps to the buffalo."

He was right, and everyone in the band knew it. One fruitless
day meant nothing. And yet, this hunt—the slaughtering of the
great animal that was so significant a part of the people's day-to-
day lives—was vitally important. Success in the hunt meant that
the people would have a good summer, a summer of relative
ease. Failure meant a season of struggle, and although it was
doubtful that anyone would starve, as they might during a winter
following a bad hunt, no one wanted to face the possibility of
having to exist for any length of time without the buffalo's
bounty.

The next day the runners went out again as the band continued
its northwestward march. Black Snake, still troubled by his
dream of two nights before but thankful that it had not returned
the previous night, glanced uneasily toward the west. Out there
somewhere was the land of the fierce Red Horn People, and

Black Snake did not want to encounter any of them. He feared not for himself but for the women and children. War was meant to be waged between men.

The spirits smiled on them, however, and at the middle of the day the runners returned, bringing with them news of the herd they had found. Camp was established, and from that point the true hunt would begin.

Black Snake was called before the Master of the Hunt along with the other men. The Master moved among them, tapping some of them on the shoulder with the sacred staff he now carried. Black Snake grunted in satisfaction when the Master included him among those so chosen. These men were responsible for discipline among the hunters. No loud noises that might frighten the buffalo were permitted, and no one was allowed to approach the herd prematurely for private hunting. Black Snake and his fellow officers would carry braided whips and mete out harsh punishment to anyone caught attempting either.

According to the runners, the herd was close enough that the hunt could be initiated this very afternoon. The Master singled out two young men to lead the approach to the buffalo. One was to carry the staff; the other was responsible for a pipestem that would be tied to the staff once the two of them had circled the herd.

Moon Hawk Sister watched in envy as the young man chosen by the Master took the staff from her. A girl was suitable for carrying the staff during the march, but not for this part of the hunt.

Beside her, a voice said, "*You* could carry the staff."

She looked down and saw Muskrat standing there. Summoning a smile despite her own resentment, she said, "This is true. I could carry the staff. But such is not the way of our people."

"Perhaps the old ways are not always the best."

"Do not let anyone hear you saying such a thing," she warned him. "You will be a holy man someday. It will be your duty to carry out the old ways and preserve them."

Muskrat sighed, making it clear that he carried a heavy burden for one so young.

* * *

Among the hunters, Black Snake was alert for any disturbance or impatience on the part of the other men as they
approached the herd. The two young men selected by the Master
trotted around the herd on foot in opposite directions, each
bearing the sacred object entrusted to him, forming a spirit line
around the buffalo that, it was hoped, would help contain the
beasts. When they met on the far side of the herd, they stopped,
and one of them tied the pipestem to the staff, which the other
raised high in the air and then thrust hard into the ground. A
great shout went up from the men.

The hunt had begun.

Arrows flew through the air as the men charged toward the
buffalo. His duties as an officer now at an end, Black Snake
joined in the shouting. He drew back his bowstring with his
powerful arm and sent a shaft whistling through the air toward
the buffalo. He was pleased to see it lodge deep in the side of one
of the creatures, just behind the front legs. A perfect shot, he
thought. Wakon-tah had guided his aim. The wounded buffalo,
startled and in pain, lurched forward a few steps before going to
its knees and rolling over onto its side.

Two more young men, also selected by the Master of the
Hunt, already moved among the herd, risking death from the
uninjured buffalo as they knelt beside the fallen beasts to harvest
the tongues and the hearts. Tonight, when the hunt was finished,
those tongues and hearts would make up the sacred feast in
which the chiefs, the Master, and a few other honored men
would take part. Black Snake hoped to be among them.

Dust rose thickly into the air, along with the shouts of the men
and the bellows of mortally wounded buffalo. Many of the
beasts had bolted, escaping death this time, but nearly as many
were down on the ground, their carcasses being skinned and the
meat cut away from the bones. It would be hauled back to the
camp, where the women were prepared to begin the process of
smoking and jerking the flesh. The hides, horns, and virtually
every other part of the animals were harvested as well. There
was a use for everything. Wakon-tah had done a good thing
indeed when he had made the buffalo to supply the people with
what they needed.

During the long afternoon of the hunt, Black Snake all but

forgot his dream. In the back of his mind, however, he knew that
it would come back to him, and sooner or later he must deal with
its portents—dark and bloody though they might be.

Chapter Three

Father Sun retreated toward the horizon, a red torch igniting
shards of cloud. Black Snake shaded his eyes as he gazed westward across the grassland. He stood on a low hill outside the village where the Crane band of the Prairie People lived on the
Nibthaska-ke, the Flat River, swollen with winter's melt-off,
early in the Moon of New Grass. The buffalo hunt was over, the
people had returned to the village, and the time had come for
Black Snake to deal with the dream that had come to him.

At twenty-eight summers, Black Snake was a warrior of
renown among his people, but he loved peace more than battle.
Sometimes he thought he had been born into the wrong time or
place; at least he might have been a peace chief or shaman
instead of a warrior and hunter. Yet among his people no one
had bested him with lance or bow or war ax, in counting coup or
killing the enemy. He approached his warrior's responsibilities
with seriousness and fervor and, for the most part, kept questions
and doubts to himself. This matter, however, was different.

His family awaited him now in their lodge for the evening
meal, but he stood his position on the hill and looked hard into
the bloody, long-shadowed sunset, trying to see the future. The
dream he had experienced during the buffalo hunt troubled him
immensely. What was it? Why was he afraid? As he stood silhouetted against the sky, a clear target for an unseen arrow, he
could see nothing upon the plain that disturbed the normal
serenity of the dying spring day.

And yet . . . the pang of unknown danger, a threat to his village of ninety lodges, knifed through his intestines. He believed

strongly in such instincts, for many times they had saved him and his friends in battle.

Thoughts of his family, his band, his people—of this young season of awakening—all crowded into his heart. The prairie had begun to blossom, and new life quickened the bellies of many women among the people. He took deeper drafts of warm, dusky air into his lungs. His vision clouded, and he blinked to wipe salty sweat from his eyes.

Finding too few words to express exactly what he felt in this moment, Black Snake offered a prayer to the Creator—the One who knew and understood all the thoughts and feelings of a man.

"I stand alone, yet with my people near, all held closely in the lodge that is my heart. It is time to rejoice in life, yet my dreams cause me to fear what is to come. I do not fear for my own life. I am prepared and willing to die if that is needed. My death will be your gift to me—and from me to my people. Yet, I know for certain that I will not die soon. Why do I know this? Why have you given *me* this gift of seeing? It troubles me deeply. My fear is for the others. How many are meant to die? I cannot know their number. Who is our enemy? I cannot see him."

He raised his hands, fingers stretched to the sky. "I ask you who have given me strength for more strength to defend my people. I ask you who have given me sight for more vision to see the trueness of this dark threat. I ask you, the Creator of the First People and the Giver of Breath to all living creatures, to bless those who will live and those who must die. Will I, or anyone among us, understand your purpose?"

The majestic silence of plain and sky coursed through his blood.

He held his muscular, tattooed arms before him. These were his chief weapons, trained, scarred, decorated with the many marks of honor that signified Black Snake's achievements during the twelve years of his adulthood. From his neck and collarbones, across his broad chest, over his shoulders, and down to his forearms, the marks told many stories. The elders performed the tattooing ceremony upon both women and men, using charcoal first to outline the design on the skin, then flint points, to which rattlesnake rattles were attached, to prick the skin. They applied another coating of charcoal mixed with berry juice, followed by a second round of pricking with the sharp flint.

The beautiful marks on Black Snake's arms seemed to glow scarlet in the powerful sunlight. Was there ever a man who had better reason to thank Wakon-tah for such a life?

He concluded his supplication: "Guide my tongue to form the correct words and my hand to perform the correct deeds as I speak to the elders this night to tell them what is in my heart. Wakon-tah, my Creator, I pray that I am wrong—that no enemy lurks beyond sight. Let my people, the Crane band, know many more sunsets in this place of peace and well-being."

Black Snake went down to a sheltered section of the hill and relieved his bladder. He felt better, lighter, suddenly. He almost laughed aloud. His fears evaporated, and he walked toward his lodge, tracking his own long shadow, the heat of Father Sun on his back. The village before him comprised several dozen earthen lodges laid out in a wide circle, with tipis scattered among the permanent houses. In the center stood the medicine and council lodges. Outlying the homes were gardens and farm plots recently planted with corn, beans, and wheat. Dogs roamed everywhere—beasts of friendship and labor that could be food in difficult times.

A few children were playing before a large house as Black Snake approached. They were older than his own son and daughter: Little Rib was five summers and Feather would turn four at the next moon. Little Rib worshiped his famous father and clung to him at every opportunity, though his mother, River Wind, and Black Snake's elder brother were responsible for his education in the way of the people. Feather, who belied the name with her stolid, dark presence, was the quieter and more thoughtful child. In a sense, she took more after her father than did the son. Black Snake loved both intensely but was careful not to spoil them with too many gifts and too much attention. Anxious to be with them and with River Wind, he loped through the village to his lodge.

An inviting wisp from the cook fire spiraled above the smoke hole.

*   *   *

After a silent meal of pemmican and boiled winter corn, River Wind served Black Snake a warm root brew. Little Rib and Feather played together away from their parents. Black Snake looked over at them. It was dark in the earthen lodge except for the glow of the cook fire. He sat uncomfortably in his place instead of easing back as his wife expected of him.

"Speak your heart to me, husband," River Wind said. She sat next to him, her face capturing shadows thrown by the fire.

He looked into her eyes. "I must sit in council to tell the others of my dream that we are in danger. You and the children must sleep early this night and rise early. I cannot tell you why—or what is going to happen."

"I believe you, husband. Your gift has been shown to me many times since we were married." She placed a hand on his cheek. It felt weathered and hard, like untanned buckskin. "I will do what you ask—if you will also obey me."

"What is it you want?" His heart lifted. Even though she was still young, River Wind was a strong-thinking woman who did not accept words—his or any other's—at face value.

"Tell the elders of your dream, urge them to prepare the people for trouble—whatever may be the cause. Then return to me and your children and rest with us. You, too, must have sleep this night so that you may be fresh to lead us through the danger that has captured your spirit."

The warrior rose and, giving River Wind a warm smile, stepped into the cold night, pulling his blanket more snugly around his shoulders. He walked directly to the council lodge where the Sacred Pole was kept and periodically anointed in now-ancient ceremonies at times of celebration and crisis among the people. The village was quiet. Beneath the star-filled sky of early spring, the many lodges sent forth smoke and cooking smells. It looked and smelled like a prosperous village—a welcoming place for a wanderer. Though it was his home, his village, Black Snake felt almost like a stranger here this night. A mysterious sorrow, not joy, welled in him at the sight and smell of these many lodges of his people.

Inside the council lodge, about twenty men had already gathered. Black Snake had sent two of his brother's sons around before the evening meal to call as many as possible to attend an emergency council. He nodded to the men and was quietly acknowledged in return. The silence was broken only by an occasional sneeze or burp or the passing of bodily gas. While their purpose was solemn, these were men who felt very much at home with each other. Together they had survived wars and hunts and hungry seasons as well as good ones. They had married each other's sisters and daughters and fathered children who would, in turn, marry.

The Master of the Sacred Pole stood near the precious relic of the ancestors. Three small fires, each an equal distance from the Pole, illuminated the interior of the lodge. Here the chiefs and elders sat to decide issues of war and peace, of religion and government. The Master, a stocky man of medium height and dark complexion flecked with blue and red tattoo markings, touched the Pole with his left fingertips and crooked his right arm upward. His name was Wind Strikes the Clouds, his rank the equivalent of subchief.

"As the smoke rises from our council fires, so our prayers rise, O Creator, to you who gives breath and movement to these men, to all creatures of the earth. Hear our words in council. Let our tongues not be false, but be worthy of our people."

The Pole itself, as the Master of its mysteries touched it, seemed to vibrate and even glow with power. Instead of a long-withered branch preserved and decorated for many generations, it assumed the aspect of a living tree: the hawk, raven, and eagle feathers became leaves in the warm flicker of the fires, and the Pole's bent lines magically smoothed and straightened as if a vein of living sap had begun to flow again within its ancient core.

Wind Strikes the Clouds took a long red-clay pipe from a pouch hanging at his waist. From another pouch he pinched a generous dollop of a tobacco-and-sumac mixture, which he then thumbed into the pipe bowl. He knelt on one knee at the nearest fire, sprinkled into it some tobacco as an offering, plucked out a burning twig, and lit the council pipe.

After a few puffs to ensure it was burning properly, Clouds lifted the pipe in each of the four cardinal directions with a chanted ritual prayer, then presented it to the senior peace chief, Black Snake's maternal uncle, One Horn.

Black Snake, sitting across the circle from his uncle, shifted impatiently on his haunches. Although he revered his people's ceremonies and traditions, he was resentful at this moment. He checked himself, stilled his legs, silently commanded his heart to cease its violent pounding. One Horn smoked, then gave the pipe to Brown Hair, Black Snake's aged father-in-law. Slowly the red pipe was passed, smoked, passed again. Pungent smoke, mixed with the warm breath of the smokers, filled the council lodge. Black Snake awaited his turn.

The tall warrior took the pipe from the man at his right, drew deeply from the pipestem, and exhaled. The taste lingered pleasantly in his mouth.

When the pipe came back to Wind Strikes the Clouds, he raised it and prayed again, then knocked out the embers and took his seat. With help from two younger men, old One Horn rose to speak. The aged peace chief pleased Black Snake by addressing the council pointedly.

"Elders, chiefs, and leaders, we are to hear the words of a young warrior who begged to speak of a vision. Listen to him with your hearts as well as your ears, as he has listened to his elders. Black Snake, tell the people what troubles you."

The old man gathered his robe about his shoulders and sat down. Black Snake stood. He was one of the tallest men of his people. He arranged his blanket around his abdomen, holding it in place with his left hand, raising his right. His long hair fell loosely to his bared shoulders. The intricate tattoos across his shoulders, chest, and arms looked like scars in the flickering yellow firelight.

"My chiefs, in this Moon of Nothing Happening, when the grass greens silently at our feet and our women plant the crops that will sustain us through another season if the Creator so wills it, I fear for our people. In my vision I have seen a strong band of many men who come to conquer our village and destroy our lodges, to kill our men and take our women and children as slaves.

"Who *is* this band? Wakon-tah has not allowed me to know. When are they coming? I can only tell you I feel it is very soon. They wish to surprise the people by stealth and swiftness. I believe it is to be before the end of this moon.

"Brothers," Black Snake continued, "I am not a shaman and I am not a war chief. I do not desire to usurp the responsibilities of any other man. Yet I cannot keep these things quiet in my heart. I must suggest we prepare to defend our village. I will help. I will lead or follow. We must ask the Creator of all things to give us the strength and wit to protect our women and children."

A bluish-white haze hung above the men sitting in the council circle. The air in the lodge was close and heavy with portent. No one stirred.

Then, deliberately, the chief shaman of the band, Walking Thunder, stood. Black Snake was not surprised that this was the first man to respond to his speech. The two had been rivals since boyhood. Thunder had risen to his position at a very young age upon the death of the old chief medicine man, who had been his uncle and mentor.

Walking Thunder was a full head shorter and half a man wider than Black Snake. His thick arms moved flamboyantly as he spoke, almost like the flapping of a hawk wounded but not killed by a hunter's shaft.

"Brothers, chiefs, friends, councillors of the people, we have listened to a strange story of visions from a man who has not been trained in the way of medicine. I do not doubt Black Snake's sincerity, but I question his ability to see and to interpret these things. He says rightly that he is not a chief or a shaman, yet he claims the robes of both. I have tried, as One Horn rightly asked of us, to hear with an open heart, but what I hear is false."

Walking Thunder had not looked directly at Black Snake during his speech. Now he turned to challenge the warrior. "Have I said any word that is false?"

Before Black Snake could respond, Brown Hair spoke. He did not rise but addressed One Horn: "Grandfather chief, these young men have passionate blood. I remember this from my own days as a younger man. I loved my wife, I loved battle, I loved debate in council. I was never gifted with visions until I was much older, yet experience placed many things in my heart that allowed me to 'see' beyond the immediate present. Does not Wakon-tah bless us as he chooses? Does not Black Snake have the trust and respect of all in this council lodge? I am his wife's father. I have finished speaking."

One Horn said, "Let others have their say in this matter."

Walking Thunder and Black Snake reclaimed their places in the circle, opposite each other. Black Snake tried to control his anger at the medicine chief and concentrate on the words of the other men. Each spoke in turn, from eldest and most senior to the youngest and newest members of the council.

Some, like the shaman, questioned Black Snake's ability and authority to proclaim such a vision, but most supported the warrior on the basis of his reputation as a fighter, husband, father, and friend.

When each man present had spoken, One Horn again struggled to his feet. "It is good that we have met. Let us go from here to our sleeping robes and take with us all the words shared this night. We will sit again tomorrow night to decide whether we shall act upon Black Snake's suggestion to us. May the one God who created all and sustains all be with us."

One by one they followed their senior peace chief from the council lodge. The Master of the Sacred Pole remained to attend to his duties and to close the house.

That night, as she lay beside him in their lodge, River Wind stirred and opened her arms to Black Snake. He entered her embrace and felt the warm friction of her skin against his. They loved quietly, then slept.

Chapter Four

As near as River Wind could calculate, Brown Hair, her father, was seventy summers old. For ten of those years the Osage shaman had lived among the Prairie People in the Flat River country. As the husband of one of their own and as an elder, he had been accepted among them and invited to sit in council. Although he was the oldest person in the band, he stood erect and clear-eyed and spoke with a firm, low voice—and all who heard his words respected and obeyed him. It was known that Brown Hair did not seek to rule but to add his voice and his experience to the councils of the people. He sought, too, to guide his young married daughter whenever she asked for help or advice or simply needed him to listen to her troubles.

The day after Black Snake's council talk, Brown Hair said to her as she sat with him outside her earthen lodge, "The man you married has the gift of seeing. It is not easy to live with such a gift."

"This I know, Father." River Wind tended a small fire she would let burn down to embers before cooking a soup for the midday meal. Right now another soupy substance simmered there in a bowl. "Sometimes it is difficult to know what to say to him, how to help him, or when to stay away from him and leave him to his visions."

"Little River, do not avoid your husband's company unless he asks you to. He needs you to stay close and to care for his children. He also has the strength to bear these visions. I only hope he is somehow wrong about them. He was not trained as a seer, but as a warrior."

"This troubles him. He thinks it is not right in some way—that he has this gift. Why do the medicine men of our people not have these visions? Why Black Snake?"

She carefully unrolled the skin of a large deer killed by her husband a few days earlier.

"Many questions have no answers," the old man said.

River Wind had heard the stories of how Brown Hair had grown up on the Snake-with-Open-Mouth River about twelve sleeps to the southeast of Black Snake's village. His people were the Wah-Sha-She, whom the Europeans later would call the Osages; the name meant Children of the Middle Waters, and they, like the Prairie People, were proud of their lineage. The men were known as canny warriors; the women were prized for their beauty and their domestic skills.

As a young man, Brown Hair had been an esteemed warrior. He had fathered six children with his first wife, who lived to be forty summers, then two more children in his advanced age with a second, a much younger woman of the Prairie People who had come to the Osages' country with her traveling-trader father and had stolen Brown Hair's lonely heart. River Wind and her brother, Fire Maker, were the products of this second marriage.

He sat erectly, his wide shoulders draped loosely with a buffalo robe that shadowed his thin but sturdy frame. There was still much power in this elder, both physical and spiritual. He had trod the path of the shaman for as long as River Wind could remember, having retired his warrior's lance and shield long before he took her mother into his lodge.

The girl and the old man had been welcomed to Black Snake's village by the Prairie People ten summers ago. River Wind, as the daughter of a Prairie woman, felt from the beginning that she had come home—and when she first saw Black Snake . . . She fingered the necklace of seashells her mother had given her. Her grandfather had traded for the shells on one of his distant journeys many, many years before.

The deerskin before her had been hard-scraped on both sides and was now ready to be tanned. She stretched the skin taut and pinned it to the ground atop the short, greening grass with small, sharp stakes.

The bowl on the fire contained some preserved buffalo brains, which had been boiled; she took up the bowl of the steaming mixture. As she and her father talked, River Wind used a brush of wild sage to apply the liquefied brains to the exposed surface of the skin. She worked quickly and efficiently, evenly spreading the unpleasant-smelling mash.

She said, "I am very much afraid."

"It is good that you tell me honestly of your fear, daughter, but you must not let your children see it. They receive their strength from you and look to you for every word and movement in time of danger. They must learn from you that it is sometimes natural to be afraid, but fear need not sap their ability to act correctly."

"I remember, Father, that I was afraid when we began our journey from the Snake-with-Open-Mouth River. With each day of travel my fear grew less and less." Her glossy hair fell in two long braids over her shoulders as she stroked the sage-scented brush with the noxious liquid over the hide.

Even as a very small child, River Wind had been open with her thoughts and heart feelings, especially with her father. Now that she was a married woman, she entrusted her most secret feelings to her husband. But in recent days Black Snake had been so preoccupied and self-absorbed that she had held back, kept silent, and busied herself with the many daily chores that seemed to have no end. Black Snake apparently did not even notice her reticence.

As if he were reading her mind, Brown Hair said, "Do not let your husband's burden cause you to stand away from him. Stand closer. His vision may take him away for a time, but his heart remains with you and his children."

"I am grateful to you, Father, for your wisdom."

"If an old man does not have some wisdom, he has very little indeed to give to his people."

Brown Hair rose as though his limbs were stiff from the morning chill. "I will go to the council house and smoke and pray for you—for all of us."

When he was gone, she returned her full attention to the tanning of the skin. After she had finished treating the second side with the brain mixture, she took the skin to the stream at the southern edge of the village and immersed it therein, weighting it at the bottom with stones.

She would leave it there overnight to soak, then retrieve it, wring it out, stretch it on a frame to dry, press out as much of the water as she could, and finally rub dry cornmeal on it to absorb any remaining moisture. At a later stage, to soften the skin, she would use a sinew loop tied to a strong post driven into the ground. She would run the skin through the loop and pull it from side to side—a finger's width or two at a time—until the skin was completely pliable.

Since this deerskin was intended for moccasins, she would brown it with smoke. Lodge skins were not smoked, but left white for later decoration with the painted animal symbols of the band. Robe skins were scraped only on one side, leaving the hair on the other for warmth.

River Wind returned to her lodge. Even before she entered, she could hear the children's voices inside, and when she went in, she found Little Rib teasing his sister, holding a small, tattered cornhusk doll just out of Feather's reach. The girl wailed as Little Rib laughed and made the doll dance in his fingers.

"Stop that," River Wind said. "Let her have the doll."

Momentarily chastened, the boy awarded the prize to Feather, who ceased crying, clutched the pitiful thing to her chest, and looked at her mother with a smile that belied the parallel tear tracks on her round cheeks.

These two young ones caused River Wind the most pain and the most happiness she had ever known. Feather's fat forearms were reason enough to rejoice for her life; Little Rib's bright, mischievous eyes told his mother that he had a quick and sensitive heart, like his father.

There was much work to be done this day—every day—to order the lodge. River Wind took quiet pride in her neat household, in her skill with the bone needle, and in her flourishing garden. She did not boast of her domestic accomplishments but let the results speak to anyone who paid attention. And in her husband's village, all the women watched the actions of Black Snake's wife.

As a girl of five summers, she had begun the lifelong process of learning from her mother what a woman of her people was expected to do. She remembered her mother's shy smile and murmurs of encouragement. She sensed from that young age that it was a privilege to be a woman, even though childbearing and strenuous labor tested and sapped a woman day in and day out through her entire life.

Men carried their burdens, too: hunts and wars and councils. But there was, in River Wind's mind, an incompleteness, a childishness about men that was difficult to fathom. Yet it was there—and it created a gulf between the sexes that sometimes seemed unbridgeable.

Feather clutched the cornhusk doll tightly to her breast and waddled purposefully to River Wind's side.

Little Rib pretended not to be jealous of his sister's triumph. He took up his bow and slung his quill-decorated boy's quiver over a shoulder. Then, as if awaiting word from his chief, he sat by the door with grim purpose. He was prepared for war.

River Wind bent and ran her slender fingers through the girl's thick dark hair. Her son's actions brought her own brother to mind. Were boys everywhere so much alike? She thought they must be, and it brought a smile along with a pang of anger. She tried to put away thoughts of war. She cursed men's boyish need to play dangerous games.

She tidied the hard-packed earthen floor of the lodge and laid out the bowls containing the midday meal. Outside, she stirred the cooking fire and placed a clean, dry cottonwood chip in the center to keep the flame alive.

Chapter Five

A furious gray rain pelted the earth outside a huge tipi that stood apart from the village of the Red Horn People. Inside, a man sat brooding before a dwindling fire. An ominous crack of thunder sent a shudder through him, and he raised his head and howled, hoarsely cursing lightning, thunder, rain, sky, man, and Creator. He flung a stick onto the fire, and it burst violently into flame.

Fallen Tree's face became a savage mask of firelight and deep shadow. His large hooked nose had been broken several times and now resembled a misshapen hawk's beak. He shook his huge head and massive shoulders as if trying to cast off an unseen demon.

This giant warrior with the dirty clay-smeared forelock was the loneliest, angriest man on the plain—at least, it was his conviction that he was.

He had not eaten or bathed in more than ten days. He'd had almost no human contact during that time, but had lived in darkest isolation amid his own urine and feces and terror. He gagged on his own bile and spat onto the earth near the sputtering fire.

A sun-bright spear of lightning struck near the tipi and shocked Fallen Tree erect. He rose, naked but for a breechclout, arms at his side. His body jerked spasmodically, as if he had been hit directly by the lightning bolt. His mouth gaped wide, but no sound came out. The pain he experienced at this moment was so overwhelming that his mind nearly shut down.

He stood above ten hand-lengths tall, a giant among his or any people, but now his hugely muscled body twisted and doubled over as he clutched his abdomen.

The sodden buffalo-skin door of the tipi opened, and a young female from Fallen Tree's nearby village stepped inside. Her hair was soaked, and she wore a robe made waterproof by several applications of grease. She carried a clay water bottle. Just inside the door flap she stopped and tried not to breathe as she watched the frightening antics of the mad, almost naked giant. His mouth was crusted with spittle and phlegm, and he moved it as if to speak, but emitted only unintelligible grunts and pitiful squeals.

The girl took a few steps toward him and bent to leave the water bottle on the floor. With the swiftness and power of a great elk, the warrior bounded over the fire and landed at her side. She trembled, nearly dropping the water bottle, and made as if to flee—but Fallen Tree seized her arm and held her fast.

She cried out, but he clamped his free hand over her mouth. She could taste the dirt and sweat and waste on his palm.

"Daughter of Lame Bull, your cries are uglier to my ears than the thunder noise. Do not be afraid. If I wanted to kill you, you would be dead now, and I would be drinking your blood. Give me the water."

Despite his long fast, Fallen Tree was incredibly strong, and his hand nearly crushed the bone of her arm as he held her in place. She gave him the bottle, and he drank the entire contents in a long swallow, then thrust the bottle back into her hands. She winced in pain; her arm became numb in his grip.

"Your name is Little Quill Girl. Are you a virgin, or do you know how to please a strong warrior?" he taunted.

"I am not married, but I am promised to a man."

She could not raise her eyes to look into his terrible face. Clutching the empty clay bottle to her breast, she turned away, but he yanked her closer.

His ugly breath engulfed her as he bent to speak directly into her face. His deeply sunken black eyes glowed. "Little Quill

Girl, you must learn to please a man if you are to be a good wife. I would show you how."

The young woman went nearly limp, as if she were going to faint, then quickly swung the bottle as hard as she could, striking Fallen Tree's head. The bottle exploded, shards of clay sticking in his matted hair. Stunned, the warrior staggered back a few paces and loosened his grip. Little Quill Girl pulled free and ran from the tipi, dropping her buffalo robe at the door.

Fallen Tree shook his head and recovered his equilibrium. He bellowed like a wounded bison and raged around the interior of the tipi. He shook the sturdy lodgepoles so violently that he nearly brought the structure down upon himself. Outside, the storm continued, and a strong wind flung the rain against the tipi walls.

By nightfall the giant warrior had spent himself, and he collapsed, exhausted, to his knees. The fire pit contained a few red embers, but Fallen Tree had not even the strength to build a new fire. He crawled across the floor to the door flap, retrieved the girl's robe, and crawled back with it to his own.

Fallen Tree stretched himself out and pulled her robe over his chest. The once-magnificent red warrior's crest atop his head was now smashed flat, and dirt streaked his chiseled, sweat-sheened face. He closed his eyes.

Even *he* knew he was crazy, but it mattered little to him. What overwhelmed everything else was the incredible pain in his head. He had been trained to ignore, to scoff at pain—and in battle he had, many times over. He had been seriously wounded a score of times. He had fought on, through blood and broken bones and severed muscles. He had won fights and killed many men. He had survived and recovered from his wounds.

But this—this was different: a curse, a test of his manhood, a pain so intense that at times he went nearly blind. He had never known such pain could exist. He was prostrate, defeated. He slept.

At first he floated above his own body, rising like mist through the smoke hole at the top of the tipi. Then he soared, a great Thunder Bird, through the sheeting rain, into the black clouds, above the clouds, into the darkling star-speckled sky where the Creator and the spirit animals dwelled and the sound of men passed through to the Other Side. This was his dream. Released from his pain and his madness, Fallen Tree flew into the heavens, free of the weight of life, yet not dead.

He saw no other man but many spirit birds flying above and below him. Each star burned vividly, a white-hot orb or ember without smoke. He flew close to many of these stars on his journey outward, until he came to a large pink star that was as round and as big as the moon. He recognized it as the Morning Star. He was aware of the presence of hundreds of spirit eagles, their magnificent heads and wing tips gleaming, reflecting the powerful light of the star. For the first time in months, since the onset of the pain in his head, he felt he was not alone.

The Morning Star's spirit called out to him. He heard the voice in his heart rather than in his ears. The spirit promised to heal him if he would perform a great deed to honor the Morning Star.

Fallen Tree felt a chill of recognition along with a surge of hope. The great star had a special significance for his people: in the spring, as planting time approached, the Red Horn People prayed to the Morning Star for a successful crop. Year after year the star's spirit blessed the labors of the people to some degree. But every few years the Morning Star demanded a propitiation in return for his favor. . . .

A heavenly gust lifted Fallen Tree like a feather and blew him to the other side of the great star. It was intensely dark there, deeply shadowed and as far from the warrior's earthly home as he could travel without passing over to the Other Side. An icy hand seized his heart and squeezed it, as he had held the girl who had brought water to him.

The cold grip on his heart presaged what must come of his dream. This knowledge lay heavily upon him, and Fallen Tree began to fall—first, below the Morning Star. He watched it recede rapidly as he hurtled through a field of lesser stars. The spirit birds flew wildly around him, squawking and calling to each other. The man flapped his arms, but he could not arrest his precipitous fall.

Suddenly he felt as heavy as a stone. He plummeted through clouds, back down through the storm. Lightning exploded around him, shocking and searing him. He smelled burned flesh.

He kept falling—plunged into a deep river, roiled the murky depth, blinded. The water soothed his burns, calmed his mind. Spirit fishes eased his dive until he rested on the muddy bed of the river. There he lay as the meaning of his dream became clearer to him.

Fallen Tree opened his eyes. He lay on his robe in a puddle of his own sweat. The rainstorm had abated. It was still the dead of night. He quieted his own breathing and listened: silence. No sound even from the night creatures who were his usual companions, the crickets, the frogs, the cicadas, the owls, the bats, the night birds. He got up from his robe and wiped the perspiration from his brow. The great pain had ceased its dreadful throbbing.

He punched through the door flap. Standing at his full height in the open air, he looked up into the becalmed sky. There he saw as if for the very first time the vast black robe stretched out above him, and like tiny knife punctures that allowed light to shine through, the stars shot their whiteness at him. He filled his tired lungs with rain-washed air and breathed a prayer of thanksgiving for this respite from madness.

Then he remembered the dream.

He returned to his tipi and was struck for the first time by the sour stench of the interior. A crazy man lived here. What were the others saying about him? He had never had many friends because he had always been an outsized, bellicose, brooding loner. But now—this bout of insanity had driven *everyone* away.

Before dawn, Fallen Tree had pulled down the tipi, set aside the skin covering, put everything else except his clothing and medicine bundle atop the lodgepole, and set it aflame. As the debris burned he bathed in the rocky shallows of the river. He rubbed sand from the riverbed over his entire body, then lay down to let the current rinse him. He noticed but did not acknowledge a number of women on the bank watching him at a safe distance.

Still naked, he left his leggings, breechclout, shirt, and moccasins to air out in the morning breeze. He put the thong of his medicine bundle around his neck. Fallen Tree had an enormous head even for such a large frame: his jaw was long, his chin a powerful jut, his ears oversized, and his nose a battered wedge of flesh. He ascended the east riverbank opposite the curious women and walked away from the village in the direction of the rising sun. Droplets fell from his long forelock, now clean and shiny black. His mind was tired and numb. Yet he knew what was required of him because of the dream. Despair and anger fueled his body forward across the treeless plain.

The eastern horizon was a lavender stripe beneath the dark cornflower of the receding night sky. There! He stopped and stared in wonder: the planet of his dream, the Morning Star had risen and hung before him like a cruel, mocking mask. The disk shone red. Through a mist of tears Fallen Tree stared in wonder.

When the sun approached its zenith he turned and began the trek back to the village. He had lost count of the number of days he had been without food. He did not want food. He wanted only water and sleep and relief from the seeming torture of insanity. He knew the only source of that relief, and he shrank from it as if from a rattlesnake. Yet he must embrace it if he was to live. The only way out of the blackness was *war*.

Fallen Tree had been schooled in the ways of war from the time when he—an awkward giant of a boy—had joined a warrior society. The warriors' practice of growing long forelocks and smearing the hair with red clay and bear grease had given the band its name. They sculpted their hair into pointed crests that resembled horns and added several inches of height. Pitching fierce, long-practiced cries from the depths of their guts, the Red Horn warriors wielded club, lance, and bow with lightning speed and awesome power. They were skilled hunters and fishermen, but were less successful farmers than almost any other eastern plains band.

Fallen Tree's band lived in four settlements scattered over a wide area about ten sleeps to the west of the Prairie People. Fallen Tree lived in the westernmost village on a tributary of the Flat River called the River of the Crane. His people were newcomers, having migrated to this grassland just two generations before his birth; they had fled a powerful enemy who had invaded their homeland many sleeps to the northeast. In the distant past these People of the Red Horn were kin to the Prairie bands now living in the east. Traditions and legends of a time of brotherhood were now dimmed. The sages and story keepers might pull an old tale from memory, but the ones of Fallen Tree's age and younger were not much interested. The years on the plain had been harsh. The people had created new and often cruel rituals and practices among themselves—and they treated their enemies with little compassion.

As one of their principal leaders, Fallen Tree was unmatched in the hideousness of his visage and the range and power of his jawbone-framed war club. In fact, with any weapon, this warrior who stood two heads taller than most men ranged over the field of battle as a whirlwind few dared to challenge.

When the yield of their gardens was meager, the people looked to Fallen Tree and the other men to take up the bow and seek more game to sustain them. The past year had seen particularly poor yields, and the hunters had provided as best they could for the band. Several youngsters and two old women had not survived the winter. Others had suffered hunger and sickness and somehow lived to see the spring. The band was crippled; it would take a number of good seasons to recover. There was not much hope among the people.

Two moons ago Fallen Tree had become possessed by a demon in his head. He had always been subject to black moods and bouts of rage—ever since he was a child. His father had been killed, his mother captured, by a raiding party when he was seven summers old. He had ever after lived with his mother's brother. He had never felt at ease in his uncle's lodge—always the outsider. Many days he sat apart from everyone and fasted and brooded and went his own way.

If he had not been such a skilled warrior, such an important—if undependable—leader, he might have been cast out long ago. The people abided his dark times, prayed for him and privately cursed him—never to his face—and reaped the benefits of his power. Ever since Fallen Tree had become an adult warrior no one had bested the Red Horn People in battle. No one had ever successfully raided their village.

The people, therefore, kept a respectful, even awed distance from their giant protector. Even the war chief and the other men in the warrior society, themselves skilled in the arts of battle and counting coup, accommodated Fallen Tree's apartness, did not tug at him too hard when he drifted into his own world. It was as if a thunderstorm raged within him at times, violently lashing his soul and causing him to pull away from all human beings.

He remembered his first raid, as a boy of fourteen summers who was as big as any full-grown man of his tribe. With a party of eight others, young Fallen Tree crossed the Flat River and ran south for three sleeps to surprise an encampment of hunters at dawn.

Fallen Tree had never before killed a human being. On this raid, however, he was one of the first to strike. The enemy was only a few years older than Fallen Tree; he had awakened at the alarm raised by his fellows. He grabbed the weapon closest at hand, a long flint boning knife notched at the tip.

Fallen Tree advanced purposefully. The young hunter stepped back warily.

He is afraid of me, the Red Horn raider realized. It made him angry in a way: he wanted to kill, but he sought a more even test of strength. With his long-handled war club in hand, he leaped at the hunter. He swung at the young man's head—missed. The hunter stabbed at Fallen Tree with the knife and missed slicing his abdomen by a hairsbreadth. Fallen Tree then swung backhand—quickly, decisively. The smooth skin-and-sinew-wrapped stone at the end of his club smashed the hunter's skull.

Stunned, the youthful Red Horn warrior stood dead still, deaf to the cries and struggles about him in the invaded camp. So this was how it felt to take the life of another. For two breaths he was completely empty of spirit. Then he awoke again to the battle his brothers had brought to this place, and he sought another target.

He had a hand in four deaths that day, one by torture after the brief battle had ended. The survivor was flayed, slowly dismembered, then decapitated before the evening meal. Fallen Tree took a finger for his medicine bundle, which he still carried.

Now he stood naked on the plain, the early grasses tickling his ankles and calves. The wildflowers of many colors shocked his eyes with their vividness.

What good, he wondered bleakly, *is a medicine bundle against an enemy that cannot be seen or touched? What have I won by killing enemies beyond number? What gain from raiding and counting coup and hunting and fighting the angry spirits?*

Because I have won nothing, I have nothing to lose. I am alone, yet I know I serve my people in some way.

I am now called by the Morning Star to bring him a gift. I will do this thing with blackness in my heart. For my people I will do this, that they may live another season. For myself I wish only to die. This is my prayer.

Fallen Tree turned his back to the sun. It burned into his skin. He would seek the Keeper of the Morning Star Medicine Bundle and tell him of this dream.

Chapter Six

With each rising of the angry planet, Striking Water Snake, the Keeper of the Morning Star Medicine Bundle, had to be prepared for any eventuality, including a dream such as Fallen Tree had experienced. The Keeper had held his position for many years and by now had become stooped with age. His was a crucial responsibility among the Red Horn People, for the Morning Star Bundle was the most feared and most sacred of all medicine bundles.

This morning he wore his buffalo bull hat decorated with thirteen eagle wing feathers and scores of hawk tail feathers. From the back of the magnificent hat two beautifully quilled bands hung to his waist. His shirt, too, was decorated with quills dyed scarlet, yellow, green, cobalt, and bleached gleaming white. Wearing his ceremonial leggings, he sat at the door of his lodge to await the events of the day.

The sacred bundle of his people lay in its place atop a small altar within the earth-and-straw lodge where Striking Water Snake dwelled without a wife, his life dedicated exclusively to his religious duties. He was a plain, stern-faced man with cropped gray hair. He did not wear a forelock crest as the warriors did.

The bundle was a buffalo-skin box made stiff with fat and

coats of wax. A representation of the Morning Star itself had been painted on one side of the box several generations ago in red and brown pigments, and a picture of the Morning Star ceremony was on the opposite side. Inside, a number of significant objects known only to the Keeper were stored. Only he was permitted to handle these objects, to preserve them or to add to their number. Herbs, grasses, dried flowers, animal remains, pottery, trade goods from far away—each item possessed a power and a meaning that the Keeper alone could interpret.

Squinting in the sunlight, he peered to the east, awaiting a sign. Before long he saw the giant approaching his lodge.

"Greetings, brother," Water Snake called when Fallen Tree was within twenty steps.

Fallen Tree strode up to the lodge and said to the holy man, "The Morning Star has spoken to me in a dream. I am sad, but I must follow the path I know to be right. You must tell me what to do, Striking Water Snake."

"Come into my house and put on a breechclout. Your nakedness does not become a war leader of our people."

Water Snake trembled inwardly at the madness he detected in Fallen Tree's black eyes. The warrior had indeed experienced a profound vision—of that the holy man had no doubt. However, could he trust Fallen Tree's vision to be authentic?

As a priest and Keeper of the most sacred totem, Water Snake himself was capable of making up visions or prophecies that were not always genuinely inspired by the spirit messenger of the Creator. He did not suspect Fallen Tree of falsifying a dream; in fact, he thought the warrior was probably incapable of such a deception. Rather, he suspected that evil spirits dominated Fallen Tree's mind and might be manipulating him.

When the giant was covered with a bleached buckskin breechclout, Water Snake bade him sit and recount the dream.

"I am crazy, like a wounded animal, though my body is healthy and strong," Fallen Tree said, disarming the holy man. "I did not seek this dream and fear what may come of it. Yet I know in my heart I must tell the truth of it, for that is the way I was taught."

"I will listen and not judge until you are finished."

"My madness left me last night for a time as I slept," Fallen

Tree began. He recounted his dream in its entirety. His fear of its meaning was still with him, but he became calmer as he spoke.

The Keeper of the most sacred bundle of the angry Morning Star closed his eyes. The warrior's words tumbled forth. Fallen Tree was not renowned as an orator, but he spoke eloquently of his dream experience. It was true—the demon that possessed him was absent from his words and his demeanor.

"When I awoke, I felt as if I had taken a long journey. Yet there is still a long path to travel. I am prepared to do whatever the spirit commands. Have I not been called to serve our people in this way?"

Water Snake said, "Truly, you have been chosen. The Morning Star spirit has found you worthy to lead the warriors on this path."

Neither man spoke directly of the task that lay before Fallen Tree. It made them uncomfortable, though each recognized its necessity. For the survival of their band, the giant must select a party of raiders and seek out a virgin from a neighboring tribe to bring back as a gift, an offering to the Morning Star. Her life must be sacrificed so that the Red Horn People would enjoy the star spirit's blessing. Other women and children would also be stolen, to serve the Red Horn People as slaves, and food would be taken to ease the pangs of bellies left hungry by several poor growing seasons in a row.

The priest sprinkled fragrant herbs over the low fire in the center of his lodge. Fallen Tree, having bathed his body and been cleansed of his soul-sickness for the moment, listened to the thrumming incantation of the medicine man. He did not absorb the words, only the familiar rhythm of supplication.

"You will break your fast and rejoin the people in the village. Your uncle and our war chief will help you select the soldiers for your mission. You are not alone, Fallen Tree, unless you choose to be. Your people are your blood and your strength."

For the first time in his life, Fallen Tree took these words into his heart. He was sick of carrying the burden of isolation thrust upon him by his madness. Was there a cure? Was there any hope? Would the Morning Star lift the pain from his soul if he was successful?

He was willing to pay the price, to put his own life at risk as he had done countless times before, as a raider of many enemies. If he did not perish in battle, but was allowed to live, perhaps he might know some relief from the black spirit.

"It is good, priest," he said. "I feel the strength. I am one with my people."

Water Snake said, "Many of the people have become frightened of you. They say you are crazy and might turn on them."

This statement cut deeply into Fallen Tree. However, he knew it had to be true—he had alienated many and angered the rest. They could not know his inner agony, only see the outward manifestations and hear his doglike howls in the night.

"I will prove to them they need not be afraid. Will you help me?"

The holy man himself felt a dry fear in the presence of Fallen Tree, but could not show that fear lest the warrior retreat into his madness again. Fallen Tree had an important task to perform. Water Snake had to ease him into sanity and keep him there for as long as possible.

"Yes, I will help you. The spirits have already blessed you with a vision. You are not alone among your people, Fallen Tree, unless you choose to be."

Something resembling a smile played upon Fallen Tree's mouth. He was aware of the effect his eccentric behavior had upon those around him. Even his fellow warriors shrank from him in his times of madness. Now this sage man who could sometimes see into the hearts of others, when words were not there, was offering his support and guidance. Fallen Tree would have to set aside *his* fear to accept the proffered friendship.

"I want only to serve my people and please the Morning Star. I need your wisdom, Striking Water Snake."

"It is good. I will pray over you now."

Fallen Tree placed his immense hands upon his knees, squared his shoulders, and shut his eyes. The Keeper of the Morning Star Medicine Bundle blessed him with purified water and crushed sage and anointed his extremities with oils of beaver and otter. Holding the great medicine bundle over Fallen Tree's unadorned head, Water Snake raised his voice to the heavens in a high chant. His prayers flew into the ears of the gods.

Water Snake watched the warrior walk away from his lodge,

looking as tall and sturdy as a cedar. A warm breeze touched the giant's forelock, and it flapped gently on the shaven head. Water Snake felt the stirrings of unease within his breast. Fallen Tree's dream meant he must alert the people to Morning Star's call for a sacrifice ceremony.

He looked after Fallen Tree for another several heartbeats, then turned and reentered his lodge. The familiar closeness eased his discomfort. During his early years as Keeper of the band's holiest and most important medicine, he had often questioned—only to himself—the truth of Morning Star's appetite for the blood of captives. Did this always ensure a successful harvest? To be truthful, it did not, in his experience. Yet who would defy the message of the star and promise the people a season of bounty? Water Snake would not.

Likewise, Fallen Tree's thoughts cascaded like water, cold and free, through the dark ravines of his mind. Now that he had shared his burden with the holy man, he felt lighter and filled with new purpose. He hated himself less. His madness waned but did not die, like an angry moon. The spring air filled his huge lungs with hope.

Beneath his feet the earth hummed with life. Why had he not felt this before? he wondered. He had many new questions in his heart. Why had the Morning Star chosen him to receive the spirit message? Why had he been selected to lead his people when he felt crippled and evil and unworthy? Perhaps he would die on this raid. The thought was like a white light that painfully illuminated Fallen Tree's entire world, yet it was the most welcome and comforting thought possible.

He spoke aloud to no one: "I am God's warrior, and my enemies are doomed before the hand God has raised."

There was no clear picture in his mind of the battle or of his own death, only clouds. Later he might be given a vision; he would pray for one. But now he possessed knowledge that had been blocked by his madness. A dangerous journey lay ahead, yet he had survived an even more perilous descent into blackness.

The wind lifted his lean forelock with unseen fingers, and the sun, father of Morning Star, shone down benevolently from its zenith upon the chosen warrior.

Chapter Seven

Fire Maker's dark eyes glistened, and sweat beaded his face. He almost smiled. A long trail lay behind, a shorter one ahead— if he and his traveling companion made it another step with their lives. The smile was eroded by fear.

The shaggy, russet-colored bear loomed like a thick tree only ten paces ahead on the forest trail. Her cubs scampered behind her for protection. Sunlight speckled the great she-bear's coat, and she slashed the air with giant gray claws.

Fire Maker raised his left hand as a signal to the fellow Wah-Sha-She man who followed: Stop. With his right hand he unsheathed a large, bone-handled flint knife. He did not want to confront or kill this angry giant, but he was ready to defend himself if she attacked. Slowly, he and the other hunter stepped back along the trail. The she-bear roared and swung her paws.

The man's eyes met the bear's. They locked on each other in question and challenge. Fire Maker had no doubt who had the advantage in this situation, and he had no desire to pit his skill against her power.

A sturdy young man of seventeen summers with a side-shaven brown head, broad shoulders, and long powerful arms, Fire Maker was traveling to seek his father, Brown Hair, and his sister, River Wind. It had been nearly eight years since he had seen them, and he wanted badly to find them. His companion, Wounded Eagle, was a year older, taller and more slender, a devoted friend.

The two stood nearly frozen, communicating silently with each other. They had known each other since their earliest boyhood, had played and fished and hunted together. At this tense, dangerous moment they moved and breathed in almost perfect unison. Fire Maker took another step back; he stood shoulder to shoulder with Eagle.

The she-bear watched suspiciously and growled.

Fire Maker's thoughts swarmed like an army of hornets. To challenge the disturbed mother head-on was foolishness. To run back would mean unacceptable delay. To circumvent the threat would take less time—possibly—but still meant a difficult trail through thicker, thornier forest without a clear place to run if she caught up to them.

No question, the bear wielded a tyrant's authority in her territory. He and Eagle must pay her obeisance if they were to progress even a step farther on their journey. But how? Fire Maker gripped his bear-killing knife but pondered how to avoid using it.

Wounded Eagle whispered, "She is ready to attack."

"We do not want to fight her. Even the two of us have little chance against her." Then the solution dawned on him: *two*.

He whispered his suggestion to Eagle, who understood. Neither man took his eyes from the she-bear's angry, heaving chest. She shifted her weight, took a tentative step closer. The cubs tumbled and jostled until she swiped at them to cease, and they docilely subsided.

At Fire Maker's tap on his shoulder, Eagle bolted into the thicket to his right. At the same moment Fire Maker dashed left and loosed a *hoop-hoop* cry. Then Wounded Eagle took up the cry, and the woods echoed as they crashed through the underbrush in opposite directions.

The brown giantess howled in frustration, tossing her great head to and fro, her trumpet shaking the forest to its very roots as the two Wah-Sha-She men pushed through unbroken webs of limb and leaf.

An hour later, the she-bear left behind, Fire Maker walked with confidence. As a scout and a hunter, he consciously blended with his surroundings, carefully placing each foot so as to make no noise and leave little or no sign. Over this much-used trail through the dense hickory, dogwood, and pin-oak woods, he glided like a cat, his powerful arms and legs pumping with each swift step. In this way he had covered about thirty miles per day. He and his friend took a light meal of pemmican and water each morning and a similarly quick supper; only one night had they taken the time to cook a jackrabbit that Wounded Eagle had killed.

The goal for Fire Maker was to make the best time possible, allowing no diversions or distractions—unless unforeseen, like the surprised she-bear. He had a youthful singleness of mind and self-assurance that would not be easily rocked.

He turned to look back at Eagle without breaking stride. Wounded Eagle had struggled to keep Fire Maker's pace for the first few sleeps, then slid into the rhythm like a shaft into a quiver. These last four days they had spoken little, but upon awakening after six hours of sleep, they moved as if they had a single head and two bodies. Fire Maker was the leader and Eagle the follower, but neither was slave to rank. Like brothers, like dual chambers of a single heart, they functioned in comfortable unison.

At nightfall the pair warmed themselves at a campfire amid a stand of willows near a narrow creek. They were sheltered on one side by a ridge the height of three men. Holding their hands over the flame, they warded off the chill of the spring evening. They had not exchanged many words about the incident on the trail. In fact, these friends often communicated more in silence than in words, each knew the other's heart so well.

But Fire Maker did speak after a time: "We were careless today. We might have been killed—at least one of us."

"Brother, if she had killed you I would have died putting her to the earth."

"And it would then be a double waste—not necessary. We have been protected by the spirits of the trail, and I am grateful."

"This I have felt since we left our home," Wounded Eagle said.

Light played magically over Fire Maker's angular face. Often he was serious, even stern in his attitude, taking matters great and small to his heart to ponder and calculate. He smiled and laughed infrequently, though he possessed a playful, incisive wit. Wounded Eagle was less somber, with a big, open laugh that could explode unexpectedly. Yet he was not frivolous about important things—such as survival.

He breathed in the pungent smoke and watched it rise into the night sky. "Your name spirit has been with us, too," he offered. An owl called to a mate.

"Just so long as the bear spirit leaves us in peace, then I will be satisfied."

Nothing could satisfy Fire Maker's restless soul for long, however. Though it was good that they had lived another day and made progress on their northern journey, he would have preferred them to be ten or even twenty bowshot lengths farther along than they were. It was his way. Never enough when it came to hunting or planting or competing in games. Never enough for an intelligent, hungry soul. That unknowable need was what had propelled these young men on their quest to begin with.

One day in deep winter, Fire Maker had come into the family lodge of Wounded Eagle and quietly paid his respects to his friend's parents and two younger sisters. The girls—fourteen and sixteen summers old—worshiped Fire Maker and vied for his attentions, but on that day he was oblivious to their feelings. He had much in his mind. Winter was long and deadening to the spirit. Therefore the men gambled and told stories and sharpened their weapons and lay with their wives. Fire Maker had no wife and consequently had abundant time to think. He had come up with a plan, which he was eager to share with Wounded Eagle.

"Let us go outside to talk," he proposed.

"You are a crazy man. It is warm and dry in here. We can talk better in this lodge."

"No. What I must say is very important—too important for ears other than your own."

Wounded Eagle's family watched and listened as Fire Maker took his friend's arm and pulled him to his feet. "Get your robe. We will go out."

Fire Maker was a persuasive fellow. Wounded Eagle saw the fire in his eyes. His friend was animated by some special spirits—or demons.

"I am curious to know what is so important that you would have me risk my life in this way," Wounded Eagle said once they were outside.

They took short, deliberate strides through the crusted snow.

Even in their fur-lined moccasins and double leggings they felt the bitter frigidity of the winter. Cruel wind spirits whipped their faces.

Fire Maker barked—as close to a laugh as he would get—and a steamy mist wreathed his dark face. "Your curiosity will end your life one day, just as it did for Mountain Cat." The popular legend of the nosy cat who was stung by bees, bitten by a coyote, pecked by birds, showered by a skunk, and finally eaten by an angry bear was well known by all of the people. "I knew I would lure you away from your warm lodge for that reason."

"Do not tease me, Fire Maker. I am not curious enough to let my ears be frozen—or my balls—just to please you."

"Remember the time we hunted the great stag elk?" Fire Maker prodded. "We were just boys, and our arrows were not straight. We wounded him, and he escaped. By that time we were lost, far from home. It took us three sleeps to get back. Remember?"

"Yes. Our mothers were very angry, though they were glad to see us alive. We had no food, but we killed some small game, ate roots. Water never tasted so good as when I was certain I'd never drink it again. These are warm memories," Wounded Eagle said skeptically, "but speak to me now of your thoughts or let me go back to my lodge. The fire there is warm."

"My thoughts are many: of my father and my sister, of old times when we were boys, of times not yet lived." Fire Maker scooped up two immense handfuls of snow, packed them together to make a large ball, and hurled it as far as he could. He looked at his friend. "Come with me to seek my father and my sister, as soon as the snow melts and the grass begins to green. We will have time to prepare properly, and this time your mother will not be so angry!"

Wounded Eagle did not laugh at Fire Maker's joke. "The people need our bows for the spring hunt and our arms to help break the soil for planting. We cannot leave them with fewer warriors to defend themselves."

"We can stay long enough for hunting and planting, then we will go. They will be safe. It is a good time for such a quest."

"How do you know, Fire Maker? Have you become a holy man? When did the Creator grant you the power of prophecy?"

"Do not be angry with me, my brother. I would not do any-thing ever to harm our people, nor to leave them in need. I only know that I must make this journey. I will make it with you or without you. It is your choice."

Fire Maker walked several paces ahead, his back to Wounded Eagle, who bent to scrape together a mass of fresh snow. He made a ball, packed it hard, aimed, and released it, throwing with strength. The ball hit Fire Maker squarely between his shoulders. Fire Maker did not turn. Eagle waited. He pulled his robe more tightly about him. A few fat flakes drifted into his face.

The young warrior's words drifted back to Wounded Eagle across the bitter white distance between them. "Nor would I ever hurt you, the brother of my heart, by any deed or word."

Wounded Eagle was taken aback by Fire Maker's solemn pronouncement. There had never been any question about the purity of his companion's motives.

Finally, after several more silent moments, the younger man turned to face his friend. His visage was dark, but with intense thought rather than anger. Fire Maker retraced his steps in now-sodden moccasins to stand beside his oldest friend and put a hand upon his shoulder.

That night Wounded Eagle had slept more soundly than he had in a long time—several moons, at least. Dreamless, deep. When he had awakened, he knew he would join Fire Maker on his journey to a place neither had ever seen. . . .

Through the wooded expanse Fire Maker and Wounded Eagle now moved swiftly and silently, more wary after the encounter with Mother Bear. They traversed the shadowed earth, leaving little sign of their passage. On their journey they had successfully avoided any contact with human beings, friendly or hostile.

Fire Maker increasingly felt the need to find his father and sister as quickly as possible. He was not sure why, but he trusted the spirits who quickened his heart and moved on.

Chapter Eight

Moon Hawk Sister awakened earlier than usual on Planting Day—more than an hour before sunrise—and boiled a bowlful of water, in which she steeped some herbs and sage. After cooling and drinking this mild, flavorful infusion, she began the many tasks that lay before her—the first, separating and arranging maize seeds that had been stored in an underground cache during the winter. There were three different strains of corn that her family planted in this season in their large garden plot, which adjoined that of Black Snake.

When the women of the village had fed and tended to their children, they would gather for the planting rite at the Sacred Pole Lodge. Moon Hawk Sister looked forward to this season's ceremony more than she ever had before.

She had no children, no husband yet. At seventeen summers she was eligible to marry, and a number of young men had made their interest known to her parents. Moon Hawk had not agreed to be courted by any one of them, however. She had so far remained aloof, not seeing her future husband among these eager boy-men. Eager they were, for she was well known in the village for her tranquil temperament and superb skill with a bone needle. Her alluring, womanly figure, having matured and ripened for love and childbirth, drew the young stags and turned the heads of many older men, too.

As she knelt outside her family's lodge with hundreds of colorful seeds before her on the hard-packed earth, she quietly hummed a prayer-song to the Creator, asking for a good day of planting.

Two strangers came to the edge of the planting field. The men who had been digging and furrowing dropped their tools and took up bows. Behind the intruders a pair of scouts from the

51

village stepped into the open, arrows fitted to their bows and aimed at the men's backs.

Moon Hawk Sister, still on her knees, watched the reactions of her people, measuring the level of threat to them and to herself. She would join the men in the defense of her village, if necessary. In her right hand she gripped the buffalo-jaw planting tool, and she would use it as a war club if it came to fighting.

She observed the newcomers, noting that one was tall and slender with very long arms, and the other was stockier, shorter, powerfully built. Each had shaved his head save for a glossy black topknot that grew from his crown. Distinctive tattoos decorated their faces, shoulders, and arms. They were young—about her own age—and their faces were yet unlined by responsibility and experience. Despite the tension caused by their appearance and the apparent danger to themselves, they were relaxed and made no threatening movements, their arms dangling casually at their sides.

The more muscular of the two moved first, lifting his hands in a sign of greeting. He announced, by signing, that he was of the Wah-Sha-She, the Children of the Middle Waters, and came with his friend from the region of the Snake-with-Open-Mouth River. He sought his father and his sister and the people of his mother. Was this the place? Were these planting people the ones he was seeking?

Moon Hawk felt a thrill of recognition. This was the brother of her friend River Wind. How happy River Wind and Brown Hair would be! She pushed herself to her feet and wiped her hands on the smooth buckskin of her shirt, her movement catching the eye of the sign-talker. Then he looked away, toward a cat-lithe man who approached from the village.

Black Snake carried a hardwood lance with a razor-sharp flint head that was a hand and a half long. Making no threatening movement, he walked to the strangers and signed to them: "You are welcome if you have come to our village peacefully. We have welcomed many strangers in the past."

The stranger signaled his name—Fire Maker—and repeated his mission. "If my sister and father are in this place, my heart will be full. What are you called?"

"I am Black Snake. I am married to your sister, River Wind."

As the two newly found brothers embraced, strangers no longer, the other young man stood somewhat awkwardly to one side. Fire Maker turned to him with hand outstretched. "Come, brother. You must know that this man Black Snake is the husband of my sister." Fire Maker brought the two men closer and introduced them. Black Snake and Wounded Eagle each clasped the arm of the other. Fire Maker smiled—a rare expression of ebullience for this most sober young man.

"Your sister is at our lodge," Black Snake told Fire Maker. "Your nephew, Little Rib, is ill today."

Fire Maker's face grew solemn again at this news. Obviously it did not matter to him that he had never met Little Rib. The boy was his nephew. "This is not a good thing," he said.

Black Snake shook his head. "Do not concern yourself greatly. The boy ate too many sweet roots, and now his belly aches. That is all."

Moon Hawk Sister and the others in the planting field moved closer to get a better view of the sign-talk. She could not help but fix her attention on the leader of the strangers. His alert movements and open demeanor impressed her, as well as the handsomeness of his face. The other women gathered near her and buzzed among themselves, but she stood apart from them, the seed pouch hanging from her shoulder. For a moment she felt as if he were looking at her, too, but in the excitement she could not be certain.

Black Snake and a half-dozen men escorted Fire Maker and Wounded Eagle into the center of the village. The women gathered their tools and seeds and followed.

One woman said loudly, "Two men with strong arms and no wives—an early harvest for our girls! Eh, Moon Hawk Sister?" The others laughed, including Moon Hawk Sister, though she was embarrassed at having her secret thought shared so openly. How did they know these men were not married?

She ran a bit ahead to catch up with the men. She knew that the woman who had made the barbed comment meant no harm, but she could feel the redness in her face and wanted to avoid further humiliation. Women of her people liked to tease each other, but most often it was in a friendly way. Jealousy and backbiting were not easily tolerated among the Prairie People of either sex.

Soon the entire village, more than one hundred souls, had gathered. After Brown Hair and River Wind had been summoned, Black Snake called upon the Master of the Sacred Pole, Wind Strikes the Clouds, to offer a prayer to honor this reunion. Wounded Eagle stood behind Fire Maker and watched the holy man, who had donned his ceremonial robe, send his prayers heavenward.

Moon Hawk Sister saw River Wind touch her brother's shoulder tentatively, as if she could not believe that he was standing there next to her. Brown Hair was beaming, as if several years had dropped from his aged shoulders.

The principal chief of the Prairie People, One Horn, spoke. "We are the Crane band of the People, and it is our way to welcome any travelers who come in peace. From our distant allies, the Wah-Sha-She, two young men have come to us seeking Brown Hair and River Wind. Our hearts rejoice with them. We are one family under the Creator. Tonight, let us light a story fire and gather to hear of the men's journey."

The people murmured approval. Several children surrounded the newcomers, gawking and touching, while the younger women, Moon Hawk Sister among them, stood back and watched.

That night, before Black Snake went to his sleeping robe, he sat near the door of his lodge and considered the significance of the arrival of the two Osages. Two able-bodied men were an immediate asset to the band, without doubt, and he was pleased for his wife and father-in-law. He sensed a benefit to the entire band in this event, but the vision was unclear.

The children slept in their section of the lodge, Little Rib's upset stomach having vanished in the excitement of meeting his uncle. River Wind had placed a robe screen between their sleeping place and that of the parents. Black Snake closed his eyes and listened to their breathing: as subtle yet powerful as the purring of a wild cat. They were unaware of his visions and his fears for the Crane band. They breathed and slept, perhaps dreaming of journeys yet untaken.

River Wind came into the lodge sometime later, and Black Snake opened his eyes. "I am happy for you and your brother," he said. "There are many seasons for you to talk about."

River Wind went to her husband and embraced him. "I never thought I would see my brother again. He has grown up but is still the little boy I teased so often. He used to run away from my friends and me. He said we tortured him."

Black Snake laughed. "I must talk with him alone and learn of your misdeeds. Perhaps we should bring you before the council for judgment."

"If my life ended this night, I would die a happy woman, for I have my children and husband with me, as well as my father and brother. Black Snake, let us go to our sleeping robes now."

She loved him aggressively; she took from him without asking. He was eager to give, wanted to please her. She squeezed him with her strong hand and thrust him inside her. They pushed the robe away and she moved atop him, her hands gripping his powerful shoulders. Perspiration sheened their nakedness. He watched her and was stimulated by the dancelike movements of her body. Her arms, her dark-tipped breasts, her oval face—he breathed in all of her and bucked beneath her like a wildly rutting dog.

Then they melted together, eyes squeezed shut, breath hard-won. His brain seemed to explode, and he cried out. She responded with an intense whimper of pleasure and collapsed upon him. They clutched each other silently, slowly breathing, drinking in the scents of their mating.

After a while she pulled the robe over them and lay down in the crook of his arm, her face against his chest. He told her of his thoughts about Fire Maker's arrival—that it had a meaning for the people he could not yet fathom.

"You seek too many visions," River Wind chastised. "You are not satisfied with knowing that all is well in your own lodge and in your own village."

"But I know that this cannot always be so, that there is a storm blowing toward us. How near is it? This I cannot see. Yet, I have the thought that your brother and his friend are important to the safety of our band. Because they will help us defeat an enemy? Perhaps. There is more, but my vision fails me. I am not a holy man." He held River Wind more tightly. "I do not want to know what is ahead. I seek only to protect the people if it is within my power."

She was flushed with passion for him and joy at her brother's safe arrival. She felt her husband's arms against her skin. A shiver touched her spine. "The people are fortunate that you are here to help them. I will stand at your side, husband."

"Your brother and his friend have strong arms. They will give the people reason to be grateful, too. We will invite them to join our next council."

Black Snake gazed up at the dark curved ceiling of the lodge. A section of night sky shone through the smoke hole. He knew a great peace in his heart that would not be disturbed by intimations of conflict and blood—he would not allow it.

"Fire Maker was always a very clever boy," she said. "He made up games and stories that his friends loved. Once he tricked several older boys—captured them in a large net he had secretly made. They were angry for a little while but soon forgave him because they respected him so much. He has always been a leader. It is his way."

Black Snake considered his wife's assessment of her brother as he stroked her thick hair. He trusted her judgment of people, for she had insights that he lacked. His thoughts often were far removed from earthbound concerns—except when he was engaged in hunting or combat. She loved this about him; it made him different from most other men and more like her revered father, Brown Hair.

She said, "The girls of our band will like him. I'm surprised he did not stay and marry among the Wah-Sha-She. He is a good catch, and his friend is nice-looking also."

"The mothers are plotting tonight, then," Black Snake responded.

"Just as I will plot when Feather is of the age," she teased.

"You have probably already chosen her mate and Rib's bride. I am made to think you have visions of such things."

River Wind laughed gently and ran her fingers over the muscled ridges of his abdomen and chest. There the tattoos of honor were engraved, marking him as a man held in the highest esteem by his people. He was so serious in his thoughts and careful in his actions. Yet there was a boy inside him, too.

"Time will reveal the truth of my seeing," she said, smiling in the darkness.

"And of mine," he said.

Moon Hawk Sister bent again to place three seeds in the small, moist dome of earth. By noon she and the women would be finished with the season's planting—a time to celebrate briefly before turning to other chores and duties. The sun warmed her head and shoulders as she packed down the soil in her own shadow. She listened to another woman singing a planting song; she had heard it hundreds of times before, but the chanted words held a special poignancy for her now.

"Creator, bless the old dry hand that holds a new seed.
Creator, breathe Your life into me that I may plant this seed of
    life in Earth's fertile breast.
Creator, weep for my children's sorrow, rain upon the seed."

She lifted her head, looked into the sky. There, dominating her vision, was the Morning Star, a scarlet-tinged ball of fire. She experienced a thrill of fear, of danger. Was the planet a sign of the Creator's displeasure—or his favor? Was it because of the man who had come? She had never felt so uncertain, so unreal before. She stared at the Morning Star, drinking in its brilliant threat, and for a moment the dark earth beneath her moccasins seemed to lift and shift like water.

Then a warm breeze lifted Moon Hawk Sister's hair and touched her round face, and other thoughts erased her unease. *It is good that I am alive this day, that my heart is full for a stranger, that I know a new kind of pain. The stranger is a gift of Wakon-tah to the people. Why do I think he is meant to be for my happiness? What if he sees another girl and desires her over me? Have I any cause to believe he or his friend has even noticed me?*

The dew had long since burned away, and the surface of the soil was dark and dry, yet rich to the touch of Moon Hawk Sister's fingers. She placed the seeds, patted the mound, and reached into her pouch for another handful. Work gave her satisfaction. *If I never marry,* she thought, *at least I will be useful at the time of planting, and the Crane band will not allow me to starve because I have no mate.*

A hunting party of ten men, including Black Snake, Fire Maker, and Wounded Eagle, passed the field and waved to the women. Planting near Moon Hawk Sister, River Wind stood and greeted her husband, watching the party walk east toward the wooded hills. The women bent to the earth like green stalks blown by a hard wind and continued to plant.

Moon Hawk Sister stepped over to River Wind's row. "Your man is a good hunter. Do you have many skins to prepare?"

River Wind paused in her work and stood erect. "Yes, I have many more skins than usual because my brother and his friend have also hunted well. I wish that little Feather could help me scrape and smoke them." She patted her brow with the back of her wrist.

"River Wind, I would help you at your work. My mother has few skins and wishes to tan them herself." The younger woman shrugged. "It is her way."

"Sometimes it is good to question one's mother—sometimes it is unwise. You have some wisdom, girl."

Moon Hawk Sister smiled. She liked River Wind and felt that she could trust her. Moon Hawk had lost her older sister, Nest of Red-tails, to sickness, and ever after, Nest's spirit sang to her—sometimes in sorrow, sometimes teasing or cajoling, often simply with the love of an older sister for a younger. Growing up, Moon Hawk experienced her sister's presence yet missed the companionship of a living being with whom she could play and quarrel. She "talked" to Nest, confided her secrets and fears and aspirations. She ached to have a sister-friend.

"My mother's spirit is good, and her hands are willing. She pleases my father, who is too old to hunt often. I do not please them enough, I think. They have wanted their daughter to be married—and, as you know, I am not."

"I feel sure they want you to marry well and to be happy in your choice of husband. They want to know their grandchildren. It is the way of all mothers and fathers."

Moon Hawk sighed. "Your father is happy now because his family has come together again."

"Will you come to my lodge tomorrow to help with the skins?"

Later, before the evening meal, everyone gathered near the Sacred Pole Lodge to celebrate the end of the planting season. The sun was nearly gone, its vermilion fingers of light touching the cloud-patched sky. The air was still, laden with expectation. Moon Hawk Sister stood with her parents, apart from her friends, who stood at the edge of the assembly and whispered to each other behind open hands. She was jealous of their freedom from care. Her heart was burdened, swollen with pain.

She caught sight of River Wind's family near the front of the crowd. She could not help staring at Fire Maker's strong shoulders and neck. His glossy topknot was combed and neatly tied. She wanted to touch his hair without anyone knowing that she did it.

She thought she was crazy. The chanting of Wind Strikes the Clouds, the Master of the Sacred Pole, lulled her, calmed her spirit. She moved with the singing, and when the unmarried girls of the clan formed a dancing circle, she joined them. Were *his* eyes burning into her as she danced? It felt that way, but she did not look in his direction. She lifted her head gracefully, like the crane for whom this band was named, melding her movements with the others', lifting her feet and raising her lithe brown arms as if they were wings. She became Crane and was as one with the girls in the circle.

The Master of the Sacred Pole sang the prayer-song to Earth and Rain and Father Sun, his voice carrying clearly on the still dusk air. He called upon the Elk Spirit to grace the planting with his generosity, as he had for the First People.

The people watched his shadowed form as he joined the dance, raising then dropping his arms, head rising and falling as he sang: "Brother Elk, we seek to know your blessing way."

He ended the prayer-song, and the ceremony was over. The girls ended their dance. A cool wind promised rain to nourish the corn crop. It seemed the Elk Spirit had heard the people's prayer.

Moon Hawk Sister walked toward her parents, but River Wind stepped to her and touched her arm. "Come."

River Wind led her to where Black Snake and Fire Maker stood, animatedly discussing the day's hunt. River Wind interrupted them.

"Husband, you know Moon Hawk Sister. She will come to our lodge tomorrow to help me tan the many skins you have harvested."

"It is good," Black Snake said. "Your family will be pleased to have new clothing and moccasins. My wife says you do excellent quill work." He ostentatiously admired the decoration of her dress. "It is good."

Meanwhile, Fire Maker stood there as if he had been struck dumb. He was trying not to look too hard at this pretty girl. She was a beauty: all slender arms and legs, eye-pleasingly curved at breast and hip. He was rescued by River Wind.

"This is my brother," she said to Moon Hawk. "He has traveled far to live with us in our lodge."

Moon Hawk Sister's words of greeting were lost in the din of a million bees buzzing in Fire Maker's head. He mustered a response and looked fiercely at the earth.

Black Snake had said it best. *It is good.*

Chapter Nine

Fallen Tree stared fixedly into the crackling fire, his black eyes reflecting white-gold tongues of flame. Above, the night sky was thickly strewn with stars. The moon shone intensely upon the cold prairie. The giant warrior sat with a buffalo robe over his powerful shoulders. Around him in the night were sixty Knife-lance warriors of the Red Horn People. It was the largest war party Fallen Tree had ever seen.

Sun Chief was their hereditary war leader, having come to his position through the maternal line. His uncle, Sky Chief (the husband of his mother's sister), had died several years earlier, and the young nephew had been invested then with the leadership of the Knife-lance Society, the warrior society of the Red Horns. Through the seasons Sun Chief had matured and gained the respect of warriors from all the clans that lived in the four towns. Even the proud, sullen loner Fallen Tree did not dispute Sun Chief's supreme position. Sun Chief, in turn, honored Fallen Tree's awesome abilities in the field and would depend mightily upon the giant in this important raid.

The Keeper of the Morning Star Medicine Bundle did not accompany the warriors but remained in his lodge, fasting and praying for the success of their mission. They were to capture a virgin, who would be sacrificed in the ancient way to the Morning Star; her "marriage," by death, would appease the sacred planet and—all hoped—ensure the success of the planting and hunting seasons for the Red Horn People.

Fallen Tree, who had set this effort in motion through his dream vision, would be largely responsible for the capture of the virgin while the other warriors were conducting a more typical raid, gathering slaves and supplies as booty. Fallen Tree barely saw the flickering campfire or heard the conversation of his fellows, so great was the storm of thunder in his head. He sat mutely among the others in the war council, who kept a wary but not disrespectful distance. After all, the entire party depended upon the giant's well-being and willingness to fight.

The sixty men of the raiding party ranged widely in age from the youngest, just approaching his sixteenth summer, to the eldest, a wiry "old man" of forty. For the young ones this was their first raid, and they were skittish and chattery in contrast to the veterans, who smoked and talked in more subdued tones, knowing that many of the Knife-lance Society would not return from this journey, successful or not. The youth were certain they would capture glory and fame; the older men knew only that they would try to kill as many enemies as possible and try to survive to return to their homes. The younger ones covered their fear with bravado; the elder ones calmly accepted their fear as part of being a warrior.

They thought about their women—wives, sisters, daughters—who stayed behind during such far-ranging raids. On the twice-yearly buffalo hunts, the women traveled with their men and worked just as hard—if not harder—to harvest the great bison. Side by side, they walked for many sleeps, slept in tipis, slaughtered and dressed as many animals as they could carry back to their village. Now, during this raid, the men missed the companionship of their women, but they also enjoyed the time away: time to be among men, to be franker and coarser, to tell jokes the women would not understand.

Darkness lay like a robe about them. Their evening meal had been light and quickly consumed. They had eaten little on their journey. It was good to fight hungry. Six men took each watch. Soon most of the warriors would be asleep, but Fallen Tree would not; he knew there would be no relief this night from the blinding pain, the lightning bolt in his skull.

His vision blurred: the campfire was a bright smudge. Voices played around his ears. The men were excited, especially the young ones who had never fought before. They listened to Sun Chief and the other leaders with eagerness and stood their watch hours anxious to stay awake and to warn the party of danger. Fallen Tree had no memory of the eager blaze of youth. He had always been quieter and darker than his contemporaries. From his first day in battle he had belonged—he had matured rapidly, without awkwardness. Now he felt as weary as an elder.

The Red Horn People had welcomed news of the raid. Upon the stagnant water of their hearts the words of the Keeper of the Medicine Bundle fell like a wild torrent. Preparation and celebration had taken several days. Fallen Tree lay in his new lodge with the frightened girl who had brought him water the night of his dream vision. Little Quill Girl had come to him and offered herself. They had mated and slept, mated and slept for three nights. She tended to his lodge and helped pack his pouch of supplies, washed and laid out his shirts and leggings. He, like all the warriors, traveled light into battle with a flint-tipped knife-lance, bow and quiver, war club, and hunting knife. Each man carried a minimum of food and water. They would win more food by defeating their enemy, along with more weapons, women, and other booty. This they fully expected.

All the people of the village had gathered to dance and pray and send off their warriors with full hearts. This was the most important mission imaginable: to capture a virgin bride to be sacrificed to the Great Star, whose blood would mingle with water and be drunk by the people. Many were deeply frightened by the violence of this practice, some repulsed, and a few anticipated the event with a flutter of pleasure in their bellies. All, however, believed it necessary to appease the Morning Star if they were to have successful harvests for the next few cycles. This had been the way of the Red Horn People for generations beyond the recollection of the oldest among them; it was expected by their Creator.

The giant warrior Fallen Tree had fasted for the past two days; he had drunk water but taken nothing else into his belly, and now his body felt as light and mobile as a bird's. He carried no excess weight in his pack. He was physically prepared for battle, was thirsty for it.

Memory of the dream had remained vivid when the pain inside his head subsided. He lapsed into silent agony, then out of it again, a few times each day. Sometimes he experienced darkness at the height of the day as the sun burned overhead and the Knife-lance warriors walked together.

The scouts, who traveled sometimes a full sleep or more ahead of the main body, had reported a large village of earthen lodges near the river that lay only one sleep to the east. That meant another long, hot day's march before the fighting began. Who were these people? The scouts identified them as the traditional enemies of the Red Horns: the Crane band of the Prairie People.

Fallen Tree listened to the chiefs and the scouts and felt bile and fear mix in his empty stomach. He drank water from a hollowed gourd and savored the wetness all the way down his throat. Sun Chief and his advisers were well pleased by the news the scouts brought. Their warriors were ready *now*, and if the action was deferred much longer, they would get stale and restless and be more difficult to discipline.

"You have done well to find the enemy," Sun Chief told the scouts. "Now the chiefs will lead the warriors against these people. How are the lodges arranged for defense?"

Around the central fire the men of the camp were silent as the head scout described the layout of the Crane band's village. "There is a strange thing. A mound of freshly dug earth rings the town away from the river, as tall as a man or taller. There seems

to be no way around it, so we must run over it." The scout's
report startled the invaders; no one among them had heard of
such a thing as this, a defensive wall made of earth.

Fallen Tree closed his eyes and envisioned the enemy village.
With startling clarity he could see the outlying fields, the paths,
the lodges, and this newly constructed mound.

Sun Chief asked for a pipe. When it was filled, lit, and passed
from hand to hand, each chief, scout, and warrior in the council
circle took a mouthful of the pungent smoke.

Enough smoking and talking, Fallen Tree complained
silently. The smoke dizzied him but relieved his head pain a bit.
He tried to concentrate on the words being spoken by his war
chief.

"It is good that we are near our goal. When the dawn comes
on the day after the next day, we shall attack. We shall be careful
not to disturb the planting fields until we know whether there are
any crops there for us to eat. It is still very early, but they may
have some winter corn or squash nearly ready to harvest. Likewise, when we have taken their lodges, we shall look for caches
of food that have survived the winter.

"We will take many prisoners—and one special captive.
Fallen Tree shall know which one she is from his vision of the
Morning Star. He shall know her from among the young
women of the enemy town, and she is not to be harmed in any
way." Sun Chief's words came slowly, each syllable carrying
the weight of law.

Fallen Tree listened, his eyes shut tightly. The leader's commands thrummed within his skull. Did the others at the council
fire hear the painfully loud and confusing noises that he heard?
His huge frame shivered. He opened his eyes. The flame was
burning down, blue and yellow now.

Sun Chief described in detail his plan of attack. Three senior
warriors, including Fallen Tree, were to lead about twenty men
each into the enemy village from the east, north, and west. They
were to strike after dawn at the chief's signal. These were seasoned warriors who could be trusted to execute such a raid with
energy and precision.

Fallen Tree forced himself to sit erectly out of respect for his
chief, and he experienced a reprieve from the blinding agony in

his head. He breathed deeply of the cold night and wondered: Would the Creator allow him to die in battle?

Wounded Eagle joined Fire Maker's sister and her family for supper after a long day in which the tall earthen mound was finally completed. It had taken the people of the Crane band five days of continuous labor to construct the defensive wall that young Fire Maker had suggested to the council many sleeps ago. It was a radical notion and had caused much debate among the warriors and the elders, as well as among the women of the band, who had counseled privately with their men.

River Wind thought her brother's idea was a very good one that could save all their lives. She thought back to when he was a child who spent many days in solitary activities such as building small villages of stone, stick, and clay. He had always posed questions to the elders about war and government, religious ceremonies and traditions of the Children of the Middle Waters. Whenever traders had come to the village he had listened intently to their stories—creation myths, tales of bravery in war, descriptions of tribal customs and ways of life foreign to his own. He had been hungry for information and experience and had quietly absorbed all that he learned.

It had been a week ago, after a successful day's hunt, that Fire Maker had first spoken of the defensive wall. He had been sitting with Black Snake, who had grown increasingly moody as he anticipated the unnamed calamity that was to befall the Crane band. The council had taken no extraordinary measures to ensure the defense of the village, and Black Snake was sorely vexed by their lack of action on this matter.

Fire Maker had said, "As a child I learned of the peoples who lived in ancient times in the valley of the Father of Waters, the Great Mi-thi-thi-pi. They built great cities and worshiped the sun, and they built great mounds and pyramids as temples to their Creator. I am made to think we can do what they did to make a strong defense of this town."

"How do you mean?" Black Snake had asked, his interest piqued. He had grown to respect Fire Maker's hunting skills and had learned that his wife's brother rarely spoke without much consideration of his words.

Fire Maker described his notion of building a shoulder-high mound of earth that would stand between the village and its yet-unseen enemies and perhaps cause them to call off their war-making—or at least make them pause and give the Crane band enough time to set their defense.

"How do we build such a barrier as this? We do not know how much time we have," Black Snake said.

"It will take many days, perhaps five or six, but if everyone in the town puts his strength to the task, we *can* accomplish this," Fire Maker replied.

After further discussion and refinement of the plan, Black Snake took it to the council, where he met the expected resistance from the more staid and traditional men. But the principal chief, One Horn, spoke in favor of the plan, and Brown Hair, who could barely contain his pride in his son's intelligence, also spoke during the council session, albeit warily, for he knew some still considered him an outsider—let alone his son who had arrived only days ago.

"Just as we have faith in the vision of Black Snake, who is not a holy man by training, so we can choose to have faith in this notion of my son, even if he is not born of the Crane band—just as I am not. In times of danger, we seek counsel and strength from whatever source the Creator provides."

There had followed much smoking and debate among the council that night, and their decision had been to build the mound wall. The next day they had called all the people together—men, women, and children—to begin work. Men and boys dug, women and girls carried baskets of rich brown soil, elders directed the placement of the baskets of earth, while the older women cooked and cared for the babies from sunrise to nightfall. In five days of intense labor, the wall that stood nearly as tall as a man had been completed.

River Wind had bidden her husband and brother good night that evening after supper and gone with the children to Brown Hair's lodge in the center of the village, since Black Snake was on watch with five other men. She had slept on and off for only a few hours. Now she lay, eyes open, in her sleeping robe. It was the still time before dawn when the Creator remade the world for a new day. The nights were yet cold, but each day seemed warmer than the last. She pushed aside the sleeping robe and sat up, rubbing her moist face.

She and Black Snake had not lain together for many nights, not since the planting season had ended and the construction of the wall had begun. When not digging or hauling earth, he and the other men had stood watch and sat in council and prayed each night. During the day they trained the younger men in the ways of war. The rest of the people continued their daily tasks, the women tending the fields, albeit with guards positioned in good hiding places all around. River Wind tried to remain calm, to keep her children always at her side, to look out for Black Snake and urge him to get some rest. She was weary by now, as were all the women.

Some of the people doubted Black Snake's warning. The scouts who went out every day came back with no news of any enemy to report to the council. The youngsters, Little Rib included, played games of war with sticks and skin balls and boys' bows. Their shouts and scuffles echoed among the quiet lodges. Even the dogs, who ran with the children and nipped at their grime-caked ankles, were warily silent at night.

River Wind never doubted her husband's visions, but sometimes she wished that another man possessed his gift. It was a burden upon Black Snake, which he then compounded by taking a leadership role in the warrior society. He worked harder, watched longer, ran farther, shot more game, sang more prayersongs than any other man—or so it seemed to River Wind.

Of course, she was fiercely protective and possessive of her man. She wanted him healthy and whole for her children and herself. She feared only for him, not for herself.

About ten handspans away from River Wind, Brown Hair snored gently in his sleeping robe. Little Rib and Feather slept as silent as stones. She was grateful to know a moment of peace such as this, but her heart worried about Black Snake. He was out beyond the breastworks, watching for the enemy he was certain would attack. When? Where? Who were they? She attempted to push these questions out of her mind but could not.

She thought back over the several days since the arrival of her brother and his companion. She was thrilled to feel a renewed link to the people of her childhood; she had not realized how much she had missed them—the familiar and welcoming faces of youth, the smell of their fires, the shade of the tall oaks, and the coldness of the distant streams. Perhaps the Prairie People, if threatened, could move to the south and join the Wah-Sha-Shes and live in safety. Life was good there in the tall woods among the hills, so different from the flat open land where trees were scarce except on river bluffs and creek banks.

I do not regret leaving with my father, River Wind reflected, *because I found Black Snake and his people—and they are now my people. But I often wonder what would have been, if I had stayed.*

She trusted the Creator and her own father; her faith was deep and strong. But one day after she had married Black Snake, she asked her father directly: "Why did you leave your home to come to a strange land and live among your wife's people? Why did you take your daughter and leave your son behind?"

Brown Hair was made to smile by his daughter's words. "The spirit of your mother moved me to leave the Wah-Sha-She country. I think she did not want me to marry one of those few-toothed widows who set upon me after she died. Nor did I wish to marry again. So, to answer her spirit I conceived a journey to her land. And because you are a woman—so like her in very many ways—I believed you would find happiness in the places she knew. Also, a spirit, not hers, made me think that I was needed somehow by these people whom I had never known."

That conversation was now a few years old. On this cold spring morning as she emerged from the sleeping robe, his words came to her as on the day he had spoken them. She listened again to her father's muffled snore and looked around his small lodge, dim and shadowed in the feeble light of the day not yet born. The lodge decorations, the few possessions, even the scent of the man touched her soul.

He had answered his daughter's questions, yet she was hungry to know more. There was meaning in the journey from the wooded country that perhaps escaped even Brown Hair himself, though she would not say that to him.

One day she would ask Black Snake—when the current alarm had passed and the village returned to its regular rhythms. She believed this would happen soon. She was almost certain that a raid—if it did come—would be repulsed by a well-prepared defense.

She did not like the fact that her husband stood with the scouts on the very point where an attack probably would come, if it came—*if*, she prayed. But it was his duty to be there, and she accepted that, for it was the way of his people.

River Wind wished the ill omens and fears would pass. She hugged her arms tightly to her breasts and admitted in her heart that she was afraid for herself, too. She did not want to lose the great treasures she possessed: her husband, her children.

Chapter Ten

The scouts were nicknamed "Wolves" because they ranged ahead of the raiding party to identify the best trails and sniff out the weakness of the enemy. Two of the Wolves led the Knife-lance warriors on the last leg of their march, to within about five bowshots of the enemy village.

There Sun Chief halted the men and gathered the subchiefs for a final council.

"Our Wolves tell us there are newly made defenses around the town. This means they are expecting a raid. But there is no sign they know we are here." He looked directly at each of his trusted lieutenants. Fallen Tree stood out as the tallest by far, as the most dangerous-looking with his hair caked red and spiked fiercely, his face, chest, and arms painted for war. "Upon my signal we will strike, as planned. Now let us each take our men to their positions."

Any encounter with an enemy scout or watch was to be dealt with swiftly and silently. If there was any alarm in the village, the attack would be unleashed. Sun Chief was a careful, experienced tactician and was not used to losing such a skirmish.

The men of the Red Horn People, decorated for battle in

the same manner as Fallen Tree, advanced stealthily toward their prey.

These warriors had endured several days of hot sticky spring sun as they walked across a grassy terrain studded with brushy sage and countless wildflowers of orange, blue, yellow, and purple. Low-crested hills and coulees had scored their trail. In the afternoons the same sun beat upon their backs and necks, pushing them forward. Then, at night, when the light was gone, it had been bitterly cold. Because they carried so little, they had no sleeping robes, but they had suffered without complaint.

From the time they could run with other children away from their mothers' lodges, these boys of the Red Horn People had been in training to be warriors. They spoke of nothing else but mischief and athletic games. They imitated their brothers, cousins, uncles, and fathers in proud attitude and belligerence toward enemies only imagined.

Girls of the people had nothing to do with boys before puberty, other than to tease and taunt them at their sports. The boys, in turn, cared little for females, except for their mothers who fed and clothed them.

War was a boy's friend. *War* was his ambition. *War* was his purpose. *War* was his identity. *War* was his manhood. Yes, he would court and marry. Yes, he would father children. But his fellow warriors were closer to him than wife, child, or parent. The Knife-lance Society gave him everything he needed to be prepared for *war*. And when his time came to die, there was only one way for him: death in battle. *War* was life and *war* was death. There was no other way for him.

Thoughts of youthful games, memories of triumphs and bruises, webbed through Fallen Tree's mind. As he walked with the others and saw the gray veil of predawn lifting ahead, he felt his heart expand and pump more vigorously. The smells of boyhood came back to him: the sweat of his young comrades, the breath of dogs, morning grass, the root-rich mud of a creek bank, the sweet-stink of old moccasins, smoke from a new buckskin shirt. Darkness had again seeped from his thoughts.

He sensed an unseen brightness. It was the promise of battle, the truest calling he knew. The girl, his prize—who was she? Was she sleeping now? Did the enemy warriors guard her lodge? No—they could not know the mission of the Red Horns, even if they did know of the raiders' approach.

The tribe should have begun preparations for the early summer hunting and for the ceremonies of passage for the youth, but the people had agreed in council to heed Black Snake's warning and prepare instead for battle. He stood near the wall of earth that ringed the village and marveled at the speed with which the men and women had completed this defensive structure. His brother-in-law, in addition to proposing the mound, had been of enormous help in the planning and construction. Black Snake was grateful that Fire Maker and Wounded Eagle had arrived when they did. He felt the Creator had dispatched them from their home far away for this purpose.

Black Snake believed that every event fitted into the Creator's plan, but that human beings could not always grasp the interconnectedness of events. They were too imperfect, self-centered, and willful to see beyond their noses or to hear beyond the rumblings in their bellies. He did not exempt himself from this judgment—for he knew his own shortcomings well. But he no longer believed in a random fate.

He remembered well the time of his youth when he was initiated into the warrior society by being consecrated to Thunder, the war spirit, in the ceremony of cutting the hair. All males of the Prairie People were expected to learn the arts of war. Black Snake, for all his athletic skills and natural strength, had not embraced the warrior's role without question. Yet he had not expressed his doubts to anyone for fear he would be shunned by his people.

Still, it had been the proper thing for him to participate in the solemn dedication ceremony. He had been twelve summers old. One at a time the boys had gone into the priest's lodge, where a man representing each clan was present in a prescribed place in the circle around a ceremonial fire. A boy entered from the east—the direction every lodge door faced—and went to the west side of the fire, turned, and faced east again. The holy man would then call upon the spirit of Thunder to envelop the boy's spirit and make him fit to defend and provide for his people. . . .

Black Snake sensed the attack before he heard the first sound.

His intestines felt as if they had been seized by a cold hand. Then his ears picked up the muffled snap of a twig in the tall grass about forty steps to the northeast. He unleashed a shout and a warning song.

Immediately the people of the Crane band awoke, and the men seized their bows and lances and flew from their lodges to move to their assigned positions along the earthen wall. There were nearly forty able-bodied warriors, including Fire Maker and Wounded Eagle. The elderly men and women helped the mothers gather their young ones in four lodges near the center of the village. Brown Hair's lodge was one of these. River Wind directed several women and their children inside, while Brown Hair stood just outside the lodge with his lance in hand, watching and listening. All this took place within several heartbeats.

An eagle flying over the village would have seen the sixty red-crested attackers fanned out among the trees and tall brush moving to hit the defensive earth wall at three points. The great bird also would have seen the Prairie men rushing—bows, axes, and lances in hand—to the wall from their own lodges within the village. The five other lookouts heard Black Snake's signal and retreated toward the wall as well.

A Red Horn raider loosed an arrow that struck a lookout in the middle of his spine and felled him. First blood was drawn. The raider whooped and went to the body to count coup. Other Red Horns shouted menacingly as they approached the wall.

Black Snake ran faster than he ever had in his life to scale the earthen wall and take a quick look at what was happening inside the village. He saw that, as planned, the women and children were nowhere to be seen, safe inside the assigned lodges, and the warriors were taking their defensive positions.

Then atop the breastworks a red-crested head appeared above Black Snake and leaped to the ground, brandishing a short lance with a sharp flint tip. Black Snake attacked with a powerful swing of his war ax and missed. The Red Horn warrior lunged. Black Snake dodged the lance tip and brought his own ax down upon the enemy's shoulder. Stunned, the invader sank to his knees. Rearing back, Black Snake swung with all his might, the sinew-wrapped stone end of his ax smashing the man's head.

The peculiar crimson scent of blood filled Black Snake's nostrils, and he felt as if he had drunk a drugged herb potion. A surge of anger and power coursed through him. These invaders would not destroy his people's lives. He would kill ten or twenty or more—if that was needed. But how many were there?

Black Snake sensed another pair of eyes on the back of his neck. He turned. The attacker—a dark, slender man with hair tallowed to a point and colored with red clay, his face painted black and white—charged with a piercing scream. As he stood to meet this new enemy, Black Snake glanced west along the wall and saw it being scaled by many more of the Red Horn warriors. No time to count or pay attention to others' battles.

The warrior feinted to his left as he charged, then tossed his knife-lance into the other hand and jabbed with the right. Black Snake was caught off guard by the move, and his legs tangled as he tried to position himself. At the last second he lunged to the side and missed being speared by a finger's width. He stumbled and fell. The Red Horn pivoted, yelled, and was upon him again. The curious-looking short lance came down as Black Snake grasped the raider's ankle and pulled. The man tumbled over, the lance point sinking into the earth. Black Snake snatched the knife-lance as the man fell. He rolled toward the attacker, armed now with the man's own weapon. He stabbed. The Red Horn cried out as the chip-sharpened flint pierced his abdomen.

Yanking the gore-stained lance from the dying man, Black Snake looked up in time to duck away from an arrow. The shaft whistled past, missing him by a handsbreadth.

He held the enemy's knife-lance in his left hand, the wide-bladed war ax in his right. He breathed heavily. The sun had just risen above the tops of the trees that skirted the river. Around him the battle continued.

Black Snake ran toward a section of the breastworks where several enemy soldiers surrounded three young defenders. Releasing a piercing, high-throated cry, he attacked, striking one enemy from the rear, nearly severing an arm. The man collapsed, screaming and thrashing. The earth accepted his blood, and soon he lay silent.

* * *

Moon Hawk Sister was in Brown Hair's lodge with River Wind. Three other women and ten children stood together in the center. One little girl clung to Moon Hawk Sister's dress and pressed her face against her leg.

Moon Hawk felt strangely calm amid the palpable fear among the women and the growing din outside. She heard unfamiliar war cries raised by many voices. How many? She smoothed the child's hair and murmured words of reassurance. She wanted to see the fighting—to be in it! Suddenly, and for the first time in her life, she wished she were a *man*.

An odd and unexpected feeling. Leading up to this moment—with all the preparations and distractions throughout the village caused by Black Snake's dire vision—she had been as afraid as any child. The little one's fingers dug into her thighs, through the leather of the dress. Fear had evaporated like the morning dew. She detached the little girl's fingers from her leg and led the child to the center of the lodge, where River Wind stood surrounded by anxious young ones.

"My friend, I am made to believe I should take up a weapon and go outside to fight," Moon Hawk Sister said in a low voice.

The air in the lodge was close with blood-fear. River Wind felt it, yet she kept her wits as she had been raised to do. Her father sat in his place now, his lance across his lap, and smoked and prayed. She glanced at him before replying to Moon Hawk.

"It is good that you wish to fight, but you are not trained—you are not a warrior woman. There are but few such women in the world. You should stay with the children. They need you."

Moon Hawk considered River Wind's words. Of course, she was correct in what she said, yet . . . something was pulling her from her place. It was dangerous, it was wrong perhaps—but she needed to go out there.

Outside, the sounds of battle rent the serenity of the morning. Men howled as flint and wood and skin met flesh and sinew and bone.

She heard a man of her people shout to the others, "Keep them from the lodges!"

Another called out, "There are too many!"

Moon Hawk Sister said to River Wind, "I must see the fight."

River Wind did not answer; she knew she could not stop the

girl. She also knew that Moon Hawk Sister was worried about Fire Maker. For many sleeps now Moon Hawk and Fire Maker had spent much time together. Had they even lain together? River Wind thought they had not, for it was taboo among the Prairie People to do so before a marriage contract had been agreed upon. River Wind guessed—hoped—that this would eventually happen. First, though, they must survive this day of death.

She pried the little girl loose from Moon Hawk, then hugged the younger woman. "Be careful. Do not lose your own life."

Nearly tripping in her eagerness to be outside, Moon Hawk Sister ran to the lodge door.

From his willow-branch chair, Brown Hair watched her. He said a silent prayer. Moon Hawk glanced backward at the women and children, and then at Brown Hair himself.

"May Thunder's spirit protect you," Brown Hair whispered.

Chapter Eleven

The blood spirit surged through Fallen Tree's body and ignited his mind. He stood on the ridge of the defensive mound and surveyed the scene below. For this moment he had been born.

More than half of his Red Horn cohorts were on or inside the newly built wall, having attacked at three points under Sun Chief's direction. The rest of them, about thirty men, were poised to scale the mound in a second wave. On the ground, among the lodges, the Red Horns engaged the defenders in vicious hand-to-hand fighting. Fallen Tree heard the shouts and grunts and death cries of combat. He saw weapon meet weapon. He had killed one man who lay below at the foot of the earthen mound, abdomen opened and head nearly severed. To kill a man in battle, to count coup against him, to bring glory to his band— this was the only antidote to the dark pain that Fallen Tree knew.

He took a deep breath of battle-scented air and looked to the sunrise; the new day was white in the east. He shouted and plunged down the inside of the breastworks, stooping to slice off his victim's scalp and to admire the intricate tattoo patterns on the dead man's bloodied shoulders, arms, and chest.

Whooping like a youngster after his first coup, Fallen Tree ran toward the center of the village. It was his task to find the girl. She must be beautiful, and she must be a virgin.

Around the side of a large earthen lodge came a young defender, unpainted and without the tattoos of an experienced warrior of his people. The youth held a brightly decorated shield and a long lance with a wide sharpened-flint head. He stopped with a gasp two paces from the giant raider, taking in the ferocious figure from the tallowed tip of the ocher-red hair to the stained moccasins on the biggest feet he had ever seen.

"Boy, you are looking at your death," Fallen Tree said in his own tongue. He knew that although the youth could not understand the words, he had immediately grasped the meaning.

The young man turned to flee, then stumbled and nearly fell. Fallen Tree was upon him in a heartbeat. With his great ax made from a buffalo's shoulder blade and a huge slab of flint chipped to a wicked edge, he swung with all his strength. The youth had the presence of mind to duck and offer his shield, but the ax splintered the shield as the defender rolled free. He jumped to his feet to face Fallen Tree again, this time with teeth gritted in fury and determination.

Fallen Tree regarded the dust-rimed enemy, who smiled, but without humor or warmth. It was a skull's gaping grin. His dark eyes were like coals, his nostrils flared. Quickly the youth fitted an arrow in his bow and shot, but the shaft flew wide of Fallen Tree's right shoulder. Fallen Tree advanced and swung again with the battle ax. This time the flint blade sliced into the youth's arm. The warrior of the Crane band dropped his bow and lifted his lance to challenge the giant.

Fallen Tree did not hesitate. With surprising agility he moved in on his enemy, lifting the bloodied knife-lance in his left hand. He jabbed. The youth jumped away and tried to thrust with his own lance, but Fallen Tree blocked the thrust with his smaller weapon and swiftly arced the war ax. The blade bit into the younger man's arm and chest; he cried out. Fallen Tree swung through, then brought the blunt end back, smashing the head of the young warrior, who crumpled like a log burned through by a campfire. Fallen Tree raised the ax and finished his work. The youth's severed head gathered dust as it rolled a few handspans from his trunk.

Feeling the barest twinge of remorse, Fallen Tree turned. The unholy din surrounded him, and he saw two defenders rushing at him from opposite sides. He stood his ground until they were closer, then spun his huge body, holding the battle ax out at arm's length.

The two Prairie warriors stopped. Each held a war club of his own. They whooped in unison and attacked: one went low, to take out the Red Horn's legs, and the other aimed high, at chest level. Caught in this pincer move, Fallen Tree could not spin away and felt the club hit behind his knees. As he went down he lifted his ax lengthwise and blocked the higher club. He fell, then pushed himself at one of the defenders, knocking the man down. He stabbed the man with his knife-lance.

The other swung once more, barely missing Fallen Tree's head. Fallen Tree slammed his big war ax into the man's gut. The warrior of the Crane band bent double, all the air pushed out of his lungs. He wobbled dizzily as Fallen Tree regained balance. Fallen Tree buried the head of the ax in the stunned warrior's back. So deep did the weapon sink in that Fallen Tree had to pull with all his strength, pushing against the body with one foot, to retrieve it.

Panting, blood spewed over his face and body paint, the giant turned again to the lodges where his quarry must be. The howls of men fighting and dying rose all about him. He scanned the scene. The defenders were tough and had somehow been prepared for the attack, but the red-crested raiders outnumbered them by a large margin. *Where is the girl?* he thought. He *knew* she was close; he could feel her presence.

Fire Maker ran along the interior side of the mound. He had already met several raiders and changed their minds about coming over in his sector. Several Prairie warriors clustered nearby. All had drawn blood this morning, and three had died within Fire Maker's sight. About six of the enemy had died here. Others had retreated over the wall and moved toward the center area, where they tried again, this time with reinforcements.

A stream of ten invaders penetrated the defense as Fire Maker's patrol approached. He wondered where Wounded Eagle stood, how many Red Horns his friend had killed. He had lost track of Eagle after the first alarm sounded. All around him men were shouting, enemies and friends alike, as Fire Maker led the men of his command to meet the warriors who had breached the wall.

With an ugly thud Fire Maker slipped behind a red-crested raider and brained him with his war club. As that man fell Fire Maker confronted another man. On either side of him Prairie warriors clashed with Red Horns, blood and spittle spraying everywhere.

He eyed the enemy before him, a man of medium height and wide, powerful-looking shoulders. The man jabbed his short lance toward Fire Maker's chest. Fire Maker swayed back but kept his feet planted, then swung up with his long war club and caught the Red Horn on the chin. The jaw shattered, but the enemy warrior fought on.

Crowded among other combatants, Fire Maker and his foe were locked together with no escape for either. The raider's face was a misshapen smear of blood—only the eyes were unmarked, and those bore in on Fire Maker. He jabbed again with his knife-lance and barely missed Fire Maker, who dodged right only a handsbreadth.

Fire Maker could not bring his club up, so he shoved at the enemy with his buffalo-hide shield. The Red Horn stabbed, the shield deflected. The broken-faced warrior opened his mouth and screamed. It was a horrifying sound that chilled Fire Maker's heart. He looked away from the terrible face, parried the lance blows with his shield, and finally was able to free his arm to raise his war club.

With all his strength Fire Maker brought the club down upon the Red Horn's shoulder. The warrior went to his knees, flailing, stabbing the air with his lance. Fire Maker kicked him in the face, pushing his nose back into his head. The man's eyes, wild in the throes of death, stabbed at Fire Maker—who turned and vomited as the Red Horn died.

Then he heard Wounded Eagle's voice raised in a high-pitched war cry. He turned and saw his friend fighting off three raiders single-handedly, feverishly ducking and parrying blows from the red-crests who surrounded him. As one knee fell to the dust and he struggled to maintain his equilibrium, Fire Maker ran to help him.

He came up behind one enemy warrior and with a mighty heave brought his club down on the man's head, felling him. The two other enemies saw what happened, and one swung a club at Fire Maker, who quickly sidestepped and drew the man's attention away from Wounded Eagle. The other Red Horn concentrated on Wounded Eagle, jabbing his knife-lance at the off-balance defender, who used shield and lance to protect himself. He spat dust and cried out in defiance.

In the corner of his eye Fire Maker caught a new movement but could not turn from his attacker to look without exposing himself. He faced the fiercely painted, red-crested enemy and saw hate and ambition and a little fear in the dark brown eyes. Dust rose in thick clouds at their feet as they maneuvered for position. Now Fire Maker could look more directly at the flash of movement. It was Moon Hawk Sister!

She hugged the rounded wall of a lodge only eight paces from where Fire Maker stood. His club met the attacker's with shuddering force. With a hand at either end of the club, he pushed against the red-crest's weapon. The enemy grunted in surprise and took two reluctant steps back, unable to meet Fire Maker's strength with equal force.

Fire Maker lost sight of the girl, and as he pushed the raider back with all his strength, sweat poured into his eyes and blurred his vision. The enemy backpedaled more quickly, gasping, and lost his footing. As he fell Fire Maker lunged and with a swipe of the club broke his arm.

Fire Maker looked up and saw a giant enemy warrior approaching Moon Hawk Sister from behind. He called out to her—but in his own language. She could neither hear nor understand him.

Then he heard Wounded Eagle cry, "Brother, help me!"

He looked toward his friend. Wounded Eagle was bleeding from a lance wound. For two heartbeats there was nothing else in the world for Fire Maker but his friend, and he rushed toward the downed man, clubbing away the Red Horns so that he could kneel beside Eagle. His friend was mortally wounded; nothing could be done to save him.

Bending over, Fire Maker placed his ear near his dying friend's mouth. Wounded Eagle struggled to speak through pink-foamed lips.

"I will die . . . have not killed enough of them—" He sucked in air with a horrible lung rattle. "The girl—marry her." His yellow-flecked brown eyes rolled back, and his face became a death mask.

The girl . . . Fire Maker scanned the battlefield and did not see her. He had attended to his injured friend, forgotten her for the briefest moment. Where was she? Then he remembered the huge red-crested warrior who had been near her. He cursed the spirits of evil and sprinted to the spot where she had stood, but there was no sign of her. The mound of earth rose like a mountain in his blurred vision as he rushed to it.

To the east he saw the giant, surrounded by several Red Horns, carrying Moon Hawk Sister like a cornhusk doll under one arm. In three huge climbing steps the enemy was up and over the defensive wall and beyond Fire Maker's sight.

Before he could get to the breastworks, another red-crested raider stepped before him. Fire Maker was angrier and more afraid than he had ever been in his life. He had to get to the girl—

The Red Horn slashed at him with a knife-lance. Fire Maker parried with his shield and violently struck the enemy's midsection, the force of the blow lifting his own feet from the ground. The enemy spat blood from punctured lungs.

Fire Maker bellowed in rage and ran up the man-high earthen mound.

She had never known fear like this: a surging, pounding, paralyzing inner storm. Yet every sense was alert, every pore open as she saw, heard, smelled awesomely new experiences. The still-dewy and pungent sod of a lodge as she skirted it, running her fingertips across the surface. The din of scores of male voices shouting, some of them familiar, some eerie and evil. A cloud of dust raised by warring feet, clogged her nostrils as she moved into the open village center where the Crane band's ceremonies, like the planting prayer-songs, were often held. It was so very different this day. Nothing, not even the shell-pink tinge of the morning sky, looked as it had before.

Moon Hawk Sister ran across the open ground and sought cover on the southern side of a lodge. Enemy warriors ran past but did not see her. They wore their hair in tall points or crests caked with reddish earth. Their heads and upper bodies were painted in bright colors: yellow, blue, white, red, green, violet. Their faces were painted black and white. She stood very still for a moment, then skipped to another lodge, then another, until she had made her way toward the earth-mounded wall where most of the fighting was concentrated. She could not count the number of red-crests because the battle was roiling all around her and more and more raiders were coming over the defensive wall. She sought Fire Maker, hoping he was unharmed.

She recalled how he and Wounded Eagle had helped the men and women of the Crane band carry thousands of baskets of earth to build the barrier that the council of elders had approved. All of this due to Black Snake's vision—and that vision had now come chillingly true.

Then Moon Hawk Sister saw Wounded Eagle. The Wah-Sha-She soldier and friend to her beloved was as quick on his feet as a wild cat. He fought two enemies at once, dodging and deflecting blows, almost seeming to enjoy the conflict as a game. But from behind him, another enemy approached. Moon Hawk called out to him.

The ambusher stabbed Wounded Eagle with a very short, strange-looking lance. Eagle howled in pain and collapsed. Tears filled Moon Hawk Sister's eyes as she watched more red-crests quickly attack, stabbing him many times over. She sobbed helplessly, and suddenly she saw Fire Maker scatter the attackers and kneel by his friend.

She started to move toward the two men. "I must help Wounded Eagle," she breathed aloud. Had Fire Maker seen her? She thought he had. Now he bent over his wounded comrade. She would help them both—

Two huge, powerful hands gripped her shoulders and hauled her backward. She lost her footing, stumbled, and fell, arms flailing. She called out with all her strength: "Fire Maker! Fire Maker!" But she knew that in the chaos of the raid he would not hear her.

She struggled against the hands—they were everywhere and all-powerful. She could not escape. Who was he? Was he going to kill her? All the tales about captivity and rape and slavery that she had ever heard flowed through her head. *Where is Fire Maker? Surely he saw me. He will come . . . he must come. . . .*

A face—uglier and more threatening than anything she had ever known—loomed above hers. She screamed.

He spoke harshly to her, spittle spraying from his lips with each word. She did not know his language but understood the meaning clearly. She closed her mouth, clutched her hands at her breast.

The huge warrior lifted her without effort, tucked her under one arm, and bounded off, calling to his fellows. In two breaths he had crested the earthen mound. From there he leaped to the ground on the other side. Moon Hawk Sister kept her eyes shut tightly, blocking out what was happening.

Chapter Twelve

Everywhere throughout the town the men of the Crane band were outnumbered by the Red Horn warriors. Yet they had fought the raiders to a near standstill when a strange, wolflike howl broke through the dusty clamor, signaling the Red Horns to end the fighting and retreat.

Black Snake fought on. He caught one of the fleeing raiders and spun him around. The painted warrior planted his feet and held lance and shield at the ready as Black Snake, arms and torso spattered with drying blood, circled, then struck like his namesake, his war ax battering the enemy's shield. The man did not yield but punched back with his knife-lance. Around them red-crested warriors ran whooping in triumph, pursued by men of the Crane band. Black Snake observed it all in his peripheral vision but had to concentrate on the enemy before him.

The Red Horn feinted left, jabbed right. Black Snake jumped away from the knife-lance and swung his ax in a wide horizontal arc, clipping the man's shield arm. The broken shield fell to the earth, and the Red Horn raider pulled a flint hunting knife from the sheath on his waist. Both men wore breechclouts and leggings but were bare-chested. Black Snake, the taller by half a head, kept moving in a circle, making the enemy follow him.

The town was engulfed in chaos as the yipping and whooping raiders hit the dark mound and ran over it to freedom, taking with them several prisoners and pouches of food they had snatched up. Many warriors of the Crane band stopped to help Black Snake with this last enemy among them, but he waved them off. Then he moved in swiftly, flashing his ax like a knife, to close the fight.

The Red Horn rocked back, surprised at Black Snake's sudden move. The war ax was a blur as it teased nearer and nearer. Now Black Snake was a spider—he seemed to have eight arms and legs. The enemy struck out with knife and lance, but there was nothing to hit—Black Snake was air. The enemy seemed to feel the wind of the war ax on his face and took a step backward, but there was no escape from Black Snake's weapon.

The Crane band warrior put all his strength and will into the ax, investing it with the power of death. When the blunt side hit, there was a thud of stone against flesh. Air exploded from the enemy's lungs, and he stood doubled over, as still as a tree, stunned by the force of the blow. Black Snake heaved back and, holding the war ax in both hands, unleashed another killing strike. This time he hit the invader with the sharpened side in the back of the head, just above the neck. Now the Red Horn wobbled, nearly decapitated, and his arms shook, and his painted body collapsed upon itself into a heap at Black Snake's feet.

The women and old people came out of their lodges. Only a few brave children poked their heads out to see what was happening, then stepped through the doors. Soon the rest followed tentatively, save for one child, who sat wailing in the doorway of a lodge. When warriors rushed to see what was wrong, they found that the Red Horns had successfully invaded this dwelling, taking captive all the women and children within except for this crying one, who had dodged the reaching hand of a raider at the last moment. More wails went up, this time from women who had lost friends and relatives to the Red Horns.

Throughout the town were scattered corpses and the wounded. The women and priests quickly identified those who needed help, who might survive.

River Wind ran to her husband. She saw he was bloodied and drained, but he seemed not to be severely injured. She stood near him and waited to be acknowledged.

Black Snake stared at the body of the man he had just killed. Here, less than half a bowshot from his own lodge, lay a stranger who might just as easily have killed *him*. He shuddered with fear and deep exhaustion. Then he looked up and saw River Wind. He was grateful. Where were the children? He reached for her, took her in his blood-crusted arms.

"My husband," she said. Tears streaked her face.

River Wind held tightly to Black Snake but anxiously scanned the immediate area, hoping to see Moon Hawk Sister. She breathed her man's war scent: the perspiration and dust and blood—his own and his enemies'—and fear and relief and death. She could hear his heart pounding as well as her own. She sobbed a prayer of gratitude. He gently placed his hand at her neck and pulled her head to his shoulder.

He had earned many new tattoo markings for his deeds, as had other men of the people—but there were many dead, too, and those must be tended to, losses counted and mourned, before any celebration of valor. And—who knew?—the enemy might regroup and return for more carnage. There seemed to be twice as many red-crests as Crane warriors. They could be back—and soon.

Black Snake's woman lifted her head, a look of grief and worry in her brown eyes. "Have you seen Moon Hawk Sister?"

"No," he said. "She was to go to Brown Hair's lodge—that was the plan."

"Yes, but she left the lodge during the fighting."

He released River Wind. His children ran to him, and he

embraced each in turn, powerfully relieved that they were safe. But he saw that his wife was troubled.

Two young scouts ran as fast as they could to the top of the earthen wall. They watched the enemy warriors melt away to the north among the close, low hills, into the cover of ravines and newly leafed trees. The scouts counted as many of the horned men as they could and noted that some were going more slowly because they held prisoners.

Black Snake saw the young men come back down the slope. He sensed something evil. River Wind was scouring the town for her brother and her young friend while Brown Hair and the other elders were gathering at the center of the village outside the Lodge of the Sacred Pole. The sun was not even at its highest, yet much death and ruin had befallen Black Snake's town.

"My brother, Fire Maker, is not here. Did he fall in the fight?" River Wind asked one old woman, who shook her head. No sign of either Moon Hawk Sister or Fire Maker. Were they lying dead somewhere within the town? No one had found their bodies. Had they run away? Why would they? When could they have done so? Someone would have seen them. With her children in tow, River Wind asked everyone she encountered. She saw, too, the corpses scattered everywhere, defenders and enemies alike.

Women attended to their husbands, brothers, and fathers who had fallen to the invading Red Horns. Fellow warriors moved the bodies to a place near the Lodge of the Sacred Pole where they would be properly honored by the band. Nine defenders, including Wounded Eagle, had died this day.

The enemy corpses were stripped of any clothing and weapons that could be used. Men and boys counted coup upon the enemies and removed their distinctive scalps, which would eventually decorate shields and war clubs. Some of the bolder boys took ears or fingers for their medicine pouches—a practice discouraged by the holy men, though the warrior society looked the other way. The bodies of the Red Horn were taken then to a place beyond the planting fields where they would be buried. The count of enemy dead was seventeen.

Two raiders were severely injured, and Black Snake and other senior warriors interrogated them but learned little about the reason for the raid. When the questioning was finished, the two were killed without torture. Now the enemy dead numbered nineteen warriors.

Five women, including Moon Hawk Sister, and seven children were missing from the town, presumed captives of the Red Horns.

And Fire Maker was gone as well.

Fire Maker was near collapse from exhaustion. After spending himself in battle, he had set out in pursuit of the Red Horn party—about forty in number, by his count—following as closely as he dared, walking, crawling, sometimes running to keep up. They moved swiftly to the north. He did not know this country well, since he was still a newcomer who had only hunted a few times with the men of the Crane band.

The land swelled in long hills and fell in deep, rocky ravines. Sturdy pin oaks, elms, willows, and cottonwoods hugged the rolling surface of the earth that Fire Maker clung to like a turtle. He moved through thick, thorny underbrush that cut his arms and legs and slowed his progress, but he dared not make any noise or swift movement that might draw attention. He had no inkling where the enemy was heading.

He came to a lake about six bowshots in length and three bowshots wide and, squatting in the tall grasses near the water's edge, watched the progress of the enemy band. They skirted to the east of the lake. Fire Maker heard crying from the children who had been taken prisoner. The women would endure their captivity in silence, unwilling to let their enemies see how frightened they were. The raiders were still moving swiftly—less in fear of pursuit, it seemed to Fire Maker, than in eagerness to reach their destination. Home, most likely. But where was home, and how far away from Black Snake's town?

A small band of geese swam past him, unperturbed by his presence. His fear and rage at Moon Hawk Sister's abduction made him want to scream to every grass blade and every creature within hearing to rise up and kill this enemy. He did not even know who they were, had never known of men such as these with their tall pointed roaches stained red and fixed with tallow to give the appearance of horns. Their body paint, too, was starkly different from any he had seen in his life. In his home in the woodlands south and east of here, the people did not decorate themselves as elaborately as the people of this prairie country did. He longed for the tall hardwoods and the cold rocky creeks and deeply shaded valleys of his home.

He controlled his breathing and became almost dead still. The enemy party was nearly opposite him to the north of the mildly rippling green water. His sharpened hearing picked up at least five different birdcalls and chirps from the poplars and cottonwoods along the banks of the lake. The silent geese were out of sight now, and the chattering grew louder.

The almost imperceptible buzzing distracted him for a moment. He carefully reached up and felt several bumps on the rear of his head and neck: mosquitoes. Suddenly his entire body itched violently, and he swatted the air around him, to no effect. The nearly invisible bloodsuckers surrounded him like a well-trained army, attacking at every vulnerable point.

Deliberately he rose and walked east, turned with the lakeshore, and picked up the horned people's trail. Alert for any of their scouts who might be hanging back to catch a follower such as he, he held a long-bladed hunting knife at the ready.

The midday sun burned his shoulders as he moved out to where there were very few trees. He had not had time to put on his shirt when the alarm had been sounded—only enough time to snatch up his weapons. Everyone in the town had slept in their moccasins—men, women, and children—for the last several nights. Fire Maker barely felt the scorching lash of Father Sun. He fell flat upon the earth when he thought an enemy scout might have glanced backward. He lay there breathing the scent of the hot earth for a hundred heartbeats before he dared lift his head.

Creator, give me the strength to continue, to survive, to take back the girl to her people and free the other captives as well. I mourn my brother's death. He killed one of the enemy and died with honor and will be long remembered by the people for whom he fought. I will always keep him in the medicine of my heart and my dreams, for I love him, my friend and brother. Oh, why must he be dead? Should we ever have left our home for this—death in a strange country?

He knew the answer: he was here because Moon Hawk Sister was to be his woman, just as River Wind had married Black Snake and settled among his people. Back in the Wah-Sha-She country he had been led to make this journey, and he had convinced Wounded Eagle to be his companion. If he had known what awaited his beloved brother, would he have undertaken this quest? He knew not the answer . . . and it grieved him so powerfully that his eyes misted. He paused before resuming his pursuit.

Across a flat green expanse that opened to his vision, he saw the enemy party moving rapidly, to the northwest now. Pockets of gray sage and stubborn tall yellow grasses dotted the open plain. There was no cover for him out there, so he lay near the top of a low-humped hill, watching, trying to put all thoughts of Wounded Eagle aside. If he finished the task at hand and survived to return to Black Snake's town, there would be time to mourn properly.

All day and into the early night the elders met in council and received reports from the men of the warrior society. Black Snake sat next to Brown Hair and listened to details of the disaster that had befallen the Crane band, his heart as heavy and immovable as stone. He said little other than to report his experience and what he had seen. He absorbed what the others said, and despite his deep physical exhaustion, he became more and more impatient to pursue the hated Red Horn party.

Several people had witnessed Moon Hawk Sister's kidnapping by what was described as a giant warrior. Brown Hair told how the girl had left his lodge in the midst of the battle. The old chief, One Horn, listened carefully to all of this, and in the early evening, after every survivor of the battle had reported to the council, he spoke to the elders and the warriors.

"When I was a boy I heard tales of these tall-headed men from the west and their evil practices," he said. "Yes, it was told, they are skilled in the arts of war—but their hearts are cowardly. They dress their hair and paint themselves magnificently—but they are cruel to their enemies and even to their own people. They will make slaves of our wives and children whom they have carried away."

One Horn continued as every man in the lodge hung on his words. "I have heard in the past that these people sometimes take unmarried women from neighboring tribes and sacrifice them to their gods." A murmur of disbelief rose in the close, smoky lodge. "I fear that our young maiden, Moon Hawk Sister, has been taken for this purpose."

An unseemly clamor erupted—very unusual among the elders and the war society leaders of the Crane band. All were taught as youngsters to observe respectful silence and behave with decorum in the precincts of the council, in any gathering of elders, and in the presence of their brother, the Sacred Pole. But nothing in their experience had prepared them for such a terrible series of events. The senior chief allowed the breach of tribal protocol for a time, because he knew that the people had never before faced such a momentous problem as this. When he felt the shock had been sufficiently absorbed, he raised his hand. A blanket of silence fell over all in the lodge.

"Our new brother, Brown Hair's son, has followed the enemy on his own—if he is still alive. Such is *not* the way of our people. We must act as one, listen to our leaders, in order to secure our survival as a band. Our children and women depend upon us to do this. Those who have been taken from us must depend upon us in the same way."

Black Snake spoke next. He draped his robe loosely over his head in a sign of anger and grieving for the dead of his band. "The principal chief of the Crane people speaks well and wisely. I am reluctant to speak because my visions—the gift and curse of my heart—have been true, and they have been dark for our people. I do not seek the visions, but I must answer them. All I seek is to help the people defend themselves from any threat to their safety."

He held out his long, tattooed warrior's arms. "My arms are for the people, as are my legs, my head, and my breast. I am made to think this war has only begun. We would do best to call together the warriors and pursue these evil men who have destroyed lives and taken our people.

"I am sickened to hear of their sacrifice ceremony, for it is not the way of the true heart of our people. We do not wish evil upon any who walk the earth created by Wakon-tah. Yet we must fight those who cause such evil as these Red Horns have. If my chief so wills it, I will lead the party to rescue the captives and avenge our honored dead with many enemy lives."

Black Snake sat down, and his words slowly penetrated the minds of his listeners. Several warriors—young and experienced—were missing from this council, dead, but their presence was felt by all who gathered in the lodge.

Later that night, when he went to his lodge and found his children soundly asleep and finally lay himself in his sleeping robe beside his wife, Black Snake told her of the council's decisions. Although he would awake at sunup the next morning to organize the search party, he patiently discussed with her all the speeches and deliberations that had taken up several hours after the battle.

River Wind said, "Do you think my brother is alive?"

"I believe he is. He fought well today but lost his best friend and the girl he wants to marry. He is probably very hungry and tired. We will track him and make him rest a little before we continue our mission. I am made to think you will see him again, wife."

Moments later, as her husband fell into a deep sleep, River Wind lay awake reliving the events of the day: the first alarm, gathering the people in Brown Hair's lodge, the shrieks of battle, the hideous smells, the shaking of the earth . . . and Moon Hawk Sister's wide brown eyes when she looked back at River Wind before leaving the lodge. *Little Sister,* River Wind prayed, *may the Creator protect you from harm and bring you back to your family.*

She did not fall asleep for a long time that night.

Chapter Thirteen

A featherlight touch on Black Snake's shoulder roused him from sleep. Instantly awake, he closed his hand around the war ax lying on the ground beside the sleeping robe he shared with

River Wind. He peered through the gloom of the lodge, seeking whatever enemy might be bold enough to accost him here in his own home.

No enemy had crept into the lodge. Instead, Brown Hair crouched there beside the sleeping robes, his position somewhat awkward due to his advanced age. In a whisper he said to Black Snake, "I must speak with you."

There was no denying the urgency in the voice of his wife's father. Black Snake stood up, moving silently and carefully. A glance through the smoke hole told him that it was still night. He gestured toward the lodge entrance.

"What is it you wish, Brown Hair?" Black Snake asked when he and his father-in-law were outside. He kept his voice pitched low so as not to start the dogs barking.

Brown Hair caught hold of Black Snake's bare, tattooed arm and clutched it with surprising strength. "I have had a vision," he said.

Black Snake frowned. He, too, had seen a vision, and it had come true. In the end that had not saved the lives of those who had died fighting off the Red Horns, nor had it prevented the raiders from capturing Moon Hawk Sister and the other women and children. He had had enough of visions.

Brown Hair was clearly disturbed, though, so Black Snake nodded and said, "Go on."

Turning his head so that he was staring off through the darkness of the prairie, Brown Hair lifted a trembling hand and said, "I have seen the buffalo lying on the ground, bleating and dying."

"They do this when we hunt them," Black Snake pointed out.

Slowly, Brown Hair shook his head. "Not in numbers without end. Always some live on so that they can feed us and clothe us another day. In my vision, *all* the buffalo were dying. They were being swept away by a ghostly horde of pale-skinned demons that overran the land of the people, trampling and destroying the great, life-giving prairie grass!"

"Pale-skinned demons," Black Snake muttered.

"Yes, and their numbers were even greater than those of the buffalo."

"Impossible! The buffalo are without end!"

Brown Hair looked at him, wrinkled face solemn in the moonlight. "So, too, were these pale-skinned killers."

Black Snake felt shaken, but he tried not to show it. When the sun rose, he would lead the war party in pursuit of the Red Horns, and he could not afford to let his confidence and anger be swayed by what Brown Hair was telling him.

Still, he could not simply ignore the old man's words, either. "You are saying the people are doomed."

"If my vision comes true, yes," Brown Hair said. "For once in my life, I pray that the spirits have spoken falsely."

"Perhaps it will be so." Black Snake put his hand on Brown Hair's shoulder. "You should return to your lodge and rest now."

"Yes," Brown Hair said. "That is what I should do. I wanted to tell you my vision, rather than taking it to Walking Thunder. I knew he would not believe it."

Black Snake was not certain that he did, either, but he said nothing of that to Brown Hair. He walked with him back to the old man's lodge. Brown Hair summoned up a brave smile as he went into the dwelling.

As he walked back to his own lodge Black Snake's mind was troubled. He did not want to believe his father-in-law's vision. At the very least he wanted to think that even if the vision did come true, there was no way of knowing how far in the future its dire consequences lay. For now, Black Snake had other things with which to concern himself: the Red Horns, the captives they had taken, Fire Maker's lone pursuit of the raiders.

River Wind was still sleeping peacefully, he saw as he entered the lodge and slipped back underneath the robes. Black Snake was grateful for that much, at least. The slumber of his wife and children had not been disturbed.

The same could not be said of his own rest. He expected sleep to reclaim him quickly, but it did not. Instead, his eyes seemed determined not to close, and he shifted restlessly in the robes. An unknowable time passed, and he looked through the smoke hole expecting to see that the sky was turning gray with the approach of dawn. But the heavens were still pitch-black, save where they were dotted with stars.

Suddenly, Black Snake heard a man calling softly to him

from outside. He did not recognize the voice, but he knew it might belong to one of the sentries standing guard over the town tonight. He came to his feet, hefting the ax once more, and hurried to the entrance of the lodge, worried that something else was wrong.

Something was indeed wrong, Black Snake saw as soon as he stepped out of the lodge, but not what he had expected. Mere instants earlier the darkness of night had reigned over the prairie and the town, but now it was as bright as day outside. Blindingly bright, in fact, like the sun on a field of new-fallen snow. Black Snake fell back half a step and lifted a hand to shield his eyes from the glare.

Within moments his eyes had adjusted to the brightness, and he could see what was around him—or rather, what was *not* around him. The town, all the lodges and the tipis and the garden plots, had vanished, were nowhere to be seen. He found himself alone on the prairie, and the grass was brown and dead underneath his moccasins.

Black Snake was a practical man, and as soon as he recovered his wits somewhat, he knew there were only two possible explanations for what he was experiencing. Either he *had* fallen asleep after all without being aware of it and another vision was coming to him . . . or he had stepped out of the lodge and actually been transported somehow to another time and another place.

Before he had a chance to consider the implications of those alternatives, a roaring noise behind him made him spin around, lifting his war ax to defend himself from attack as he did so. What he saw advancing toward him would not be turned aside by the ax, however, or by any other weapon. It was a force of nature, a tornado of pure white, spectacular, awe-inspiring, fierce, like nothing he had ever seen before. The storm raged across the prairie toward him like the breath of the Creator, uprooting the grass and scarring the earth as it came. In its wake came the very demons spoken of by Brown Hair.

Black Snake cried out at the sight of them. They were as hideous and frightening as Brown Hair had described them, monsters with hair on their sickly white faces and long lances held propped against their shoulders. Fire flashed from the ends of the lances, and thunder rumbled across the plains. As if the demons were not enough by themselves, they rode devil-creatures: long-tailed, four-legged animals that raced across the prairie like the wind under the dominion of the pale-skinned demons.

Black Snake fell to his knees, trembling with fear and awe. He understood now why Brown Hair had been so shaken. There was no doubt that Black Snake was now sharing the vision that had come first to his wife's father. Why he had been so blessed—or cursed—he had no idea.

The white tornado was still coming toward him, but it seemed little closer now than it had been when he first saw it. The demons were clear in his sight, however, and as he watched, other riders became visible as well: the Red Horns, astride the same devil-beasts the pale-skinned demons commanded! Their presence was almost more than Black Snake could comprehend. The Red Horn people were evil; they had proven that by attacking the town of the Prairie People and carrying off the captives. But would even such ruthless raiders as the Red Horns ally themselves with demons? Black Snake could not believe it. Yet there they were in his vision, as plain as day.

Brown Hair had been right. There were evil times ahead for the people. Soon the very prairie itself might lie silent in ruins and death.

But there was no silence now. The roaring of the tornado shook the earth and battered Black Snake's ears as it swept closer and closer toward him. As it approached it traveled faster, and within the space of a few heartbeats it was looming over him, ready to snatch him up into its gaping maw.

Just when it seemed that death was upon him and all was lost, the tornado lifted up into the air, passing over him, taking with it the pale-skinned ones and the Red Horns. Black Snake fell face-down onto the ground, shuddering. He lay there for a moment, until he heard a rapid fluttering of wings. Lifting himself and turning his head, he caught a glimpse of a hummingbird—his spirit animal—darting and hovering near his ear, always moving so that he could never quite see it clearly. But he saw it well enough to experience a new surge of fright, because the tiny spirit was as white as the tornado and the demons that had followed the storm.

Over the pounding of his heart, within the humming of the wings, Black Snake heard a voice, a soft voice that whispered, *Embrace the land, and you embrace the people. The storm blows the people to the four winds, but they shall return. The land shall call them home.*

Black Snake lifted a hand, reaching for that which he could not truly see. His fingers closed around the white hummingbird, stilling its wings, and against his palm he felt the beating of its heart, soft and faint like the breath of a sleeping child. He rose to his feet, extended his arm above his head as far as he could reach, and opened his hand.

The hummingbird shot out of his grasp, spiraled into the bright, silvery sky overhead, and vanished.

Black Snake awoke with a gasp.

He sat up, kicked away the sleeping robes, and surged to his feet. A few quick steps took him to the entrance of the lodge, where he thrust aside the flap of hide and peered out into the night, into the blessed darkness. There was no white tornado. The town of the Prairie People slumbered quietly around him, unmolested by white-skinned demons riding on devil-beasts.

"My husband!" River Wind's hands fell on his shoulders from behind. His abrupt rising from their robes had awakened her, startled her, even frightened her. "Black Snake, what is it?"

His heart still pounded heavily, but his hammering pulse was beginning to slow. He had not wished for yet another vision, but it had come to him anyway, and although he was not certain what all of it meant, he knew somehow that this vision was even more important than the one that had warned him of the attack by the Red Horns. He knew what he had to do. His mind and his heart would question his fate no longer. He would fight for his people, fight for his land, fight for whatever hope remained for this once-peaceful band.

"Black Snake!" River Wind said again, shaking his shoulder gently. "What is wrong?"

He turned to look at his wife. "I am Black Snake no longer," he said, not knowing where the words came from but trusting them completely. "I am now called Storm Seeker."

"Storm Seeker," River Wind repeated in a whisper.
And both of them knew it would be so.

Chapter Fourteen

She was jolted awake as the front bearer stumbled and almost
fell. Now, the third day out from the skirmish, they were carrying her in a makeshift litter. They had covered more ground
than any of the men had thought possible, because Fallen Tree
had urged his leader, Sun Chief, to keep moving at all costs.
Only twice each day had they stopped for rest and water. Caring
nothing for the other prisoners, Fallen Tree himself had made
the litter that held their prize. The warriors grudgingly shared
carrying duty. The other women and children could weaken
from the strenuous pace and even die; more slaves could always
be captured in another raid. But Moon Hawk Sister's time had
not yet come.

A different destiny awaited her.

She did not know any of this because she had lain unconscious after being forced to drink a potent herb concoction prepared by the Keeper of the Morning Star Medicine Bundle. Now
Moon Hawk Sister opened one eye to a slit, afraid of what she
would see.

Directly above, the deep azure sky held a blinding brightness;
she felt the sun burning into the skin of her upturned face. She
lifted her head slightly and saw the bare torso of the man in front
of the litter, trotting in time with the rear bearer, whom she could
not see and dared not turn to look at. All around her were the red-
crested warriors, moving like a single-minded herd.

She tried to think but could only construct her situation in
fragments and patches. She had not been beaten: she felt no
aches or bruises. She could recall a struggle when the giant—she
remembered the huge ugly enemy warrior, a giant! his hands
around her mouth and neck!—captured her. Then he had carried

her away from the town. How long ago? It had happened so quickly. . . .

A powerful jolt of memory nearly forced a spasm through her body, but she gritted her teeth and held on to the edges of the litter and willed herself still. Fire Maker! She knew now that he *had* seen her being taken, that he had survived the battle—and that he was somewhere on the prairie, somewhere close to her.

She realized she must not give in to fear and panic but must stay alive at all cost. Fire Maker would come for her. He must come for her. She prayed with eyes clenched and tears brimming. She prayed with all her strength.

They kept moving until well past sundown. Fallen Tree begged Sun Chief to keep pushing the men on because he could feel in his bones that they would be followed—at least for a while, until the defenders tired and returned home. The first few days were the most likely time for a counterattack. Fallen Tree's black eyes scanned the green hills and flats. Nothing—at least nothing he could see. And the scouts, the Wolves, had nothing to report.

Every waking moment he relived the battle, each step and each blow, the capture of the girl, running up the breastworks to survey the scene . . . the diminishment of the ball of pain in his skull. There was no time to savor the triumph, not yet—too far still to go before they were safely back to their own town. Then the ceremony would seal a blessing for his people, and his dream vision would be fulfilled. The memory of the fight surged through him, giving him the power to act, to command, to counsel Sun Chief, to walk proudly among his fellow warriors.

On the fourth day out, the Red Horn party rested at midday near a creek that cut deeply into the grassy surface of the plain. Here there was a large enough stand of cottonwoods to shelter the tired men and their captives. Fallen Tree did not rest but walked apart from the others, onto a low hill where he sat and let the sun beat down upon his head. He had maintained his tall red crest and war paint during the march. Like the others, he had not bathed. Their first task was to move and keep moving. Even this respite that Sun Chief had called was to be only long enough to catch their breath and fill their waterskins.

Some of the warriors had been angry that the Red Horns had pulled out of the enemy town so quickly, instead of killing all the warriors, making all the women their prisoners, and completely looting the strange-looking lodges made of earth. The town seemed prosperous, surely with an abundance of food and other goods for the warriors who had marched long days to get there. Sun Chief had held some of the men back, preventing them from even participating in the attack. These men were especially displeased. Fallen Tree had argued vehemently that no renewed attack, no siege, should occur, that the Knife-lance warriors immediately trek back to their home with their prize for the angry Morning Star.

Sun Chief, after much thought, weighing the demands of his warriors against Fallen Tree's strong argument, had decided it was best to return home, not to leave their village undefended for so long and to be certain the ceremony of sacrifice was held as quickly as possible.

Everywhere that Fallen Tree looked from his hillside vantage point, he saw a riot of colors: wildflowers, multihued sages, various green and yellow grasses, dark stones that jutted angrily from the earth. The sky itself was a brilliant, shadowless blue blasted by the white sun. Not a cloud was within his seeing— only a vast, empty, sovereign sky.

Warily, snakelike, his glance darted from one landmark to another, searching for signs of pursuit. He saw no signs but knew in his entrails that at least one enemy lay nearby watching. Who? And how close was he? Was there more than one? Fallen Tree thought not.

With his hand he lazily swished away the tiny insects that swarmed near his face, buzzing and stinging like flying thorns, drawn by perspiration and dried blood. He did not much mind them at this moment. Life was good, better than it had been for nearly as long as he could remember.

He pulled his legs up, wrapped his arms around his knees, and stared straight ahead to the west, toward home. He was returning as a dreamer of visions touched by the gods, the Morning Star most especially. He had chosen to be an outcast, a man almost completely apart from the society of his people. He had been— yes—a crazy man whom others feared and avoided. Now there might be a chance to live otherwise, perhaps to take a wife . . . perhaps the girl who had brought him water the night of his dream vision, the daughter of Lame Bull. She had said she was promised to another, but many things were different now. Fallen Tree himself was different.

He felt as excited as a boy, sitting there beneath the blue-hot sky, surveying the rambling and endless prairie whence he and his Red Horn companions had come on their quest for the Spirit Star. Any feelings for the girl he had captured were subsumed by his pride and his hope that his own people would now love and accept him for his deeds. They must!

She was beautiful, fresh, very much alive, and until he gave her over to the priests, she was his possession. He sensed that she was untouched and untried—a perfect bride. But he did not allow himself to go much further in his thoughts; he could complicate his life and ultimately destroy his own people if he were to question his mission at this point.

His people had known a difficult existence for many generations. The storytellers related a history of wars and droughts and famines and trials that had caused the people to migrate often and isolate themselves from other human beings as much as they could. Except in belligerence, the aloof Red Horn People avoided foreign tribes and even bands who spoke a common tongue; they traded little because they had so little to trade; they stole much because their crops were usually poor and they needed to feed their young. They looked more to the spirit world than to the world of people for hope and sustenance.

Growing up, Fallen Tree had never seen a time when he or his people had not known shortage and want. Hunger was his brother; sickness from cold and starvation, his cousin who visited every winter. As soon as he was old enough, he had taken his bow and his knife and hunted for his people. By the time he was twelve summers old he had become especially skilled at bow hunting—better than some of the adults. At fourteen summers he had killed his first buffalo, a bull calf, and had used the calf's testicle bag as a belt pouch wherein he kept his fire-starting flint and kindling; tufts of hair lay even now in his medicine bundle as a testament to the spirit power of that first kill. But this was uncommon among his people: they did not participate with other bands in the spring and fall bison hunts. They went their own way in these practices, and it was a way of loneliness and deprivation. Their priests enforced this differentness, telling the people that the Morning Star Medicine Bundle must be kept safe from foreign hands and meddlesome outsiders; constantly did the holy men sow seeds of distrust among the people.

Sometimes Fallen Tree suspected that the priests had selfish motives for such practices and teachings, though he would never speak to anyone of this suspicion. Instead, he held it in his heart and watched with brooding eyes. Always he would follow his chief and respect the beliefs of his people, whatever doubts bedeviled him.

The sun burned through uncertainty and memory. He lay back upon the breast of the hill and sucked in hot air, closing his eyes. He heard the talk and activity among the men. The girl was down there among them. He had thought much of her since he had given her over to be carried. She belonged to the Morning Star, but Fallen Tree had captured her, and for this act he would be recognized by his people. It was better than counting coup a thousand times or killing a hundred buffalo.

He heard Sun Chief's command to resume their march and went down the hillside to join the others.

Chapter Fifteen

On the second morning after the council, Storm Seeker led a party of twenty warriors from the town to find Fire Maker and to free Moon Hawk Sister and the other prisoners from their captors.

Before embarking upon such a long and dangerous journey, Storm Seeker spent an entire day praying and preparing, and River Wind worked with him and the other women of the band to gather provisions. The warriors repaired weapons and collected arrow shafts that could be reused on this mission. The village, astir with preparations, had little time to grieve for its dead.

From the winter caches River Wind and several women companions took dried corn and ground it into meal to cook a flat, hard bread that would sustain the men in the days ahead. They took the dried, pressed deer meat that had been stored for many weeks and cut and bundled it into packets, several for each warrior. The men packed their parfleches and pouches with provisions and filled their skin bags with water, for there would be no time to hunt, precious little to spend eating.

The council had directed that the men be out no more than forty sleeps. Any longer than that and the town would cease to function properly, and the lives of all would be endangered. Several warriors and elders would remain to hunt and to protect the children and women from further raids. The women, of course, stayed busy in any circumstances: tending the crops, preparing hides, cooking daily meals, caring for the children, advising their husbands and fathers in all matters.

Over a single sleepless day Storm Seeker had planned the pursuit with two trusted friends from the warrior society: Yellow-tail Deer, a stolid young soldier, and Follows the Wake of the Herd, an orphaned protégé of Storm Seeker's who considered the visionary war leader a man he would follow even to death. Each man was assigned his first command for this mission, a two-man patrol. Three scouts reported directly to Storm Seeker, who held overall command of the party. He outlined this structure and his general plan to the two younger leaders.

With eyes worshipfully fixed upon his leader, Follows the Wake of the Herd nodded enthusiastically at every detail of the plan. The more reserved and skeptical Yellow-tail Deer showed no outward indication of his understanding or agreement, but Storm Seeker could see that he was absorbing everything and knew he would speak up if he had any opposing thoughts.

He trusted both young men as well as the others in the small party. He knew them well and believed they would all give their utmost to bring back the prisoners; what he did not know was where their quest would take these soldiers of the people—and how many were destined to come back. The Crane band could ill afford to lose more of its young men.

Then there was Fire Maker, River Wind's brother, a new and valued friend of the band and perhaps a husband to Moon Hawk Sister, if she was recovered. Fire Maker was out there somewhere—alive, Storm Seeker fervently hoped. His party's first goal was to track Fire Maker; if he was alive, he could then join the party, adding another strong pair of arms to the cause.

At dawn on the day of departure, Storm Seeker led his men to the Lodge of the Sacred Pole. There they received the blessing of the Master of the Sacred Pole.

It was a somber occasion. The elders and the holy men wore robes of mourning, as did the women gathered outside. They would attend to burial rites when Storm Seeker's patrol had gone. The widows and mothers of the dead wept in the presence of their band and before the Sacred Pole. All the people of the Crane band knew their sorrow; all felt overwhelmed by uncertainty.

Storm Seeker's tattoos, the bold markings of an accomplished warrior, set him apart from all other men. Etched upon his skin for all time were the records of his deeds and his progress through manhood. The intricate black, blue, and red lines shimmered like a million spiders in the just-risen sun as he stood on a bare hilltop, skylined for the span of several heartbeats, and looked out upon the forbidding, eternal plain. His dark, smooth head was shaved and plucked nearly bald, with only a stubbornly tufted roach that shivered in the breeze.

No one had asked him why the name Black Snake was no more and why he was now to be known as Storm Seeker. No one had dared, though all were curious. The answer would come in time.

Each of his twenty men—except for three acting as scouts, who had to move more swiftly than the rest—carried back and shoulder bags of provisions. Each, scouts included, carried two water bags because they did not know how much water was available in the land through which they would be traveling.

Neither Storm Seeker nor his men had ever journeyed so far from their home into unknown country, among hitherto unknown people who were now their blood enemies. He had shared his concerns with River Wind but otherwise kept them to himself.

"Do not doubt your leadership," she had said to him as they lay together. "All the people look up to you as a man who has visions and who counts many coups."

"I do not doubt—the vision that came to me left no room for that—but I do worry. Before the attack came, I was afraid, but when I fought the enemy I felt no fear."

"It is the way of many warriors. My father has told me of this. He once told my brother—" She did not finish her thought but lay still in the darkness.

Storm Seeker pulled her closer. "I will find him, wife. I know he is alive and will come back to you."

Tears welled in her eyes. "And Moon Hawk Sister? What is to become of that foolish girl? What is to become of the other women and children who have been ripped away from their families?"

He had had no answer for River Wind then, and now as he scanned the teeming horizon, he found no answers there, either, only the certainty that pursuit and blood-misted battle lay ahead.

Storm Seeker wore the toughest buffalo-hide moccasins he possessed, expecting that the journey ahead would be long and arduous. He had handpicked the twenty men for his search party and advised them to dress only for comfort and utility—no decorated war shirts or other ceremonial gear. They were on a hunt that must be executed with stealth and precision. No show of color or tribal flamboyance.

The prairie unfolded like a great skin before Storm Seeker's eyes, rippled and dimpled and scarred with rocks, ravines, and coulees, dotted with sage and blue wildflowers. Little rain had fallen this spring, and the grasses drooped and swayed in the light breeze as the sun rose higher to the east.

To his left was a great prairie-dog town, larger in area and number of inhabitants than any settlement of human beings. The wary creatures popped into and out of their burrow holes like children playing hide-and-find games. They scurried through the grasses in search of food, carefully watching for hawks, snakes, and other natural enemies for whom they were prey.

The sign of the Red Horns' passage was clear, and Storm

Seeker's party followed it exactly. He charged the scouts to find
Fire Maker's sign and directed his party to set a fast, loping pace.
They had little time and much distance to cover.

Soon they fell into an easy ground-eating rhythm. Yellow-tail
and Follows ran on either side of Storm Seeker. He said to them,
"Before this day is finished, we must cut our brother's trail and
know he is alive." Their pace slowed as they moved up a broad
hillside.

Follows the Wake of the Herd said, "The scouts will find his
sign. They are good. But what we see this day will be two sleeps
past. It will not tell us where he is now or whether he lives."

"By seeing and touching his sign we can know about his
spirit," Storm Seeker replied. "We can know without seeing
him, and he can know of us. The Creator makes it so."

Follows and Yellow-tail exchanged looks that said, *It is true
that Storm Seeker sees things differently than most men, beyond
the present—but how can we know this about Fire Maker?*

The two lead scouts had left the town an hour before the rest
of the party and were not seen again until sunset. A third scout,
an apprentice who had shown much promise, ranged ahead of
the main body and watched for his teacher's sign directing him
and the others. In this way everyone came together at dusk
where the lead scouts awaited, in a tree-cloaked ravine cut by a
slow-moving brown creek.

Storm Seeker had directed that they would cold-camp until
they knew how close to the Red Horns they were. He was
pleased the party had come this far on the first day. They had
passed the place where the Red Horn raiders had camped their
first night—several miles south—so they were gaining already
on their quarry.

A veteran scout named Proud Antelope spoke first to Storm
Seeker. "The enemy numbers about forty men. They made a
litter to carry someone, either Moon Hawk Sister or one of their
wounded men. Fire Maker is following them; we see his sign
always about one bowshot to the east of the large group. He was
bleeding for a while early in the journey, but it stopped. I believe
he is not badly hurt but must be very tired."

"I am made to think he will have to stop and sleep sometime,"

Storm Seeker said. "We may catch up with him if he rests long enough."

"This is unlikely to happen," the scout volunteered. "He is trying hard to keep up with the enemy."

Storm Seeker pondered this information. It was dark now, and a thin, gauzy layer of clouds moved across the black sky. The prairie rolled out in every direction from where they were camped, and he felt very small and alone beneath the whispering cottonwoods. Fire Maker was out there by himself—if he was still alive—somewhere on the same giant plain.

Storm Seeker sat with his scouts to plan the next day's march. With no fire and the moon and stars obscured, he could barely see their faces.

"We must travel even farther tomorrow. The enemy moves too swiftly. We are in danger of losing much ground unless we run harder than we have."

Proud Antelope agreed. "They made no fire and probably left before first light. They are in a hurry."

"We need little sleep," Yellow-tail Deer said.

"Yet I do not want our men too tired to fight. They have just come from a terrible battle." Storm Seeker pondered the situation for a moment. "We will rest for half the night. There will be two watches. I will take the first with three men. Before sunup we will cover as much country as we can. Our scouts have good eyes!"

The men smiled in the darkness. They would follow Storm Seeker into a stampede of a million bison if he wished them to. His courage and vision bound them to him like brothers. He went apart from them to pray to the Creator for that very courage and ability to lead such loyal warriors.

She lay in the travois, her hands bound carefully by the giant who had captured her so as not to hurt or bruise her in any way. But bound they were now, because she was no longer drugged to sleep. She was fully alert to the morning sounds and rhythms of the campsite as the Red Horns prepared to depart.

Through the dreamlike haze of the past days Moon Hawk Sister had moved in and out of consciousness; in truth, she had not wanted to know where she was or what was happening to her. She had wished to be dead. No man except her original captor had touched her, but she had felt their eyes, like hard fingers, probing her every waking moment. She tasted tension in the enemy party—tension caused by the presence of a woman among more than thirty men, a woman they were not allowed to touch. She heard the cries of the other female captives as they were assaulted and knew it went harder for them because of her presence and the strange way her captors regarded her.

Had it been five days or six? Why should she care to count?

Her body was covered with a sheen of many days' perspiration, and her hair was soiled and matted. More than anything else she craved a bath in a swift-moving stream and clean clothing. Even on the buffalo hunt—where the work was dirty and difficult—the women took time after the evening meal to bathe themselves if they were camped near water.

Oh, River Wind! she almost cried aloud. Her chest heaved in a powerful sob. Why had she not stayed with her friend and the children in Brown Hair's lodge? They would all be safe in their own lodges now, if only . . . But Moon Hawk Sister knew in her heart that this was not true—that she had been *led* to go out of the lodge, that the Red Horns had been seeking *her*.

The night before, the skies had delivered a powerful downpour upon the earth. Thunder had roared and lightning crashed so near the enemy campsite that she thought they would be struck by the violent fingers of fire. Rain had lashed the earth as if to punish it for some misdeed. Moon Hawk had been placed under a hurriedly constructed lean-to and stayed dry throughout the storm.

Why did they treat her this way? Why was she so different from the other captives?

Whenever she finally found out the answer, she knew she would not like it.

On the day after the rain Storm Seeker's party covered more distance than on any previous day. The earth was wet and soft and sucked at their moccasins as they loped across the low, flat terrain.

They had covered about two leagues when, with the sun rising at their backs, Proud Antelope and his scouts stood at the foot of a long green hill waiting for the party to catch up to them.

"He is near," the chief scout told Storm Seeker. "The enemy is about a quarter of a day's march ahead. Fire Maker must be very tired. He has fallen farther behind than he was before."

Storm Seeker considered this news. He was more hopeful than he had been since leaving the Crane band's town; his wife's brother was near. They must find him and see that he was healthy. That was the first task. Then the Red Horns . . .

He gazed up into the sky and breathed in the moist, rain-cleansed air. He put all questions out of his mind and turned to Proud Antelope.

"I want you and your scouts to catch up to him as soon as you can. Announce yourself. Hold him where you find him. We will catch up soon."

The scouts disappeared over the hill. Storm Seeker gathered his men, Yellow-tail Deer and Follows the Wake of the Herd next to him. He addressed them briefly: "We will see our brother soon. The scouts have run ahead to meet him. He will need rest, and we must take the time for him, but as soon as he regains some strength, we will again press toward our enemy. With our brother back among us, we will have the means to attack with stealth and power. Follow me now."

He led them over the hill and across a stretch of near desert that had drunk greedily of the rain, sucking the moisture underground to sustain the short, tough grass on the surface. Storm Seeker soon spotted Proud Antelope and the others ahead, Fire Maker sitting on the grass beside them. He started to run, ignoring his own aches and exhaustion.

Then Fire Maker stood, and Storm Seeker saw immediately that he was weakened, no doubt by lack of food. Storm Seeker went to him and embraced him as the others of the Crane band watched.

"I am happy we found you alive, brother."

"It is I who am happy—to see you and to be alive to fight our enemy. I have followed them as best I could, but now I am far behind them."

"Come. We will eat and sleep. We will regain our strength—all of us."

They made camp close by a narrow river near a small stand of tall poplars, now fully leafed. A late wind turned the leaves and made them whisper. The sun bathed the leaves in green and gold light. Fire Maker and Storm Seeker sat side by side on the riverbank with their backs to the small, smokeless cook fire. They spoke to each other without words, signing instead.

The younger man asked about his sister, and Storm Seeker reported that she and his father were unhurt. The children? Same. How many warriors of the Crane band had died? Had Wounded Eagle been properly attended in his death? How many of the enemy had been killed? Storm Seeker answered these questions and more.

Fire Maker closed his eyes. He saw the battle again in his mind, as clearly as if he were back in the dust and confusion. He heard the cries of dying men, of the attackers, of the frightened children. He saw her—Moon Hawk Sister—in the arms of the huge, dark enemy warrior. Then he saw his closest friend from boyhood lying on the blood-soaked earth and heard Wounded Eagle calling his name. As if from above, he saw himself holding his friend . . . and his friend dying and all other thoughts dying and all of his own life leaking away like Wounded Eagle's blood into the welcoming dust.

Fire Maker heard Storm Seeker speaking to him and opened his eyes. "Sleep first, then eat and drink," he was saying. Fire Maker raised his hand to argue but realized his sister's husband was right.

Storm Seeker's men took their nourishment quickly and silently. There was a sense of accomplishment in their finding Fire Maker, as well as a deep foreboding over the more difficult task ahead. They would be outnumbered by a large margin, but it would do no good to brood about that fact. They all needed rest. Four stood the first watch as the small fire died.

Storm Seeker lay upon the dark grass near his wife's brother and listened to the youth snore gently. He laid his weapons at his side, rested his head on a parfleche, and closed his eyes. Sleep did not come for a long time.

Then it was morning, two hours before dawn, time to rise and begin this day's journey. All the men drank a little water and broke the night's fast lightly.

Storm Seeker dispatched the scouts. Proud Antelope and the others would surely encounter the enemy before midday. The Crane band warriors felt this in their guts. They watched the scouts leave the camp on their lonely mission and quietly prayed for these brave men who marched ahead ever more deeply into unknown country. Then they turned to their leader.

"Before the next sunrise we shall again meet these hated men who stole our sisters and children. May the Creator give us courage and strength. May we accomplish his will. We hope he will grant that these lost ones be returned to our people." He gazed into their dark, tired faces and saw that Fire Maker, renewed by food, water, and sleep, now stood among the men as the proud warrior he was. "I am made to think that if we are bold and unafraid, we shall be back with our families in six or seven sleeps. Wakon-tah is good."

With his war ax in one hand and a water bag in the other, he headed west. His warriors followed.

Chapter Sixteen

Darkness would be their greatest ally. Though Fire Maker, Yellow-tail Deer, Follows the Clouds, and the other men wanted to attack as soon as they spotted the Red Horns far ahead of them on the prairie, Storm Seeker issued orders to hold back. He even slowed the pace at which they were moving over the plains so as not to get too close to their quarry.

"The Red Horns will have men watching the path they have taken," Storm Seeker said as he and the others paused to catch their breath. "Now that we are close to them, they cannot travel beyond our reach in what is left of the day. While Father Sun is in the sky, we can have no hope of getting close enough to attack them without being seen. But tonight, when the darkness comes, it will be different."

His words were reasonable, but Fire Maker still raged

inwardly at the delay. The thought of Moon Hawk Sister in the hands of the Red Horns for even such a short time longer was almost intolerable. But he knew that getting himself killed in a futile foray in broad daylight would not help her, either.

After the short respite, Storm Seeker and the other men resumed the chase. The tracks left by the Red Horns were easy enough to follow now, so it was not necessary to remain within sight of them. They probably believed they were beyond any pursuit, Fire Maker thought.

Soon they would find out differently, he vowed. And they would pay for the evil they had done to his new friends—and to the woman he intended to marry.

The crying caught the attention of Moon Hawk Sister, a series of wails and moans that bespoke great grief. Now that she knew the Red Horns would not harm her—at least, not yet—she dared to twist around on the litter and seek out the cause of the disturbance.

The party had come to a stop. Moon Hawk Sister saw the group of captives that had been herded along at the rear of the group ever since the raid on the town of the Prairie People. The prisoners stood fearfully apart from two of their own, a woman and a young boy. The woman cradled the child's head in her lap. He lay motionless. As the grief-stricken woman writhed and cried she turned the boy's head toward Moon Hawk Sister. Moon Hawk's breath caught in her throat when she saw the bloody, crumpled-in side of the boy's skull.

Standing over the wailing woman was the giant warrior who had captured Moon Hawk Sister. In his hand was his war club, and the stone head was matted with crimson and gray. The giant had clearly just smashed the skull of the boy—for what reason, Moon Hawk Sister knew not. Nor did she understand why he now unbound her hands.

The other prisoners were so frightened of the massive warrior that they would not go to the woman to comfort her. Moon Hawk Sister did not fault them for feeling that way. She would have been afraid, too—she *was* afraid—but she was also convinced that she could take a few liberties not permitted to the other captives. She swung her legs off the litter and stood up.

Immediately, the two Red Horn warriors who had been carrying the litter moved to block her path, their hands going to the strange knife-lances they wore, but a sharp word from the giant stopped them from threatening her and forced them to step aside. Moon Hawk Sister went to the side of the grieving woman.

Moon Hawk Sister knew the woman; she was called Laughing Waters—but she was not laughing now. Her son, Spotted Beaver, was dead. There could be no doubt of that.

Moon Hawk Sister put her hand on Laughing Waters's shoulder, and the woman looked up and said through her tears, "He kept up as well as he could. He was ill. I would have carried him, but the Red Horns would not allow it."

"I am so sorry, Laughing Waters," Moon Hawk said.

She was not prepared for the expression of anger and hatred that suddenly contorted the face of Laughing Waters. "They wanted *you*," the woman said. "The rest of us matter but little to them. *You* are the only one they consider important!"

Moon Hawk Sister took a step back, flinching under the lash of the words. She could not believe that Laughing Waters was blaming her for what had happened. She searched her heart and mind for something to say, something to make the woman understand that she had had nothing to do with the tragedies that had befallen the people, but there were no words that would breach the wall of sorrow around the older woman.

One of the Red Horns grasped the arm of Laughing Waters and jerked her to her feet. Again Laughing Waters cried out as the mutilated head of her son fell from her lap and struck the ground. The Red Horn warrior gave her a shove, sending her stumbling over to the other prisoners. They were ready to move on again.

Moon Hawk Sister pointed at the boy's body and spoke to the giant warrior. "Will you not even give him a proper burial?"

The monster did not understand, of course. He pointed with his war club toward the litter, and his expression left little doubt what he wanted. Moon Hawk swallowed and went back to the litter, unable to meet the burning stare of the giant.

The litter bearers picked up their burden and broke once more into a ground-eating trot. The others followed, moving the prisoners along at the point of their lances, leaving Spotted Beaver's corpse behind for whatever scavengers might find it.

Storm Seeker's heart was heavy in his breast as he looked at the sprawled body. Spotted Beaver's uncle was among the members of the patrol, and he had fallen to his knees to chant a death song for his nephew.

Fire Maker stood next to Storm Seeker and asked quietly, "Will we bury the boy, or continue to seek his murderers?"

Storm Seeker took a deep breath. "Though it grieves me to do it, we will leave him until we return. Then he shall be laid to rest properly so that his spirit will not wander."

With a grim set to his mouth, Fire Maker agreed. Storm Seeker knew the young man was anxious to catch up to the Red Horns and wreak vengeance on them. Father Sun had almost slipped away beneath the world, and soon it would be time to do battle with the raiders, before the rising of the moon. Discovering Spotted Beaver's body had only made each member of the patrol more determined to slay their enemies and free the other captives.

"Moon Hawk Sister will be all right," Storm Seeker told his wife's brother. "They will not harm her until they return to their own town."

"But unless we stop them, they will sacrifice her to their dark spirits."

"We will stop them," Storm Seeker said. "We will stop them soon."

Fire Maker lifted his war ax and started to let out a shout, but at a warning look from Storm Seeker he stopped himself. This close to the enemy, that would only give away their presence. Outnumbered as they were, their only hope for success lay in surprise.

After a few moments, when the death song was finished, Storm Seeker went to the dead boy's uncle and placed his hand on the man's shoulder. "We must go now," he said.

"But . . . but my nephew . . . Can we not do something—"

"There is nothing we can do now, my friend. We have no robe in which to wrap him, no stones to cover his body. When we have dealt out justice to the Red Horns and freed our people from them, we will honor Spotted Beaver."

"But wolves will take him!"

"I am made to think it will not be so," Storm Seeker said. "The Creator will watch over his body and protect it until we return."

"You are certain of this, Storm Seeker?"

"As certain as I can be."

The man stood up. Storm Seeker, always a respected warrior, had proven himself to be even more worthy of their compliance in recent days. He had been touched by the spirits, and the grieving uncle had no choice but to obey his commands. "Where you lead, I will follow. And when we find the Red Horns, I will kill many of them."

"So say all of us, my friend," Storm Seeker assured him.

They moved out quickly, trotting into the gathering darkness, leaving the body of Spotted Beaver behind.

Creator, grant that what I told the boy's uncle is true, Storm Seeker thought. *Protect Spotted Beaver, body and spirit.* This was one more injustice that demanded vengeance. And avenged it would be, Storm Seeker vowed.

Fallen Tree tried not to lift his hands to his head and press them to his temples. He knew it would do little good, and he did not want to let the others know that the pain had returned.

It was worse now than ever before, a blinding agony that dimmed his vision and stopped up his ears, so that the words of his companions as they talked around the campfire came only vaguely to him. He understood little of what they said. He sat by the fire, peering down at his crossed legs, not knowing or caring if any of the others spoke to him. If they did, and he failed to answer, they would think nothing of it. To them he had always seemed less than sane to begin with.

Unable to sit still any longer, he stood up and paced to the edge of the circle of light cast by the fire. He wanted to flail his arms and rage at the heavens in defiance of the pain in his head, but he would not allow it even that small a victory. He turned and stalked toward the girl, passing the other prisoners on the way. They flinched away from him, eyes wide with terror, but he never noticed, nor would he have cared if he had.

The virgin was frightened, too, but she was stubborn and looked up at him boldly as he loomed over her. She would make a fine sacrifice, he thought. The wrath of the Morning Star would surely be appeased by her death.

Holding out a massive hand toward her, he said, "You will save my people. And through you, *I* will save my people."

His words meant nothing to her, of course. And when she spoke in return, practically spitting the words at him, he understood nothing of what she said, though her attitude was clear enough. She despised him. No doubt it would have pleased her to watch him roasting slowly over a fire, his skin charring and smoking, his eyes swelling and popping like ripe fruit from the heat. Yes, Fallen Tree thought with a grunt, she would have liked that.

He touched her hair, stroking it with surprising softness, but she jerked away from him, her voice trembling as she cursed him. By the Creator, she was filled with courage! If anyone else had spoken to him in that manner, he would have dashed the offender's brains out with his club. Instinctively he lifted the weapon, then sensed the sudden silence that gripped the camp. He turned his head, trying to ignore the horrible pounding inside his skull, and looked at the rest of the Red Horns. Sun Chief was watching him intently, as were the other warriors. They had come so far, risked so much, lost friends and relatives in the attack on the town of the Prairie People, all so that this virgin could be brought back and sacrificed to the Morning Star. And here was Fallen Tree, about to kill her before she could fulfill the purpose for which she had been destined.

Slowly, he lowered his war club. He turned and strode into the darkness, desperate for solitude, filled with the knowledge that he had to be alone with his pain.

The shape came at him out of the shadows, lance held low before it for a killing thrust.

Chapter Seventeen

The giant Red Horn warrior moved faster than Fire Maker would have thought possible. He brought up his club, blocking the lance and shattering its shaft. In the same motion he slammed the stone head of the club into Fire Maker's left shoulder, sending him spinning backward into the darkness.

Fire Maker landed hard on his injured shoulder, bringing a cry of pain from his lips despite his efforts to hold it back. He rolled over, fumbling for the knife at his waist. It would be little defense against the giant, but it was all he had.

The Red Horn was already engaged in battle with another member of the patrol, however. Fire Maker and two more men had been chosen to rush the camp while the others used their bows to cut down the odds against them as much as possible. Even now, arrows whistled through the night, then thudded into the flesh of the Red Horns. As Fire Maker pushed himself into a sitting position, he saw that three of the enemy warriors were already down by the fire, writhing in pain from the arrows embedded in their bodies.

Angry shouts from both sides filled the night air. Fire Maker heard the giant bellow in rage as he used his war club to block the ax of the man attacking him. The huge Red Horn was strong enough to wield the heavy cudgel with one hand, leaving the other hand free to pluck the knife-lance from the rawhide belt tied around his waist. Knocking aside his opponent's war ax, the Red Horn lunged forward with the knife-lance, burying the chipped-flint head in the Crane man's chest. At the same time that Fire Maker witnessed the brutal death, he saw Moon Hawk Sister in the glare of the flames, and his heart leaped. She looked tired and disheveled, but she seemed to be all right. He scrambled to his feet and started toward her.

Another of the Red Horns blocked his path and swung an ax

115

at his head. His left arm dangling uselessly from his shoulder, Fire Maker ducked under the blow and rammed into the man's midsection with his other shoulder. They both fell, Fire Maker on top. He plunged the knife in his right hand into the belly of the Red Horn warrior, ripping it from side to side in a disemboweling stroke before jerking the blade free. The grass was suddenly slick with blood and belly juices as Fire Maker leaped up again.

He had started once more toward Moon Hawk Sister when the entire world seemed to rise up behind him and strike him in the back of the head.

Moon Hawk Sister screamed when she saw the giant swing his club toward Fire Maker. All during her captivity she had prayed that Fire Maker would come to save her, and the spirits had seemed to tell her he would, but now that he was here, really here, and not alone but with other warriors of the Crane band, it seemed that he had come after her only to die.

But then someone jostled the huge Red Horn warrior, spoiling his aim, and only the thick wooden handle of the war club struck Fire Maker instead of the deadly stone head. The impact of the blow was nevertheless powerful enough to pitch Fire Maker forward, stunned senseless.

Her heart pounding furiously, Moon Hawk leaped to her feet and flung herself toward Fire Maker's sprawled form. She dared not think too much about what she was doing and had to act on instinct instead. The day the Red Horns had attacked the town of the Prairie People and she had been seized with the urge to be a warrior woman, she had only gotten herself into trouble.

Now she had one more chance to be a warrior.

She snatched up the knife that Fire Maker had dropped and darted toward the startled Red Horn giant. The hand holding the knife lashed out. The blade raked across the man's bare chest, leaving a gash that welled blood behind it. The wound was a shallow one, though, accomplishing little except to enrage the giant even more. With a roar he swung the hand holding the knife-lance at her. She saw it coming but could not get out of the way in time. The back of the monster's hand cracked against her cheek and sent her sailing backward. She tripped over Fire Maker and fell.

At least I drew blood, she thought groggily. *I counted coup on my enemy, and if I die now, it will be as a warrior.*

Storm Seeker had never heard such a tumult. The captive women and children were crying out, the Red Horns were shouting in anger, and the men of the Crane band lifted their voices in return. The clash of clubs and axes against shields, the ugly thudding of weapons against flesh, the gasping for breath, the rattle of air in a dying man's throat . . . all of it blended together in Storm Seeker's ears and made the sound of madness.

Even if his spirit animal, the white hummingbird, had come to him now, he would not have been able to hear the beating of the delicate creature's wings.

He and the other members of the patrol had fired two volleys of arrows while Fire Maker and two men rushed the camp. The arrows had performed their tasks well, drinking deeply of the blood of nearly a dozen Red Horn raiders. Although that was a significant loss, it still left the Crane warriors badly outnumbered. They would have to fight fiercely and be smiled upon by the spirits to survive this battle, let alone have a chance of winning.

Storm Seeker dropped his bow after the second volley, hefted his ax, and charged into the confusion of the camp. With the first swing of his ax he felt the satisfying crunch of the weapon shattering the skull of an enemy. He whipped it around, and its keen edge opened the throat of another Red Horn lunging at him. The man stumbled and died in a gush of blood.

The point of a knife-lance raked across Storm Seeker's side. Grimacing, he pivoted and this time used both hands to swing the ax. The blade bit deep into the chest of the man who had just wounded him. Storm Seeker jerked the weapon free as the dead man fell away from him.

He had accounted for three of the Red Horns, four counting the man who had fallen to one of his arrows. From what he could see of the battle, his fellow warriors were acquitting themselves almost as well.

But there were still so many of the Red Horns.

* * *

This was like the nightmares that had haunted his sleep when the pain was upon him. The leaping shadows cast by the firelight, the darting figures, the cries like those of spirits in torment . . . all of it made Fallen Tree wonder for an instant if this battle was indeed real—or just another product of the madness that sometimes gripped him.

But it *was* real, he knew. The pain of the knife drawn across his chest was little more than the irritating sting of a mosquito, but it was enough to convince him the attack was actually occurring. Without thinking about what he was doing, he backhanded the girl who had cut him and watched in horror as she flew backward and then fell over the body of the young man.

She was not dead, Fallen Tree saw to his relief. Her breasts rose and fell under the buckskin dress as she drew in great drafts of air. She lifted her head and glared at him, her eyes burning in defiance.

Such a sacrifice to the Morning Star would she make! The spirit would surely be pleased.

Fallen Tree lifted his club and stalked toward her. The warrior who lay on the ground beside the girl still breathed, but Fallen Tree intended to put an end to that. He would crush the young man's skull, then carve out his still-warm heart with the knife-lance. Such an atrocity would be barbaric even for the Red Horns, but none would dare reprimand him for it later, not even Sun Chief.

Fallen Tree was suddenly filled with power. The pain in his head had gone away, and in the frenzy of battle he had not even noticed its departure. He realized now that he could do anything—anything! He was godlike in his strength. All down through the long seasons to come, his people would sing songs of this fight and the glory and power that were his.

He dropped the knife-lance on the ground next to the youth. The girl tried to scramble on top of the unconscious figure, as if hoping to save his life by offering up her own, but it was too soon for that. She was not fated to die yet. Fallen Tree reached down and caught hold of her dress. With the strength of the bear, the strength of the mighty rivers, the strength of the very earth itself, he cast her aside. Crying out, she rolled over and over.

Fallen Tree lifted his club over his head, solemnly preparing to bring it down and crush the life out of his enemy.

The light from the campfire cast a reddish glare over everything, but even so the red crest of the giant warrior stood out. Storm Seeker spotted him across the camp, standing over a fallen foe, war club uplifted for the deathblow. To his horror, Storm Seeker recognized Fire Maker lying at the giant's feet. Nearby lay Moon Hawk Sister, also stunned.

With a shout Storm Seeker leaped over the fire and threw himself at the giant, whirling his ax over his head.

The massive, red-crested warrior turned with amazing speed and parried the blow that Storm Seeker aimed at his head. Storm Seeker's momentum carried him into the man, and it was almost like running into a mountain. Storm Seeker caromed off and went to one knee. The giant Red Horn warrior staggered as well, but he managed to stay on his feet.

The gazes of the two men met, locked.

Without understanding how he came to be aware of it, Storm Seeker knew he had been brought here to kill this man.

This huge, ugly warrior with the red crest and the contorted face was the heart and soul of the Red Horn people. A tiny voice seemed to whisper that certainty into Storm Seeker's ear, and he almost turned his head in hopes of catching a glimpse of the white hummingbird. But he kept his attention centered on his foe, who took a step back and waited while Storm Seeker regained his feet.

The Red Horn understood, too, Storm Seeker sensed. There was a connection between the two of them, and although men were fighting and dying all around them, they might as well have been alone on the endless prairie. This . . . communion, as it were, stretched out a moment longer.

Then, with hoarse yells, each man threw himself at the other.

Club met ax again and again; blows were launched and parried, launched and parried, the impact so great that Storm Seeker's arms almost went numb from the shivering force that traveled through them. If he died, he thought, the Red Horns would return to raid the town of the Crane band, believing they could attack with impunity. And they would not be the only ones. Other bands would steal the women and the children and the food of the Prairie People. The warriors of the town would try to put up a defense, but in the end it would be futile. There would be too many enemies anxious to take advantage of them, an unending tide of troubles.

But if Storm Seeker could survive—not only survive but *kill* this giant—then the Prairie People would be safe, at least for a time. The stories of this battle would be told, the songs would be sung, and anyone who envied the prosperity of the Crane band would know that to attack them meant revenge and death, swift and sure.

That had been the meaning of his vision, he knew now. True, an ending might someday come to the tale of the people, but for now—for all the seasons until that inevitable tragedy—they would be strong, and they would fight, and they would *win*.

With an inarticulate cry, Storm Seeker swung his ax in his most powerful blow yet.

And missed.

He stumbled forward, thrown off balance by the blow that had not landed. Somehow the giant had avoided his ax. For an instant Storm Seeker was defenseless, unable to block any blow the Red Horn warrior swung at him. That instant would be long enough, he knew, to mean his death. He could see it blazing in the eyes of the giant.

But then Storm Seeker's huge foe staggered, too. He reached down to his right leg, where a knife-lance had been thrust deep into the back of his thigh. Fire Maker had driven it there. The young man had been restored to his senses in time to save Storm Seeker's life.

Storm Seeker did not intend to let this new opportunity pass him by.

His ax bit into the giant's chest and drove him back another step. The Red Horn tried to lift his club, but a great weakness had come over him. Storm Seeker pulled his weapon free and struck again and again, driving the giant back. Blood sprayed through the air. The battle around them came to a halt and silence fell over the camp, a silence broken only by Storm Seeker's grunts of effort, the striking of ax against flesh and bone, and the sobbing of terrified children. The war club slipped from the giant's blood-slick fingers and fell beside his feet as he stumbled backward again. Storm Seeker wondered what force was keeping the man upright. Any normal man would have been dead by now.

This was no normal man.

But he was mortal, and finally he fell, toppling like a great tree. Storm Seeker stood over him, panting, drops of crimson falling from his ax.

The giant, scarcely resembling anything human now, looked up at him and said thickly, "You have not won."

It took a moment for Storm Seeker to realize that he understood the man's words, even though they spoke different tongues. He said, "How—"

"We are . . . two sides . . . of the same stone. Closer . . . than brothers."

Storm Seeker wanted to cry out that this was untrue. There was nothing about him even remotely like this monster in human form.

"You and I . . . we have our visions. . . . You can kill me now . . . but I consecrate my death to . . . the Morning Star. The spirit will bless . . . my people . . . and your people . . . will die. Many seasons may pass . . . but your people will die. . . ."

"All people die," Storm Seeker said. "Your time is now."

He brought his ax down in the middle of what was left of the giant's face.

He left it there, embedded in the corpse, and stumbled back a few steps. Lifting a trembling hand, he wiped away the sweat that coated his face, then turned his head and looked around. The only Red Horns he saw were lying dead upon the ground, almost too many to count. Some of the warriors from the Crane band were dead, too, but several were still on their feet, including Fire Maker, who limped toward him with Moon Hawk Sister at his side. Storm Seeker could not have said which of them was supporting the other.

And perhaps that was the way it should be.

"Where are the Red Horns?" he asked.

"Those who still live fled when they saw you defeating their mightiest warrior," Fire Maker said. "Their chief was already dead, and you killed their final hope."

"They still outnumbered us," Storm Seeker said with a frown.

"True. But you stole their spirit." Fire Maker looked at him intently. "I thought I heard you speaking to the giant, just before you killed him. How did you—"

"It was nothing. We were . . . cursing each other in our own tongues."

It was best that what the giant had said died with him, Storm Seeker decided. Perhaps there had been some truth to the man's rantings. Storm Seeker hoped fervently that it was not so, but he had been deeply shaken by what he had just experienced. This was a matter that would require much prayer and thought.

There would be time for that later. For now, there were more immediate tasks awaiting him. He turned toward the women and children of the Crane band who had been prisoners of the Red Horns and managed to put a smile on his blood-spattered face.

"Let us go home," he said.

The next day, Spotted Beaver's body was treated with the honor and dignity usually reserved for a fallen warrior, despite the fact that he had been only a child. Storm Seeker would have it no other way, and no one in the group argued with him. They buried the child in the side of a hill, sitting up and facing east, so that he could see the sun rise each morning. A war ax of the Prairie People was placed in the grave with him. After the burial had been conducted with great solemnity, the survivors began their homeward trek.

The journey back to the village of the Crane band took more time than when the same distance was covered in pursuit. Storm Seeker set a slow pace for the women and children, trying to ignore the urgent need he felt to see River Wind, Little Rib, and Feather. Finally the earth lodges of the people came into view, still surrounded by the wall that had slowed but failed to turn back the attack of the Red Horns.

The wall had been a good idea, Storm Seeker thought, but they had reckoned without the overwhelming numbers of the raiders and the ferocity with which they had fought.

Even a vision, true though it might be, could not tell a man *everything* about what was to come.

Storm Seeker took some comfort in that thought. The

prophecy of the dying Red Horn giant might yet prove to be false—or at least not completely true. Storm Seeker found greater comfort in the feel of his wife in his arms when she ran from the town to meet them. Other women, wives and mothers and daughters of the men in the patrol, followed her, drawn by the smoke of the fire Storm Seeker's party had kindled to signal their return. Those who saw that their men were not with the group stopped short and began to tear at their clothes and wail. There would be much mourning in the town tonight.

But there would be celebration as well. The captives had been rescued, the enemy had been defeated, and for now the Prairie People were once more secure.

His arm around his wife as he walked toward his home, Storm Seeker prayed to Wakon-tah that it would always be so.

PART TWO

The Black Robe

Chapter Eighteen

1725 C.E.

"Wake up, Your Excellency. It's time to move. You'll want to have your blessed Mass and set your arse in the bateau. Get up now!"

Father Charles de St. Aubyn of the Society of Jesus opened his eyes in the predawn darkness. He smelled the rancid breath and felt the cold hard hands of the voyageur captain and could not remember the blasphemer's name for a moment. The long brown beard fell over the big man's chest in two tightly woven plaits. Beyond the large head was only purple-black sky, the color of mourning vestments. . . .

Claude Grenet. That was the brutish captain's name. And— Missouri—the country of gray bluffs and deep forests so far from his beloved Normandy. He blinked the sleep and stiffness from his eyes and quickly sat upright. He sucked in lungfuls of frigid foreign air.

"One of the boys'll assist you in your toilet, gentle friar, when he is finished puking his guts clean of last night's drink. We missed you at our celebration."

God, take this crude, towering demon, the chancre upon my life and Thine earth, Charles thought. He clenched his jaw and amended his wish: *Father, bless Your child Claude, the lieutenant, and all their companions that they may know Thy goodness and mercy: likewise grant me Thy mercy and protection in this wild place that I may do Thy will. Amen.*

Charles stood slowly, his joints and muscles aching violently. "Thank you, my helpful friend, but I shall attend my own needs on this cold and beautiful morning. We shall have Mass in half an hour. Do you wish me to hear your confession?"

"Baagh! I left my homeland to escape the cursed clergy and their pious, greedy ways."

A black woolen cap was pulled tightly over Grenet's head, covering the tops of his red ears and nearly touching the single thick eyebrow that shadowed his dark and deep-set eyes. Black gaps and yellow teeth colored his crooked smile. His lips were dry and purplish. He was forty-odd years old by Charles's estimate—hard and sinful years, no doubt.

"You are different, Reverence, of course," the captain added with only a hint of sincerity. "The bateaux will launch in one hour. Time enough to save a few souls—even among these natural-born heathen Frenchmen."

The party that had left St. Louis four weeks earlier numbered seventeen voyageurs and one French officer, Lieutenant René Dubois, bound for the beaver-rich upper Missouri valley; one Iowa Indian guide and interpreter, who was paid in brandy; and one thirty-year-old Jesuit, assigned to the Platte River mission by his superiors in Paris and Rome. Each member of the party was a subject of Louis XV, by the grace of Almighty God King of France in this year of Our Lord 1725.

Father Charles craved nothing more than a clean hot shave to shed the unwonted whiskers that shadowed his grave white face. He had been the neatest and cleanest child and seminarian, always striving for purity in every aspect of his life. But out here in the wild there was no opportunity for such luxuries of personal hygiene.

He therefore crouched on the pebbly bank and splashed handfuls of cold brown river water on his face and had to be satisfied with that alone. He rose to his full height—a slender six feet, extremely tall among his clerical peers—and wiped his face on a black sleeve. He went back to his bedroll beneath a stumpy willow and gathered stole, chalice, and host (from a sorely dwindling supply of wafers). Using a river-smoothed rock for an altar, he said Mass, attended by the lieutenant and a few of the trappers.

"*Dominus vobiscum.* May the Lord be with you."

He gazed into the sleepy, illiterate eyes of the voyageurs and tried not to consider them less than human. It was difficult for a worldly, university-educated cleric to see those coarse adventurers as peers or anything close to that status. Yet . . . all such men—indeed *all* men—were children of the same Father in heaven. This he believed. But to practice such a belief took concentrated, prayerful effort for this Jesuit priest.

Lieutenant René Dubois was different. In his eyes Charles saw a cunning ambition.

Dubois stood about five and one-half feet tall, with broad shoulders and a thick peasant's neck, long wheat-colored hair, and a carefully maintained beard—a virtual impossibility in this place, but maintained nonetheless. Charles guessed the army officer was a later son or perhaps illegitimate issue of minor gentry. No money, but brains and drive. More dangerous even than the apelike trappers. He took Communion daily but rarely spoke to the priest except to issue orders. He spent time apart from the party when he could, brooding and planning.

Mass ended, sacred vestments and chalice packed and stowed among other supplies in one of the bateaux, Charles was ready to join his comrades on the water for another long day's travel.

The river narrowed and bent northward. The sun did not emerge from behind its gray shroud, but eventually the day would grow slightly warmer. The priest, like his fellow oarsmen, faced the stern and was unable to see where they were headed. It made little difference, for the approaching land was virtually identical to the endless miles already traversed. And so Charles closed his eyes and rowed mechanically, keeping pace with his hardy countrymen. They plowed deep furrows against the strong current, straining for every slow circle of progress. The oars thrust and flashed and pushed the water in swift waves. Father Charles angled his own blade and dug furiously into the river, winning his own piece of forward motion.

What did these men think of him? Other than Grenet's crude antipriest sentiments and the lieutenant's haughty disdain, he had no idea of the feelings of the others. Did they have thoughts of anything other than women, whiskey, beaver pelts, and gold? Did they ever think of God? Even the ones who faithfully attended his pitiful Masses—did they care for their immortal souls at all? And the Iowa guide—in his heathen heart was there a door through which the living Christ might enter to save him from eternal damnation? What of *all* the natives in this boundless wilderness? Did God love them as He loved the Frenchmen? Was God capable of loving any of these motley sinful humans?

An hour into the day's voyage he combed slender fingers through the moist matted tangle of black beard that hung like tree moss from his gaunt face. His neck and shoulders burned with pain. He held his oar across his lap, felt the hard wood against a callused palm. Wind gusted over the river and created cold, rippling waves upon the surface. In his heart and mind he knew that God loved him. But here in this most strange and hostile land the immediacy of struggle and the absence of the sun overruled all sentiment and logic: if God were anywhere near this place, He must be asleep or distracted by other, distant sinners.

Charles de St. Aubyn prayed: *In my work I shall find His glory. In His glory I shall find my salvation.*

On his thirtieth birthday, January 5, 1725, Charles had landed in the New World at Mont Royal on the St. Lawrence River. There, after only a month to recover from the arduous winter sea voyage, he embarked to St. Louis in the center of the continent, thence upon the Missouri River to the Platte, which widened and stilled in the country beyond the great limestone bluffs of the Missouri.

Father Charles rubbed his dirty horned hands together, careful to keep the oar balanced on his lap. The gravid sky hung low and heavy. It was still cold in the morning, so he was grateful for the labor of rowing the bateau to keep his body active and generate warmth. His breath plumed before his face, and the mist evaporated quickly. There was no ending to the gray sky or the dark river. Occasional stands of budding trees jutted along the banks as if clawing at the heavens. He raised a hand and flexed his long fingers in salute to the land and his God and the unknown. For the thousandth time he questioned the wisdom of his mission here.

He had forgotten what it felt like to be warm and thoroughly dry; he had forgotten how to participate in a theological discussion; he had forgotten the sensation of silk against palm or cheek. He desperately wanted to shave his four weeks' beard, but his companions—soldiers and trappers who looked more like bears than humans—scoffed at the notion and allowed Charles no opportunity for such a frivolous pastime. They tolerated his priestly needs, such as an abbreviated daily Mass and time for his breviary and his journal. But they were a gruff and restless lot who needed to be on the move; they were motivated by something other than religious duty.

Charles was seated on the forward thwart, and he gazed guiltily at the broad backs of the three oarsmen before him. Their shoulders moved with power and grace as they dipped their oars deeply into the brown water of the river. He felt idle and useless. Certainly he pulled his share, but exhaustion and fear claimed him at this moment, and again he questioned his presence and purpose in this forsaken country so far from his beloved Norman home.

The six long, narrow bateaux—two filled with supplies, the others bearing five men each—worked against the current, making a line that broke and re-formed throughout the sunless day. Charles rowed again in rhythm with the voyageurs, rowed until it became like breathing, until he and the others seemed unable to stop. The slender oar with a carved blade to push the water became an extension of his arms, of himself.

Lift, dip, pull.

Lift, dip, pull.

Lift, dip, pull.

The current slowed somewhat at the wide bend. Cold water lapped against the bateau and spilled over the bow as the priest bent to his labor.

Lift, dip, pull.

Lift, dip, pull.

Lift, dip, pull.

Charles was the third son of an elderly landowner's second wife. For most of his growing up, no one except the servants paid much attention to the boy, so he roamed the estate and spent most of his days alone. He loved to read in the woods, especially books about the lives of the saints. He had brought one of those childhood books with him on this voyage to New France. The book was beautifully printed on soft paper and contained a score of brightly colored plate illustrations of the saints in their martyrdom. He kept the volume wrapped in a waterproofed cloth in a small safe box with his most precious belongings.

That the priesthood would be his vocation had been accepted by Charles and his family from his earliest recognition. The local abbé, Father Basil, a stern rail of a man with a soul of iron, had instructed Charles from age five to age sixteen. He had poured his own hard understanding of Christ and canon into the boy's mind.

The pupil drank of the scholar's wine and became a drunkard for knowledge.

For months, since he first received this mission from his provincial, Charles had been in nearly constant motion. Preparations, packing his few belongings, a visit to his mother, readings on geography and the theology and practice of evangelizing, booking his passage, finally boarding ship and sailing into the cold Atlantic: all of it was a blur, half-remembered, half-dreamed.

"See him?" a low voice called.

Charles looked beyond the oarsman to where Claude Grenet was seated at the stern, working the rudder to keep them heading straight. Just now his single bush of an eyebrow hung portentously over eyes as hard and dark as coal. His lips drew back thin and tight, and Charles thought he detected the hint of a smile.

"Behind that thicket." The voyageur captain gave a brusque nod to the left, and Charles and the others turned to examine the riverbank, lined with thin alders and some type of thorny bushes not yet in leaf.

Charles strained to see something—anything—out of the ordinary. As if anything were ordinary in this forgotten wasteland. Some branches rustled, and he stiffened with fear, the blade of his oar hovering inches above the waterline. But then a large black bird lifted from the bushes and shot north across the river, just raking the bow of the forwardmost bateau.

Charles forced his breath to relax and gingerly dipped his oar back into the river. But his eyes kept searching the riverbank, seeking the cause of the bird's discomfort.

"Ain't seen him myself, but he's there, all right," Grenet hissed, just loud enough for Charles to hear. "Don't know how many—maybe just the one. We'd best keep our muskets primed." He spoke to the nearest voyageur, who put up his oar and proceeded to unwrap the weapons from their oilcloth bags.

"Don't worry, *Your Excellency*," Grenet called forward, not bothering to mask the smirking disdain in his voice. "These Indians are like lambs. The first sound of a musket, they'll be bleating and running in all directions. All they need is the right shepherd to gather 'em back in."

"Would that it were so easy," Charles muttered to himself.

His words must have carried on the wind, for the voyageur chuckled and replied, "Easy enough for a Jesuit, I daresay. Give 'em a touch of the fear of God—and a taste of our black powder—and they'll be turning them loincloths into sackcloth."

The priest pretended to be amused and continued rowing. Realizing he had hunched lower in the bateau, he forced himself upright, determined not to let Claude Grenet or the others sense his fear.

That he was afraid did not surprise Father Charles de St. Aubyn. Passing through these wild lands with nothing but one's faith and a handful of muskets would frighten the Holy Father himself. What so disconcerted Charles was not the prospect of dying but of being forgotten. Undoubtedly he already had been reduced to an object of idle conversation among his fellow clerics back home in France. It would not take much, or long, to be forgotten altogether.

To be forgotten . . .

He shook his head, forcing the image from his mind. *I did not forget her,* he told himself. *She was the one, not me. . . .*

"No," he muttered. He would not let himself think of her again. It was so long and so many dark, empty miles ago. Before he had donned the robe and taken his vows. When she had turned from him and chosen another, he had sought the only comfort left to him, in the arms of Mother Church. And now she, too, seemed to be turning her back.

He pulled furiously at the oar, almost knocking it from its oar-lock. *You will not forsake me!* his heart raged, the words stamped in creases upon his brow. *Not here! Not like this!*

His oar blade slapped the water, shooting a plume of spray behind the bateau. He slowed his breathing, forced his arms and hands to relax. He was not forsaken, he told himself. There had to be a reason, some sort of divine plan. If only he had the courage and the strength to discover it.

The rigid set of his jaw softened ever so slightly as he invoked the words of his Lord in a whispered invocation: " 'And I will bring the blind by a way they knew not; I will lead them in paths they have not known: I will make darkness light before them, and crooked things straight. These things will I do unto them, and not forsake them.' "

But while this favorite passage from Isaiah helped to calm his thoughts, it did little to unburden his troubled spirit.

In time, he told himself. *All will be revealed in time.*

"There he is!" Claude Grenet shouted.

Charles twisted on the narrow thwart seat and followed the voyageur's raised arm to a point along the riverbank. He saw nothing among the low, thin alders. But then he glanced above and beyond, toward the crest of a low hill. Someone was running up the slope, and when he reached the top, he halted and gazed back at the river.

From what Charles could make out from such a distance, it appeared to be a boy, though perhaps it was a short man. He wore leather leggings and had a dark robe—probably buffalo—slung across his left shoulder, covering part of his bare chest. He stood watching the bateaux for a few moments, then turned and raced from sight down the far side of the hill.

Father Charles felt his muscles stiffen, and he wanted to reach for his left upper arm. But he forced himself to keep rowing and tried to forget the arrow that had pierced his robe and laid a long gash across his skin.

They had called themselves Wazhazhe, and they occupied a region two weeks' journey to the east. They had seemed friendly enough when the voyageurs encountered them and had even invited them to sit at the tribal council with representatives of all five of their kinship groups.

The trouble had come two days later, and Charles blamed it on the young war leader Nobeze, or Yellow Claw. The voyageurs never figured out precisely what caused the bad blood, though Charles suspected it involved Yellow Claw's sister, Mitaiga. The young woman, whose name meant New Moon, had shown more than passing interest in one of the

Frenchmen. The voyageur was keen to return her attentions, but their Iowa guide warned him against it. No indiscretion took place, yet soon the Wazhazhe turned against them, and they were forced to fight their way out of the village. Vastly outnumbered, they were saved only by their muskets, which put the enemy into such disarray that they were able to make their escape up the river.

But not before Father Charles had tasted the sting of Yellow Claw's arrow. One other Frenchman had also been shot, but neither of their wounds had been serious. The same could not be said for the Wazhazhe, who lost at least two warriors to the muskets. For several days after that encounter, Charles had been convinced that they were being followed. But their guide, Two Crows, had checked their back trail several times and saw no signs of the Wazhazhe.

The lead bateau slowed down until it was alongside the one bearing Father Charles. Two Crows was normally at the bow but had moved to the stern, where he was speaking with Lieutenant René Dubois.

"Was that one of them Wazhazhe bastards?" Claude Grenet called over to the lieutenant.

The officer finished his conversation with the guide, who scrambled back to the bow. Turning to the voyageur, he replied, "Doesn't appear to be. Two Crows says it's just a boy from one of the local tribes. We'll know soon enough, no doubt. See?"

He gestured toward where the boy had first appeared. Three other youths—in their young teens at most—had ventured into the open and were scurrying up the hill after their friend.

"What shall we do?" Grenet asked.

"It won't be long before the men come looking to see what's going on," Dubois said gravely.

"Shall we make a run for it?"

The lieutenant shook his head. "No point—especially against the current. The river takes a bend up ahead." He indicated a point upstream where the river hugged the base of the hill over which the boys had run. "My guess is their village lies at water's edge on the far side. Rather than sailing right up among them, we'll let them come to us. Better to face them on land, muskets in hand, than spread out in these boats. Anyway, we could stand to resupply, and they may prove to be friendly."

"Like the Wazhazhe?" Grenet commented, his brow lifting with merriment. Without awaiting a reply, he pushed the handle of the rudder, angling the bateau toward the riverbank.

"St. Aubyn!" the lieutenant called as the two vessels moved apart. "You'd best dust off that Bible. I'd say there'll be more than enough heathen souls for you to save." He chuckled, then turned his own bateau toward land.

Dust off? Charles thought, shaking his head ruefully. *Dry out is more like it.*

As they glided toward the riverbank Charles put up his oar and reached into the pocket of his robe. He gingerly touched the oiled-cloth case that protected the leather-bound book, his fingers tightening on it as he breathed, "Be strong and of good courage, fear not, nor be afraid of them, for the Lord thy God will be with thee; he will not fail thee, nor forsake thee, until thou hast finished all the work for the service of the house of the Lord."

Chapter Nineteen

Hornet of the Crane band knelt in the center of the medicine lodge and tended the prayer fire, sprinkling dried sage clumps into the center of the yellow flame. Smoke enveloped his face. He sat back on his haunches to pray. Before him stood the Sacred Pole of his people, a sturdy remnant of a once-great cedar, now decorated with carvings and feathers and colored strips of hide. In the Sacred Pole resided the identity of Hornet's people, who lived in a large town at the edge of the Nibthaska-ke, the Flat River.

At the foot of the pole lay the sacred medicine skins upon which were told the stories of the Crane band of the people who lived in the Land of the Two Rivers. The Crane band had three sister bands: the Hawks, Otters, and White-tails. Each lived in towns located within three or four sleeps of the Cranes to the north and west of where Hornet sat.

As the chief of the holy men of all the bands, Hornet often had contact with members of these other bands. He was unmarried but hoped to find a woman, from his own or another band, to bear children, maintain his lodge, and tend crops for the family. He wanted a woman of intelligence who would also share his most secret thoughts and visions and offer counsel. There were many times when he wished he had someone close, not the chief or one of the elders, with whom he could discuss the things he saw in his mind.

Just last night, for example, he had experienced a most disturbing dream that reminded him of something he had seen on the old story skins—something similar to Storm Seeker's great vision many generations earlier.

A boy burst breathlessly into the medicine lodge without asking Hornet's permission. Such a breach of etiquette was punishable by shunning and withholding of food for a period of time. However, as Hornet looked up from his task, he saw that the youth, a boy of twelve summers named Badger, was agitated, perhaps in danger.

Hornet stood and frowned at the intruder. "What brings you here, boy?"

"Uncle, forgive me. I was out by the riverbank playing with the other boys. We have seen strangers. Pale ghosts who look like bears. They are coming up the river in strange-looking dugouts." Badger gulped for breath. "They will be here soon. I am frightened."

"Ghosts? Bears? Have you told others of this?"

"Yes. My mother. She is telling the other women and has sent my brother to tell the chief. She said I should seek you."

"How many were there?"

Badger struggled a moment with his memory. "There were six dugouts; two of them were empty."

Hornet eyed him closely. "And how many were in each of the other dugouts?"

The boy held up one hand, his small fingers outstretched. "Four? Five?"

"No more than twenty, then," Hornet said. "You and I will go to the chief, Badger."

The boy stood as if frozen by the door, his brown eyes wide with terror and wonder at being within the sacred lodge. It was rare for anyone who was neither a holy man, an elder, nor a victim of sickness to be admitted here. He realized suddenly that he had made a mistake by running inside.

"I am sorry, Uncle. I—"

"Do not bother about it. Let us hear our chief's words."

Hornet returned to the fire. He carefully built a bank around the flames, singing quietly as he worked. From the corner of his eye he saw the awed boy watching him. He remembered his own boyhood and smiled. Boys were the same in all times: curious as foxes but rarely as clever. They learned from hard experience; they pretended to be brave when they were often scared to death. This child, Badger, had a reputation for incessantly questioning his elders. Perhaps he would make a good apprentice holy man. Hornet would keep an eye on him.

What had Badger seen? Probably nothing more than a party of hunters—perhaps from their cousins the Gray Heads, who had traveled with the people to this region many generations before. They were given the name Pa'xude, or Gray Heads, because when they crossed the Uha'i-ke, a windstorm covered them with sand, giving them a grayish appearance. Their paint might well make them appear like pale ghosts to a boy.

Yet something within Hornet—a stirring of memory, of recognition—told him these were no ordinary visitors. He turned toward the Sacred Pole, toward the story skins of his people. On the skins were recorded events and visions from as far back as Storm Seeker's days. The famous prophet and leader had lived five generations earlier and was Hornet's direct matrilineal ancestor. He had studied the visions of Storm Seeker and the events of that spring and summer of warfare with the Red Horns. The boy had called the strangers "ghosts who look like bears." Was it possible these were the men described in Storm Seeker's great vision?

The holy man stood again to his full height. His skin was hickory brown, his head shiny but for a stiff black roach decorated with hawk feathers. His face bore the intricate blue-black tattoos of clan and office. He wore a buckskin shirt and leggings with little decoration. Broad-shouldered and slightly stooped, Hornet moved with the easy grace of a warrior and the measured pace of a holy man. He considered his words with care before he spoke to anyone—chief, friend, child.

He led Badger from the medicine lodge. The town of the Crane band was full to bursting with people, some from sister bands who were attracted to the prosperity and stability here. Through the generations the people had improved their lot substantially and learned new techniques to make their lodges sturdier and more permanent. Their farming and hunting skills also proved successful year after year under the aid and guidance of the Creator. Perhaps, Hornet thought, the people had become too settled in their ways.

There was tension in the gray air as he strode past cook fires and family lodges. Women looked up at him from their work with unspoken questions in their eyes. Small children hid behind their skirts.

Badger scurried at his side, trying to stay even with Hornet's long strides. Smoke stung the boy's eyes. He, too, sensed fear in the people but saw that they went about their tasks without interruption. They would await directions from their leaders before reacting to the rumor of the strangers' approach. After all, families must eat.

Hornet's long stride took him to the chief's lodge at the northern edge of the town. He said to the boy, "Wait here. I may need your help."

He announced himself and heard the chief bid him enter. As he pushed through the buffalo-skin door flap he saw that six men had already gathered by the chief. They were Hornet's friends, fellow members of the band, leaders among the clans, and they greeted him with raised hands. He sat opposite the chief, Red-tail Hawk, in the circle around the low-burning fire. The lodge was full of the scent of smoke and sweat. Red-tail Hawk, principal chief of the Crane band, spoke as Hornet settled upon his haunches.

"From the children and the women I hear of strangers who approach our town in dugouts."

The Cranes' war chief, Cedar That Does Not Bend, a reed-thin man a few summers younger than Hornet, raised his head and spoke next. "I have posted scouts along the river to watch these invaders. They will fight if the invaders attack."

"It is not yet time to fight," Red-tail Hawk cautioned. He had seen nearly sixty winters, and the last one had almost been his last due to an ailment in his lungs. Hornet had treated him and pulled him through the Moon of Starvation into the first days of springtime. The chief was still weak, but slowly recovering.

"The boy says they are ghosts," Hornet said. "Has their number been counted?"

Cedar flashed both hands to indicate twenty. "About this many. They have skin the color of whitened buckskin and hair on their faces. They are dressed in heavy clothing. There is one who is dark-skinned like us, perhaps from a faraway tribe like those who trade with us." He could barely sit still, so eager was he to supervise the defense of the town against what he assumed to be a hostile force.

Another man, an elder named Buffalo Scent, gestured widely as he spoke. "Yes, we must prepare to defend our women and our gardens from any who would take them. But we do not yet know who these creatures are—if they are men or spirits. We must all see them, perhaps sit in council with them. Then we can make our choice of what to do."

"My brother Buffalo Scent says words that are wise. Cedar That Does Not Bend tells us that these creatures have landed their dugouts at the Flat Rock." The chief named a spot along the riverbank about a mile downstream from the village. "Let us gather the women and children in one place in the center of the town, and our warriors and elders will go to the Flat Rock to see the strangers. All will be armed in case of attack. Yet—we will speak words of peace and greeting. If these are spirits, they could be here to help us."

The chief's speech met with agreement, and the leaders rose. Cedar helped Red-tail Hawk to his feet and supported him across the floor of the lodge and outside. The chief moved unsteadily but with purpose. Hornet offered his shoulder in support also.

Throughout the village word of the plan spread. Swiftly the women came from their gardens and homes and, with the children, met near the council lodge in the center of all the lodges. Warriors took up their weapons, bows and stone axes. Boys and girls chattered giddily, not knowing whether to be afraid or excited at such a momentous event—something that had never happened before.

Soon all the band's warriors were gathered around the chiefs, making a party of about forty armed men. There were six scouts already posted along the river, so the leaders and men of the Crane band felt confident in their strength to repel an attack, if it came. Hornet, however, kept remembering the images upon the story skin in the medicine lodge: white, ghostly figures riding great animals of many colors. These man-ghosts wore blue shirts and carried long smoking war clubs. And they seemed to be shouting as they rode to battle.

The procession moved slowly from the village, keeping pace with the chief. Though Red-tail Hawk walked supported by Cedar on one side and Hornet on the other, his strength did not flag as they climbed the hill to the east of the village. Indeed, he seemed younger, rejuvenated, as they gained the crest of the hill.

Hornet gazed down upon the strangers and the large, angular dugouts that had brought them from another land or another world. It was exactly as Badger had described. The creatures took the forms of men but were as hairy as bears, brown locks cascading onto their shoulders and dark, curly hair sprouting from all over their faces. What little skin could be seen was as pale as the inner layer of a cornhusk. Hornet was grateful that their shirts were not blue and their war clubs did not smoke. But those clubs were unlike any he had ever seen, and they shimmered with an eerie light, like the morning sun upon the river.

One of the young Crane warriors brought forth Red-tail Hawk's war lance. The old man held it with the sharp stone head pointing to the sky. Leaning upon it, he turned to Hornet. "You will offer words of welcome from our people," he told the medicine man. "And you will go with him, Cedar That Does Not Bend," he added, turning to the man at his other side. "If they will not meet us in peace, we will meet them in war."

Hornet handed his weapons to the young man who had brought the war lance, then started down the incline. Cedar kept his bow and arrows but remained several feet behind the medicine man as they strode toward the place of the Flat Rock.

Below, the strange creatures stood with their backs to the river, their hands gripping those curious weapons without sharpened heads or striking stones. They stood without moving, watching the two leaders of the Crane band approach.

Chapter Twenty

Charles tried not to show his fear as the two Indians walked down the hill toward the voyageurs. As far as he could see, only one of the men was armed; the other had handed his weapons to a companion before descending the slope.

But there were more Indians on the other side of that hill, Charles knew, and he was certain that all of them would be armed. The Scriptures commanded him to love his fellowmen, but that was much easier to do when they were not painted and armed and perhaps thirsty for blood.

He took a deep breath. There was no way of knowing yet if these natives were hostile; they might not be like the Wazhazhe at all.

"They seem interested in talking," Claude Grenet said to Lieutenant Dubois.

"Good," the officer said. "We wish them no harm. But keep the muskets ready, and be alert."

There was no danger of failing to be alert, Charles thought. Every man in the party was stiff with tension.

When the two Indians stopped at the base of the hill, barely twenty feet from the Frenchmen, Dubois moved forward a few steps. One of the men was tall and slender, with a look of strength even though he was not overly muscular. The other was shorter, thicker-bodied, with broad, powerful shoulders. He was the one who still carried his bow, and there was a quiver of arrows slung on his back as well as an ax tucked behind his belt. Both men wore buckskin leggings and shirts.

Loudly Dubois said, "I bring you most cordial greetings from His Majesty, Louis the Fifteenth, King of France."

The taller of the two Indians, who stood slightly in front of his companion, frowned and stepped back slightly. Whether his reaction was due to the strange language or the fact that Dubois was shouting, Charles did not know.

"He probably doesn't speak French, Lieutenant," Grenet said to the officer. "Two Crows can probably talk to him, though."

The unarmed Indian, who was still frowning at them, opened his mouth and spoke, but the words were unintelligible to Charles. He had always been fluent in languages and had had no trouble learning Latin in his youth, but the convoluted tongue of these natives had so far been beyond him. The voyageurs had never been around any one tribe long enough for him to learn more than a few words, and each group seemed to have its own language, although Charles was sure there were similarities he had simply failed to pick up.

Dubois turned and gestured for Two Crows, the Iowa guide, to come forward. As Two Crows did so and the strange Indians got their first good look at him, Charles thought he saw them stiffen. Perhaps they did not like the idea of one of their own traveling with these white interlopers. Or perhaps their band and the Iowas were old enemies. These Indians might try to capture Two Crows and take his scalp.

Charles prayed they would not soon have another fight on their hands.

The strange human being spoke the tongue of the Prairie People, but not well. Still, Hornet could understand what he was saying.

"These men come from far away, over the great waters, from a place called France. They seek not trouble, only the skins of the beavers and other animals that live in this land. I am called Two Crows, of the Iowa people. I lead them through this land."

"You are their chief?" asked Cedar That Does Not Bend.

Two Crows shook his head. "No. The one who first spoke to

you leads them. He is called Du . . . Dubois." He stumbled over the French name, even with the experience he had had saying it.

"The beaver is our friend," Hornet said to the guide. "Why should we allow these men to take his skin?"

"There are many, many beaver in this land. When these men leave, there will *still* be many, many beaver."

That made sense, Hornet thought. There were only a few of these strangers; surely they could not kill and skin so many beavers as to make any difference. They might as well try to wipe out the great herds of buffalo that roamed the prairie.

Hornet looked over at Cedar. The war chief was still suspicious of the strangers, but that did not surprise Hornet. It was Cedar's responsibility to protect the people of the Crane band. Therefore he would regard every new situation as a possible threat.

One of the traditions of the people, however, was hospitality. Visitors were to be made welcome, unless and until they gave proof that they were unfriendly. Hornet said to Two Crows, "We will speak with our chief and then return to tell you if these men may visit our town."

Two Crows nodded emphatically. His demeanor made it seem that the outcome of the discussion mattered little to him.

Hornet cast a glance at the strangers again as he and Cedar turned to walk back up the hill. Badger had been correct; these men had the palest skin Hornet had ever seen in his life.

Once again he recalled the tales written down on the story skins concerning the vision that had come to his ancestors Storm Seeker and Brown Hair. In that vision, which the two men had shared, a horde of such pale-skinned demons had overrun the prairie, destroying everything in their path. They had trampled the grass, slaughtered the buffalo, even killed the people themselves. Those demons had ridden devil-beasts and carried clubs that smoked and thundered. These men had strange-looking clubs in their hands, true, but there was not a devil-beast to be seen.

Hornet suspected that the creatures in the vision were, in fact, horses. He had never laid eyes on a horse, here along the Nibthaska-ke, but in the past, traders who had visited the town of the Prairie People from the south had claimed to have seen such beasts.

Riding with the demons in the vision had been warriors of the Red Horn people, who still lived to the west of the Crane band, much farther upstream along the Flat River. Perhaps the thing to do, Hornet thought, was to kill these pale-skinned ones right now so that they would never bring their horses to this land or form an allegiance with the Red Horn people. That way the vision of Storm Seeker and Brown Hair could never come to pass.

But even as the idea went through Hornet's mind, he knew he should never advise Red-tail Hawk to order such an extreme measure. The thought of killing all the strangers was contrary to everything Hornet believed; it was repugnant to him.

Not so to Cedar That Does Not Bend. Even though he was a warrior, not a holy man, Cedar was familiar with the legends written down on the story skins, and when they were out of earshot of Two Crows, he said with conviction, "I think we should kill them all *now*."

Hornet disagreed. "War is not our way. We will fight to defend ourselves or to avenge a wrong, but we are not murderers."

Clearly Cedar thought that was a shortsighted attitude, but he said no more as he and Hornet ascended the hill to stand before Red-tail Hawk. The aged chief regarded them gravely and asked, "Are the pale-skinned creatures demons?"

"They are men," Hornet said. "The one who travels with them is of the Iowa people, and he says they come from France."

"I have never heard of this place. Is it beyond the Father of Waters?"

"Far beyond, from what the Iowa Two Crows says."

Cedar said, "They come to kill the beaver and take his skin."

That statement put a puzzled, angry frown on Red-tail Hawk's face. "Why would they do this thing? The hide of the buffalo warms us in the winter and forms the walls of our tipis, but the beaver is much too small for that."

Hornet replied honestly, "I do not know. But as the Iowa says, the beaver are plentiful. These men cannot kill all of them."

Red-tail Hawk pondered that for a moment, then said, "The war clubs these men carry—do they thunder and smoke?"

Once again Hornet confessed, "We do not know that, either."

"They must," Cedar said. "The clubs are too spindly to serve as weapons in any other fashion."

Red-tail Hawk had come to a decision. "I would talk with these men about the things that puzzle me. They may come to our town." He looked directly at Cedar. "But you and your warriors will be charged with watching them closely so that there is no trouble."

Despite the grim expression on the war chief's face, Hornet could tell that Cedar That Does Not Bend was pleased. Cedar jerked his head in a curt nod and said, "It shall be done."

"I will go and tell them," Hornet said. He turned and started down the hill once more, alone this time. The fact that Cedar was not with him did not bother him; Wakon-tah walked at his side, always. Hornet trusted in the Creator to protect him.

Two Crows was waiting at the base of the slope. Hornet said to him, "You and the men with you may come to our village." He pointed toward the bend in the river. "It is beyond there. You and your companions are welcome. We wish no trouble."

"Our visit will be a peaceful one," Two Crows promised. The Iowa turned away to take the news to the pale-skinned visitors.

Red-tail Hawk's decision had been the proper one, Hornet thought. If he had been chief, he, too, would have allowed the strangers to enter the town. But memories of Storm Seeker's vision tugged at his mind as he walked back up the hill to join the others of the Crane band. By allowing these pale-skinned visitors to come among them, the Prairie People were taking a chance with the peaceful existence they had enjoyed for many years.

Hornet hoped they were not risking the very lives of the people as well.

Chapter Twenty-one

Charles was relieved when the tall, unarmed Indian came down the hill alone. The man talked to Two Crows for a moment, then started back to the others. The Iowa guide rejoined the party of voyageurs on the bank of the river.

"Chief of this band says we may visit town," Two Crows said to Lieutenant Dubois. He gestured. "Follow river. Find town around bend."

Dubois said, "Just as I thought. You assured them we are peaceful?"

"Tell them we not want trouble. Want only beaver skins."

Claude Grenet turned his head to look at Charles and gave the priest a broad wink. "Looks like you'll be keeping your hair awhile longer, eh, Father?"

Charles did not bother answering the question. He lowered his head and muttered a brief prayer of thanksgiving. Although there had been no trouble so far, he was not convinced matters would remain tranquil. The Wazhazhe had been friendly at first, too, before one of the voyageurs had roused their ire.

Perhaps everyone would be on their best behavior here. Perhaps Lieutenant Dubois should issue orders to that effect. Charles resolved to discuss that with the officer at the first opportunity.

For the moment, however, the voyageurs piled back into their bateaux and pushed off from the bank of the river. Charles joined them, getting the hem of his robe wet, as he did every time he climbed into the bateau. Were it not a sin, he might have envied the trappers their high-topped boots and leather breeches.

Settling down on the thwart, Charles took up the oars again and began to row with the other men. At least they had to travel only a short distance before stopping; Charles would not have to endure an entire day of rowing until his arms were on fire and

147

almost too heavy to lift. Within moments the sleek vessels reached the bend in the river, slid around it, and came within sight of moundlike earthen lodges built on the northern bank. Scattered among the more permanent lodges were several conical structures made of sewn-together hides of some sort, probably buffalo.

Women and children lined the bank, awaiting the arrival of the strangers. Dogs crowded around them, barking at the bateaux. The men who had gone to the hill to meet the visitors were now returning to the town, and they moved up alongside their wives and children, cautiously intent as they watched the bateaux angling toward the shore.

Once again, the bateaux landed and were pulled up onto the muddy bank by the men as they disembarked. The voyageurs stood together, holding their muskets at the ready, as a delegation led by an aged Indian, probably the chief of this band, advanced toward them. Beyond that group, the women talked animatedly among themselves, and the children gaped at the newcomers with wide eyes. Despite the excitement, however, Charles discerned more than a trace of fear lurking in the eyes that watched the visitors. He wished he could reassure these innocents that he and his companions wished them no harm. Perhaps this time the party would remain in one place long enough that he could learn the rudiments of the native language. He might even be able to teach some of the Indians a bit of French.

The old man who led the official welcoming party lifted a wrinkled hand in greeting and spoke at length to Lieutenant Dubois, who failed to conceal his impatience as he listened. When the chief was finally finished with his speech, Dubois turned to Two Crows and snapped, "What did he say?"

"He is Red-tail Hawk, chief of Crane band," the Iowa said. "Says welcome to land of Prairie People. Good land here, grow much corn. Many buffalo to west, good hunting. Says we stay here, be friends to Prairie People."

Grenet emitted a harsh laugh. "Stay here, my arse! Only until we clean out the beaver. I didn't come all this way to spend the rest of my life grubbing in the dirt with a bunch of savages."

While the Indians had no idea what the unkempt voyageur

had said, they could tell by the tone of voice that it had been contemptuous. Dubois shot a glare at the man and then turned quickly to Two Crows. "Thank the chief for his generous offer," he said, "but explain to him that we will not be staying here permanently."

As Two Crows translated the lieutenant's statement Charles repressed a shudder. The idea of staying here forever was as appalling to him as it was to Grenet, albeit for different reasons. He would do his very best to fulfill the mission given to him by the Jesuits, even in these primitive surroundings, but one of the things that gave him the strength to endure the hardships and deprivations was the knowledge that one day he would return to France—if he survived his time in this new world.

The chief—what was his name? Red-tail Hawk?—indicated his understanding as Two Crows spoke to him, apparently mollified by the Iowa's words. He replied, again at length, and Two Crows passed along the response to Dubois. "Chief say visitors are welcome for as long as they want to stay. Have feast tonight." When Two Crows continued, it was clear he was speaking for himself rather than translating the words of Red-tail Hawk. "Not be much of a feast. Crops barely in the ground, not time yet for spring buffalo hunt. Food not too good."

"We didn't come here for the cuisine," Dubois said coldly. "Express our appreciation to the chief and suggest that perhaps we might get in out of this weather." A fine mist had begun to fall from the leaden sky.

While Two Crows was translating, Charles felt someone watching him. He looked to the side and saw the tall man who had first met the French party unarmed. The man was carrying his bow now and had his quiver of arrows slung on his back, but he did not seem overtly dangerous, unlike some of the other warriors of the Crane band, who watched the visitors with narrowed, suspicious gazes. This man looked squarely at the priest, interest in his dark eyes.

Perhaps it was his robes that had drawn the man's attention, Charles thought. It was true that his garments made him stand out from the other men. He was as wet and grimy as they were, and his beard was almost as tangled. But the black robe was decidedly different.

As Charles met the man's gaze the Indian stepped forward, coming straight toward him. Charles stiffened in fear. *God be with me! What does the savage want?*

The man stopped in front of Charles and reached out, extending a long, slender finger. He prodded the priest's chest, then touched his own chest and said something. The word was a mélange of unfamiliar sounds. Then the man poked Charles's chest again.

"Looks like you've got an admirer, Your Holiness," Grenet said. "You fancy a red savage, priest?"

The man touched his own chest and said the same words again, and this time Charles realized it must be his name. When the man reached toward his chest again, he said, "Father Charles de St. Aubyn."

The man frowned. He prodded Charles again, and Charles repeated his name. The man shook his head and said something else. His finger poked Charles's chest. He repeated the words.

He had just been given a new name by this man of the Prairie People, Charles realized, something that the man could understand and pronounce. A part of him was offended by the casual dismissal of his real name, but at the same time he was glad the man seemed to be accepting him. Charles summoned up a smile. He touched his own chest and tried to repeat the words the man had spoken. It was difficult, however, and the man had to repeat Charles's new name several times before the priest could pronounce it well enough that his newfound friend indicated grudging acceptance. Charles was not yet ready to attempt the Indian's name.

The man turned, gestured toward one of the lodges, and motioned for Charles to follow him. Charles became aware that the other members of the party were watching him, as were the rest of the Indians. He looked at Lieutenant Dubois and asked, "What should I do?"

Grenet started to snicker, but Dubois silenced him with a look. "Go with the savage," Dubois said. "I do not think you are in danger. They seem friendly enough, and this man obviously means you no harm."

Charles wanted to believe the officer, but he looked at Two

Crows for his opinion. The Iowa shrugged. The choice was up to Charles.

Our Lord and Savior went among the people and ministered to them in their own places, he reminded himself. If he was to follow in those holy footsteps, he had no choice but to do likewise.

He followed the Indian toward the lodge.

The man her brother had dubbed Black Robe was frightened, Bright Water saw, but he followed Hornet toward the holy man's lodge anyway. That took great courage; for a stranger to come among an unknown band and place his trust in them was a common thing among the people, but these visitors were true outsiders. The Prairie People had only the word of the Iowa guide that the pale-skinned ones were even human. Hornet was a brave man, too, to invite one of them into his lodge.

So there was bravery on both sides, and Bright Water was impressed. She fell in step behind Black Robe, who glanced back at her in surprise.

Hornet had noticed her presence as well. He said, "This is my sister, Bright Water. She will cook for us."

Black Robe did not understand the words, of course; Bright Water could see his confusion. But he continued to follow Hornet. He had placed himself in their hands. Perhaps he was relying on the Great Spirit to watch over him and protect him.

Bright Water realized suddenly that she had no idea what these pale-skinned creatures ate. She hoped she would not disappoint him.

Tall and slender like her brother, Bright Water was two summers younger. For the past eight seasons she had shared Hornet's lodge, cooking and sewing and performing all the other womanly tasks a wife would have done had Hornet ever taken a wife. But he had not, and neither had Bright Water accepted any of the suitors who had pursued her in the years since the death of her husband, Lame Deer. She had married Lame Deer during her eighteenth summer and was widowed when he was gored by a buffalo during the spring hunt of their second year together. Bright Water would always remember the pale, lifeless face of her husband when he was brought back to the camp. It was an image that haunted her dreams to this day.

When her period of mourning was over, she had moved back into her brother's lodge. The parents of Hornet and Bright Water were both dead, so there was nowhere else she could go. She could have taken another husband, of course, but none of the other men in the band stirred her the way Lame Deer had. Still, her breath came quickly and a hollow formed in the pit of her stomach if she thought too much about the way he had made her feel when he came to her in their sleeping robes.

Better to remain dead inside, Bright Water had resolved long ago, than to torture herself with memories.

Black Robe looked back at her several times as they approached the lodge. Bright Water was glad her brother had given the man the new name; the first one he had spoken when Hornet touched his chest would have been impossible for Bright Water ever to pronounce correctly. "Black Robe" she could say with no trouble, and it fit the stranger so well.

It was all she could do not to stare at him. His skin was so white underneath the dark hair on his face. She had heard the boy Badger describing the strangers as pale-skinned bears who walked upright, and Bright Water had had a difficult time believing that such creatures could even exist. Yet here they were, just as they had been described. Not only that, but at this moment Hornet was ushering one of the visitors into his lodge.

Hornet turned to Bright Water as she followed the two men inside. "We would eat," he said.

"What? What do pale-skinned demons eat?"

"These are men, not demons," Hornet said sharply. "They eat what all men eat."

She began preparing a stew of dried roots and corn and strips of salted, jerked buffalo. Supplies were running low following the harsh winter, and Bright Water was glad that spring was near. She longed for the taste of fresh greens and meat.

While she was busy with that, her brother gestured for Black Robe to sit. Hornet brought out a pipe, packed it with some of his meager supply of tobacco and sumac, and lit it with a blazing sliver of wood from the cooking fire. When he had it drawing well, he offered it to the visitor. At first Black Robe looked as if he wanted to decline, but then with a sigh he took the pipe, puffed on it, and coughed heavily. Hornet smiled in approval. Black Robe managed to give him a weak smile in return.

It was good, Bright Water thought unexpectedly, to have another man in the lodge. She began chanting softly to herself, the first time in many seasons that the words of this particular song had passed her lips.

It was a song of welcome.

Chapter Twenty-two

The stew was quite good, Charles discovered, hot and savory but not too spicy. The woman served it to him in a wooden bowl and handed him a spoon made of horn and wood. Charles balanced the bowl in his lap, being careful because it was hot, and took a small taste of the stew. His next spoonful was larger, the one after that even larger. He had not realized how hungry he was.

Even so, he found his eyes following the woman as she served the man who had brought him here. Her movements were smooth and graceful. Charles had assumed that she was the man's wife, but as he studied her more closely and watched the two of them together, he began to think that he might be mistaken. There was a strong resemblance between the two of them, and there were none of the little touches, the private looks, that often passed between married people. Not that he was an expert on the state of marriage, Charles reminded himself; he was wedded to Holy Mother Church. But he began to think that perhaps the couple were brother and sister rather than husband and wife.

When the woman looked at him shyly, he lifted the bowl of stew and said, "It is very good. Thank you." The words would be meaningless to her, but perhaps she could understand the sound of his voice and the smile he put on his face.

The man said something, and Charles caught the sound of his new name mixed in with the rest of the incomprehensible statement. The woman cast her eyes toward the floor of the lodge, but she was smiling. Probably her brother had complimented her as well, Charles thought.

He pointed at the remaining contents of the bowl and said, "Stew."

The man caught on immediately. He pointed into his own bowl and slowly pronounced a word in the native tongue. The priest attempted to say it. His host corrected him politely. By the third try, Charles came close enough so that the man smiled again.

Excitement filled Charles's heart. He had finally encountered an Indian who seemed anxious to teach him the language of these people. It would be much easier to save their immortal souls if he spoke their language.

Charles was ready to move on to something else, and he was looking around the lodge for another object whose name he could learn, when the man pointed at the bowl in his hand once more and said, *"Stoooo."*

"That's very close," Charles told him. "Stew." He said the word clearly and distinctly, rounding the sound of it in his mouth.

"Stew."

"Excellent!" Charles said. This was even more exciting than he had expected. Not only was this Indian willing to teach him the tongue of the Prairie People, but he obviously wanted to learn Charles's language as well. French might sound a bit odd coming from the mouth of a painted heathen, but no more so than the Indian tongue being spoken by a black-robed Jesuit.

He was so caught up in his anticipation of being able to truly communicate with the man that he did not notice the woman mouthing the new word along with her brother.

Hornet had no trouble speaking and understanding the different dialects used by the other bands along the Flat River that he served as medicine man. But Black Robe's tongue was completely foreign to him. As the two men stammered at each other

Hornet tried to contain his frustration. He wondered if these strange visitors had a different word for *everything*.

Hornet noticed that his sister was paying close attention to the exchange of words. He had not been surprised when she followed them into the lodge. After all, she cooked for him and tended his lodge, and when he had a guest, it was her duty to serve the visitor as well.

But something about Bright Water's behavior now struck Hornet as strange. She was acting almost as if Black Robe were a man of the people, and one who might be looking for a wife, at that. Hornet tried not to frown; the thoughts going through his head were almost unthinkable.

He concentrated instead on the exchange of words between himself and Black Robe. He was more convinced than ever that Black Robe and the others, pale-skinned though they might be, were truly men and not demons. If that were true, then they were surely not the destroyers from the vision of Hornet's ancestor, either. That was what he wanted to believe, but he was not sure.

Men could destroy as easily as demons. The Red Horn people were proof of that. Their raids had continued sporadically through the generations.

A voice called from outside the lodge, a voice belonging to one of the strangers, Hornet realized. The words the man spoke meant nothing to him, except for a mention of the name Black Robe had claimed was his true name. Black Robe glanced around, surprised. He said something to Hornet, perhaps an apology for leaving, then stood up, placing his empty bowl on the ground. He looked at Bright Water, smiled, and spoke directly to her. "Stew" and "good" were the only words Hornet understood. Bright Water might have understood even less, but again she smiled and looked down, as if complimented by a warrior she considered handsome.

Hornet did not think Black Robe was handsome—but Hornet was not a woman. The only things he cared about were that Black Robe was intelligent and friendly. Hornet hoped to learn much from him; a shaman never truly stopped learning, not if he wished to serve his people well.

When Black Robe had left the lodge, Bright Water gathered

up the empty bowls and, without looking at her brother, said, "He is a good man."

"Black Robe?" Hornet scowled. "I think he is. But I would know him better."

"As would I."

Hornet looked at her intently. "He has just come among us. He is not of the people, Bright Water."

"I know these things."

"Then you should care about them. Care as well about your brother."

"You know I do," Bright Water said. She turned away, ending the conversation.

But not the worry that suddenly filled Hornet's heart.

"What do you think, Father?" Lieutenant Dubois asked. "Can we trust these people?"

Charles hesitated, then said, "I believe so. The man who invited me into his lodge is quite friendly. We've been trying to learn each other's language."

"Good. If you can talk to them, so much the better. I don't completely trust the Iowa. I'm never sure if he's translating correctly or not." The lieutenant glanced up at the sky. The mist had stopped falling, but the clouds, flat and gray, promised more moisture later. "I should get back to the lodge of Red-tail Hawk. I told him through Two Crows that I wanted to make sure the bateaux were secured. Actually I just wanted your opinion of these people, Father."

"I have given it to you." Charles was anxious to return to the lodge and continue learning the language of the Prairie People.

"Indeed you have." With that, Dubois turned away and started toward the chief's lodge in the center of the town.

Charles watched after the lieutenant for a moment, then swung around toward the lodge of his newfound friend. To his surprise, the man pushed through the entrance of the lodge, cast an unfathomable look at the priest, and stalked away.

Charles frowned in a mixture of surprise and regret. He thought he had been getting along well with the man, but the expression on the Indian's face had been almost angry, as if Charles had unwittingly offended him. Baffled as to what it might have been, Charles started to go after him, thinking that perhaps they might discuss the problem. Then he realized how futile that would be. They had learned nowhere near enough of each other's language to carry on such a complicated conversation.

The woman stepped out of the lodge then and spoke to Charles. He recognized nothing of what she said except the name he had been given. She pointed toward her brother and shook her head, and Charles understood that; she was telling him to leave the man alone. Charles did not want to make the situation worse through his ignorance.

The woman gestured for him to come back into the lodge. Charles hesitated, then followed her. She let the covering fall back over the entrance, so that the interior was lit only by the fire and the faint light of the overcast day that came through the smoke hole. Charles sat down again, grateful for the warmth of the fire. His eyes followed her as she brought him a hollowed-out gourd with some sort of drink in it. She held it out to him, and as he took it from her his fingers brushed hers.

Given the natural hue of her skin and the reddish glow of the flames, it was impossible to tell if her face was flushed or not. But Charles thought it was, and as he brought the gourd to his lips and sipped the hot liquid within it, he tried to figure out why she would display such a reaction from a simple, meaningless touch.

Unless it was not so meaningless to her, he thought. Perhaps all the veiled looks she had been giving him were not without meaning, either.

His fingers tightened on the gourd. This woman had no idea what his cassock meant, nor the significance of the crucifix that hung from a chain around his neck. She had never heard of the Society of Jesus, and vows of poverty and chastity had no meaning at all for her.

She saw him, Charles realized with a shock, as a man.

Under his breath he muttered a prayer for strength and fixed his gaze on the gourd in his hands. Inevitably his eyes were drawn back to the woman, who had backed away and now sat solemnly on the other side of the fire. As seemed to be her habit, she was not looking directly at him, but he knew he commanded her entire attention.

She was lovely, Charles thought. Any man with eyes could see that, even a priest.

Her face was rounded; her hair, black as a raven's wing, was parted in the center and drawn into two braids, the ends of which were caught together at the back of the neck so that the braids formed symmetrical loops. Around her neck hung a necklace of painted, braided rawhide. Her dress was pale buckskin with colorful quillwork and tight enough at breast and hip to show her womanly curves. Beneath it she wore leggings and moccasins.

Charles burned with shame as he considered her body. He wished she would look up and meet his gaze so that he would be so embarrassed he would have to tear his eyes away. But she did not; obviously she was willing to sit there the rest of the afternoon and allow him to study her in a way that no priest should ever look at a woman.

The breath in his throat sounded loud and harsh to him.

Dear God! he thought wildly. He was as consumed by lust as the trappers who had nearly gotten them all killed at the hands of the Wazhazhe. What was wrong with him? Was he so overcome by the wildness, the dreary isolation of this land, that he was willing to turn to a woman for comfort? Willing to turn his back on his faith and his order and abandon the mission that had brought him here?

Of course not. I am stronger than that.

He clung to that thought.

And he was exceedingly grateful, a moment later, when the man whose lodge this was thrust aside the hide covering over the entrance and strode back in. He took his seat by the fire and nodded toward Charles. The expression on his face was friendly once more; he had gotten over whatever had upset him earlier. Not only that, but he was ready to resume the language lesson. He took off one of his moccasins, held it up, and spoke the name for it among the Prairie People.

Charles repeated the word several times until he got it right, then straightened one of his legs, pointed at his own foot, and said, "Boot."

The Indian accepted the challenge, trying to form the word with his mouth.

Charles fervently hoped that his host would not become angry with him again. *And* that he would not be left alone with the woman. That way lay danger, not only for himself and his companions—he thought uneasily of the Wazhazhe—but for his soul as well.

Chapter Twenty-three

Charles sat in front of Hornet's lodge, his journal propped open in his lap as he wrote in it. The nib of the quill pen scratched furiously on the fine paper. He wrote quickly, looking up from time to time as he considered the words he was inscribing into the black, leather-bound volume. The journal looked something like a Bible, but it was not Holy Scripture, of course. No divine inspiration guided the pen of St. Aubyn. What he wrote were only the thoughts and observations of a mortal man.

So much, he thought. So much to write. These people and their land were a boundless source of material.

The sun warmed him. It felt good to be dry and relatively clean. The spring storms were over, and most of the time the sky was a deep, cloudless blue. The crops planted in the gardens of the Prairie People were growing well. The spring buffalo hunt had been conducted only the week before, and Charles had been allowed to go along. Never had he seen such a thrilling spectacle. It had been a good hunt, and the people were satisfied.

Difficult to believe that a little less than two months had passed since he had come here among the Prairie People. In some ways it seemed as if he had been with them his entire life.

"Ho, Black Robe! I see you are adding more to your story skins."

The greeting made Charles look up. "Hornet, my friend," he

said. "Sit with me for a time and enjoy the warm sun and the breeze."

The medicine man sank cross-legged onto the ground next to Charles. They conversed easily now, speaking the language of the Prairie People for the most part, with an occasional word of French thrown in. Charles had grasped the language of the people better than Hornet or Bright Water or any of the other members of the Crane band had mastered French. But nearly everyone in the town could now communicate with the pale-skinned visitors, at least to some extent.

"The Flat River is lower this morning," Hornet said. "Soon you and your friends will be able to leave."

There was regret in his voice as he spoke. Despite a certain friction between them during the early days of their relationship, Charles and Hornet had become close friends. Both of them had been glad that the current of the Nibthaska-ke, swollen by the snowmelt in the distant mountains and the spring rain, had grown too strong to allow the voyageurs to leave for a time. While there were many beaver along the streams of this area, the animals' numbers were even greater in the mountains. Lieutenant Dubois, Grenet, and the other men had soon been ready to push on, but they had been unwilling to travel overland. They would wait for the river to go down, Dubois had decided.

Now, according to Hornet, that was exactly what was happening. Charles could not help but be disappointed. He had barely gotten started on his magnum opus.

He was not certain when the idea had come to him—sometime early during his stay in the town of the Crane band, he was sure of that. He would write a book, he had decided, a book about this new world, about the Prairie People and their land and customs. To that end, he had begun keeping a journal that would form the basis for the book, recording his thoughts and impressions. Hornet had proven extremely helpful, sitting for hours on end with Charles and answering every question the priest asked. In addition to that, he had taken Charles along on his visits to the towns of the Hawks, the Otters, and the White-tails, farther upstream on the Nibthaska-ke. With Hornet's assistance Charles had been able to talk at length with the chiefs and medicine men of those bands.

When he returned to France and wrote his book, it would be magnificent; Charles was certain of that. Not only would it win him great acclaim among his fellow Jesuits, but it might even attract the attention of royalty. Charles could imagine himself in an audience with the king, explaining how he had come to write such an impressive volume.

But now Hornet was telling him that the party of voyageurs would be leaving soon, and all Charles's plans would be ruined if he was forced to depart with them. There was still so much to learn about the Prairie People!

"I don't want to go," he said dully.

Hornet glanced over at him in surprise. "Then do not. Stay here with us."

Charles looked down at the ground. "When I was sent to this land, I was supposed to accompany the voyageurs wherever they went. I was charged with bringing the word of God to the inhabitants of this land."

Shame weighed heavily inside him. Since arriving here in the town of the Crane band, he had spent hardly any time ministering to the spiritual needs of the people. From the first he had been too excited about learning their language and their way of life, their culture. True, he had preached to Hornet and some of the others about Christ the Savior, but in return they had told him of Wakon-tah, the Creator, the Giver of Breath. The discussion of religion had been simply part of the exchange of ideas rather than a conscious attempt on his part to convert these people, whom any priest worthy of the title would consider to be a group of sinful, godless savages.

And yet, Charles had never met a more fundamentally decent man than Hornet. Even though until recently Hornet had never heard of the Savior, Charles knew him to be kind and just and brave. How could any man who had not been touched by the Lord Jesus Christ possess those qualities?

Charles had no answer for that question.

He had a more immediate problem now. He put the journal aside and looked intently at Hornet. "Are you offering me a home here?" he asked.

Hornet considered for a moment, then said, "Brown Hair, my honored ancestor, was an Osage, as was his daughter River

Wind, the wife of Storm Seeker. Fire Maker, the brother of River Wind, was a mighty warrior and a great friend to the Prairie People. They became part of us, as have others from different bands." He smiled and clasped Charles's arm. "You are Black Robe . . . of the Norman band of the Prairie People."

Charles was as touched as he had been by anything in his life. He swallowed hard and said, "I thank you, Hornet. But I still do not know if I can stay."

Another moment of silence passed between them, and then Hornet said, "Bright Water would be sad if you left us."

Charles knew that admission cost Hornet an effort, even though they were now the best of friends. They never discussed how Bright Water felt about Charles. Yet even a blind man unable to see the light in Bright Water's eyes whenever Charles was nearby would have heard the happiness in her voice and known what was in her heart. Hornet was neither blind nor deaf. He knew that his sister loved the man called Black Robe.

Charles was equally aware of it, and her feelings for him—along with his for her—had become a conundrum he could not solve, no matter how much he pondered or prayed. Did he love Bright Water? He loved the way she smiled at him. He loved the warm touch of her hand when it sometimes lingered on his arm. He loved her laughter and the way she sighed. The songs she chanted as she worked around the lodge soothed him and made him forget his worries.

And, shameful though it was to admit, even in the depths of his own mind and soul, he desired her, desired her with a need and an urgency he had thought to be successfully banished from his existence long, long ago. More than once since coming to this place and meeting Bright Water, he had awakened in the night sweating and shivering, his whole body a-throb with wanting.

If that was love—and he was woefully lacking in the experience to tell if it was—then yes, he was in love with Bright Water. He realized that now as he sat in the warm morning sun with Hornet.

All the more reason not to stay.

The thought was painful, even agonizing, but he knew it was the right decision. He had to leave the town of the Crane band, had to journey on to the mountains with Dubois and the other voyageurs. *Get thee behind me, Satan.*

Bright Water was no fallen angel, but she *was* temptation. Charles knew he had to put that temptation as far behind him as possible.

"I am truly sorry, Hornet, but I cannot—"

A series of urgent shouts interrupted him, and Hornet came to his feet in a lithe, uncoiling motion, looking toward the river. The shouts came from that direction.

"There is trouble," he said sharply to Charles.

Several men were running along the riverbank from downstream. Charles could not recognize them from this distance, but he knew they were members of the Crane band.

Beyond the running men, at the bend in the river, several canoes came into view, gliding along the surface past the hill, propelled by paddles. More of the sleek, hide-and-bark vessels followed, all of them filled with men like the first ones. Charles's eyes widened in surprise and more than a little fear as he watched their approach. These were not French bateaux, and they were not manned by voyageurs. Inside these canoes were warriors, grim-faced and painted for battle—and they were coming straight toward the town of the Crane band.

"Wazhazhe," Hornet said, his voice hushed. "Osage."

Charles had known that the Wazhazhe were also called Osage by the French, and he knew as well that there were ties of family and friendship between them and the Crane band. He had said nothing to Hornet or anyone else about the trouble between the voyageurs and the Wazhazhe downstream, thinking that they had not been pursued from the Wazhazhe town. Charles had hoped that was all over. Two Crows had assured them that too much time had passed, that they would not be followed by any vengeance-seeking Osage.

It appeared that Two Crows had been wrong.

Bright Water emerged from the lodge behind Charles and Hornet. "What is it, Black Robe? What is wrong?"

Charles was too upset to do more than note in passing that she had addressed him rather than her brother, as would have been more proper. He turned to her and said, "It looks like an Osage war party."

Bright Water shook her head. "That cannot be. The Osage are our friends."

Charles did not want to tell her that what she said might be true for the Crane band, but it did not necessarily apply to their pale-skinned visitors.

"We must meet them, Cedar That Does Not Bend and I," Hornet said. "We will talk with them and find out what they want." He looked at Charles. "Will you go with us, Black Robe?"

That was the worst thing he could possibly do, Charles thought. He still had a rip in his robe and a small scar on his arm from his last encounter with the Osage. If he walked down to the river to greet them, he would likely be riddled with arrows before he got to the bank.

"You go, Hornet," Charles said. "I must find Lieutenant Dubois."

Hornet gave him a brief, puzzled frown, then nodded. He started toward the river while Charles hurried toward the lodge where he had last seen the lieutenant.

Dubois emerged from the lodge before Charles could reach it. The officer was sleepy-eyed, as if the commotion caused by the arrival of the Wazhazhe had awakened him, but he clutched his musket tightly in his hand and seemed ready to use it. Several more of the voyageurs came out of other lodges where they had been staying as guests of the Prairie People.

"What is it?" Dubois asked when he saw Charles. "What is all this disturbance?"

"Osage," Charles said simply. "They have come from downriver."

Dubois's eyes widened for a second, then narrowed angrily. "So the savages followed us, did they? Well, they will regret being so stubborn." He turned and called, "Grenet! Dublanc! Étienne! Gather all the men!"

The trappers congregated around Dubois, who did a quick head count, grimly satisfied that all the voyageurs were there. Each man had his musket, and those weapons not already primed and loaded were being rapidly prepared for action.

Dubois turned to face the river. "If the Osage want war, then by God, we shall give it to them!"

Charles wished the officer had not invoked the name of the Lord. Now the men, despite their rough, profane exteriors, would probably look to him for a prayer or two.

And he no longer knew if he could pray for their deliverance if it would mean trouble for his new friends in the Crane band.

Chapter Twenty-four

Once more, Hornet went forth to meet the unknown with Cedar beside him. Just as when he had first greeted the pale-skinned ones, he was unarmed, although Cedar was ready for trouble, as usual. The encounter with the trappers had turned out well enough, Hornet supposed, though he did not like any of the Frenchmen except Black Robe. The voyageurs were rough in their ways, and arrogant, and many of them smelled bad to Hornet, but for the most part they had caused no problems in the town. Their leader, the man called Dubois, had given strict orders that the females of the Crane band were not to be molested, and although some of the men looked with lustful eyes on the women, they kept their distance. Still, Hornet was ready for them to move on—with the lone exception of his friend Black Robe.

He hoped that this visit by the Osages would go as well, but his instincts told him it might not.

The first canoe slid up onto the bank as the men inside hopped out and pulled it halfway from the water. A young man dressed in beaded buckskins and armed with bow and arrows, a war ax, and a lance stalked toward Hornet and Cedar. His face was painted, his expression taut and angry. Cedar made a sound of disapproval low in his throat. The Osage warrior was dishonoring them by coming to them in this manner, as if he expected war instead of the cordial welcome always extended by the Prairie People.

"I am Yellow Claw," the Osage said as he came to a stop

directly in front of Hornet and Cedar. "I am the war chief of the Wazhazhe."

"I am Hornet of the Crane band, shaman of my people. This is Cedar That Does Not Bend, war chief of the people. We are friends of the Wazhazhe. Wazhazhe blood runs in many of us. So it has always been, so it will always be. Why do you come among friends painted and armed for war?"

"You harbor our enemies," Yellow Claw said. "That means you are now our enemies, too, no matter how things have been in days gone by."

Hornet stiffened, not fully understanding Yellow Claw's accusation. He did not like the idea that had come into his head, though. "Who are your enemies?"

Yellow Claw lifted the lance in his right hand and pointed. "There! The devils whose skins are as pale as Sister Moon!"

Hornet turned his head, knowing already that Yellow Claw's lance was leveled at the party of French trappers. They stood in the center of town, a tight knot of men, bristling with the war clubs that shot smoke and fire and death. Black Robe stood just to one side, among them but not truly with them.

"What have these men done to become the enemies of the Osage people?" Hornet asked.

"They stole the lives of two of our fine young warriors with their thundersticks. These deaths caused great suffering among the people. Before that, they insulted our women, especially my sister. They are evil! They should all be killed before they can bring their evil to your town, Hornet." Yellow Claw hefted his lance again. "We would be pleased to kill them for you."

"We kill our own enemies," Cedar said, an angry edge to his voice. Hornet knew that Cedar was not particularly fond of their French visitors, either, but Yellow Claw's arrogant offer was irksome.

"These men are our guests," Hornet said. "We do not want war with the Wazhazhe, but we have offered our hospitality to the French, and it cannot be withdrawn without good reason. To do so would dishonor us."

"It dishonors you more to have such demons among you," Yellow Claw pointed out.

Hornet drew a deep breath. "We must think on these things

and speak of them in council. Our chief, Red-tail Hawk, and our elders will decide what to do."

"Decide quickly," Yellow Claw warned. "We prayed and fasted for many days after the pale-skinned demons left us mourning our dead, and the Creator told us to pursue them and kill them. We must do this. But we would not kill the people of the Crane band unless we are forced to do so. I would come to your council and speak to your chief and your elders."

Hornet glanced at Cedar. It was a reasonable request, and Yellow Claw had framed it in a way that was not quite as insulting as some of his earlier declarations.

"Come and speak to us," Hornet said to Yellow Claw. "But the French will have a representative at the council as well so that we may know what each of you considers the truth."

Yellow Claw stiffened, and for a moment Hornet thought he was going to balk at that condition. But then he nodded. "You will hear the truth," he said. "I will speak it."

That remained to be seen, Hornet thought. Now he had to find out who among the visitors wanted to speak at the council. There was really only one man suited for the task.

"I . . . cannot," Charles said. "Please, Hornet, do not ask me to do this."

"You must," Hornet urged. "If only Yellow Claw speaks, Red-tail Hawk and the rest of the council will have little choice but to agree with him. We will have to step aside and allow the Osage to settle this matter with you."

Lieutenant Dubois stood nearby, listening to the conversation and following enough of it to realize what Hornet had just said. "Those heathens will not find it easy," he said as he hefted his musket. "We gave them a taste of powder and shot before, and we can do it again."

"Aye!" Grenet added. "They'll go back down the river with their tail feathers shot off!"

Charles held out his hands toward the voyageurs. "Please, let us not rush into anything. There has already been enough trouble. We must not bring down more on our friends here—"

"Did Yellow Claw speak the truth?" Hornet asked. "Did two of the Wazhazhe die at the hands of these men?"

"Yes," Charles said miserably. "We did little to provoke the trouble, but when it began, our men shot to kill. The Osage were trying to kill us, though, my friend. I myself bear a scar from that battle." He thrust back the sleeve of his robe to reveal where Yellow Claw's arrow had torn his flesh.

Hornet nodded gravely. "I am sorry, Black Robe. No matter what your companions might have done, I know you did not deserve that injury. But that does not change things now. The Osage, our allies in many wars past, demand that we step aside and allow them to seek their revenge."

Charles glanced toward the river. All of the Osage canoes were drawn up on the bank, and the warriors had left them, spreading out around the town so that it was almost completely surrounded. Cedar That Does Not Bend and the other warriors of the Crane band had formed a loose ring just inside the town, a line of defense should the Osages decide to rush the center of the settlement. The numbers of defenders and besiegers were roughly equal. If runners were sent to the other bands of the Prairie People upriver, whatever reinforcements they might send would swing the balance toward the defenders—but by then it might well be too late. Regardless of the outcome, if fighting broke out, men would die. It was as simple as that, Charles thought.

And why should any of the Prairie People die defending them? he asked himself. The voyageurs were interlopers in this land, uninvited guests who had no right to bring down trouble on the heads of their reluctant hosts. It would be best if Hornet, Cedar, and all the others stood aside and let the Frenchmen and the Wazhazhe settle this among themselves. Perhaps he ought to go to the council and advise that very course.

But to do so would be to betray his own kind: white men, Christians—though hardly devout—and fellow Frenchmen. Could he bring himself to do that? His own death would be a certainty, too; the Osages would not spare him because of his robes. The vestments had not shielded him from Yellow Claw's arrow during the earlier encounter.

Charles sighed. Hornet was waiting for an answer, and so were Lieutenant Dubois and the other voyageurs. It was probably impossible to prevent a confrontation, but he had to try.

"I will speak to the council," he said.

Hornet looked relieved, although still worried. "Good. I will come for you tomorrow."

"Tomorrow?" Dubois said. "What's wrong with today?"

"It is too late to call a council today. We must pray and fast for a time before deciding this matter."

Grenet asked angrily, "How do we know those damned Osages won't try to slit our throats in the night?" His question was echoed by several of the other men.

"You will still be in our lodges and under our protection," Hornet said. "I will speak to Yellow Claw and make it clear that you are not to be harmed until after the council has met and spoken. The Wazhazhe will respect this; it is their way, as well as ours."

"I hope you're right," Dubois said. "We'll fight our way out of here if we have to."

Hornet held up a warning hand. "That will not be necessary. Return now to your lodges. It will be better if you stay out of sight as much as possible today."

Charles understood the logic of that request. No one wanted to goad the Osages into starting a battle when Yellow Claw had already agreed to wait until after the council.

Muttering threats and obscenities, the trappers went back to the lodges and disappeared inside them. Charles would have gone back to Hornet's lodge, but the holy man asked Charles to accompany him to the lodge of Red-tail Hawk.

"Black Robe has agreed to speak to the council on behalf of the Frenchmen," Hornet told the aged chief when he and Charles stood before him.

Red-tail Hawk spoke solemnly. "This is good. Black Robe is a man who speaks the truth."

Charles bowed his head in acknowledgment of the praise. Unfortunately, this was a case in which the truth might not set them free. In fact, it could well get them all killed.

The air was oppressively still as Charles walked through the town of the Crane band that evening. In the distance to the southwest, lightning flickered in the heavens, too far away for the sound of thunder to reach the town.

Tomorrow the thunder of gunfire and the lightning of black powder might fill the air, Charles thought. A storm such as that could destroy these peaceful people. He prayed that the Savior would guide his words and allow him to find a middle path to satisfy those on both sides of the dispute. It had fallen to him to be a mediator, a bringer of peace.

The town was quiet at the moment, save for a few dogs growling and yipping at the fires of the Wazhazhe, who had settled down for the night in camps ranged around the lodges of the Crane band. The voyageurs stayed inside for the most part, out of sight, to avoid provoking their enemies. Father Charles was the only one moving around, too restless to sit still after the meal Bright Water had served to him and Hornet. The holy man had offered to come with him, but Charles had refused. He needed to be alone with his thoughts.

But now, after strolling around the town several times, he was no closer to an answer. His steps carried him back to where he had begun.

He thrust aside the flap over the entrance and stepped in. Bright Water sat on the far side of the fire, mending one of her brother's buckskin tunics. There was no sign of Hornet. Bright Water looked up, meeting Charles's eyes squarely.

"Where is Hornet?" Charles asked.

"He has gone to the lodge of Red-tail Hawk to fast and pray with the chief," she replied. "He will not return tonight."

Charles wondered briefly why she had seen fit to add that, but he said nothing. He sat down and sighed. Life weighed more heavily on him at this moment than it ever had before, and he wished fervently that he were back home in Normandy, where no one had to face such dilemmas. His superiors in the Society of Jesus had no idea what this new world was like, no idea at all.

Bright Water set aside the tunic. "Black Robe is sad."

"I don't know what to do, Bright Water," Charles said. "If I tell the truth, it means betraying my companions and turning your people against us. If I lie, Yellow Claw may convince Red-tail Hawk to believe him anyway. Either way, there will be trouble."

"Your words have told me the truth," Bright Water said

softly. "Do you not fear that I will go to Red-tail Hawk and tell him?"

Charles raised his eyes to meet her gaze. "It never occurred to me to tell *you* a lie, Bright Water. I could not do that, no more than I could lie to your brother. The two of you are the best friends I have ever had."

She rose and came around the fire toward him. As always, he admired the gracefulness of her movements. She sank to her knees beside him and reached out to rest a hand on his shoulder.

"There is so much pain inside you, Black Robe," she murmured. "I would take it away, if only for a time."

Charles did not move as she leaned closer to him. Her lips brushed his cheek. He felt the warmth of her breath on his skin, the soft pressure of her breast against his arm. He had told her in the past of the vows he had taken when he entered the priesthood, but although she understood the words, they had little real meaning for her. He knew she had not comprehended. Now she was reaching out to him in the only way she knew.

He wanted to turn to her, take her in his arms, accept what she was offering so freely. God, he wanted to! But he could not. It would be a sin thus to cast aside his vow of chastity.

"My life is your life," Bright Water whispered. "Wherever you go and whatever you do, I am bound to you by my heart, Black Robe. I have known this since the day you came among us. I can no more stop it than I can stop Father Sun from rising in the morning."

"Bright Water . . . I cannot. Hornet is my friend—"

"Hornet is not here tonight. And the reason he left is so that you and I can be together. This is a good thing, a right thing. The Creator will bless our union."

She sounded absolutely convinced of that. For the two of them to lie together would not be a sin in her eyes. Charles wished he could look at it the same way.

"I want you." The words forced themselves out of his mouth.

"You have me," Bright Water said. "For as long as the two of us shall live, Black Robe, I am yours and you are mine. This is the way it must be. My heart is blown to you as the wind blows the prairie grass."

A force of nature . . . yes, that was exactly what this was. He could not deny such a force.

Despising himself, he reached for her, drew her into his arms, and brought his mouth down hard on hers.

Chapter Twenty-five

Hornet cast a wary glance at the sky as he emerged from the lodge of Red-tail Hawk early the next morning. It was already hot and bright and flat, with not a breath of air stirring. To the southwest, almost beyond the range of Hornet's sight, lay a low, dark blue line of clouds. Hornet shook his head. He did not like any of this—the weather, or what might happen today.

He was weary from the night of fasting and praying, but his mind was clear. No matter how much he had grown to like Black Robe, his first duty was to his people. Black Robe had admitted to him that two of the Wazhazhe had fallen to the thundersticks of the voyageurs. Yellow Claw and his people had a right to vengeance, and it was not proper that any of the Crane band should die from standing in the way. Hornet's heart was heavy with this knowledge.

He would do everything in his power to see that Black Robe was spared. The priest had done nothing to deserve the anger of the Wazhazhe, and Hornet would lay down his life to protect his friend—especially if what he suspected had happened the night before had actually taken place.

Bright Water might well be with child this morning. A man who denied himself the comfort of a woman, as Black Robe evidently had for a long time, would undoubtedly be quite potent. Hornet had a duty as well to this child, a duty to see that its father was kept safe.

As Hornet approached, Black Robe emerged from the shaman's lodge. He stopped short and dropped his eyes. Hornet sensed the shame in him and knew it had no place there. He stepped closer, threw his arms around Black Robe, and said, "Good morning, brother."

"Hornet, I—"

"The Creator and Giver of Breath has blessed us with another day," Hornet said firmly. "We must use it as best we can."

After a moment Black Robe acknowledged his friend's truth. "Yes, I suppose you are right." He stepped back as Hornet released him. Holding up the book in his hands, he continued, "I intend to use part of it making a few final entries in my journal. If anything happens to me, Hornet, will you protect it and give it to the next one like me who comes to your town?"

Hornet wanted to assure him that it would not come to that, but it was a promise he could not honestly make. "I will protect Black Robe's sacred story skins. But there will never be another like Black Robe who comes to the town of the Crane band."

"Thank you." Black Robe clasped Hornet's arm. "You are a good friend."

Hornet returned the clasp. "And you as well, Black Robe . . . Charles de St. Aubyn."

Black Robe's eyes widened in surprise, and a smile touched his mouth under the tangled beard. "You have been practicing."

"I wanted to call you by your true name."

"Will you summon me when it is time for the council?"

Hornet agreed gravely.

"Very well. As I said, I believe I will jot down a few more notes."

Hornet watched him go, then turned toward the lodge as Bright Water came out. She, too, lowered her eyes.

Hornet stepped over to her, caught her in his arms, and hugged her as hard as he could. He knew the truth, and for now, at least, he was happy.

Dubois looked around at the men crowded into the lodge with him. Their bearded faces were grim and determined. The lieutenant uncorked his powder horn and began measuring a charge into the pan of his musket. "I'll not place my faith in a group of red savages, nor my life in their hands," he said.

"We're with you, Lieutenant," Grenet said.

Carefully, everything in place, Dubois lowered the hammer

of the weapon so that it rested against the pan. A fresh charge of powder, wadding, and ball had already been rammed home in the barrel. The other men's weapons were loaded and primed as well.

"Here is what we will do," Dubois said.

Charles's eyes burned with tears, but he blinked them away and continued to write in his journal. His book, his magnificent book that would bring him fame and a stronger position in the hierarchy of his order, would probably never be written now. He fully expected not to survive this day, but he would not stop until he had written down everything he knew of these people who had welcomed him among them.

A part of him felt dead inside. His faith was gone, destroyed by the mortal sin he had committed. Yet another part of his soul was alive, more alive than it had ever been. He might no longer be a priest, but he was still a man, fallible, certainly damned, but *alive*.

It felt good.

A tendril of breeze plucked at his hair and beard. The air had been so heavy and motionless all morning that the touch made him glance up in surprise. The clouds that had been far off to the southwest earlier in the day were closer now, and as he watched them for a moment they seemed to come closer still. A hint of coolness brushed him. The storm was finally coming.

Hornet touched his shoulder and said, "It is time."

Charles turned his head and looked up at the holy man, whose face was set in bleak lines. Charles understood. He felt the same way.

He closed the journal and put his pen and ink aside. "I want to take this back to the lodge."

Hornet said solemnly, "Bright Water will care for it until we return."

Charles swallowed hard. He wished he could have Bright Water at his side during the council, but he knew she would not be permitted to enter the lodge of Red-tail Hawk. He stood up, his back aching for a moment, and walked first toward Hornet's lodge. The shaman walked beside him.

Bright Water met them at the entrance, her face set in the

same grim lines as those of Charles and Hornet. Yet in her eyes Charles saw something shining, something fresh and new and good. He held out the journal toward her and said, "Take care of this. I will be back for it."

All three of them knew that might not happen, but none of them wanted to put that thought into words. Bright Water took the journal.

He let his hands linger as they touched hers, then slid them away with a sigh. Turning to Hornet, he said, "I am ready."

Together they walked toward the lodge of Red-tail Hawk. The town was crowded this morning; no one was working in the garden plots because of the threat from the Osages. As he and Hornet walked among the people, Charles felt their eyes on him. Most of the stares were accusing. He and those like him had brought trouble to the land of the Prairie People, and Charles could not blame them for feeling betrayed.

He saw no sign of Dubois, Grenet, and the others. They must still be inside the lodges, he thought. *Hiding.* No, that was too harsh a judgment. The old habit of trying to be fair was well ingrained in him.

Cedar That Does Not Bend was waiting for them outside the chief's lodge. He pulled back the entrance flap and stood aside so that Charles and Hornet preceded him. Charles hesitated for a second, then drew a deep breath and stepped into the shadowy interior of the lodge.

The Master of the Sacred Pole stood by that holy relic, his ceremonial robe pulled closely to his neck. Red-tail Hawk, in a position of honor, and the other elders of the band sat around the small fire in the center of the lodge. Sweat beaded Charles's face. It was hot and stuffy, even more so than outside.

Cedar stepped inside and dropped the flap behind him, cutting off some of the morning light. He took a seat with the others. Charles and Hornet remained standing. Charles opened his mouth to speak, but a soft nudge from Hornet's elbow and a warning look made him remain silent. He did not know the proper procedures for a council such as this, so he would be quiet and look to Hornet for direction.

A moment later another man thrust aside the entrance flap and stepped into the lodge. Yellow Claw moved around the circle of elders, stopping when several feet separated him from Charles and Hornet. He glared at the white priest, then turned his attention to Red-tail Hawk. "The people of the Crane band do me great honor by allowing me to speak in their council," he said, taking a place in the circle.

Red-tail Hawk inclined his head in acknowledgment but said nothing in reply. Another elder brought out a pipe and carefully filled it. A low murmur rippled among the men as the tension inside the lodge eased a bit. This might be a solemn occasion, when matters grave and even dangerous were about to be discussed, but still it was good to sit and talk. That was the mood Charles sensed. He wished he could make a note in his journal.

Under other circumstances he would have been fascinated by the ritual of smoking the pipe, but now it seemed endless. He wanted to speak his piece, even though he was still not certain what he would say.

Finally Red-tail Hawk lifted his robe to his head and said, "We are here to decide whether or not the Wazhazhe should have these men who have been guests in our lodges and are under our protection. The Wazhazhe war chief, Yellow Claw, who honors us with his presence, will speak first. Then we will hear Black Robe, shaman of our pale-skinned visitors."

The chief's lined and weathered face turned toward Yellow Claw, who stood up and again glared at Charles before opening his mouth to level the accusations that Charles, in all honesty, would not be able to deny.

The shattering sound of a gunshot echoed from outside the lodge before Yellow Claw could say a word.

The deafening roar of exploding black powder made every man inside the lodge jerk around. Outside the lodge someone yelped in pain. A figure loomed in the entrance, followed closely by others. Lieutenant Dubois pushed through the flap and aimed his musket at Red-tail Hawk, shouting in the tongue of the Prairie People, "No one move!"

"Lieutenant!" Charles exclaimed in French. "What is the meaning of this?"

More voyageurs crowded into the lodge behind Dubois, pointing their guns menacingly at the men of the council. "We submit only to the justice of our king," Dubois said. "The decisions of these Indians mean nothing to us! We are leaving this place, and we are taking that one"—he gestured toward Red-tail Hawk—"and that one"—Yellow Claw—"with us. The savages won't dare harm us while they are our prisoners."

Charles bit back a groan of despair. "You cannot do this, Lieutenant," he cried. "You do not know what you are doing—"

"I am saving our lives, Father," Dubois snapped. "You should be grateful. These red devils mean to kill us, and they would not spare you, either."

The officer was correct about that, Charles knew. If the council decided against them, his own life would no doubt be forfeit, too. He could see how this plan had appealed to Dubois's military reasoning. The most important men in each group of potential enemies were here for the taking, gathered together in the lodge.

But Dubois did not know the Prairie People as Charles did. Even in the relatively short time he had been among them, he had learned much, and he knew they would never stand for this insult. They would prevent the Frenchmen from leaving even if it cost Red-tail Hawk and Yellow Claw their lives.

The voyageurs had muskets, however, and with them they could fight their way out of the town. At the very least they would kill many people. Somehow Charles had to stop this.

As he took a step toward Dubois a gust of wind whipped into the lodge and a low rumble of thunder sounded. Charles lifted a hand. "In the name of Christ Our Lord, Lieutenant, I implore you—"

"Look out!" Grenet shouted. "He has an ax!"

Charles looked around. Yellow Claw lunged fearlessly at the voyageurs, his war ax raised. As Charles cried, "No!" Grenet's musket roared and spat flame. Yellow Claw was thrown backward by the lead ball that struck him with an ugly thud.

Furious, Charles reached for the barrel of Grenet's musket, intending to wrench the weapon out of the trapper's hands, but someone gave him a hard shove before he could reach it. "Get out of the way, Father!"

As Charles staggered back strong hands grabbed him and

steadied him. Hornet was beside him. "Be careful, Black Robe," the medicine man said urgently.

"Stop it! Hold your fire!" Dubois was practically screaming. He thrust the barrel of his musket at Red-tail Hawk. "You! Get up! You will take us out of here!"

The chief of the Crane band calmly shook his head. "You may kill me," he said, "but I will not help you. I will not leave this place."

Grenet tugged at the sleeve of Dubois's uniform jacket. "Come on, Lieutenant. One way or another, we have to get out of here!"

Dubois's eyes were wide with fear. His great plan had failed, and he did not know what to do now. Grasping at any hope, he said, "Yes, we'll go to the bateaux. We'll go upriver. The current's not too bad now." He backed toward the entrance of the lodge. "Come on, Father!"

Charles did not move. He looked down at Yellow Claw, who was clutching a bloody shoulder as he lay in a half-sitting position. At least he was not dead. Perhaps there was still hope that more tragedy could be averted.

"Oh, Lord!" The cry came from one of the men at the entrance. "Here come the rest of them!"

The Osages were closing in, drawn by the gunshots. They would know that some sort of treachery was afoot and would be ready to spill the blood of their enemies.

"We're going, damn it!" Dubois shouted raggedly at Charles. "Are you coming, Father, or are you going to stay here and be a heathen savage, too?"

There might be worse fates, Charles suddenly realized, much worse indeed. To stay here and live with Hornet and Bright Water seemed very like paradise to him.

Yet there was still the call of blood, and the hope that he might one day regain his faith. That would never happen if he stayed with the Prairie People.

Thunder shook the earth.

One of the voyageurs screamed and stumbled back through the entrance of the lodge, an arrow buried in his belly. Dubois spun around, forgetting about Charles. "Come on!" he shouted. "Kill anyone who gets in your way!"

It was happening all over again, Charles thought. Just like their first encounter with the Wazhazhe, this one would end in blood. But this time the trappers were not going to emerge unscathed. Already they had lost one man.

A new fear washed through Charles as his former companions charged out of the lodge, shouting and firing their weapons. The voyageurs were shooting indiscriminately, and with so many lead balls flying through the air, one of them might hit—

Bright Water.

Charles started after them, calling her name, as Cedar and the other elders of the Crane band also surged to their feet to pursue the Frenchmen, yanking knives and war axes from their belts. Charles was buffeted aside, and again only the strong hand of Hornet on his arm kept him from falling. They were the last two out of the lodge, except for Red-tail Hawk and Yellow Claw, neither of whom moved from his place, the Osage chief because of his wound and the principal chief of the Crane band because of his advanced age. Charles stumbled.

A cold wind slapped him in the face as he turned toward the river. No rain was falling, but dark, heavy clouds had hidden the sun. Lightning flickered, shards of brilliance that lanced down to the ground all around the town.

Charles de St. Aubyn saw Dubois and the others running toward the Nibthaska-ke and their bateaux, but they were cut off by Crane warriors who moved to intercept them. The trappers had made their decision; every hand was against them now, Crane band and Osage alike.

Darting off in a different direction to avoid the warriors who blocked their path, the voyageurs ran for their lives. Those who had discharged their weapons tried awkwardly to reload as they ran. Another volley rang out, and several Wazhazhe who were rushing in from the perimeter of the town collapsed. That created a gap in the closing circle, and the trappers, led by Dubois, plunged through it, leaping over the bodies of the men they had just killed.

The whole town was whirling in chaos. Men shouted in outrage, women cried in fear and sorrow, children and dogs darted everywhere. Charles caught hold of Hornet's arm as he watched the voyageurs run toward the open prairie. "Can't your people let them go?" he asked. "They will not dare to come back, and they will probably die out there without their provisions."

For an instant Hornet considered what Charles had said. He was the holy man, the spiritual leader of these people. He could persuade them to halt their pursuit.

Hornet opened his mouth to speak.

As he did, his head snapped back and a black hole appeared above his right eye. He expelled the air in his lungs, the last sound he would ever make, and fell.

Chapter Twenty-six

Bright Water came out of the lodge and searched frantically for Hornet or Black Robe. The sound of the thundersticks wielded by the pale-skinned demons mixed with the real thunder and made her ears hurt. People were running everywhere, shouting and crying. There was no doubt in her mind what had happened: war had come, war between the Prairie People, the Wazhazhe, and the Frenchmen.

Where was Black Robe? He must be all right, she thought. He had to be.

Bright Water ran toward the lodge of Red-tail Hawk, where the council had been held to decide the fate of the visitors. That was where she would find Black Robe and Hornet. Through the crowd thronging between the lodges, she thought she caught a glimpse of her brother's tall form, a smaller figure in dark robes beside him.

"Black Robe!" she called. "Hornet!"

But at that moment something happened to Hornet. She saw the sudden movement of his head, saw him slump to the ground as if every bone in his body had turned to sand. Bright Water's breath caught in her throat. She wanted to scream, but she could not. She stumbled to a halt.

Her brother was dead; she was certain of it.

Slowly, a new sound penetrated her shock. The cries of the Prairie People had taken on a different tone. Something else was wrong, and when Bright Water turned her head and looked south, she saw what it was.

Smoke blacker than the clouds in the sky billowed upward from the plains. At the base of the smoke, barely visible now but becoming clearer with each passing second, was a line of red, leaping flames. A lightning strike must have ignited the thick grass that had begun to dry with the onset of summer, and now one of the most dreaded things in all the world she knew was racing toward the town.

Prairie fire.

"No!" Charles screamed as he fell to his knees beside the body of his friend. He grabbed Hornet's shoulders and shook, but he knew it was no use. The medicine man of the Crane band was dead, a musket ball in his brain.

That thought made Charles look up. Through the confusion that swirled around him, through the opening in the Osage forces that the trappers had used to escape, he saw that one of them had stopped and turned around for a final shot. The man was just now lowering his musket, gray smoke still curling from its barrel.

Claude Grenet. And he was *smiling*.

With an incoherent shout Charles reached for the war ax still tucked behind Hornet's belt, jerked it free, and lunged to his feet. They had accused him of wanting to be a savage—well, a savage he would be! He would join the chase, would crush Grenet's skull with Hornet's own ax—

A hand caught his arm, and a familiar voice shouted in his ear, "Black Robe! Black Robe, come!"

Wild-eyed, he looked around and saw Bright Water clutching him. Tears glistened in her eyes. "Bright Water!" he cried. "I'm sorry, so sorry—"

"There is no time!" She swept her arm toward the southern horizon. "The fire comes!"

For the first time Charles noticed the billowing clouds of smoke and the rampaging flames, driven by the strong wind.

"Come!" she said as she tugged on his arm. "Come to the river!"

"But . . . but Hornet—" Charles gestured helplessly at the body of his friend.

"I mourn for him more than you can know, but we can do nothing for him now. We must go to the river. The fire will be here soon."

Charles shook his head numbly and tried to force his mind to work. If they went to the river, as Bright Water was urging, they would be going *toward* the fire. Surely that was not right. He pointed toward the other direction, the way Dubois and the others—including that murderer Grenet!—had fled. "We should run away from the fire."

Bright Water shook her head. "No time! The flames move too fast. Come, Black Robe!"

Perhaps she was right. Perhaps the river offered the only protection. The rest of the Prairie People had been alerted to the menace of the fire by now, and Charles saw them scurrying for the water, as Bright Water was urging. Even those who had pursued the fleeing voyageurs had turned back and were racing toward the Nibthaska-ke.

Abruptly he made his decision. He must trust her. He would go with her. But that would mean leaving Hornet's body to the flames.

Hornet would want it that way, Charles made himself think. With Bright Water he ran toward the stream.

The fire had already reached the far side of the river, the flames towering in the air, casting smoke and sparks even higher. Some sparks had already been carried across the river by the hard wind, and new fires were breaking out all through the town.

"My journal!" Charles suddenly cried. Bright Water did not have it, which meant that it had to be in the lodge. He veered in that direction.

"No! No time!" She pulled hard on his robe, tugging him toward the river. "If you go, I go with you!"

Charles swallowed the bitter taste that welled up in his throat. He had lost his friend, he had lost the faith that had sustained him for so long, and now all the work he had done on his journal was to be taken from him as well.

But he would not lose Bright Water. Not if he could help it.

Together they plunged into the river, joining the other Prairie People and Osages who sought refuge there. More than a hundred souls all told, they hid from the flames, lowering themselves beneath the surface of the water until only their faces remained above. Charles and Bright Water followed their example, burrowing into the cool mud of the riverbed so that they could submerge themselves almost completely. The cool embrace of the water and mud was welcome relief from the heat of the fire. Charles took only short breaths, plunging his head underwater in between. Each time he came up for air, he gasped harder. He kept one arm looped around Bright Water's shuddering body so that they would not be separated. The entire world seemed to have turned crimson, the nightmarish red of the flames.

This had to be what hell was like.

"They're turning back!" Claude Grenet shouted as the pursuit fell away behind them. "The red bastards are turning back!"

The trapper called Étienne clutched Lieutenant Dubois's arm and pointed at the smoke. "The plains are on fire! What should we do?"

Gasping for breath, Dubois wiped sweat from his grimy face. The pulse pounding in his head seemed as loud as the thunder rumbling over the prairie. "Surely the river will stop the fire," he said. "Since the Indians have turned back, we will push on."

"Our bateaux, our provisions—" one of the men yelled.

"Damn the bateaux!" Dubois burst out. "We can build more bateaux. And as long as we have powder and shot, we will not go hungry. This is a rich land. We can live off it for as long as we need to."

He hoped that was true. He could not let the men see how frightened he really was.

"Lieutenant," Grenet suddenly said, "why are those bastards running back *toward* the fire?"

Why indeed? Dubois asked himself. Then, before his horrified eyes, he saw the answer: new fires were breaking out on *this* side of the river, ignited by wind-borne sparks.

"Come on!" Dubois called urgently. "We have to keep moving! We must keep ahead of those flames."

He broke into a run once more, and the rest of the party went with him, casting fearful looks back over their shoulders as they did. The fire even now consumed the lodges and tipis of the Prairie People. But he and his men had a good lead on the flames, Dubois thought desperately, and if they could keep moving . . .

Why was no rain falling? There had been thunder and lightning aplenty, but where was the damned rain? That would put out the fire, Dubois thought. A good hard downpour would save them.

But the rain did not come, and the fire leaped unabated across the grassland. Each time Dubois glanced back, the flames were closer. He could feel the heat beating against his back, the smoke searing his lungs as his legs pumped in what now seemed like a futile attempt to escape the fire. He tried to tell himself that was just his imagination—his *fear*—but he knew better. The fire was moving much faster than the men could run, and the face of the inferno was too wide. They could not escape by veering to the side.

If they could find a creek, some low place where there was water . . . Now Dubois knew why the Indians had gone back to the river. They had known where their only hope of salvation lay.

Some of the men cried out in terror as they ran. They knew they were doomed. Suddenly Grenet's foot caught in a sinkhole, and he fell. Dubois turned back at the man's alarmed shout as the others raced on.

To his horror Dubois saw that the flames were even closer than he had thought. Tufts of grass were igniting less than a hundred yards away. He shouted, "Grenet, get up and come on!"

Grenet ignored him. The trapper pushed himself up onto his knees and reached for a pistol tucked behind his belt. As he drew the weapon and cocked it Grenet shouted at the flames, "I won't burn! I won't burn, damn you!"

He jammed the barrel of the pistol under his chin and pulled the trigger.

Dubois winced, looking away as the heavy powder charge blew away half of Grenet's head. The voyageur's body slumped to the side. There was nothing Dubois could do for him now.

There was precious little he could do for himself, he realized.

He turned to run again, but with astounding speed the fire spread all around him. He gasped for breath, though the smoke-filled air offered little to sustain him. He stumbled, caught himself, ran on for a few more yards, then lost his balance again. As he fell the flames surrounded him, clutching at him like blazing hands. He screamed and thrashed as his clothing ignited. A horrible stench filled his nostrils, and he realized, with one of the last coherent thoughts of his life, that it came from his own burning flesh.

The fire moved on as quickly as it had come, its remnants extinguished by the drenching rain that at last began to fall. The Prairie People and the Wazhazhe emerged from the river to a land of mud made black by ashes. Those who had survived such conflagrations before knew that the fire, for all its terror and destruction, would renew the land. The grass would come back thicker and greener. From death would come new life.

But the people who had died would not come back. Charles de St. Aubyn knelt beside the charred body of his friend Hornet and wept.

Finally Bright Water, her own face etched by grief, came to him and gently led him away. There was much work to be done in the months to come, a town to rebuild, loved ones to bury.

Life would go on. It was the way of the people.

By the time the new grass had begun to sprout through the earth and reach greedily for the sun, Bright Water knew she was with child. She could feel the new being growing within her. When she counted the moons, she knew the child would be born that winter, probably during the Moon of Starvation. It would be a difficult time to bring a child into the world.

But all times were difficult in their own way. There was no perfect time for a baby to be born.

She went to tell Black Robe the news and found him by the

river, apart from the new lodges that had been built. He was staring off to the east, and she knew he was thinking of his homeland, so far away across the great water. Perhaps he was thinking as well of those who had come with him to this land, those who had all died out there on the prairie when they were overtaken by the fire. A band of warriors led by Cedar and Yellow Claw had found their bodies; the bones had been left where they lay to bleach in the sun, a fitting end for those men who did not belong here.

Bright Water placed a hand on Black Robe's shoulder. "My husband," she said. "You are unhappy? You want to leave this place?"

Black Robe took a deep breath and turned to her. "Never," he said. "My place is here now, with you—and the child."

Bright Water smiled at him. "You know?"

"I know."

Then he took her hand, and together they walked back to the town, to the lodge in which Charles de St. Aubyn of the Society of Jesus had made his home.

Chapter Twenty-seven

Nineteen years later

Hummingbird ran lightly over the prairie, her movements as quick and darting as those of the bird she had been named after. Only when she caught sight of those she was pursuing in the distance did she slow down, careful not to get too close. If they noticed her, they would be angry and send her back to the town of the Crane band. A hunt was no place for a girl, they would tell her.

At the age of fifteen summers, Hummingbird no longer considered herself a girl. She was a woman now, and soon it would be time to start thinking about a husband.

Her heartbeat quickened as she knelt in the tall grass and looked at the shorter of the two figures ahead of her. Even though he was out of earshot and his back was turned to her, Hummingbird could hear his laughter and see his face as clearly as if she were standing before him. Young Man Coyote was much in her thoughts these days.

The taller of the two hunters paused and pointed in a new direction, then trotted that way. Hummingbird's brother, Black Snake, usually took the lead in these little expeditions. Only eighteen summers old, he was already a member of the Elk Society, and it was widely accepted among the people that someday the son of Black Robe and Bright Water would be a leader, perhaps even a chief, of the Crane band. After all, was he not named after one of his ancestors who had been both a mighty warrior *and* a visionary?

To Hummingbird, however, he was first and foremost an older brother, to be either admired or loathed as the situation warranted. Today she was very annoyed with him for not allowing her to accompany him and Young Man Coyote on their hunt. In fact, he had made it clear that she was not welcome.

They had not yet killed any game or even shot at any, and Hummingbird suspected they did not care whether the hunt was successful. It was simply an excuse to roam the plains together, talking and enjoying each other's company. Ever since they were children Black Snake and Coyote had been the closest of friends, and despite her current feelings, Hummingbird could almost understand why her brother did not want her to disturb that.

But she could not live her life according to the wishes of Black Snake. She knew that the Creator intended for her and Coyote to be together, and she hoped, even suspected, that Coyote felt the same way.

She shifted the strap of the quiver of arrows she wore into a more comfortable position and resumed her pursuit of the two young men. In her left hand she carried a bow carved for her by her father, Black Robe. While it was shorter and had an easier pull than the weapons carried by the men, it was larger than those used by the boys of the band when they practiced hunting and war. With it she could send an arrow almost as far as her brother could with his bow, and with almost as much force. Her aim was better than Black Snake's, too, which added to his customary exasperation with her. It was bad enough to have a sister who wanted to be a warrior; the fact that she was actually good at manly things only added to his embarrassment.

Hummingbird would have given up all of that, however, to marry Young Man Coyote. She would happily cook for him and keep his lodge and bear his children without complaint.

Her quarry stopped again, so Hummingbird came to a halt as well. Black Snake and Young Man Coyote stood still, listening to something. After a moment they started up a small hill that would give them a view of the river that flowed across this land. Their movements were quick but careful, and Hummingbird could tell they were trying to be quiet. She frowned. Was something wrong? Or had they simply come across some game they did not want to scare away?

Their attention was turned away from her now, so she threw caution to the wind and hurried after them, her instincts telling her that it was important she share in their discovery, whatever it was.

Black Snake and Coyote reached the top of the hill and stretched full-length on the ground just below the crest, raising their heads until they could peer over. Hummingbird could tell by the tense bunching of their shoulders that something was wrong. She started up the slope after them and glanced to the west, where the town of the Crane band lay about an hour's hard run away. If an enemy was approaching, the people would have to be warned. It was unlikely an enemy would come from this direction, however. The Osage lived to the east, and they were very friendly to the Crane band. There had been much intermarriage between the two bands since the time when the Osage were called the Wazhazhe. The traditional enemies of the Prairie People, the Red Horns, lived far to the west now, and they seemed to be retreating farther with each passing season. War was not unknown in this area, but it was rare.

Hummingbird would get no answers down here, she told herself. She kept climbing toward the top of the hill, but she was not quiet enough to avoid the attention of the two young men, both of whom turned their heads and saw her.

Black Snake grimaced and slid down the slope a short distance before standing up to meet her. He grasped her arms and said angrily, "What are you doing here, Hummingbird? I told you this was no place for a girl!"

A mixture of satisfaction and anger surged through her: satisfaction that she had known exactly what he would say when he saw her, anger that he could be so narrow-minded. She looked boldly at him and said, "The prairie does not belong to you, brother. I come and go as I please."

"Be quiet, both of you!" Coyote hissed at them. "Do you want them to hear you? Bring Hummingbird up here, Black Snake."

Hummingbird felt a fierce jolt of elation. Coyote wanted her to be with him. Black Snake looked disgusted, but he released one of Hummingbird's arms and tugged on the other one. "Come with me," he whispered, "but be quiet."

They went to the top of the hill, and Hummingbird lay down on the grass between her brother and Coyote. Her shoulder lightly touched Coyote's, but she tried not to think about the warm pressure of his bare flesh through her buckskin dress. She wished that she, too, could wear only leggings and a breechclout and let the hot summer sun play over her skin.

As she edged her head up to look over the crest of the rise, she forgot about the sun and bare skin. The prairie spread out before her, the thick brown grass still dotted with patches of green and an occasional wildflower. In the near distance, perhaps two bowshots away, the Flat River flowed sluggishly. It was broad and shallow, its course twisted and turned. Making their way easily upstream against the gentle current were ten boats, eight of them holding five or six men each, the other two loaded with provisions and towed by ropes. Paddles rose and fell in a steady rhythm, droplets of water cascading and sparkling in the sunlight with each stroke.

"White men," Black Snake breathed.

There was no mistaking them, even at this distance. Most of them sported beards, a feature that immediately set them apart from men of the Prairie People or the Osage. Several wore coats of blue cloth and breeches even paler than their skin, while others were clad in buckskins.

"Trappers and French soldiers," Coyote said, and Hummingbird agreed. Like the two young men, she had seen such visitors before. They had passed through the town of the Crane band, where they were welcomed coolly and sent on their way as soon as possible. Many of the elders in the town still remembered the big fire and all the trouble that had been caused by the first visit of the pale-skinned demons.

Of course, her own father had been one of those demons, Hummingbird thought, although she could barely conceive of such a notion. Black Robe was as much a man of the Crane band now as anyone else. He had been one of them for nineteen summers.

Black Snake suddenly nudged her arm and said in a low, urgent voice, "Look." Hummingbird's gaze followed his pointing finger, and for the first time she noticed that a figure in one of the boats was not dressed like any of his companions. The man wore a black, hooded robe.

"Father," Hummingbird breathed.

The man was not Black Robe, of course. Their father was back in the town with their mother, Bright Water. And Black Robe, despite his name, had dressed in buckskins for years; he no longer wore the cassock that had prompted Hummingbird's uncle, Hornet, to give him a new name. The man in the boat had to be another . . . what was the word? Priest? Yes, that was it. The man was a priest—a white holy man.

"We must tell the people," Coyote said.

Black Snake agreed. "We will carry the warning."

"How do you know these men mean trouble for our people?" Hummingbird asked. "Others like them have visited our town before, and nothing bad happened."

Her brother looked at her as if she were a young child, which infuriated her. So did his tone of voice as he said, "This is the largest group to come to our land in many years. There are even more of them than came with Father, before the big fire. And they all have thunder-lances."

"Muskets," Coyote said. "They call the weapons muskets."

"Whatever they are called, they can kill many of our people if we are not prepared." Black Snake moved down the hillside and stood up again. "Come. We are wasting time."

Coyote joined him, and Hummingbird had no choice but to

follow. Coyote turned to her and said, "You can go back to the town by the long way. Stay away from the river, Hummingbird. You do not want these men to see you."

Hummingbird frowned. "I do not understand. I am coming with you."

Black Snake snorted in disbelief. "We will be running hard. You could not keep up, little sister."

"Let me try. The worst that can happen is that you will outrun me."

"She speaks the truth," Coyote pointed out.

Black Snake looked as if he wanted to continue arguing but instead said sternly to Hummingbird, "If you cannot keep up, you will let us go on to the town. You will stay away from the river and those white men."

"Of course," Hummingbird said.

"Very well. You can come with us."

With that, Black Snake turned and launched into a run. His smooth, ground-eating stride carried him swiftly over the gently rolling hills. Silently Coyote and Hummingbird fell in behind him, willing to let him lead the way. Though they did not speak, Hummingbird felt a closeness to Coyote that was more than mere physical proximity. She was glad to be here running beside him.

As they ran she was aware of him glancing over at her from time to time, and she sensed as much as saw his surprise. She ran easily, her legs flashing back and forth beneath the dress, her moccasined feet landing surely and cleanly with each stride. She matched Coyote's pace with no difficulty, even when he increased his speed so that he drew even with Black Snake. Her brother grunted in surprise when he saw her from the corner of his eye. Hummingbird felt a surge of satisfaction. Perhaps next time they went out for a hunt, they would not insist on leaving her behind. Of course, they probably would; their attitude would not be changed overnight or by the events of any one day. But one thing was certain. After today, Young Man Coyote would never look at her in quite the same way again.

That, Hummingbird thought, was a good thing.

Chapter Twenty-eight

Black Robe chanted softly to himself as he worked. He smoothed the shaft of the arrow, scraping it gently with the keen edge of a flint knife. The shaft was from an ash sapling, seasoned over a fire, then cut to the proper length. He removed the knots from it now, and when that was done, he would take handfuls of sand from the riverbank and rub the shaft with them, making it even smoother so that its flight would be true. Once he was satisfied with the shaft, the arrow maker cut a slit into one end for the arrowhead, which would be tied with sinew soaked in a glue made by boiling turtle shells. Once the sinew dried and hardened, it would be as strong as straps of iron. A slit in the other end of the shaft would provide the archer a place to nock his bowstring. Then came the part of the process that Black Robe enjoyed the most: carving the shallow, wavering grooves that ran the length of the shaft. Those grooves prevented the shaft from warping, and they symbolized lightning. The arrows of the Prairie People struck like lightning, the young warriors liked to say.

Black Robe had never been a good hunter. Nor was he a warrior. But he made arrows for the hunters and the warriors, and he was good at his self-appointed task, perhaps the best arrow maker among the Crane band.

Bright Water came to him where he sat beside the river with the tools of his trade. "You should come back to the lodge now," she told him. "It will soon be night. You cannot work in the darkness, though I think you would if you had eyes like the owl."

Her tone was affectionately chiding. She put a hand on his shoulder, and he picked it up and brought it to his cheek. "If I worked all night," he said, "when would I lie with my wife?"

"Do not think I would die of disappointment if you never

came to my sleeping robes again, husband," she said. The warmth with which she leaned over and embraced him belied the mocking words.

Nineteen summers they had been together, Black Robe thought. *Dix-neuf ans,* he added to himself, using the French words so that they would stay in his mind. He had to be careful not to lose them. In his lodge he spoke only the tongue of the Prairie People, the language Hornet had taught him so long ago. It would have been easy to let his French slip away. Often it seemed that Charles de St. Aubyn was a different man entirely; he was Black Robe of the Crane band, always had been, always would be.

There had been a time, right after the big fire and the deaths of Hornet, Dubois, Grenet, and the other men, when Black Robe would gladly have put all those terrible memories away forever and never called them back. The events of those bloody, early summer days had been too close, however; he could not banish them. Now he was glad he had failed to block them out. Even though he would never return to the life he had once led, he did not want to lose his past completely.

In fact, he had begun to write again, using pieces of buffalo hide scraped to an almost parchmentlike thinness and the same inks with which the Prairie People painted their faces in times of war. The process was slow and painstaking, but he had managed to re-create much of what had been lost when the fire swept through the town and destroyed his journal. He planned to go far beyond that, however, and tell the entire story of the Prairie People, including his own time among them. Bright Water watched him working on his story skins, as she called them, near the fire at night or seated with his back to a rock near the river during the day, and he knew she had to be wondering about his sanity.

Black Robe could not have said why he wrote. His hopes of someday writing a book that could be published in his native country, that would attract the attention of royalty and enhance his standing in the Jesuit order, had long since been abandoned. He would never see Europe again, and that was the way he wanted it.

He could not pass his writings along to his descendants

among the people and expect them to make anything of his words, either, since he wrote in French. If his work had been true story skins, the kind first created by old Storm Seeker, those who came after him could use them to learn the history of their people.

No, if pressed he would have had to say that he wrote for himself, to understand the tapestry of memories that had been his life. His time with the Crane band had been good; Bright Water had been a loving wife, and she had given him two fine children in Black Snake and Hummingbird—though the girl was a trial at times, no doubt about that. Black Robe loved them all dearly. He was content to live here, and he would be content to die here. But still he wrote and through his writing sought understanding.

"—as far away as the Shining Mountains."

He looked up at Bright Water as her words finally penetrated his reverie. "I am sorry. What did you say?"

She gave a bark of laughter. "I said your mind had gone as far away as the Shining Mountains, and you proved that I spoke the truth. Come, Black Robe. Let us return to our lodge."

He put the arrow shaft aside. He would return to it tomorrow. Bright Water took his arm to help him stand. His body was tired and did not work as well as it once had. Her hand remained on his arm as they turned toward the lodges.

The echo of an urgent shout floated to them.

Black Robe's eyes narrowed as he peered toward the east. Three figures were running toward the town, shouting. He stiffened in surprise when he realized that two of the runners were his own children. Young Man Coyote was with them.

"Something is wrong," Bright Water said.

Black Robe did not want to believe that, but in his heart and soul he knew she was right. "Let us hurry," he said.

By the time he and Bright Water reached the center of town, Black Snake, Hummingbird, and Young Man Coyote were there, too. The three young people came to a stop in front of the lodge of Cedar That Does Not Bend, who was now the principal chief of the Crane band. Cedar was getting along in years, but as he emerged from his lodge to see what all the commotion was about, he stood straight and strong.

Black Robe grasped his son's arm. "What news have you

brought us?" He knew that it had to be important to bring Black Snake and Coyote running back from their hunt. Black Robe had no idea what his daughter was doing with them. He had thought Hummingbird was with Bright Water all afternoon.

All three were out of breath from what had obviously been a long run. Black Snake recovered enough to say, "We saw boats . . . on the river . . . full of white men."

The words brought a stir of reaction from the people who had gathered around to hear. Black Robe exchanged a glance with Cedar, and the chief asked, "Were they coming toward our town?"

Black Snake said, "They will be here soon."

"How many?"

"The fingers of my hands, four times. Perhaps a few more."

Forty, Black Robe thought. A good-sized party. Probably the largest group of white men ever to visit this town.

"There is more," Hummingbird said. "One of them wears the black robes—like you, Father, when you first came to the Crane band."

Black Robe stiffened in surprise. Another Jesuit priest, coming here at last? Since he had never been in contact with his superiors back in France after leaving the St. Lawrence, he had expected them to send someone after him. But the years had passed, and no one had arrived, and gradually Black Robe had come to believe that he was forgotten. That was truly the way he preferred it now.

So the news that another priest might arrive at any moment did not come as a welcome surprise. He looked at his wife and saw worry on her face. Was she afraid he would turn his back on them and return to France? Surely she knew him better than that; there was nothing in France for him now. His life was here, among her Prairie People.

"Our band is known as one that makes visitors welcome," Cedar said. "We will extend our hospitality to these white men, as we have done with others in the past. But the warriors should watch them closely and be alert for any sign of trouble. We must be ready in case they mean us harm."

Black Robe hoped fervently that it would not turn out that way. If he were still the man he once had been, he would have prayed that the visit of the white men would be peaceful. But that man's Catholic faith had been shattered a long time ago.

With Cedar at their head, a group of warriors started toward the river so that they would be waiting when the boats came into view. Black Snake and Young Man Coyote, still catching their breath, went with them. Hummingbird tried to accompany them, but Bright Water stopped her.

"Come back to our lodge," Bright Water said. "You are tired."

"Not too tired to see the white men," Hummingbird protested.

"You will see more than enough of them later. We all will."

Black Robe could not help but agree with his wife's statement. Truly, he would have been content never to see another white man again.

Lieutenant Henri Guerre balanced carefully as he stood in the lead bateau. The bateau was easy to tip over, and if that happened, he would be dumped into the broad, shallow, muddy river. Such an assault on his dignity was not to be allowed. It was important that the rest of the men look up to him, even the rough trappers, who seemed to have little respect for anybody or anything.

He knew he cut a dashing figure in his blue coat and tight white breeches. The black tricorn on his head was decorated with a bright red cockade. The grizzled old trapper named Jacques LeCarde had told him the cockade made a good target and little else out here in the wilderness, but Guerre was not about to remove it.

He turned his head to look at the men in the bateau. Father Paul Maîtresse had moved up here into the lead bateau at their last stop along the river. The Jesuit wielded a paddle along with the rest of them, but the weakness of his slender body and the awkwardness with which he moved made him as much a liability as an asset. Still, he was one of the reasons Guerre was here; one of his orders was to assist Father Paul in discovering the fate of another priest who had disappeared in this area almost twenty years earlier. It was a foolish errand as far as Guerre was concerned, but even the army, at least to a certain extent, answered to the Church.

The sky to the west was reddening as the sun lowered in front of the bateaux. Behind Guerre, in another bateau, LeCarde called, "See that smoke up there? That will be the Indian village we heard about."

Guerre looked but could not see the smoke because of the glare of the sun. He hated to squint; it creased the skin around his eyes. So he would take LeCarde's word for it that they were approaching the village of the natives. LeCarde's face above the gray beard was already lined and seamed and baked to the color of old leather. He never had to worry about squinting.

The river, which seemed incapable of flowing for more than twenty rods without twisting and turning, bent up ahead around a small hill. As the bateaux floated around the bend moundlike dwellings made of earth came into view. Lodges, they were called, Guerre remembered from their visit to the Osage village downriver. These Indians called themselves the Crane band of the Prairie People—whatever that meant. To Guerre it was ridiculous the way these un-Christian savages associated themselves with animals and birds. Why could they not have proper names?

"Looks as if we've got a welcoming committee waiting for us," LeCarde said. The bateau he was in had pulled almost even with Guerre's.

The lieutenant peered toward the shore and saw that LeCarde was right. Several dozen men ranged along the bank, waiting and watching impassively as the bateaux approached. All were armed.

Guerre felt a tiny shiver of fear, but he quickly repressed it before anyone could notice. He pointed at the Indian town and the men who stood along the bank, then called loudly enough for everyone to hear him, "Bring the bateaux in to shore! We will stop here!"

Chapter Twenty-nine

Bright Water took a still-complaining Hummingbird back to the lodge while Black Robe followed the warriors to the river. As he went to join them Charles de St. Aubyn wondered if it would be possible not to reveal his identity to the visitors. He kept his beard shaved with a razor he had gotten in a trade with a trapper who had come through the town several years earlier. His dark hair was graying, but so was that of Cedar That Does Not Bend; there was nothing unusual about an Indian's hair turning gray. And his skin, though not as coppery as that of his friends, was certainly much darker now than it had been. He spoke the language of the Prairie People fluently. If he kept his knowledge of French to himself and stayed in the background, there would be no reason for the visitors to think him anything other than a lifelong member of the Crane band.

But as soon as he saw the men in the bateaux, he knew he could not do that. He felt a hollowness deep inside, a longing to talk to and be with those who were truly his own kind.

The sight of the priest, especially, touched something in Black Robe he had not known was there.

The Jesuit was so young, in Black Robe's eyes little more than a boy. He tried to paddle the bateau along with the others, but he was doing a poor job of it—much as he, Charles de St. Aubyn, had all those years ago. This priest seemed as unsuited for life in the wilderness as Charles had been.

But Charles had adapted—adapted so well, in fact, that the Church would now consider him an apostate and a heathen. Well, so be it, Black Robe decided. None of these men had the authority to make him go back to France and face his superiors.

One by one, the bateaux reached the shore and were pulled up onto the bank by the men who hopped out of them. The first to step off, an officer, took great pains not to get his high-topped black boots wet in the stream. Nor did he help pull his bateau from the water, leaving that task to the other men. He was young, tall, and handsome, and he strode with easy confidence over to the delegation waiting to greet him.

"Good afternoon," he said briskly. "I am Lieutenant Henri Guerre of His Majesty's army."

The sound of someone speaking French was strange to Black Robe's ears.

"Welcome to our town," Cedar said, also in French. His enunciation was labored, but the words were understandable. "We are the Crane band. I am Cedar That Does Not Bend, chief of the Crane band."

Lieutenant Guerre smiled, but Black Robe judged the expression none too sincere. "We have come to your land from across the great water, from a kingdom called France."

Cedar nodded solemnly. "We know of this place. Others from your homeland have visited us before."

"Good. Then you know why we are here."

"You go to the far mountains to trap the beaver and take his skin." Cedar's tone made it clear he still considered this a foolish activity, but if these pale-skinned Frenchmen wanted to engage in it, he would do nothing to stop them. As long as he and his people had the buffalo and the prairie, what happened in the far mountains mattered little to them.

"We would like to stop in your village for a time so that we can rest and replenish our supply of meat by hunting," Guerre said. "If this meets with your approval, of course."

Cedar waved a hand at the prairie. "The land is here for all. It does not belong to my people. We merely live upon it and use its bounty. You are free to do the same."

Guerre made a precise bow. "Thank you, Chief. There is one other matter." He turned and gestured to the priest, who came forward. "This is Father Paul Maîtresse. He is looking for a man of his order who vanished in this region many years ago, a man who wore black robes such as this and spoke of God. I am certain this man is dead by now, but if you know of his fate—"

Charles—that was suddenly the way he was thinking of himself again—had taken a deep breath as Guerre introduced the priest and began his questioning. Now he released it and stepped forward, moving between two of the warriors.

"The man you seek is not dead," he said in a loud, clear voice. "I am he. I am Charles de St. Aubyn."

Father Paul Maîtresse gave an audible gasp. Guerre was shocked, too, but he controlled his surprise with a visible effort and allowed himself only the raising of an eyebrow.

"Father Charles?" the young priest said, extending a hand. "Of the Jesuit order?"

Charles did not take Father Paul's proffered hand. "I should say, I *was* the man you seek. No longer. Now I am Black Robe, of the Crane band of the Prairie People."

One of the trappers, a rough-looking man with a gray beard, spoke up. "What he's trying to say is that he's gone Indian, Lieutenant. He's one of them now."

"I know what the man means, LeCarde," Guerre said. "I simply cannot understand *why* anyone would do such a thing."

Father Paul came closer to Charles. "This cannot be! No sane man could turn aside from the order, turn away from the Lord God—"

"Perhaps God turned away from me," Charles said, trying to control a sudden surge of anger. He did not need this callow youth to pass judgment on him, to condemn the last nineteen years of his life.

Father Paul backed away, shaking his head, then hurriedly crossed himself and began muttering prayers in Latin. It was clear he thought himself to be in the presence of a madman, a heretic, or both.

"Well, Father," Guerre said to the young priest, his tone surprisingly jovial, "you seem to have accomplished this part of your mission. When you return to France, you can tell them what happened to St. Aubyn. First, though, we have some more voyaging to do." He turned to Cedar again. "We would like to camp here for a few days, perhaps just upriver."

"I have already said that the land belongs to no one, and to all," Cedar replied. "You are welcome in our town." He motioned for his warriors to withdraw back to the cluster of lodges. As far as he was concerned, the conversation was over.

Charles still stood there, however, and he heard Guerre

mutter, "The King of France might argue that point with you." Charles knew what the lieutenant meant: Louis considered this part of the territory called New France.

Father Paul was still staring at him. "I . . . cannot understand this," he said.

Charles felt a touch on his arm. Bright Water stood beside him. He did not know when she had left the lodge and come to join him, but he was glad she was here and smiled at her. Father Paul had already suffered one shock today; perhaps another would not harm him. "This is my wife, Father. Her name is Bright Water. Will you come to our lodge and eat with us?"

He had made the invitation on impulse, but he hoped the priest would accept. Although they would probably disagree about everything, he really did want to converse with the young man. He wanted to find out how things were in France—a natural enough curiosity, he told himself.

Father Paul said hesitantly, "I suppose I can do that."

Charles clapped him on the shoulder, as he would a friend of the Crane band, and ignored the way the priest winced. "Good! We will eat and smoke a pipe and talk."

Father Paul seemed to swallow hard. He went along with Charles and Bright Water, looking for all the world as if he were being led to slaughter.

Hummingbird slipped through the gathering twilight, a patch of shadow moving among other shadows. Her mother, anxious to be with her father, had left the lodge sometime earlier and started down to the river, leaving Hummingbird behind after extracting a promise from her. Hummingbird had pledged to remain inside the lodge.

It pained Hummingbird to have lied to her mother, but she wanted to take a closer look at the white strangers. She left the lodge and circled through the town, finding a good spot from which to watch the meeting on the riverbank. When the talking was done and the Crane warriors began to return to their homes, Hummingbird moved into a small clump of trees near the stream.

From there she watched as the white men got back in their boats and shoved off from the bank. For a moment she thought despairingly that they were leaving. Then she saw that they were merely moving upstream a short distance. They brought the boats back in to shore and unloaded them less than a bowshot from where she crouched in the shadows. Some of them set up shelters that resembled tipis, but only faintly. They were not made of buffalo hide, either.

The ways of the Frenchmen were strange, Hummingbird thought, but fascinating. She wished that night would not fall so that she could watch them some more.

As they moved around setting up camp one of the men suddenly stopped, seized by a coughing spasm so violent that it bent him over almost double. Hummingbird frowned, wondering what was wrong with the man. He walked over to the river and spat several times, loudly, into the water, then wiped the back of his hand across his mouth and went back to what he had been doing.

A tall man in a blue coat strode around giving orders while the rest of the group set up the shelters, unloaded supplies, and got a fire started. Hummingbird watched him in the dying light. He was quite handsome, she saw to her surprise. She had seen other white men before and always thought they were ugly, with their pale skin and their beards. This man's face was clean; no bushy whiskers obscured his features. He stood tall and straight and strong, and he was good to look upon. Hummingbird could tell from the way he acted that he was the chief of this band of Frenchmen.

She was so caught up in watching that she did not hear the movement behind her, was not aware anyone was there until a hand fell on her shoulder. She gasped and turned sharply, wishing she had a knife or club or other weapon.

It was no enemy who had touched her, however. Young Man Coyote stood there, a grin on his face. "What are you doing here, little one?" he asked in a voice pitched quietly enough so that the nearby men could not overhear.

Hummingbird's chin lifted defiantly. "I am not a little one. And what I do here is my own business."

"So you are spying on the white demons," Coyote said as he crouched beside her and looked at the camp of the Frenchmen. "They are very strange."

Hummingbird glanced at the young chief and said, "Not all of them."

Coyote frowned. "You should not be here. Your mother and father will be searching for you when they find you are not in their lodge. The new black robe went with them. Your father asked him to come eat and talk."

"There is only one Black Robe," Hummingbird said.

"You know my meaning."

It was true; she did. But it was difficult for her to accept that anyone else could be like her father, even though she knew that he had had a life elsewhere before he came to be a member of the Crane band.

"I will go back to the lodge soon, but only when I am ready."

"You should be tired. You ran a long way with us today. You ran well."

"Well enough that I can go with you and Black Snake the next time you hunt?"

Coyote grunted. "Hunting is not a woman's job. It is meant for men, for warriors."

"The story skins say that Moon Hawk Sister was both a woman and a warrior. She helped Storm Seeker and Fire Maker kill the giant Red Horn demon."

"That is just a story, and even if it is true, it happened long, long ago. Besides, after she was rescued from the Red Horns, Moon Hawk Sister came back to the Prairie People and married Fire Maker and was a good wife to him. She bore him many fine children and kept his lodge and did not complain. You have forgotten *that* part of the story, Hummingbird."

"I did not forget." She had just never liked that part of the tale nearly as well as the first part.

Coyote considered her for a long moment, then spoke solemnly. "I think you will make some warrior a good wife. You are strong. You do not mind working. You talk too much, but—"

"Talk too much!" She struck him on the arm with a clenched fist, but not too hard. "I speak when I have something to say. Men rattle like dried beans in a pod!"

Coyote rubbed his arm where she had hit him and sighed.

"Your husband, whoever he is, will have to teach you to respect him. But I think you will probably be worth the trouble."

A warm glow suffused Hummingbird. This was courtship talk. She and Coyote should not have been alone together like this. He should have come to the river early in the morning when the women went to fetch the day's water. According to the customs of the Prairie People, a suitor waited there for an opportunity to speak with the young woman he favored. Coyote could sing a song for her or play a tune on a special lovers' flute carved from a hollowed-out branch and decorated with floral symbols, and thus tell her of his interest.

But Hummingbird had never been one to abide strictly by the customs of the people, not when they interfered with what she wanted. Now, as she smiled at Coyote, the handsome young Frenchman she had seen and admired earlier was forgotten. Coyote was smiling back at her, and she wondered how long it would be before he asked for her hand in marriage.

The next moment all thoughts of romance vanished as a twig snapped nearby and the barrel of a musket suddenly thrust past the trunk of a tree and pointed at them. "What have we here?" a voice asked, surprising Hummingbird and Coyote even more because it spoke in the tongue of the Prairie People. "Young lovers, eh? You had best come with me."

Chapter Thirty

Lieutenant Henri Guerre had gone inside his tent, lit a candle, and started an entry in his journal when he heard the commotion outside. Grateful for the interruption, he set pen and ink aside. Keeping meticulous records of the mission was his least favorite duty, one he would gladly have handed over to an adjutant had the army seen fit to assign him one. Instead, the corporal and three privates under his command could barely write their own names, let alone the careful record of how far the party had traveled, the route they had taken, and detailed information about everything they had seen along the way. Most of the trappers, of course, were hopelessly illiterate and barely followed his orders.

So Guerre continued to keep the journal himself, knowing that if he did a good job on this mission, there would be a promotion waiting for him in France. That was what he kept telling himself. It would all be worth it.

For the moment, though, he was glad of the distraction. Settling his hat on his sleek dark hair, he stepped out of the tent to see why the voyageurs were hooting and laughing.

A frown creased Guerre's smooth forehead. One of the trappers, Jacques LeCarde, herded a pair of Indians through the camp at gunpoint, heading toward the lieutenant's tent. The natives, a young man and a girl, looked angry and not the least bit frightened.

"What is the meaning of this, LeCarde?" Guerre demanded sharply.

"Found these two lurking out there in the brush, Lieutenant. Thought you might want to question them, find out if they were up to any mischief." LeCarde took a hand off his musket and tugged at his whiskers. "Maybe they were planning to sneak into the camp tonight and slit all of our throats."

"I hardly think that's likely. These people seem friendly enough."

"Things aren't always what they seem out here in the wilderness."

Guerre swallowed his annoyance at the man's impertinence. LeCarde's attitude often bordered on outright insubordination. Looking at the two Indians, Guerre asked, "Who are you, and what do you want?"

"They probably don't speak French, Lieutenant," LeCarde said. "I'll jabber at them in their own tongue."

"I speak your language," the girl said, taking Guerre and LeCarde by surprise. "My father taught me."

"Your father is the priest, St. Aubyn?"

"He is Black Robe. Once that other name was his, but no more."

Guerre looked at her with rising interest. If the old priest was her father, that meant she was half-white. And she spoke French, which he had not expected. He put her age at fifteen or sixteen years, on the verge of womanhood. Already she had the curving hips of a woman, and her breasts had a lovely shape to them under that buckskin dress. In the light of the campfire, she was undeniably beautiful.

"Who is your friend?" Guerre asked, indicating the young warrior.

"He is Young Man Coyote," the girl said. "I am called Hummingbird."

It was a good name for one so lovely, Guerre reflected. "Why were you and Young Man Coyote spying on us, Hummingbird? Did you plan to do us harm?"

She shook her head emphatically. "I was curious, that is all. And Coyote came after me to see what I was doing."

"They were making courtship talk, Lieutenant," LeCarde said. "But that doesn't mean they weren't up to no good."

"I don't believe we have to worry about these two young people." Guerre gestured sharply at the trapper. "Put your gun down and go about your business." He ignored the hostile glare LeCarde sent in his direction and turned his attention back to Hummingbird. "You may go back to your father's lodge now, but you are welcome to visit our camp anytime you wish, Hummingbird." He pointedly did not extend the same invitation to Coyote.

The girl did not indicate whether she would accept or not. Instead she said something to Coyote in the language of the Prairie People, and then the two of them turned and walked away from the fire, moving between the tents and then striding toward the nearby town of the Crane band. Guerre watched them go, wishing that the light was better so that he could observe the motion of her hips as she walked. He swallowed and licked his lips; they had gone dry.

"I don't trust them," LeCarde said, breaking into Guerre's thoughts. "You got to keep a close eye on all these red Indians. I've been out here before, Lieutenant—"

"Yes, I'm aware of your vast experience, Monsieur LeCarde, but I'm still in command of this mission, am I not?"

LeCarde shrugged and turned away.

Guerre reined in his temper. They still had a long way to

travel, and he sensed that to make an issue of LeCarde's behavior here and now would be a mistake. But someday he would have to deal with the trapper, perhaps harshly.

For the moment, however, his thoughts were of the young woman called Hummingbird. He had never expected to encounter a female native who was so appealing to him. Well, she *was* half-white, he reminded himself. That helped.

He hoped she would take him up on his offer and return to visit the camp.

"I simply can't understand," Father Paul repeated for what seemed like the dozenth time. "To abandon your life of faith—"

"I have a life here," Charles said, sweeping his hand to indicate his surroundings. "A life that suits me very well." He was trying hard not to be insulted by the younger man's attitude.

Father Paul shook his head. "But what about your vows, your faith?"

"What about it?" Charles replied, sounding harsher than he intended. *My faith did not save the life of my friend Hornet. My faith did nothing to turn aside the evil of Dubois and Grenet and the others.*

This young priest would not understand that, either. The Jesuits had done a good job on Father Paul. His mind, alert and eager to quest for knowledge and new answers in some areas, was utterly closed in others.

Charles tried to focus his attention on the conversation with Father Paul as Bright Water prepared the evening meal, though part of his mind was worrying about Hummingbird. Bright Water had said the girl was here in the lodge, but when he and Father Paul had arrived, she was gone. His daughter had a strong will and a mind of her own, Charles knew, and most of the time he would have had it no other way. Now, however, with strangers camped near the town—French trappers at that—he wished she were here so that he would know she was safe.

Black Snake had gone to look for his sister. A few quick words from Charles, spoken in an undertone in the language of the Prairie People, had seen to that. Charles suspected that wherever Hummingbird was, Young Man Coyote would not be far away. Coyote was a good man, an able warrior despite his youth, and Charles was somewhat comforted by his certainty that Coyote would protect Hummingbird with his very life. It would only be a matter of time before Coyote asked for his daughter's hand in marriage, Charles thought, and he knew Bright Water agreed with him. Strange how the old ones were often aware of such things before the young people were.

His mind had wandered, and he noticed now that Father Paul was still talking about the need for him to return to France. Charles shook his head firmly and interrupted the young priest again. "We can speak of this later," he said. "Tell me about yourself."

Reluctantly Father Paul explained that he was from a small farming village north of Paris and that he was the youngest of four sons. With little if any legacy to look forward to, his options in life had been either the army or the priesthood. He had wound up under the command of a military officer even though he had chosen the priesthood, he said ruefully. "But I have been chosen to minister to the heathens, and I shall do so regardless of the circumstances. The Holy Word must be brought to the godless."

"They are not godless," Charles said, knowing that he was about to scandalize the young priest. "They simply call Him by a different name. But they pray to the Creator just as you do."

As expected, Father Paul frowned darkly. "How can it be the same? They have never heard of Jesus, they do not know our rituals—"

"Have you heard of Wakon-tah? Do you know the rituals of the Prairie People?"

"It is not the same," Father Paul said stubbornly. "They are pagans! They will burn in hell unless we save their souls!"

Charles took a deep breath, once again controlling his anger. He glanced at Bright Water, so lovely and graceful, so gentle, so strong. To call her a pagan merely reflected the depth of Father Paul's ignorance.

Charles managed to smile. "This, too, we shall discuss another time. Now we will eat."

Bright Water brought them bowls of stew, and Charles noticed that Father Paul ate his hungrily—even though it had been cooked by a heathen! That thought made him look down at his own bowl and smile again.

They had almost finished the meal when the hide flap over the entrance was pushed aside and Hummingbird came into the lodge, her expression as dark as a storm cloud rolling over the plains. Black Snake followed, looking angry, too.

"I found my sister and Coyote returning from the camp of the white men," Black Snake said in his native tongue.

"I told you to stay in the lodge," Bright Water said to Hummingbird. "Why did you not do as I said?"

Hummingbird did not look at all contrite as she said, "I am sorry. I wanted to see the white men."

"You have seen white men before. I am white," Charles reminded her. "And another sits in our lodge at this very moment."

"They went into the camp," Black Snake said. "Coyote told me. One of the trappers found them in the woods, pointed a musket at them, and took them to the chief of the white men."

That would be Lieutenant Guerre, Charles thought. He had disliked the officer on sight, but whether that was because his instincts were trying to tell him something or simply that Guerre reminded him of Lieutenant Dubois, he could not have said. He frowned, disturbed that his daughter had been in the midst of the voyageurs.

He stood up and went to her, placing his hands on her shoulders. "Did they do anything to hurt you?"

Hummingbird shook her head. "Their chief was very kind. He made the other man put away his gun. He spoke with respect to me. And he said that I could go back and visit their camp whenever I liked."

Charles's concern deepened. Hummingbird did not need to be encouraged to act willfully. "You will not go there again," he said to her. "There is no reason for you to be there. Your life is here, not among the whites."

"I was only curious."

"Just do not go there again."

Hummingbird accepted his command, but Charles still had his doubts she would obey. Mischief lurked in her eyes.

All he could do was pray that her stubbornness would not lead
her into more trouble.

Chapter Thirty-one

For several days Hummingbird remained close to her parents'
lodge so that they would think she had accepted their decree to
stay away from the camp of the white demons. Black Robe and
Bright Water were not the only ones watching her to make sure
she behaved properly. Her brother, Black Snake, was insuffer-
ably smug as he kept an eye on her. Often Young Man Coyote
was with him. She was pleased by Coyote's attentions, but she
did not care for the way he sometimes assumed they were
already betrothed. He had not sung a song for her yet. He had no
right to treat her as if he owned her.

Hummingbird watched the camp of the Frenchmen from a
distance. No one could stop her from doing that. She saw their
hunting parties set out and return. More than once she saw the
tall, clean-limbed figure of their chief striding about. Although
she had no doubt that Coyote was her man, her eyes were still
drawn to the Frenchman called Lieutenant Guerre.

Black Robe and Father Paul had spent much time in the lodge
after that first night, arguing in the tongue Hummingbird's father
had spoken when he first came to the Land of the Two Rivers.
Though she could speak it as well, listening to the two of them
made her head hurt, so she paid little attention to their endless
discussions about religion. Besides, Bright Water was keeping
her busy most of the time with chores. Hummingbird knew why;
her mother wanted to keep her thoughts away from the pale-
skinned visitors.

Hummingbird was fetching water from the river—even
though she knew her mother did not really need more water—
when she noticed that one of the other women, Grass Waving,

was doubled over coughing. Hummingbird put down the earthen pot and hurried over to her. "Are you all right?" she asked.

"A . . . sickness has come over me," Grass Waving replied. "But I am sure I will soon be well again. Hawk Wing has prayed and sung the healing song for me."

The coughing fit subsided, and Hummingbird patted Grass Waving's shoulder and went back to her errand. Hawk Wing was a good medicine man, although Hummingbird was certain he was not the equal of her late uncle Hornet, whom she had never known. Now that she thought about it, she had heard more and more of the people coughing in recent days, which was unusual for this time of year. Such sicknesses were common in the winter, but not in midsummer. Hawk Wing would care for those who were ill, she told herself.

After two more days had passed, Hummingbird noticed that her parents, her brother, and Coyote were not watching her as closely as before. Obviously they had decided her fascination with the white men had subsided. That was what she had been waiting for. She feared the visitors would be leaving soon, since they still had far to go on their journey to the mountains and their supply of fresh meat was surely replenished by now. For more than a week they had been camped beside the river. If Hummingbird was going to see them again and speak with Lieutenant Guerre, she would have to seize the next opportunity to do so or perhaps never have the chance again.

The opportunity came that very afternoon. Black Snake and Coyote went downriver to hunt, and Black Robe was engaged in one of his interminable discussions with Father Paul. Bright Water had left the lodge to help care for another woman in the town who had fallen ill. The sickness seemed to be spreading, but Hummingbird was not worried about catching it. She was young and healthy, and except for a fever that had struck her when she was a young child, she had never been ill. This new malady would not touch her.

While Black Robe and Father Paul were arguing, Hummingbird slipped out of the lodge. It was the middle of the afternoon, the hottest part of the day, and most people had sought the shade of their lodges. Others were inside because they were sick. As Hummingbird walked quickly through the town no one noticed her.

She headed for the camp of the whites. It, too, looked sleepy, almost deserted. Some of the men were out hunting, no doubt, and the others were inside their tipis-that-were-not-tipis. One young man, who was wearing his blue coat despite the heat, stood near the tipi of Lieutenant Guerre. He leaned on his musket, resting the stock of the weapon on the ground, but when he noticed Hummingbird coming toward him, he straightened.

"What do you want here, Indian?" he asked in French.

"I am Hummingbird," she replied in the same language. "I was told by your chief, Lieutenant Guerre, that I could visit your camp whenever I wished."

Some of the suspicion died out of the young man's eyes. "I remember you now. Jacques brought you and a young buck into camp the first evening we were here." He snickered. "Brought you in at the point of his musket."

Hummingbird said nothing.

"Well, I suppose it's all right for you to be here," he went on. His eyes dropped to her breasts. "What is it you want?"

"I want to see Lieutenant Guerre."

He sighed. "Of course you do. That's what all the ladies want, all the way from here to France. And the rest of us do without."

Hummingbird did not know what he was talking about. "You will take me to Lieutenant Guerre?"

"All right. Come with me."

She followed him as he went over to the lieutenant's shelter and rapped on one of the poles that held it up. "Excuse me, Lieutenant," he called, "but you have a visitor out here."

A moment later Guerre stepped through the slit cut in the French tent. He was wearing high black boots and tight white breeches, but he was naked from the waist up. His fair skin stood out in sharp contrast to his tanned face and hands, and it was all Hummingbird could do not to stare. She had never seen such pale skin, nor such a mat of dark, curling hair as adorned the lieutenant's chest.

Guerre looked surprised when he saw her, but an instant later he smiled. "Hummingbird! I'm glad to see you. I was afraid you weren't going to come back to visit me."

"I have been busy," she said, thinking of all the unnecessary chores with which her mother had burdened her in recent days.

"Well, I'm glad you've made the time for me." He held open the entrance to his dwelling. "Come in, come in."

Hummingbird hesitated briefly before stepping into the French tipi. She had thought that Lieutenant Guerre would show her around the camp. Of course, there was not really anything there to see other than what she had already observed. And she *was* curious about the way these Frenchmen lived.

She stepped through the opening into the shadowy interior. Guerre came after her, dropping the entrance flap closed behind him.

Henri Guerre could barely believe his good fortune. He had decided with some disappointment that the beautiful Indian girl was not going to return to the camp. He had seen the interest in her eyes during her first visit, the evening LeCarde had caught her and that boy hiding in the trees.

Of course she was interested, Guerre had told himself. What woman would want a red man when a handsome young officer such as he was available? And now she was here, obviously ready to take him up on his offer.

It was about time, he told himself as he let his gaze play over the clean lines of her body. He had been without a woman for weeks. The voyageurs were ready to rut with any available female, no matter how ugly and dirty, and his troops were only a bit more discriminating. But Henri Guerre deserved better. He deserved a woman with some measure of beauty and grace. Hummingbird was well endowed with both.

These Indians had no morals, of course. They were like animals. Guerre was certain he could have found any number of them willing to share his bunk, but he had waited.

Now, as he looked at Hummingbird, he was very glad he had. He was going to enjoy this.

She looked in what seemed to be awe at his cot and the small table beside it, both of which folded up so that they could be stowed away in a bateau. She reached down and picked up an object from the table. "What is this?" she asked as she turned toward him and held it out. "It shines."

"It's a looking glass," Guerre explained. "Here, I'll show you."

He put his fingers on her wrist, enjoying the feel of her bare skin. He lifted her hand until she was peering into the looking glass.

"See that pretty girl? That's you, Hummingbird."

Her eyes widened, and she jerked the looking glass away. "A demon!" she said. "This is a demon that tries to steal my soul!"

Guerre laughed and shook his head. "Not at all. Have you ever seen your reflection in the surface of the river?"

Hummingbird raised her eyebrows dubiously.

"This is the same thing." He slid his fingertips over the smooth face of the looking glass. "This is like the surface of a river, only you can pick it up and carry it with you. Most beautiful young women enjoy looking at themselves."

She frowned. "Do you think I am good to look upon?"

"Oh, yes. Very good indeed."

That seemed to please her. A little flattery, perhaps a trinket or two, was all it would take, Guerre thought.

She turned back to the table and picked up something else. "I know what this is," she said proudly as she displayed it to him. "You use it to scrape the hair off your face."

"Yes, it's a razor. You've seen one like it before."

"My father has one. He will not allow me to touch it, though."

"You can open that one," Guerre told her with a casual gesture.

She looked quickly at him, as if checking to make certain he was serious, then carefully, almost gingerly, pulled the blade away from its wooden handle. She stared at it, once again awestruck by something that seemed incredibly simple to him.

"Careful," Guerre said suddenly as she touched the keen edge of the razor with the index finger of her other hand.

She let out a little cry and jerked her finger back. A tiny spot of red appeared on the tip where she had pricked it. Guerre took the razor out of her hand, pitching it back onto the table beside the bunk. "It will be all right," he assured her. "It's just a little cut. Let me see."

He took hold of the injured hand and brought it up close to his face. Without warning he pressed his lips to her finger, tasting the faint saltiness of the drop of blood, then sucked her finger into his mouth so that his tongue could circle it. Hummingbird's breath came faster, and her eyes grew even wider.

Guerre finally took her finger out of his mouth, tightened his grip on her wrist, and pulled her hard against him.

"No!" Hummingbird cried. "What are you doing?"

"What we both want," Guerre said. His other arm went around her waist and clamped into place. He felt the warm thrust of her buckskin-covered breasts against his bare chest and nudged the hardness of his groin against the small, soft mound of her belly.

"You cannot do this," she said desperately.

"Do you know what a man and a woman do, Hummingbird? I can show you."

"I know. I cannot lie with you! We are not betrothed!"

"That does not matter. Let me love you, little one."

Of course, love had nothing to do with it, Guerre thought fleetingly. His only goal was pleasure, a slaking of the lust that had been growing within him since the first time he had seen her. She would enjoy it, too, he told himself. Once she got over being frightened, he would give her more passion than any of these untutored savages possibly could. After all, was he not French?

He let go of her wrist and closed his hand over her breast, tugging at the buckskin dress as he did so. He wanted her naked and spread out on his cot awaiting him. With any luck, she would not scream. He did not want to be forced to hit her and knock her unconscious before he took his pleasure with her. It would be much better if she was awake and cooperating.

Keeping one arm tightly around her, he moved toward the bunk, forcing her backward. She trembled wildly in his embrace, reminding him of an animal in a trap, an image that only heightened his desire.

Suddenly she struck him in the chest with both hands, shoving him back a step. His grip loosened enough that she was able to slip out of it. As he lunged for her again she reached behind her, and her flailing hand closed on the handle of the razor. She lifted it from the table.

Then she slashed at his face with the blade, and he felt a kiss of fire on his cheek.

Chapter Thirty-two

Worry gnawed at Black Snake like a beaver felling a tree. He had one arm around Coyote, who had become feverish and started coughing while they were looking for game along the river earlier that afternoon. His friend's sudden illness troubled him. Although no one of the Crane band had died from the sickness that had appeared so mysteriously in the town, many were quite ill. Hawk Wing claimed that the spirits would cure them, but Black Snake thought that the medicine man secretly doubted the efficacy of his chants and herbs. Black Snake knew that his father and mother were very worried, too.

Now the illness had come to Coyote. Black Snake wished he could take his war club and drive out the demons that were making his friend sick.

"I am sorry to have ruined our hunt," Coyote said as they neared the town.

"There will be other hunts," Black Snake said, forcing a note of heartiness into his voice. He did not know what he would do if death claimed Coyote; they had been friends since childhood. He would lay down his own life if it would save Coyote's. "In the fall we will kill many buffalo," he went on. "Our families will grow fat from the meat we bring them."

"I . . . hope this is so," Coyote said, his words interrupted by another racking cough.

Coyote's skin was hot to the touch, like a rock that had been sitting in the summer sun. He needed to be bathed in cool water. Black Snake thought about taking him to the river but decided it would be best for Coyote to be with his own parents. They along with Hawk Wing would care for him.

Dogs barked at them as they entered the town, drawing the attention of several men and women who hurried out to meet them. Coyote's parents were summoned, and as his father and uncle took him into a lodge, Coyote's mother asked Black Snake what had happened.

"He sickened while we were hunting," Black Snake explained. "I brought him back as quickly as I could."

Another of Coyote's uncles clasped Black Snake's arm. "You have our thanks," he said.

Knowing he could do nothing more for his friend but offer up prayers to the Creator, Black Snake turned toward his own family's lodge. His father and mother met him before he could reach it.

"Have you seen Hummingbird?" Black Robe asked.

Black Snake shook his head. "How could I have seen her? She is here in the town, and I went hunting with Coyote." He sighed. "Coyote is very sick. I brought him back—"

"Your sister is gone," Bright Water said.

The fear in her voice made Black Snake forget Coyote's plight for the moment. "Gone?" he repeated.

"She left the lodge while I was talking to Father Paul and your mother was not there." Black Robe's voice was harsh with guilt. "I should have asked her where she was going."

Black Snake grunted. "Hummingbird is stubborn, and she lies. She would not have told you the truth, Father. But I know where she has gone."

"I think I know as well," Black Robe said. "To the camp of the Frenchmen."

"I will find her," Black Snake said. "It will not take long. She will be sorry to hear that Coyote is ill, and she will come back to the town with me."

Bright Water put a hand on her son's shoulder. "Go," she said. Fear put an edge on her voice.

Black Snake was more angry than afraid. Hummingbird had no right to upset their parents this way, he thought as he trotted toward the camp of the white men. With all the trouble that had already come to the Crane band, she should not have been so selfish. He would speak very strongly to her when he found her, he decided. He loved Black Robe very much, but sometimes he was not strict enough, especially where Hummingbird was concerned.

As he neared the French camp one of the soldiers came

forward to meet him. The man lifted his musket and called sharply, "Halt! What are you doing, Indian?"

Black Snake hated speaking French, but he forced his lips and tongue to wrestle out the unfamiliar words. "I look for . . . my sister . . . called Hummingbird."

"Oh, her." The soldier grinned, and Black Snake thought the expression made his pale, bearded face even uglier. "She's here, but you can't see her now. She's with the lieutenant."

"Lieu . . . tenant?" Black Snake repeated.

"Our chief. Do not worry, my friend. He will be finished with her soon, I am sure."

Finished with her? Black Snake did not like the sound of that. He started to step past the guard. "I will find her myself."

"Now, hold on," the man began, barring Black Snake's path again. His thumb looped around the hammer of his musket. "You can't just barge in here with your red ass—"

That was when, inside one of the French tipis nearby, a man shouted suddenly in pain and anger. An instant later a woman screamed.

Hummingbird.

Lieutenant Guerre cried out when Hummingbird slashed his face with the razor. As he stumbled back a step she attempted to dart past him toward the entrance. His left hand went to his cheek, where dark red blood spilled between his fingers, while his right hand closed over Hummingbird's wrist. He twisted her arm brutally, and she screamed as she was forced to drop the razor.

He took his hand away from his face, and she saw the gash she had opened up in his cheek. The back of his hand cracked painfully against her own cheek as he struck her. "You bitch!" he shouted. Still holding her tightly, he stooped and picked up the fallen razor. "When I'm through with you, I'll carve you so that no man will ever want you again!"

Despite the terror welling inside her, Hummingbird fought back, trying to jerk herself free from his grasp as she clawed at the bleeding face with her other hand. She was vaguely aware of shouts outside, and then a musket exploded. Guerre turned his head toward the entrance.

Black Snake burst through the opening. Hummingbird had never been so glad to see him in her life. She had no idea what he was doing here when he was supposed to be out hunting with Coyote, but she did not care. All that mattered now was that he would save her from this mad Frenchman.

Black Snake took his war club from his belt and lifted it for a killing stroke aimed at Guerre's skull. Guerre pivoted, pulling Hummingbird along with him. He yanked on her arm and then released it, sending her staggering directly into the path of Black Snake, who had to stop his war club in mid-blow to keep from hitting her with it. That threw him off balance, and when she fell into him, their feet tangled and both of them went down.

Guerre, still holding the razor, leaned over and slashed at Black Snake, who barely lifted his war club in time to block the blade. The keen tip of it bit into the wood of the club. Black Snake brought his foot up and kicked the lieutenant in the belly.

Hummingbird rolled toward Guerre's cot as Black Snake scrambled back to his feet. Guerre had lost his hold on the razor; it was still stuck to Black Snake's war club. Clutching his midsection with one hand, with the other he reached for a musket propped in a corner of the tent. His fingers closed around the barrel, and he swung it toward Black Snake's head.

The stock slammed into the side of Black Snake's head above the left ear and shattered. Black Snake fell, knocked half-senseless by the blow. As he tried to push himself back to his feet, several trappers plunged into the tent. One of them took in the scene in an instant and shouted, "The Indian's gone mad! Shoot him!"

"No!" That urgent cry came from Guerre. "He is mine!"

Who was the madman here? Hummingbird asked herself. Black Snake, who was only fighting to protect his sister's life and honor? Or Lieutenant Henri Guerre, with blood dripping from his face and eyes blazing with rage? She knew the answer, and she looked around desperately for some sort of weapon so that she could help her brother.

As Black Snake struggled upright Guerre turned toward the other side of his bunk and snatched up something Hummingbird had not noticed before. It was a long knife such as she had seen some white soldiers carry. With a rasp of blade against sheath, Guerre pulled the weapon free.

"No!" Hummingbird cried as she lunged to her feet and threw herself across the cot toward him. He met her with an outstretched hand that easily shoved her aside. Then he stepped toward Black Snake, who had dropped his war club and was defenseless.

"You never should have interfered," Guerre hissed. He feinted with the blade once, twice, forcing Black Snake into a corner. Seeing no escape, Black Snake uttered a yipping war cry and threw himself forward just as Guerre thrust a final time.

The blade ripped into Black Snake's belly. The muscles of Guerre's bare back and shoulders bunched as he twisted the blade and jerked it back and forth. Hummingbird could see her brother's face over Guerre's shoulder. She saw his eyes and mouth open wide, saw the gout of blood that surged between his lips.

Then her eyes fell on the razor lying on the ground where it had fallen, forgotten. She picked it up, intending to attack Guerre from behind and avenge her brother's death, even if it cost her own life.

But as she stepped toward Guerre one of the trappers noticed and moved to intercept her. He swung a clenched fist at her face, and though Hummingbird saw the blow coming, she could not avoid it. His fist caught her just above the right eye and sent her plummeting into a pool of blackness.

After everything that had just happened, she almost welcomed the oblivion.

Panting from both exertion and emotion, Guerre tore his sword free from the Indian's belly and stepped back so that the man's body could fall to the ground, his organs spilling out through the hideous wound Guerre had inflicted. The Indian youth had sagged against him as he died, and his blood had smeared Guerre's chest. With a grimace of distaste the lieutenant wiped at it but could not remove the gore from his skin.

His face throbbed where the girl had cut him, but there was no time to worry about that now. The thought of the girl made him look around for her. He saw her sprawled on the floor and for an instant thought she was dead, too.

"I had to hit her, Lieutenant," one of the men said. "She's just knocked out."

Guerre said, "Good. Bind her hands and feet, and put a gag in her mouth. There's already been too much shouting."

He hoped none of the cries had been heard in the neighboring town of the Crane band. If they had, they would surely draw unwelcome attention. But if not, he might still be able to salvage this unholy situation. There had been a single gunshot, but the Indians probably would not think anything of that; his men discharged their weapons frequently.

Why hadn't the girl just gone along with him, damn it? She had caused this whole fiasco by resisting him.

He sighed and brought his fingers to the wound on his cheek. The blood had begun to dry and form a crust on his skin. There would be a terrible scar there, he feared. Hummingbird had marked him for life. She would pay for her crime. By God, she would pay!

But again, there would be time for that later. He said to the trappers who had finished tying up Hummingbird, "Get ready to break camp. Spread the word that we're pulling out."

"We still have men out hunting," one of the voyageurs protested.

"They know to rendezvous with us upstream if there's trouble," Guerre said. "When they get close enough to see that we're no longer here, they will avoid the Indian town and come to meet us."

Those were the standing orders, at any rate. Guerre did not really care if the men who were not in camp at the moment ever rejoined them or not. He had to put as much distance as possible between himself and the natives before this incident was discovered.

"Wrap the girl and the other Indian in blankets and put them in the bateaux. We'll take the girl with us and dump the boy's body in the river when we get a good distance upstream. The other Indians will never know what happened to them."

One of the men nudged the corpse with his foot. "This isn't

the buck who was with her the first time, is it? Wonder who he was."

"He's a dead Indian," Guerre said coldly. "He's less than nothing."

"He's trouble for us if the rest of those red bastards find out about this."

"That is why we must make sure they do not. Now get busy, all of you. I want to be away from here in less than an hour."

The trappers hurriedly left the tent to execute his orders. Guerre found the looking glass, which had somehow survived all the commotion without a scratch, and studied his reflection in it. He wet a cloth with water from a canteen and washed away as much blood as he could. The wound was a couple of inches long, but the edges were smooth and clean, and it was not as deep as he had feared. At first he had believed that Hummingbird had laid his cheek open to the bone. With any luck, the injury would heal and leave behind only a thin scar. That might not be too bad. A dueling scar—that was what it would be when he returned to Paris. A mark of distinction. The romance of it would set the ladies' hearts aflutter.

In the meantime there was Hummingbird. He intended to use her until he grew tired of her, and then he would turn her over to the men. That would be a more suitable punishment than killing her right away. She would regret ruining his plans for her. He would have enjoyed teaching her to make love, and then he would have left her here, perhaps with a French baby growing in her belly if she was lucky. Now that would never come to be. Even if she survived the next few months as a captive, she would never return to her home.

Because before they left the mountains for the return journey, Guerre intended to slit her throat.

Chapter Thirty-three

"I don't understand," Father Paul said as he paced back and forth in the lodge of Black Robe and Bright Water. "I simply don't understand. Why would they leave without me?"

Charles de St. Aubyn, Black Robe, had other worries at the moment. Not only had his daughter vanished, but now Black Snake was nowhere to be found. Bright Water was frightened, and his own fear was growing.

"You're welcome to stay here for as long as necessary," Charles told the young Jesuit. Father Paul had arrived at the lodge a short while earlier, upset because he noticed that Lieutenant Guerre and the voyageurs had broken camp and departed while he was visiting some of the sick in the town of the Crane band. That was the first Charles had heard of the Frenchmen leaving, and every instinct told him that their departure was related somehow to the disappearance of Black Snake and Hummingbird. Right now he was waiting for Cedar That Does Not Bend, and when the chief came, they would go to the place where the white men had camped and see what they could discover.

"I appreciate that generous offer," Father Paul was saying, "but what about my mission? I was supposed to travel all the way to the mountains with Lieutenant Guerre's party and minister to the Indians I found there."

"There are people in need of help right here," Charles pointed out. "Perhaps when you care for their physical bodies, are you not caring for their spirits at the same time?"

Father Paul frowned. "I suppose one could say so . . . but how will I ever return to France?" A note of desperation entered his voice. "Will I never see my home again? After all, *you* are still here, Father Charles!"

"Only by my own choice," Charles told him. "There will be other parties of trappers, perhaps even other priests from the

223

Society of Jesus. And it is always possible that Lieutenant Guerre and the others will stop here and pick you up when the trapping season is over."

Charles secretly doubted that. The stealth and swiftness with which Guerre and his men had left strongly suggested that they would not want to come back this way. Charles thought again of Hummingbird and Black Snake. His mind sickened.

Cedar That Does Not Bend arrived at the lodge a few moments later, along with Hawk Wing and several warriors. "Stay here with Bright Water," Charles said to Father Paul. He did not want to leave his wife alone while she was so worried. The priest understood.

Charles left the lodge with Cedar and the other men. They walked quickly upstream to the place on the riverbank where the French camp had been. As they neared it Cedar said, "One of the white men's guns made the sound of thunder not long before they left. This is what several of the warriors have said they heard. And there was some shouting as well."

"I never noticed," Black Robe said, trying to fight off the guilt that was already wrapping its fingers around him. "I was concerned with Young Man Coyote and the others who have fallen sick."

Cedar lifted a hand to his mouth and coughed softly. Black Robe shot a startled, anxious glance at him. Cedar shook his head. "I am all right. I must be. My people depend on me." When they reached the campsite, he looked around grimly. "Let us see if we can tell what happened."

As usual, the white men had left many reminders of their presence: the ashes of their fire, holes and gouges where the ground had been disturbed, and flattened areas on the grass where they had spread their bedrolls. In one spot, sand had been brought from the riverbank and spread out on the ground, for what purpose Black Robe could not see.

Cedar was more suspicious. He knelt beside the sand, brushed some of it aside, and picked up a handful, which he rubbed between his fingers. He brought his hand to his nose and sniffed. His expression was grim as he looked up at Black Robe and said, "Someone bled here, a great deal, I would say."

Black Robe's own blood turned to ice. "Hummingbird was

here," he said. "She and Black Snake both. I can feel it. Those Frenchmen . . ." His voice cracked. "They did something to my children."

Cedar straightened. "We cannot know this. But we can send men to follow them—"

Again he stopped to cough.

Black Robe, his face bleak, looked around at the other men. They were his friends; he had made arrows for every one of them. Several looked pale and haggard, and Cedar was not the only one trying to stifle a cough. The illness was spreading almost as fast as the prairie fire that had destroyed Dubois and Grenet and the others so many years ago, Black Robe thought. Even the men who were not ill were grieving for those who were. He could not ask them to leave their homes on his behalf, not now.

"No," he said, "I will go."

Cedar placed a hand on his shoulder. "Black Robe, my friend, you are not a warrior. You must have help."

"I am one of the Crane band. Wakon-tah will help me. He will give me strength and guide my path."

"The decision is yours. But know that we will go with you if you wish."

Black Robe passed a trembling hand over his face. "Let us go back to our lodges. I must gather my weapons."

Cedar had spoken the truth: Black Robe was no warrior. He had no idea what he would do if he caught up to the party of trappers. If Black Snake and Hummingbird were their prisoners, he would try to rescue them, he supposed. If his children were dead—and as much as he hated to acknowledge the possibility, it seemed a likely one—then he would avenge them somehow.

But Charles de St. Aubyn had one advantage—he could still think like a Frenchman. He would find a way to achieve his revenge.

As he and Cedar and the other men returned to the town, those thoughts filled his mind, but they vanished when he stepped into his lodge and saw Father Paul bending over Bright Water. She was stretched out, unmoving, on a buffalo robe. Father Paul turned a frantic face toward Charles de St. Aubyn and exclaimed, "I don't know what happened! She moaned suddenly and then collapsed. I managed to get her onto this robe so that she might be more comfortable, but I don't know what else to do."

Black Robe pushed him out of the way and knelt beside the robe. He put his hand on his wife's cheek. *Hot!* She was burning with fever. Black Robe stared down at her, aghast, as a racking cough shook her.

Bright Water burned—and Black Robe turned to ice inside.

Hummingbird was dead—or might as well have been. She lay unmoving, barely breathing, as Guerre thrust himself back and forth inside her body. The ordeal seemed to go on forever, but time meant little to her now. Finally, he spilled his seed within her, drew away, and rolled to the side. He had not seemed to notice her unresponsiveness—or if he had, he had not cared.

"My God!" Guerre said breathlessly. "You are beautiful, Hummingbird."

The compliment meant nothing to her. Her face remained expressionless as she stared up at the top of the tent. Suddenly an unwanted vision intruded into her thoughts. She remembered how Black Snake's blanket-wrapped body had splashed into the river and sunk quickly, weighted down by the rocks that Guerre's men had placed in the blanket with him. She had regained consciousness in time to witness that hideous sight, and it had stayed with her during the two weeks since her abduction from the town of the Crane band. Unless she guarded her thoughts carefully, the memory stole into her head like a thief and tortured her.

For that reason—and that reason alone—she was almost glad when Guerre came to her and took her. His attacks distracted her, forced her to retreat into that secret part of herself where she was isolated from everything happening to her. For a time it was easier to forget the awful vision and the knowledge that she had been responsible for her brother's death. But the memories always came back. . . .

"Breakfast, Lieutenant," a soldier called from outside the tent. Guerre stood up from the sleeping robes spread on the ground. He never bothered setting up the cot and the table anymore, since the party never camped for more than one night in the same place. They moved upriver every day. Besides, with Hummingbird sharing his quarters, there was more room in the robes than the bunk would have provided. He generally used her every night and then every morning upon awakening, just as he had this morning. In between, he slept soundly, his soft snores scraping away at Hummingbird's soul as she stared into the darkness. Sleep always eluded her until sheer exhaustion claimed her. Some nights that never happened.

Guerre was smart; she had to give him credit for that. He always removed his sword and left it outside the tent so that she could not get her hands on it. No weapons were allowed inside the tent at all, and a guard was posted right outside. She lacked the strength to strangle him in his sleep, and he made sure there were no rocks around she could use to smash his skull. There was nothing she could do except lie there, submit to him, and hold fast to the feeble hope that someday she would have her revenge on him.

Dressed now in his uniform, Guerre glanced at her and said, "We will be breaking camp shortly. I would advise you to be ready." His tone was cold, the endearments he had muttered earlier long forgotten. She knew that if she did not cooperate with him, he would give her to the trappers. That would be a far worse fate. She forced herself to acknowledge his words.

A few minutes later, when she had pulled her buckskin dress over her head and slipped into her moccasins, she stepped out of the tent. The sun was barely up, its rays flowing over the plains finally to strike against the mountains, far in the distance to the west. *The Shining Mountains,* Hummingbird thought as she looked at them. Progress was slow, but each day the party was a little closer to those towering peaks. She had never seen anything like them before. She would have preferred never to have seen them at all.

But perhaps, she thought as she looked at them now, it would be easier to get away from her captors once they reached the mountains. She would hold that hope within her, nourish it until it became a reality.

She had already given up hope of anyone following them from the town of the Crane band. She wondered about her mother and father, wondered why no one had pursued the Frenchmen, wondered if they even knew where she had gone.

Black Robe chanted the funeral song, and those of the Crane band who had come to this hilltop with him to bury Bright Water sang with him. With his knife he cut off locks of the hair he had grown long over his years with the Prairie People and tossed them into the still-open grave with his wife's body. Bright Water was dressed in her finest clothes, and several of the household items she had used had been placed in the grave with her. She was sitting upright, facing east. A framework of sticks had been erected around and over the grave so that earth could be piled upon it to make a mound. Black Robe wished he had been the one to die instead of his beloved wife.

Bright Water's spirit had been valiant. She had struggled against the sickness for more than two weeks before it finally conquered her. During that time her body had wasted away, drained of its strength by the fever and the coughing, and as he watched her dying slowly Black Robe's heart had broken beyond repair. Not only had he lost his mate, the woman who had been his strength and his joy for so many years, but he had also been unable to leave her side to pursue the Frenchmen who had stolen his children from him. Bright Water had never been lucid enough to ask about Hummingbird and Black Snake before she died, and Black Robe counted that a blessing.

He was certain now that he would never see his son or daughter alive again.

There had been no pursuit from the town. The situation here was too grave for any warriors to be spared. Everyone who was still healthy—and there were fewer of those with each passing day—had sick relatives to care for. Only a handful of mourners had come with Black Robe today to lay Bright Water to rest. Everyone else in the band was either too sick or too busy caring for those who were ill.

Cedar That Does Not Bend was dead, having bent finally to the force of the disease. Hawk Wing was dead, too; his prayers, his herbs, his healing roots had done him no more good than they had anyone else stricken with this killing sickness. The band was leaderless, but it no longer mattered.

The people were dying, and all knew that unless a miracle took place, they would eventually be wiped out.

Black Robe turned away from the grave as the other men began to cover it over. A fire would be lit atop the mound of earth and be kept burning for four days so that Bright Water would have light to guide her on her journey to the spirit world. The Jesuits who had sent young Father Charles here so long ago would have said that her soul already burned in hell because she was a heathen, but Charles refused to believe that. He no longer knew what he believed. The faith of the Prairie People had proven as empty as that of his youth.

Halfway back to the town, he stopped short and lifted his arms to the heavens. "Why have I not been stricken?" he asked aloud, his voice a plaintive wail. "Why can I not be taken, too?"

There was no answer, of course. For reasons unfathomable, the sickness had passed him by. He was as healthy as ever, one of the few in the town who seemed immune to the disease. Black Robe could not understand it. All he knew was that he wanted to rejoin his wife and his children in whatever world lay beyond this one—if indeed such a world existed.

He trudged on toward the town, and when he was almost there, he noticed a figure coming to meet him. He frowned as he asked, "Coyote, what are you doing?"

Young Man Coyote's steps were unsteady but determined. He was thin, much of his weight having been burned up by the fever that had gripped him for over a week before it broke. The fever *had* broken, however, and the coughs had diminished. He had regained some of his strength, but undoubtedly he would never be the same again. The laughing young warrior was forever gone.

Still, he was alive, and that was something of a miracle in itself. He was not the only one to have fallen victim to the sickness and then recovered, but the disease rarely took that course.

Coyote carried a bow and had a quiver of arrows slung on his back. In his other hand was a war club, and tucked behind his belt was a knife. He was armed for battle.

"I am going after Hummingbird," he said.

"You cannot!" Black Robe exclaimed in alarm. "You are still too weak."

"I must," Coyote said stubbornly. "With each day that passes, Hummingbird is farther from me. I must go to her while I can."

"I fear my daughter is dead."

"No! I would know if it was so."

"You would claim that your heart is closer to Hummingbird than is mine?"

Coyote scowled and said, "I am certain in my heart Hummingbird is alive. I must go to her and save her from the pale-skinned devils who have stolen her."

"How do we know the French have her?"

"What other explanation is there for her disappearance?"

Coyote was right, of course: if Hummingbird still lived, she was with the Frenchmen.

And that was one more reason to damn the Frenchmen to the depths of their souls. Black Robe was convinced they were responsible for the disease destroying the Crane band. They must have brought it with them when they came to this land uninvited.

He sighed. Coyote would not be swayed. "May the Creator guide your steps and protect you," he said. "I would go with you if I could, but I am needed here." As one of the few healthy people remaining in the town, his days were filled with caring for the sick.

"I will find her," Coyote vowed. "I will bring her back, and I will take revenge for the death of Black Snake."

"You believe him to be dead?"

"He has been my friend since childhood. Death is the only thing that would have stopped him from returning. If he were alive and healthy, he would have brought Hummingbird back to us by now."

Black Robe could not argue with that, either. The only difference was that he believed both his children to be dead.

He clasped Coyote's wrist. The young warrior's grip was but a shadow of what it had once been. But perhaps it would be enough.

If what was in Coyote's heart counted as much as what was in his body, it would be, Black Robe thought. He stood and watched for a long time as Coyote walked slowly alongside the river, finally vanishing in the distance to the west.

Chapter Thirty-four

The mountains were beautiful, soaring almost straight up to snowcapped heights. And this broad green valley through which flowed a fast, clear, icy stream was lovely, too. Hummingbird had never seen such wonders. But most of the time her eyes—and her soul—were too dulled by despair to appreciate fully what she was seeing.

She had been with Guerre and the voyageurs for two moons now. It had been seven weeks or perhaps a little more since she had been taken from the town of the Crane band, she estimated, using the measure of time her father had taught her. Convinced that they were now safe from any reprisals, the Frenchmen had set up a large permanent camp here in the valley just east of the tallest mountains. There were many streams in this region where they could set their beaver traps, and the stacks of pelts they took mounted every day. They would be rich men when they finally got back to wherever they had come from.

Hummingbird still shared Guerre's tent. She had thought he would tire of her by now and hand her over to the other men, especially since she had never been able to bring herself to even pretend to enjoy what he did to her. But he was a stubborn man, she had learned. Perhaps he was determined to bring at least one cry of pleasure from her lips before he gave her to the others.

If that was the case, he would have a long wait. She still felt nothing when he thrust himself into her. She was too numbed by her ordeal even to loathe him.

The only thing that touched her was the fear that his seed might grow into a child inside her. Every night she prayed to Wakon-tah that it would not be so.

She was scraping beaver pelts, one of the jobs she had been given by Guerre, when the old trapper LeCarde walked by. He paused and looked down at her, and after a moment Humming-bird glanced up. She thought she saw a flash of pity in his eyes.

To her surprise, LeCarde was the only one of the men who had not leered at her or made bawdy comments. Guerre per-mitted them to act like that, knowing that it only added to her humiliation. She could not bring herself to think of any of these men as a friend, but perhaps Jacques LeCarde was less of an enemy than the others, despite his rough exterior.

"You're doing a good job, Hummingbird," he said to her now as he watched her scrape the skins with the wide piece of buffalo bone, a tool too blunt to be considered a weapon.

She said nothing in reply and looked once more at the beaver hide in her hands. After a moment LeCarde went on, "I've been in these mountains before, you know. I've known your people and the Red Horns and the tribes that live up here. It's a good land. Good people. I wouldn't mind staying up here. There's nothing I have to go back to, either in France or Canada. Be easy enough to do. Just gather up some supplies and slip off when I'm supposed to be checking the traps. Head up into the mountains and never come back. It would sure be warmer at night, though, with someone to share my robes."

It was the longest speech she had ever known LeCarde to make, and that surprised her almost as much as what he had said. She said nothing as she turned over the proposal in her mind. Since they were so far from her home, Guerre had become more lax about having her guarded. She might be able to slip out of the camp and meet LeCarde at a prearranged rendezvous. She was confident the two of them could not only survive in the moun-tains but also elude any pursuers Guerre might send after them.

But did she want to stay with LeCarde? He was not as brutal as the other men, to be sure, but he *was* white, a demon-spirit in the shape of a man. No matter how kindly he treated her at first, sooner or later he would hurt her. She was certain of it.

She took a deep breath. "I will think on what you have said."

"Do your thinking quick. I'm not going to stay around here much longer." He walked away.

Perhaps he could be persuaded to take her back to her people, she thought. She knew now the things that a man liked, because Guerre had forced her to do them with him. She could bend

LeCarde to her will if she went with him. Eventually she might be able to return to her home.

But would anyone there welcome her? She had been responsible for Black Snake's death, after all. If she had not gone to the French camp in the first place on that terrible, fateful day, her brother would still be alive. That guilt weighed heavily on her.

It might be better if she never returned to the town of the Crane band. She could make a new life for herself here in the mountains with LeCarde.

But if she did that—if she escaped from the camp and disappeared into the mountains—she would never have her vengeance on Lieutenant Guerre. His crimes would go unpunished.

Unless she could manage somehow to kill him before she fled with LeCarde. She might even be able to persuade LeCarde to kill Guerre for her, although she doubted the trapper would be willing to run such a risk. The murderer of a French officer would be in much more danger of reprisals than a simple deserter from a party of voyageurs.

She had to weigh vengeance against survival, because she was sure that Guerre would either kill her or make sure she was dead before he left the mountains. He hated her that much for the scar she had put on his face, even though the wound had healed cleanly and left only a thin red line on his cheek.

As she had told LeCarde, she would think on his offer, and she would try to give him her answer that night.

Young Man Coyote trotted alongside the creek in the gathering twilight. His head hung forward in exhaustion. For many, many days he had moved west, until now he had no idea how long he had actually been gone from the town of the Crane band. It might as well have been forever; his mind was as foggy as these mountain valleys early in the morning, not long after dawn. The only thing that remained clear to him was the need to find Hummingbird.

His memory of her was a beacon that drew him on despite the sickness that had returned to him. When he burned with fever, she seemed to come to him, and the cool touch of her hand on his brow soothed him. When the fits of coughing shook him, she called to him and assured him he would be all right. With that to give him strength, he had pressed on day after day. He had no trail to follow save the one his instincts presented him.

It had led him across the great prairie, through the foothills, across several smaller ranges of mountains, and finally here to this long, wide valley. On the western side the mountains rose in a straight line, towering peaks that seemed to march toward the north. Coyote moved inexorably toward them, and when his mind was clear enough to worry about such things, he wondered if he would be able to find a pass through the high peaks. He lifted his head now and studied them, silhouetted by the fading red glare of the sun that had set behind them a little while earlier.

He lowered his eyes and stopped abruptly when he saw a pinpoint of light ahead of him in the valley. A campfire, he thought.

He watched it as the shadows of night gathered and thickened. The light grew brighter. The trappers were up there, he told himself, and so was Hummingbird. The fire had to mark their camp. They let it burn boldly, secure in the knowledge that with their guns they could hold off any attack by the people of these mountains.

But they had reckoned without Young Man Coyote. He started toward the fire again, and this time as he ran he chanted a song of war.

Before the night was over, they would learn to fear him.

Hummingbird had decided to go with LeCarde. Though she hated to let go of her desire for vengeance on Lieutenant Guerre, she knew that her only real hope of living through this ordeal lay in escape, and leaving with LeCarde would increase her chances of survival in the rugged mountains.

She was watchful as she waited for an opportunity to talk to the trapper and tell him of her decision. The men were all gathered around the fire, laughing and talking and eating. The corporal and the three privates had grown beards and allowed their uniforms to become as wrinkled and dirty as the voyageurs' buckskins, and now they looked every bit as disreputable. Only Guerre maintained a semblance of military discipline this far from what the French considered civilization. He shaved every morning, using the razor and the looking glass.

At the moment he was the only one not joining in the raucous behavior around the campfire. He sat a little apart from the others and stared broodingly into the flames. Hummingbird knew what that meant; she had seen him this way many times before. He would be rougher tonight when he came to the sleeping robes. On such occasions she wondered if he was trying to make her cry out in pain, since he could not rouse her to cry out in passion. But she gave him no satisfaction either way, enduring his assaults as if they had no effect on her.

She saw LeCarde stand up and start around the fire toward her. He seemed to be paying no attention to her, and she was sure he would disguise his interest with some other reason for circling the fire. But for an instant his eyes met hers, and she read the question there. She was about to nod, hoping LeCarde would understand her meaning, when she heard a thud and the trapper suddenly stood up straight on his toes and stiffened. A harsh sigh gusted from his lips as he tottered there for a brief moment.

Then he pitched forward onto his face, the shaft of an arrow protruding from his back.

Instantly, the camp was filled with chaos. Men leaped to their feet, shouting curses and questions as they reached for their muskets. Lieutenant Guerre was up, waving his sword. Hummingbird sat where she was, her eyes fixed on the arrow that had killed LeCarde. Though the flickering fire offered poor light, she thought she recognized the shaft.

She should have, since her father had made it.

That thought penetrated her stunned mind just as a figure loomed out of the darkness and flung itself at the trappers, who were milling around in confusion. A shrill cry split the night. The attacker whirled a war club over his head and lashed out with it, the heavy stone on the end smashing into a man's head, shattering the skull like a robin's egg.

"Stop him!" Guerre shouted wildly. "Stop that man!"

Coyote! Hummingbird lunged to her feet. Young Man Coyote had finally come for her! Perhaps he had brought more Crane warriors with him, a war party that would kill these white men, especially the hated lieutenant.

But Coyote seemed to be alone. Fear shot through Hummingbird. Though he twisted and turned like a dust devil on the prairie, evading the blows of the voyageurs as he swung the war club, his movements were growing slower and less controlled. He seemed to be having trouble breathing, and his war song came in tired gasps. He was not only exhausted from his long pursuit, Hummingbird thought, but he might be sick as well.

"Coyote!" she screamed as one of the trappers struck him across the back of the legs with the barrel of a musket. The young warrior staggered forward and fell to his knees, and another slashing blow drove him to the ground. One man stepped forward and kicked him in the head. The war club slipped from Coyote's fingers.

"Get his weapons!" Guerre called angrily. "I want him disarmed."

It took only seconds for the trappers to yank Coyote's knife and arrows away from him. Guerre stepped forward, hooked a booted toe under his shoulder, and rolled him over. Coyote began to cough.

He had the disease that had stricken so many in her town before she was abducted, Hummingbird realized. She took a step toward him, but Guerre's head snapped around as he barked, "Hold her! Don't let her anywhere near the devil!" As two of the men grabbed her arms and pulled her away, he added, "Not too far. I want the bitch to be able to see this."

Hummingbird trembled with rage and terror as Guerre looked down at Coyote. When the coughing fit had passed, Guerre said, "I remember you. You were with Hummingbird that first day. LeCarde said you were her lover." He cast a glance at the body of the dead trapper. "Now you've killed him. I'm sure he would have been surprised to know that you have followed us all this way. I certainly am. Are you alone?"

Coyote glared up at him in silence.

"Yes, I think you are," Guerre answered his own question. "If there were more of you red devils, you would have attacked at the same time. Striking out of the darkness like cowards."

Hummingbird could remain silent no longer. "Coyote is a braver man than you will ever be!" she cried.

Guerre turned his head to look at her. The cheek with the scar on it was toward her, and the mark shone bright red in the fire-light where it cut across his face. "Coyote is nothing," he said. "Nothing but a dead man."

With that he reached over, took a musket from a nearby man, and pointed the weapon at Coyote's forehead, almost touching the skin with the barrel. Hummingbird screamed again and lunged forward, but the strong hands of the trappers held her back.

Guerre pressed the trigger of the musket.

With a roar of black powder, the weapon fired. Coyote's arms and legs jerked as the upper half of his head was practically blown away. Hummingbird collapsed, racked by sobs, and this time the voyageurs let her go. She slid to the ground, beyond horror, beyond grief, filled with a despair deeper and darker than any night.

"Get rid of this filth," she heard Guerre say. "Throw it out of the camp for the scavengers. We'll bury the two men he killed first thing in the morning." He stepped over to Hummingbird, bent over, and grasped her arm. As he jerked her to her feet he went on, "You're coming with me." He shoved her toward his tent.

Later, after he had taken her with more violence than he had ever shown before, he took hold of her chin and turned her head so that she had to look at him. "This is the end of it," he said, his voice as icy as the mountain streams. "Tomorrow night, the men get you to do with as they will."

Hummingbird barely heard the words. He had already hurt her as much as she could be hurt. Nothing he or anyone else could do to her now would be any worse than seeing Coyote killed before her eyes—and being powerless to stop it.

Chapter Thirty-five

"Father? Are you there?"

Charles reached out to take hold of the trembling hand Father Paul lifted toward him. Though unsure if the young Jesuit was calling for another priest or for his own father, Charles answered in a soft murmur, "I am here, my son."

Father Paul's fingers closed tightly on his. "You must . . . administer . . . Extreme Unction," he breathed.

Charles tilted his head back and closed his eyes. He did not need to see the roof of the lodge arching over him to know it was not the vaulted ceiling of a cathedral. The walls around them were not even the walls of a humble country church. The two men were in an earthen lodge of the Prairie People, and Charles—he thought of himself as a priest and a Christian in this moment—had not administered any of the sacraments in two decades. He would have considered himself a hypocrite to do so, since his own faith had been bled from him so long ago.

Yet with such a simple act he could bring at least a little peace to a dying man. He crossed himself and reached far back into his memory for the words. The Latin phrases came awkwardly from his lips, but the pain that had etched deep lines in Father Paul's face seemed to ease a bit.

There was no point in trying to tell the man he would be all right. Father Paul had only a short time, perhaps even moments, to live, and they both knew it. The sickness had claimed him, just as it had claimed nearly everyone else in the town. Only Charles and a very few others had escaped its deadly touch.

Father Paul's eyelids fluttered and then slowly closed as Charles finished performing the last rites of the Holy Roman Catholic Church. His chest rose and fell a few times more, then, after he had drawn in a deeper breath, became still for a long moment. Finally the last breath came in a rattling sigh, and it was over. He was dead.

Charles de St. Aubyn wept.

He could not help it. He had been surrounded by death for so long. He had never understood Father Paul, had never even liked the young man particularly, but still the priest's passing touched him deeply.

After a few moments Black Robe wiped the back of his hand across his eyes and stood up. He stepped heavily to the lodge entrance and pushed his way outside. His journal lay on a large flat rock near the lodge, where he had placed it earlier, along with his pen and ink. He went to the rock, picked up the roll of buffalo hide, and sat down. With a hand that shook, he laboriously dipped the quill in the ink and then brought it to the story skin, as his wife had called it.

I am alone in a city of death.

Earlier in the day, the few survivors of the epidemic had left the town, heading southeast toward the land of the Osage, where they hoped to find a new home. Black Robe had stayed, unwilling to leave Father Paul. Now the priest was dead, but he found himself still somehow drawn to remain here.

I am a pariah, the lowest of the low. I have brought suffering and death to all those I love. Had I not been here, the men who brought this sickness might never have come.

My faith has returned. My belief in God is stronger than it has ever been before. For now I know the truth. I cannot speak for heaven, but I know there is a hell.

I dwell there.

Hummingbird awoke to pain. Her jaw ached where Guerre had slapped her the night before, and her left eye was swollen almost shut. Her body hurt as well, and she felt bruised all over. Her muscles protested as she rolled over and pushed herself to a sitting position among the tangle of sleeping robes.

Guerre had not forced himself on her this morning. What he had done to her the previous night had been his way of saying farewell before he gave her to the other men. All that came flooding back into Hummingbird's mind: his attack on her, the cold-voiced decision to turn her over to the trappers, and before that—worst by far—the murder of Coyote. Hummingbird remembered it all.

She was alone in the tent. Forcing herself painfully to her feet, she walked out into the morning, squinting against the rays of the newly risen sun. A sound caught her attention, and she looked around. The tent was only a few feet from the river, and Guerre stood beside an aspen on the bank. He had propped his looking glass in the juncture of two branches and was shaving as he sang softly to himself. The song was in French, and Hummingbird could not force her mind around the words, not this morning. But the tune was a bright and happy one.

He was *singing*. The night before, he had blown away half the skull of the man she loved, and he was *singing*.

She stepped lightly toward him, paying no attention to anything else that was going on in the camp.

If she had, she would have seen that the men were busy with their own activities, getting ready for another day of checking and setting beaver traps. The bodies of LeCarde and the other voyageur had been wrapped in blankets for burial, and several men were digging graves some distance back from the river. A few white clouds floated in the blue sky overhead, and a warm breeze blew. It was a beautiful day.

Guerre set his razor aside, placing it on a stump where another small aspen had toppled sometime in the past. He reached for a cloth to wipe his face. From the corner of his eye he spotted Hummingbird's reflection in the looking glass.

"What are you—"

Even as he spoke her hand flashed forward and closed over the handle of the razor. Where she found the speed and strength to accomplish what she did next, she would never know. Perhaps the Creator and Giver of Breath guided her hand.

Before Guerre could turn, Hummingbird grabbed hold of his long, thick, dark hair with her other hand, jerked his head back, and slit his throat with one swift, clean stroke.

He tried to scream, but no sound came except a grotesque gurgle as blood fountained from his throat. Hummingbird held him upright by the hair as he trembled wildly for a few seconds. He pawed at his throat with one hand, failing to stem the tide of blood. After a moment his knees folded, and Hummingbird let him fall. He rolled onto his back, his bare chest patched with crimson, and stared up at her with the last of the rapidly fading light in his eyes.

She smiled as that light died, thinking it very apt that her bruised and battered face was the last thing he would ever see.

With that, reason returned to her, and she glanced over her shoulder. There had been no outcry, and amazingly, none of the other men seemed to have noticed yet what had happened. True, Guerre's tent was set somewhat apart from theirs, and they were occupied with their own tasks. But it was only a matter of time before someone spotted the lieutenant's crumpled form and raised the alarm.

Hummingbird stepped past Guerre's body and slid down the sandy bank of the river. She crouched so that the bank would conceal her and started walking quickly downstream. She had gone quite a way when she heard the sudden shouts behind her.

That was when she began to run, and she never looked back.

Without being aware of it, she had held Guerre's razor in her hand when she escaped from the Frenchmen, and during the next several weeks the keen little blade came in handy more than once. She used it to cut small branches from trees for making snares, and to skin the rabbits and prairie dogs she caught before eating them raw. She might have been able to kindle a fire with sticks and dried grass, but she chose not to. She wanted nothing to lead the men to her.

Not that she was convinced they were still pursuing her. They had chased her when she had fled from the camp, of course, but she had run that day as she once had with Black Snake and Coyote, all those moons ago when the white men first came to the land of the Prairie People. She had been running all her life, and the trappers were no match for her. Even when she felt certain she had outdistanced them and they had given up the chase, she continued running.

She was going home.

Regardless of the guilt she felt for her part in what had happened, she had to return to the town of the Crane band so that she could tell Coyote's parents he had died bravely, as a warrior should. She would tell her own parents the same thing about Black Snake. They had a right to know.

The mountains fell behind her as she traveled, dwindling in size with each day until she could no longer see them at all. Once again she was surrounded by seemingly endless prairie, the rolling hills and lush grassland that had been her home, her entire world.

Now she knew there were worlds beyond what she had known, evil beyond any she could have dreamed might exist. Something inside her was broken and would never be whole again.

She thanked the Creator when her flow came and she knew she was not with child. If a part of Guerre had been growing inside her, she might have taken the razor and cut it out of her, along with her own life.

Finally, after uncountable days, she came to a river she recognized as the Nibthaska-ke. Broad, muddy, and sluggish, it was still beautiful to her. For the first time in months she sang a song as she trotted alongside it. Soon she would be home.

There were no dogs. That was the first thing Hummingbird noticed as she approached the town of the Crane band. Normally, whenever anyone came near the town, the dogs charged out to challenge them, barking and growling.

The lodges had been visible for some time now, and she realized that no smoke rose from them. It was late in the day. The women should have been cooking the evening meal. The men would be finished with the day's hunting or other chores and would be moving around the town, talking to their friends, perhaps sharing a pipe. But Hummingbird saw no movement. The town appeared empty, deserted.

She stumbled to a stop and cried, "No!"

Her people were gone. This was her home no longer.

She forced her legs to move. Her injuries had healed during the weeks of travel, her body becoming as lean and strong as a willow. But she felt empty inside as her gaze searched everywhere in the town for a sign of life.

Suddenly, she stopped short. She had seen something. A gaunt figure pushed through the entrance of a lodge and, swaying slightly, looked toward her. She knew that lodge; she had grown up in it. And she knew the man staring at her.

Black Robe.

"Father!" she shouted as she ran toward him. He stood unmoving, except for the swaying. As Hummingbird went up to him she saw to her dismay how haggard his features were. His hair, which had been graying when she left, was now almost pure white, and his beard had grown back in white patches. He was little more than skin and bones under the tattered robe—the raiment of his former people. For some reason, that made Hummingbird despair, too.

"Father?" she said again as she held out a hand toward him.

"Bright Water?" he said, his voice croaking from long disuse. "Is that you?"

She choked back a sob. "It is Hummingbird, Father. Your daughter."

"I . . . I do not remember." He looked past her, and suddenly his face brightened. "Cedar, old friend! You have come back."

Hummingbird spun around, expecting to see the chief of the Crane band. No one was there. Wind stirred the grass and blew through the empty spaces between the lodges, spaces that had once been filled with the people of the Crane band, filled with life and laughter.

"What happened, Father?" She turned back to him and caught hold of his arms, wincing as she felt how frail he had become. "The sickness—did it take them all?"

Black Robe blinked several times, and for a moment something resembling lucidity came into his eyes. "All gone," he murmured. "All gone now, every one." Then he looked past her again and said, "Hawk Wing!"

Hummingbird knew better than to turn around. The holy man would not be there. Her father was the only one alive here in the town, and his mind had slipped away in his desolation and solitude. She might never know exactly what had happened, what tragedy had befallen the once-proud Crane band, but she was fairly certain the sickness that brought fever and coughing had wiped them out. She put her arms around her father and hugged him, being careful not to hurt him. He felt as if he were made of sticks and rags.

"We must leave here, Father," she said.

"Leave?" he repeated.

"We will go to the land of the Osage. They are our friends. They will take us in. We will make a new home there."

He seemed to consider the suggestion for a moment, although his blank eyes belied that. Then he said, "I have to get something first."

He pulled away from her, and she let him go. He went into the lodge and came out a moment later clutching something to his chest. It was a sheaf of buffalo hides, she saw, several pieces rolled together in one bundle: his story skins, the tales he had spent months writing down, much to the puzzlement of everyone around him.

Well, if they were important to him, that was all that mattered. She held out her hands and said, "Here. I will carry them."

He hesitated. "You won't let anything happen to them?"

"I will care for them, just as I will care for you."

"All right, then." He gave her the story skins. "Where did you say we were going?"

"To the land of the Osage."

Together they began walking, putting the town of the Crane band behind them—the only home Hummingbird had ever known, and now she was leaving it forever. Tears sprang into her eyes.

She had not known she could still cry. It felt good.

They had gone only a short distance when Black Robe asked, "Who did you say you were?"

Hummingbird wiped her eyes. "A friend."

That was enough. Black Robe smiled at the sky and walked on.

PART III

The Thunder Bird

Chapter Thirty-six

1807 C.E.

"Move along! Move along there, damn it! Hit them mules up beside the head if you have to! Move them son-of-a-bitchin' wagons!"

Maximilian Adolphus had never seen—or heard—anything like it. The scene before him was astonishing, absolutely astonishing. Those . . . mule skinners, that was what they were called . . . were the most colorful characters he had ever encountered. With their buckskin clothing and broad-brimmed hats and obscenity-laden vocabulary and long whips that coiled and hissed like snakes, they were like nothing Max had ever seen in Vienna. He twisted around on the wagon seat and reached behind him for his drawing pad. He selected a piece of charcoal and began sketching.

He drew the scene from his own perspective, placing one rugged mule skinner in the foreground along with the two leaders in the team of mules pulling the wagon. As he worked toward the background he sketched in several more wagons dwindling in size as they rolled down the trail. The road curved down a heavily wooded hill, and at the base was the broad, placid expanse of the Missouri River. Next to the river, on high ground cleared of trees, rose the wooden battlements of Fort Osage, the destination of this wagon train.

But beyond the river and the forest that bordered it—that was what caught Max's eye. There the prairie rolled endlessly, lush with grass and wildflowers. Patches of shadow sailed majestically across the plains as billowing clouds scudded through the blue sky.

"Glorious!" Max muttered to himself. "Absolutely glorious!"

"Eh? What'd ye say?"

Max paused in his sketching and looked over at the man perched on the wagon seat beside him. Daniel Dupree was a red-faced, rawboned man wearing a broad-brimmed black hat, a linsey-woolsey shirt open at the throat, brown whipcord pants, and high black boots. His eyes flashed darkly and his cheekbones resided high in that hard face; as an artist, Max had noticed those features immediately. There were rumors among the men that Dupree was a half-breed, that his mother had been Choctaw, his father a Scots trader. Looking at him now, Max could easily believe that.

"I said this was absolutely glorious country."

Dupree agreed. "Aye, that it is. Plenty of money to be made, what with all the buffalo, beaver, an' elk out there. Aye, glorious."

Max looked down at his pad again to hide a smile. He and Dupree obviously had different definitions of the word "glorious." To Max the American frontier was a land filled with opportunity to practice his art. There was something fascinating to paint or sketch around every bend in the trail. To Daniel Dupree the frontier represented a chance to increase the profits of his employer, the Columbia-American Fur Trading Company—and thereby increase his own wealth.

He should not begrudge the man that, Max told himself. Not everyone saw the world with an artist's eyes.

His hand moved as if it had a will of its own, darting over the paper and leaving behind lines and smudges of charcoal that transformed almost magically into images that exactly represented the scene before him.

Max knew he had a gift. But his skill as an artist was not his only advantage in life. At twenty-five years of age, he was slender, dark-haired, and handsome enough to have caught the eye of many a lady in Vienna. More than one wealthy aristocratic family would have been pleased to see him marry their daughter. Max had resisted those temptations, concentrating instead on his art. He had developed a keen interest in this land called America. When Prince Otto Wilhelm of Saxe-Coburg had announced his plans for this expedition and asked Max to accompany him, Max had jumped at the chance.

Prince Otto rode at the head of the column on a magnificent

golden-red sorrel stallion, next to Captain Vincent Standard, the commander of the party's military escort. Max had sketched the prince several times during the journey from Europe and across the American territory, and he planned to do a full-fledged portrait in oils before they all returned to the Continent. Prince Otto had promised a hefty payment for such a portrait, although truth to tell, Max might have done it for free, so grateful was he for having the opportunity to visit the frontier.

Captain Standard turned and rode back along the line of wagons, checking to make sure as he did several times each day that no one was having any difficulty. The captain was responsible not only for Prince Otto's party but also for the supplies bound for Fort Osage. That responsibility, at least, would soon be behind him, because the wagonloads of goods would be delivered to the sutler at the fort later today.

Standard drew rein as he reached the wagon on which Max and Dupree rode. As he fell in alongside the vehicle, matching the gait of his horse to its slow pace, he indicated the pad in Max's hand and said, "Drawing again, Mr. Adolphus?"

Max turned the pad so that Standard could see the sketch. "That is Fort Osage up ahead, is it not?" Max asked.

"It is." Standard unfastened the strap of his military hat and took it off. He ran gloved fingers through his thick, sand-colored hair. He made a dashing figure in his long blue coat, tight white pants, and sheathed saber. Max was hoping he, too, would sit for a portrait sometime during the expedition. Standard gestured toward the fort and went on, "It was just commissioned last year. As far as I know, it's the westernmost fort we've established so far. The first step toward pacifying the frontier, I'd say."

"And the next step is the establishment of commerce," Dupree pointed out. "Wouldn't you say so, Captain?"

"Definitely, Mr. Dupree."

Max looked back and forth between the men. Standard and Dupree were much alike, he sensed, despite the fact that one was a rough-and-ready businessman and the other a polished officer in the regular army. Both were ambitious, willing to do whatever it might take to get ahead in their chosen endeavors. More than once Max had heard Captain Standard talking about the need to drive the Indians off this land. The territory belonged to the

United States of America now and had ever since President Jefferson had bought it from the French three years earlier, in 1804. It was damn well about time, Standard had said, that they started civilizing it.

In a way, that would be a shame, Max thought as he again gazed out over the plains. He had seen the great cities of Europe, and they no longer impressed him as they had when he was a mere lad from a farming village going to Vienna for the first time. This vast, magnificent land was much more awe-inspiring.

"Well, I'd better be checking the rest of the train," Standard said as he wheeled his horse around. "Good day, gentlemen."

"Good day, Captain," Dupree said, but Max stopped the officer by calling out to him.

"Yes, what is it, Mr. Adolphus?" Standard asked, sounding impatient.

"Will we be seeing Indians at the fort?"

"Almost certainly we will." Standard smiled. "But don't worry, Mr. Adolphus, they will be tame ones. We have little to fear from the natives in this region."

Max did not care for the trace of contempt he saw in Standard's smile and heard in his voice. Being afraid of Indians they might encounter was not on Max's mind at all. Rather, he was anxious to meet them and talk to them and, most of all, to draw and paint them. The wagon train had crossed paths with a few natives, but in Max's opinion they had been fairly pathetic specimens. Where were the fearsome warriors of the plains, about whom he had read so much? The Indians he had seen so far, for all the colorful qualities they possessed, might as well have been beggars on the streets of Paris or London.

"I hope the savages are ready to trade," Dupree said, as usual reducing every conversation to his own concerns.

"They will be," Standard said curtly. "If they're not, we'll convince them to be. That's one reason the army's here, after all."

He turned his horse again, and this time Max let him go. He could not bring himself to like Captain Vincent Standard's company very much.

But a man did not have to be pleasant to be a good subject for a painting, nor did the artist have to be fond of him. All that was really required was a keen eye and a steady hand, and Maximilian Adolphus had both.

Prince Otto Wilhelm turned to one of the soldiers riding nearby and pointed to a red flower growing near the trail. "What is that plant called, Corporal?"

The soldier frowned. "I'm afraid I don't know, Your Excellency. I'm from Vermont, and I don't recall ever seeing a flower just like that before."

"Well, there are a multitude of them." Otto swept his hand toward the gently sloping hillside, which was blanketed with the red flowers. "I shall make some sketches of it and have young Maximilian do a drawing of one. I am certain I shall be able to identify it and note it in my journal later on."

The corporal shrugged absently, clearly uninterested in what Otto was saying. He was humoring the royal visitor. Otto knew that but did not care; he had not come to America to be fawned over. He was here to learn, to add not only to his own knowledge but to that of the entire scientific community.

Also to challenge himself, he had to admit. He could have lived a very comfortable life indeed in Saxe-Coburg, where his family had ruled for generations. But here he was, forty years old, and he had never done anything truly worthwhile in his life. It was time to change that.

Of course, some would have said that exploring this rugged, largely untamed continent was hardly worthwhile. After all, there was still plenty of room in Europe. In the opinion of virtually everyone Otto knew among the aristocracy, no one but malcontents and failures came to America to live. While he did not plan to settle here, he saw nothing wrong with an extended visit. Already he had filled nearly an entire volume with his notes on what he had found in this new land called the United States. His fellow scholars would be very impressed when he returned to Europe.

Captain Standard galloped back to the head of the column. "Fort Osage dead ahead," he said to Otto as he pulled his horse back to a walk. "I hope the accommodations suit you, Excellency."

"After more than a week of sleeping on the ground under a

wagon, I am certain they will be fine, Captain," Otto said with a smile. "Although I attempt to be very egalitarian about such things, I must admit it will feel good to have a real bed again."

"Don't forget, we'll only be staying a few days."

"Just as well. Though the respite shall be welcome, I am anxious to move on up the Missouri. There is much to see."

"That artist of yours has done a good sketch of the landscape hereabouts. Between his drawings and your journals, you ought to have a fine record of your trip."

"Indeed. I shall convey my appreciation to your superiors and to the officials in Washington City for seeing that everything has gone so well."

Standard said, "That's one report I'll be pleased to be a part of."

The captain was ambitious; Otto had realized that as soon as he met the man. Not that there was anything wrong with that. Captain Standard hailed from Massachusetts, the younger son of a shipping family that had lived there since early colonial times. Though the Americans, with their casting off of the British monarchy, had also done away with such things as strict lines of succession and the system of primogeniture, Vincent Standard's best chance for success in life was to make a name for himself in the military. This assignment to the frontier was tailor-made for him.

The gates of the fort swung open as the column approached. Otto and Captain Standard rode side by side through the entrance and found several officers waiting to meet them. The visitors dismounted, and Standard saluted the officers.

"Welcome to Fort Osage, Captain," one of them said. "I'm Captain Eli Clemson, the commanding officer."

"It's an honor, sir," Standard said. "May I present His Royal Highness, Prince Otto Wilhelm of Saxe-Coburg."

Otto extended his hand to Captain Clemson. The captain was a fairly young man with the usual stiff military posture and a neatly trimmed mustache. "We're pleased to have you join us, Your Excellency. I'd like for you to meet my staff."

Otto shook hands with the junior officers, all of them fresh-faced, earnest-looking young men, much like the officers in the

Prussian army. Well, perhaps not quite *that* earnest, Otto corrected himself.

While the introductions were made, the wagons had rolled into the fort, and the supplies were already being unloaded, Otto saw when he looked around. Daniel Dupree, who would be the factor for the trading post to be established upriver, was deep in conversation with the sutler. And Max Adolphus, Otto was pleased to see, was sketching so fast that the motions of his hand were a blur. The young man was wide-eyed as he eagerly took in all these new sights.

Evidently a large garrison was posted here; quite a few blue-coated soldiers hurried about the fort. Some were unloading wagons while others were standing watch or drilling on the parade ground. The atmosphere was as exciting as Otto had expected it to be, except in one respect.

He turned back to Captain Clemson and asked, "Where are the Indians?"

Chapter Thirty-seven

Brother Owl chanted a song of thanks and supplication to the Creator. Alone on the prairie beneath an endless blanket of stars, the young man sat cross-legged beside a small fire, swaying slightly, eyes closed, waiting for his vision to come to him.

He hoped he would not be disappointed again.

For days now he had fasted and prayed, preparing for the spirits to speak to him. He had left the town of the Wah-Sha-She, the Osage, and come out here on the prairie to be alone, as his ancestors had done for generation upon generation, all the way back to the great warrior and mystic Storm Seeker.

Owl knew all about Storm Seeker, who had been born Black Snake. The stories told through the generations by his people would have been enough to teach him about his mighty ancestor, but in addition Owl had the story skins that had been passed down to him from his great-grandmother Hummingbird. He had been charged with keeping them safe. They were not the original story skins of Storm Seeker, of course; those had been lost with the passage of years and the various disasters that had befallen the Prairie People. These skins had been written by Hummingbird herself; it was unusual for a woman to have done it, but she was the only one who could translate the strange writing of her father, Black Robe. Both sets of story skins—the one written in the language of the Prairie People and the earlier version in the language of the French—still existed. Owl cared for them and studied them with equal diligence, for one day soon he would be a medicine man, and they contained the story of his people.

A lost people.

Owl's thoughts wandered; he tried to force them back onto the paths of respect and reverence that would please the spirits and perhaps move them to give him the vision he awaited. But it was difficult not to think about the tragic history of the Crane band.

To the best of his knowledge, he was the only one left who claimed to be of that band. There were others, of course, who had the blood of the Crane band flowing in their veins, but they were Osage now. The few survivors of the terrible sickness that had all but wiped out the Crane people had been accepted into the lodges of the Wah-Sha-She, and they had put the past behind them.

Hummingbird would not allow that to happen to her. After she had escaped from the white-skinned demons who had carried her off to the Shining Mountains, she had come back to the Land of the Two Rivers to find all her people dead except for her father, and only his body lived. His mind and spirit already wandered in the mists of the world beyond this world. Hummingbird had brought him to the Osage and had cared for him all the rest of his days, which had been relatively few. She had stayed with the Osage, and in time she had married one of the warriors, a man named Caller of Crows. Their children, and the children of their children, had led to Brother Owl, and always they had considered themselves members of the Crane band. Owl still did.

He remembered Hummingbird, tiny and wrinkled, ancient of days, nothing like the young woman who had stood straight and strong as a willow—the woman who had killed the chief of her captors and fled from the others for many weeks across the great grasslands before finally coming to her home. But when he had looked in her eyes, even though he was only a child, he had seen the fire there and knew that she was indeed the woman of the story skins.

"One day it will fall to you to guard the sacred story skins," she had told him. "Care for them well, because they are your heritage. They are all that is left of your true people." Her bony finger had touched his chest, frightening him a little. "The story skins, and what is in your heart."

He had done his best to honor her memory and obey her command. His mother, Wanderer, had given him the story skins as she lay on her deathbed in this, his eighteenth summer, but even before that he had read and studied them until he knew everything that was in them.

The Osage had been good to his family, and Brother Owl was grateful. He loved his Osage relatives. But he was of the Crane band of the Prairie People, and after his mother had been properly buried, he had come out here as their representative, seeking whatever message the spirits might have for him.

So far, there had been nothing.

He lowered his head, opened his eyes, and sighed. He was tired. There would be no vision this night. Soon he would have to return to the town of the Wah-Sha-She, his quest a failure.

Owl rolled over in his buffalo robe and waited for sleep to claim him. It was elusive, and he found himself staring up at the stars. He wondered if the spirits were looking down on him. Why had they found him lacking? Why had they not come to him and presented him with his vision? His prayers had been sincere. He had fasted and followed all the rituals faithfully. But something had gone wrong—either that or the spirits truly had nothing to tell him.

He found that possibility even more disturbing.

Owl rolled onto his side and sighed again. Eventually, he drowsed.

The sound of hoofbeats woke him.

He sat up hurriedly. Many horses were approaching. These days it was common enough to see the animals on the prairie.

Traders from the south had brought them first, and then they had appeared in increasing numbers, ridden by French and American fur trappers. But still it was odd to see them in such great numbers. From the sound of the hooves, more horses were approaching than Owl had ever seen in one place before, even at the Fiery Prairie Fort two days' walk northwest of the Osage town. He scrambled to his feet, ready to dart right or left to keep from being trampled.

They loomed up out of the night, and Owl saw to his shock that there were more than ten times as many as the fingers on his hands. The group spread out across the prairie—he could not possibly avoid them—and a strange light shone upon them, brighter than the illumination from the moon and stars. In that light he saw the riders clearly.

He saw their pale skin and blue coats, their hats and long guns. Along with the pounding of hooves, he heard the clatter of sheathed sabers and the rattle of harness. They shouted and rode straight toward him, and the rifles in their hands erupted in smoke and flame.

Owl emitted a shout of anger and fear and threw himself forward on the ground, expecting to hear the whine of lead balls passing close over his head. The riders did not seem to be shooting at him, however; none of the bullets came close enough for him to hear. One manner of death was much the same as another, though, and in a matter of moments the horses would trample him into the ground, killing him as surely as if he had been shot down. He lifted his head and stared in horror at the onrushing doom.

To his shock, he saw that others were riding with the white men: Indians mounted on small, wiry ponies, warriors with their hair pulled up into roaches that looked like horns.

The Red Horns. Horned Heads. Pawnee. By all those names were they known, the enemies of the Prairie People. They always had been, as far back as the time of Storm Seeker.

Suddenly Owl knew what he was seeing. *This is the vision of Storm Seeker come to life, the ancient prophecy finally become real.* In these last moments of life Owl felt a bond between himself and his ancestor—though Storm Seeker would not have died cowering on the ground, he told himself. That great man would have stood and shouted defiance at the enemy, daring them to ride him down.

Brother Owl could do no less.

He leaped to his feet and snatched up the war club he had brought with him. Brandishing it over his head, he sang a song of war. Let the enemies come! Owl would face them without fear. The riders were practically on top of him when he swung his war club at one of the blue-coated white men.

The stone head passed right through the rider.

Thrown off balance, Owl half turned and fell to one knee. The riders swept past him, leaving him untouched. No, not *past* him. *Through* him.

This was the vision he had sought.

Just as it had come to Storm Seeker, he saw it now. He saw the buffalo being shot down, slaughtered, by the white men and their Pawnee allies. He saw the prairie itself dying, its tall grasses and flowers destroyed by the sharp hooves of the horses. And still the ghostly figures rode on, until Owl heard the cries of people dying. His people . . .

He slumped to the ground once more, overcome by what he had seen and heard.

When he finally looked up, the vision was gone. The riders had disappeared as if they had never been there. Nearby, the flames of his campfire leaped and danced as if they had never been disturbed. As indeed they had not. The white men, their horses, their Pawnee allies . . . none of them had been real.

Yet the threat they represented was real enough. Owl stumbled to his feet, went over to the fire, and fell to his knees beside it. He threw back his head and prayed.

"O Creator! O Master of Breath! Thank you for this vision. Give me now the wisdom to understand it and to know what you would have me do! Give me the strength to carry your message to the people!"

He lifted his arms to the heavens, and for a moment he no longer felt alone. A hand touched his shoulder. He looked to the side, saw the strong fingers resting on his bare flesh, saw the tattoos running up the arm. A stern but kindly face looked down at him.

"Storm Seeker . . ." Brother Owl whispered.

Then blackness enfolded him, and that was the last he knew.

The peace chief of the Osage was named Elk Came Down from the Mountains, because in his youth he had had a vision in which that very thing occurred. Elk had come from the Shining Mountains, crossed the great prairie, and paraded into the town of the Osage. That had not yet happened, of course, but the chief was still confident it would, despite the more than eighty summers he had lived to see.

So he believed strongly in the power of visions, and he nodded gravely as he sat in council with the other elders of the tribe and listened to what Brother Owl told them.

"It was the same vision that came to my ancestor," Owl concluded. "I knew it was so when I saw it, and then Storm Seeker himself came to me. He said nothing, but seeing him was enough."

Elk said in his cracked, wheezing voice, "You are the keeper of the sacred story skins of the Crane band?"

"Yes. Such is my honor."

"And the vision of Storm Seeker is contained in these story skins?"

"It is," Owl confirmed. "I have studied it many times."

Muddy Water, the Wah-Sha-She medicine man, leaned forward and said sharply, "Then how do you know this was a true vision and not simply a dream brought on by studying the story skins?"

Owl blinked in surprise. He had not even thought of that explanation, but as he considered it he knew it to be false. "It was a true vision," he insisted. "Each man knows the truth when the spirits speak to him."

Some of the other men seated around the council fire murmured in agreement. After a moment Elk said, "If this was a true vision, what do you think it means, Brother Owl?"

Again Owl had to consider. During his return to the town of the Osage, he had thought much on the meaning of the vision, but the answer had not come to him. All he had felt was an overriding urgency to ask for a council so that he could share his experience with older, more knowledgeable men. He had halfway hoped that *they* could tell *him* the meaning of the vision.

Now, with the faces of the men around the council fire regarding him solemnly, he felt a moment of panic. If he confessed his ignorance, they might be inclined to disregard the vision entirely. Muddy Water did not like him; the shaman thought that *he* should be the guardian of the story skins. He had done everything he could to discourage Owl's ambition to be a member of the medicine society. Owl suspected that the other men had never been comfortable with his claim that he was still a man of the Crane band, not an Osage, and now he could not allow them to see his confusion and his fear—or Elk might decide to take the story skins away from him.

He stiffened his backbone and stood up straight. "My vision calls me to return to the land of my people. This is what Storm Seeker came to tell me. I will go back to the Land of the Two Rivers, to the place where the Crane band of the Prairie People lived."

"That is not your home," Muddy Water said. "You are one of us now. This is not the meaning of the vision."

He might have said more, but Elk raised a hand to stop him. The aged chief said, "It is not for one man to decide the meaning of another man's vision. Brother Owl must follow his heart and spirit."

Muddy Water frowned but said no more. He would not go against the decision of his chief.

Elk turned to Brother Owl and went on, "Would you go alone?"

Owl said, "It was my vision. It is my responsibility." Now that he had begun this, he knew, he must finish it, but he would not involve anyone else in what might be a foolish misadventure. He had blurted out the idea of returning to his homeland simply to have something to say; he had no idea if that was what the spirits willed or not.

"Very well," Elk Came Down from the Mountains said. "May the Creator and Father of All Waters guide you and protect you. How will you go back to the home of the Crane band?"

One of the other men spoke up. "The best way would be to go to the Fiery Prairie Fort and follow the river from there. You can trade there with the white men and provision yourself for your journey."

Owl saw the wisdom of that idea. "That is what I will do."

"Do not trust the white men too much," Muddy Water warned. "Some of them are demons."

Owl remembered the vision that had come to him, the way the white riders had destroyed the buffalo, the people, the grasses of the prairie itself.

He did not believe that trusting the white men too much was a possibility.

Chapter Thirty-eight

"Max! Come here, lad, and bring your drawing pad."

Max looked up from the sketch he had been composing of a cannon and the soldiers who were leaning against it. Prince Otto, standing on the porch of the headquarters building with several other men, motioned to him.

With a sigh, Max turned to a new page in his pad and started toward the building, which also served as the officers' quarters. He would have to finish the other sketch later. While he was not under the direct orders of the prince, he cared to stay in Otto's good graces. The nobleman had, after all, financed this journey, including Max's part in it.

The men on the porch with the prince were Captain Standard and Captain Clemson, whom Max had met earlier in the day when the wagon train arrived. Standing with them was a squat man in buckskins and a cap of animal fur. Extending from the side of the cap was a stiff piece of hide shaped like a long triangle and painted with several different designs, including the shape of a hand. The man's dark hair was drawn up in short braids that fell behind each shoulder. His skin was as dark and weathered as a leather saddle.

Otto put his hand on the Indian's shoulder and said to Max, "This is Birds Fly Against the Sun, headman of the Little Osage tribe, who live near here. Would you be so kind as to do a sketch of him, Max?"

"Certainly." Max got to work with his charcoal. The Little Osage chieftain stood proudly, unmoving, but while he was more impressive than most of the Indians Max had seen farther east, his eyes lacked the fire Max had expected to find. More than anything else, Birds Fly Against the Sun looked like a tired old man.

Max attempted to correct that impression in his drawing. He made the man's stance a bit straighter, the tilt of his chin a little higher and more defiant, the eyes slightly narrower, as if he was searching across a great distance for an enemy. The alterations from real life were subtle, yet they made a great deal of difference.

When Max was finished, he turned the sketch so that Otto, the chief, and the two army officers could see it. Captain Standard and Captain Clemson murmured polite, admiring responses, although Max could see that neither man was genuinely interested. But Otto, beaming, slapped the Indian's back and said, "The lad really captured you, my friend."

Birds Fly Against the Sun said to Max in awkward English, "Picture is . . . good."

"Thank you. You're a good subject, Chief."

Birds Fly Against the Sun turned to Captain Clemson and said, "Give me food for the tribe now?"

"Of course," Clemson said brusquely. "You and your people would have gotten your ration anyway. Posing for young Mr. Adolphus wasn't required for the sutler to dole out the food."

Despite the captain's words, Max had the feeling that the man's posing *had* been part of the price. The insight disappointed but did not surprise him.

The Little Osage chief went off with Clemson and Standard toward the sutler's office, leaving Max with Otto. The prince said, "Magnificent, isn't he?"

"If you say so, Your Excellency."

Otto was too keen to miss the tone in Max's voice. "You disagree?"

"I . . . expected more," Max said. Unlike many of the

sycophants who normally surrounded the prince, Max was not afraid to disagree with him.

"Ah, you want to see 'noble savages,' " Otto said. "Warriors of the plains."

"Something like that."

"I can't say that I blame you, my boy." Otto leaned closer and went on in a conspiratorial tone, "You know, I was a bit disappointed myself when we got here and I didn't see a single Indian. Captain Clemson explained, though, that they live in a village nearby. He sent a man to fetch the chief."

"One man?" Max asked.

"From the sound of it, these Little Osage aren't savages at all. They're rather mild, in fact. Farmers instead of warriors. The captain assured me his man would be all right alone."

"And the village is close by, you said?"

"That's right. Just a short distance upriver. Another band called the Big Osage used to live near here, but the captain persuaded them to move because their numbers were sufficient to make the men nervous."

"I'd like to see the Little Osage village, then," Max mused. "I'm sure it would be an interesting visit, even though the inhabitants might not be what we expect from our reading about the American frontier."

"That's the spirit," Otto said. "Everything we witness and document advances the causes of natural science and the study of man, even the things that don't seem very exciting."

The prince was right, Max knew. He intended to do as many sketches as he could when he visited the Indian town and record the details of their daily lives as completely as possible. The paintings he would do later, based on those sketches, would make him the toast of Vienna. While the lure of fame was not the only reason he had made this long journey, of course, it was always at the back of his mind.

Max returned to the cannon and finished the sketch he had started earlier, then prowled around the fort for a while. It was built in roughly triangular shape, with several log blockhouses and eleven-foot walls made of sharpened logs forming its boundaries. From the parapet around the inside of the stockade walls where the sentries patrolled, he looked out over the wooded hills to the east and the rolling prairie beyond the band of forest to the west. As he peered at the seemingly endless grassland he spotted a figure moving over it at a steady, fluid trot. Max turned to one of the soldiers on duty. "Do you have a spyglass?"

"Yes, sir, I do." The sentry drew the instrument from the pocket of his coat and handed it to Max. "Please be careful, sir. That's government property."

"I won't damage it," Max assured the man. He held the spyglass to his eye and squinted through it, trying to locate the figure he had seen a moment earlier.

It took a minute, but finally Max focused in on the running man, an Indian. Max had assumed as much. The image he saw through the spyglass was enlarged but rather blurry. It was a young man clad in loincloth, buckskin leggings, and a vest of some sort, with long black hair drawn back in two braids. He had something slung on his back which Max took to be a bow and a quiver of arrows, suggesting that he was ready to do battle with his enemies. The expression on his face, though difficult to read at this distance, seemed to be one of determination.

Max felt his heart pound. Indians such as this one were the reason he had come to America. The young man on the prairie appeared to have enough fire and vitality to run all day if he had to. What a subject for a portrait he would make!

For several minutes Max tracked the Indian with the spyglass. At first he thought the man was bound for the fort, but then it became evident that his route would take him to the north. He was headed for the village of the Little Osage, Max decided, the community led by Chief Birds Fly Against the Sun. Was the man a Little Osage, a hunter or a scout who had been sent out from the village? It was possible, Max thought, but the young man seemed cut from a different cloth.

Max lowered the spyglass and pointed out the figure in the distance. "Excuse me," he said to the sentry, "do you know that lad?"

"I don't know any of these redskins 'cept for Chief Birds," the guard said. "Don't want to know 'em, either. As long as they behave themselves, I don't have any business with 'em. We're here more to keep an eye on the Spaniards and the damned

Englishmen who've got their sights set on this part of the country. They'd like to take it away from us and make President Jefferson look like a fool for buyin' it from ol' Bonaparte."

Military discipline had obviously done little to curtail the man's natural garrulousness. Max let the sentry talk, but at the same time he brought the spyglass to his eye and peered through it again. The Indian disappeared into the distance upriver. Max might never see him again.

But that would be all right. He had been heartened by the sight of so lithe and powerful a representative of the native people. Surely there would be more such encounters along the way.

Brother Owl was tired, though he did not want to reveal that fact to his hosts. He had run most of the day, anxious to reach the town of the Little Osage near the Fiery Prairie Fort. He carried a message for their peace chief, Birds Fly Against the Sun, from his own chief, Elk Came Down from the Mountains. Elk had asked his old friend to give shelter to Brother Owl and assist him in any way possible in fulfilling his quest.

Owl sat now in the lodge of the chief and drank from a gourd of water that had been brought to him by one of the man's daughters. The young woman looked at him rather boldly, but he did not return her interest. He had other things on his mind right now.

"What are these soldiers like?" Owl asked the chief of the Little Osage. "I have never visited the Fiery Prairie Fort, though I have heard much of it since it was built."

"The pale skins treat us well," Birds said. "Our spring harvest was bad this year, and so was our buffalo hunt. The chief of the soldiers has given us food to help us. He would be our friend." The old chief said solemnly, "I have told him this is a good thing. Perhaps next winter during the Moon of Starvation not so many of the babies and the old ones will die."

The idea of the people depending on the charity of strangers—and pale-skinned strangers, at that—rankled Owl. Yet he could understand the chief's dilemma. The Little Osage were a small, poor band. Help from outsiders might be the only way they could endure.

Birds broke into his thoughts by saying, "Tell me about your vision, Brother Owl. How can we help you to fulfill your quest?"

"I must return to the true homeland of my people," Owl said. "I am not really Osage, though they have been kind enough to give me a home. I am the last of the Crane band of the Prairie People. My ancestors came from the Land of the Two Rivers, and that is where I must go. This is the vision that came to me."

He described the strange dream—or whatever it had been— that had come to him during his vigil on the prairie. When he was finished, the chief asked, "Are you sure this journey to the home of your people is what the spirits would have you do?"

"I am certain," Owl said. "The spirits would not mislead me."

By this time he had truly come to believe that. Although he had been less sure when he was addressing Elk and the other members of the Osage council, he had since convinced himself of the truth of his impulsive words. He had had much time to think about the matter during his trip here to the town of the Little Osage.

"Very well," Birds said. "You should go to the Fiery Prairie Fort and speak to the one they call the sutler. He will give you supplies for your journey. Do you speak the tongue of the white men?"

"White men speak different tongues," Owl pointed out, thinking of the French in which his great-great-grandfather Black Robe had written the original story skins. "I can speak two of them, French and English, well enough."

"I will go with you to the fort anyway. I speak English well. I will help you."

"I will be forever thankful and honored that the peace chief of the Little Osage was so kind to me."

Birds waved a wrinkled hand. "I am glad to do it. While I am there I will ask the chief of the soldiers if my people can have more food."

If that was what Birds wanted to do, then it was not Owl's place as a guest to dispute his actions. Yet as he thought about the chief's words he wondered if the many horses and rifles he had seen that night on the prairie would be necessary for his vision to be made real.

There was more than one way, it seemed, to destroy a people and a way of life.

Chapter Thirty-nine

The visitors dined with Captain Clemson in his quarters that evening. The fare was simple—sage hen cooked with potatoes and wild onions—but the chance to sit down at a real table again was welcomed by Max and Prince Otto. While this was not the fine dining to which both men were accustomed in their homeland, they appreciated the effort to which Captain Clemson had gone. The captain had even brought out a bottle of wine.

"I daresay this may be the only bottle of wine west of the Mississippi, gentlemen," Clemson said as an orderly filled their glasses. "The sutler has a few jugs of whiskey and rum on hand, strictly for medicinal purposes, of course, but normally we don't allow spirits."

"That wouldn't be *Scotch* whiskey, would it?" Dupree asked.

"Actually, I believe it is."

Dupree said, "Then 'tis good medicine indeed, Captain."

That brought a laugh from the other men. As they ate, Clemson said to Otto, "I understand from Captain Standard, Excellency, that you plan to ascend to the upper Missouri."

"That is correct, Captain. We shall not follow exactly the same route used by your intrepid explorers Lewis and Clark, but it will serve as a general guide. I doubt we will venture as far as they did. They reached the Pacific Ocean, I was told in Washington City."

Clemson sipped his wine, then said, "That's right. Last winter, not long after the fort was established, one of the men who went with them came through here. Jacob Reznor, I believe his name was." The captain chuckled. "A pretty disreputable character, if you ask me, but he had plenty of interesting stories to tell. Too bad you missed him."

"Perhaps we shall encounter him elsewhere," Otto replied.

"Could be. A lot of those who have already been west seem to have gotten it in their blood. They go back east and can't stand it anymore. They have to come out here again. I'd wager that within a few years there will be white men settled all over the prairie and the mountains between here and the Pacific."

"You could well be right, sir," Captain Standard put in, "but I won't be one of them." He looked at Otto and went on, "Begging your pardon, Your Excellency, and I certainly mean no offense, but when your expedition is over I'll be happy to return to a command back east."

And you'll use every bit of fame and glory you may garner from this journey to achieve that command, won't you, Captain? Max kept the question to himself and concentrated on his food.

Otto, Clemson, and Standard spent several more minutes discussing the trip up the Missouri River, stopping only when one of the captain's aides, a lieutenant, came into the room and said, "Excuse me, Captain, but the chief of the Little Osages is here again, and he has another Indian with him. They want to speak to the sutler."

Clemson scowled. "Then why are you disturbing me with this matter?"

"The sutler just issued some rations to the savages earlier today, sir. He wanted to check with you before he handed out any more supplies."

"Well, that's probably best, I suppose." Clemson drank the last of his wine, patted his lips with a napkin, and pushed his chair back. "If you'll excuse me, gentlemen, I must attend to this."

"Duty calls," Dupree grunted, and continued eating.

Max and Otto were both finished, though, having taken smaller portions than Dupree had. Otto asked quickly, "Could we join you, Captain? I was most impressed by Chief Birds Fly Against the Sun, and I should not mind seeing him again."

"Nor would I," Max said. He was curious what had brought the chief back to the fort so soon.

"Very well," Clemson said. "Captain, why don't you come along, too?"

"Of course," Standard agreed without hesitation, although

Max saw him cast a brief, wistful glance at the wine remaining in the bottle.

The men got their hats, left the commander's quarters, and walked toward the sutler's office. It was a lovely evening, with a warm breeze blowing and a few clouds overhead faintly tinged pink from the setting sun. Max inhaled deeply. True, he caught the odors of unwashed flesh and horse droppings, but other than that the air was crisp and clean, so invigorating that he could almost understand why many of the men who left the east to come out here never went home again. And this was only the edge of the vast plains. The mountain air was supposed to be even better.

They found the sutler standing on the porch of his office with two natives. In the light of the lantern hanging from the porch roof, Max recognized the squat figure of Birds Fly Against the Sun. There was something familiar about the other man, too, and Max stopped short as he realized the second Indian was the distant figure he had seen loping tirelessly across the prairie that afternoon.

"Captain," the sutler said, "the chief here has asked if we can give him more salt and flour and bacon for his people. He wants us to outfit this young fella for some sort of trip, too."

"I need none of your provisions," the young Osage man said. "As long as I have my bow and arrows, I will eat."

"A little salt makes the game taste better, though," Clemson said.

Max had no doubt that the man's pride kept him from asking for supplies. The captain had to walk a fine line here. The military was attempting to maintain friendly relations with the Indians; provisioning the determined young native for his journey would be a wise thing to do. Yet Clemson had to accomplish that without being insulting or patronizing.

"I don't believe I know you, son," the captain said.

Max thought the man looked a bit offended by the captain's familiarity, but he replied politely, "I am Brother Owl, of the Crane band of the Prairie People."

Clemson peered sharply at the speaker. "Sorry, never heard of that band. I'll take your word for it. What sort of trip is this you're talking about?"

"I return to the land of my people, the Land of the Two Rivers, far upstream on the Nibthaska-ke."

"I think he's talkin' about the Platte River, Captain," the sutler put in. "It's a pretty good ways from here."

Clemson turned back to Brother Owl. "Will you be coming back this way after you visit your homeland?"

Brother Owl seemed a little surprised by the question, but he answered promptly, "I can do this."

"Good. We need somebody to scout up the Platte for us, and I think you're the perfect one for the job. All you have to do is come back here when you're through with your visit and tell us what conditions are like along the river. Since you'd be helping us, we'd be glad to let you have some supplies."

Brother Owl seemed to be on the verge of accepting the offer when Prince Otto spoke up. "The lad may travel with us part of the way," he said, "at least to the point where the Platte splits off from the Missouri. We should be glad to have him accompany us. We were planning to take some Indian guides, weren't we, Captain?"

"That's right," Standard agreed. "We'll need several redskins along with us."

Max watched and listened to the discussion with keen interest. He wanted to do a portrait of Brother Owl, and having the young man with their party would make that easier. Besides, Brother Owl spoke fairly good English, and Max looked forward to talking with him about the Indian way of life.

Clemson turned back to the young man. "Well, what do you say? Would you like to go with the prince and his party? We'll still outfit you for the rest of your trip."

Owl looked at Otto and Max and said, "You are not soldiers, like these others?"

"No. I am Prince Otto Wilhelm, and this is my good friend Maximilian Adolphus. We have come here to learn as much as we can about your land and your people so that we may return to our land and tell our own people all about you."

"It is good. I will go with you."

"Excellent!" Otto said.

Clemson looked at Chief Birds, who had waited patiently

with his arms crossed over his chest. "Now, Chief, about these extra supplies *you* want . . . "

"Chief of soldiers is good friend," Birds said solemnly. "The spirits will smile on him for gifts given to the people."

Clemson sighed. To the sutler he said, "Issue the chief a few more rations. We can't be making a habit of this, though."

"Yes, sir."

Birds Fly Against the Sun beamed benevolently.

While the other men were occupied, Max stepped up to Brother Owl and extended his hand. "As the prince said, my name is Maximilian Adolphus. Max to my friends. I'm pleased to make your acquaintance, Brother Owl."

Owl hesitated, then took Max's hand, clearly puzzled by the gesture. The handshake was a brief, awkward one. Then Max went on, "I'm an artist."

"I am of the Crane band," Owl said.

Max smiled. "No, being an artist is what I *do*. I draw pictures and paint them. I'm from a city called Vienna. That's in Austria. In Europe."

Owl's quizzical frown deepened. "You have many names for your homeland."

"Well, you said you were from the Land of the Two Rivers, and then you called it another name. . . . "

"Nibthaska-ke. That is the name of the river before it splits in two. Our word for it also means . . ." Owl had to think for a moment. "Flat River."

"So you see, your homeland has many names, too."

"This is true." Owl paused. "You paint story pictures?"

"Yes, I suppose I do. I paint and sketch on paper and canvas."

"We paint also, on buffalo hide. We make our robes and shields with it and use it to cover our lodges. And there are the story skins, too."

Max's interest quickened. "Story skins?" he repeated. "What are those?"

"The story of our people."

"I'd be very interested to see them," Max said, trying to contain his excitement. The story skins sounded like some sort of historical document. From everything he had heard, the native peoples had no written history, despite their rich oral tradition.

To study written documents would be an extraordinary opportunity to learn about their way of life. When the prince learned of this, he would be even more excited than Max.

Captain Standard walked along the porch to join them. "You two seem to be getting on well."

"Yes," Max said. "I was just about to ask Brother Owl for permission to paint his portrait."

"Por-trait? What is this?" Owl asked.

"A picture of you," Max explained. "A large picture, painted with oils on canvas. I think you would be very pleased with it."

Owl looked dubious. "I am not sure this is a good thing. A demon can steal a man's soul by capturing his image."

"I'm not a demon," Max said with a laugh. "And I promise I don't want to steal your soul. I just want people back in my homeland to be able to see what you look like. I'm going to paint a portrait of Chief Birds while we're here at the fort."

That news surprised Brother Owl. "You and your friends are not leaving right away?"

"No, we'll be here for three or four days," Standard replied. "We need to let our mules and horses rest and replenish our supplies."

"I wish we were to leave sooner," Owl said, as much to himself as to Max and Standard.

"As far as I'm concerned, we could leave right now," Standard said. "The sooner we finish this foray into the wilderness, the sooner we can return. But the men and the animals *do* need rest."

"And I have that portrait of the chief to do, as well as my other sketches," Max said. He turned to Owl. "I'll paint you while we're on the trail, if that's all right with you. You can pose each night."

"Pose?"

"Don't worry, I'll explain everything to you," Max assured him. "You won't have to do anything except stand very still. You can do that, can't you?"

"Of course he can," Standard said. "All of you savages can stand still while you're waiting to ambush an enemy, isn't that right?"

Owl stiffened. "Warriors of the Crane band do not attack our enemies from hiding. We fight them face-to-face."

"Of course. No offense meant." Standard's casual tone made it clear he didn't really care if he had offended Owl or not.

Why should he care? Max thought. To men like Vincent Standard, Brother Owl and all the other Indians of the prairie were just savages, heathens who were either grudging allies or annoying obstructions, depending on their attitude toward the white men who had come uninvited to their land.

Max shared Owl's resentment of the captain's callous words. He said, "I'm sure Brother Owl will have no trouble posing for his portrait. It shall be the best painting I have ever done."

Bold words—but this was a bold land, and some of it, Max thought to his satisfaction, was beginning to rub off on him.

Chapter Forty

Brother Owl watched in fascination during the next two days as Max Adolphus painted the portrait of Birds Fly Against the Sun. The chief stood on the porch of the headquarters building wearing a buffalo-horn headdress, a bone breastplate, and a buffalo-hide robe on which was painted the record of his feats in war. With a lance in one hand and a fierce expression on his face he looked very impressive. In the back of Owl's mind, however, was the memory of how Birds had come to the fort and practically begged the chief of the white soldiers for food.

There had been a time when Birds was a revered war leader. That time, Owl thought regretfully, had passed.

It was better to watch Max at work and not think too much about such things. Owl's eyes followed the brush in the painter's hand as it moved from palette to canvas and back again. With each stroke the image took on new shape, color, and dimension. As he worked Max tried to explain to Owl what he was doing, and Owl listened politely, somewhat bewildered by the concepts

Max described. Owl offered his own descriptions of his people's art, of the artists who painted the stories of the tribe on buffalo hide with tints made from plants and earth and crushed rock. Fascinated, Max countered with endless questions. Owl enjoyed the exchange, and they spent hours in this manner. It was almost enough to make him forget about his vision and the quest on which it had led him. Almost, but not quite. The need to return to his homeland still gnawed at him.

Owl was also distracted by the questions of the white man called Prince Otto. The man perched on a barrel while Max painted and asked about various aspects of the life Owl and his people led. He wrote down each answer in a book. Black Robe had written in a book, too, Owl remembered from the legends, but it had been destroyed in the great fire. Now there were only the story skins. The book in which Prince Otto wrote had much in common with the story skins, Owl decided.

On the third day, Max put the finishing touches on the portrait, then stepped back and announced, "There! It's done."

Owl moved closer to the painting and studied it. It certainly looked like Chief Birds, and in some subtle ways it looked more like the chief than the chief himself did. How could a picture be more real than its subject? Owl did not understand, but his eyes told him it was so.

Birds lowered the war lance and came around the easel to look at the portrait. His chest swelled with pride as he declared, "This is a mighty warrior and a great leader of his people."

"I paint what I see," Max said, and the chief looked even more pleased.

"What will you do with the picture?" he asked.

"It will be taken back to Washington City and then shipped to my country," Max explained. "There I will either sell it or display it in a museum or gallery."

Birds eyed him narrowly. "I would have it."

"I can't do that, Chief," Max said, and Owl could tell he was trying to be patient. "But I do have this for you." He picked up a roll of paper tied with string. When he unfastened the string and let the paper unroll, Owl saw that it was a drawing of the chief, made with charcoal. "I always give my preliminary sketch to my subjects," Max went on.

Birds hesitated, then took the drawing. "I am honored."

"No more than I am," Max assured him. "Thank you for posing for me."

When the chief had gone, taking the sketch with him, Max turned to Owl. "You've seen what I do. Do I still have your permission to paint your portrait?"

"I have decided you are not a demon," Owl said solemnly. "But I want you to paint me as I truly am."

"I always try to be true to my subjects—"

"No." Owl gestured at the portrait of Chief Birds. "That warrior would never accept the charity of the white man—or any man. He would die first, and his people would gladly die with him if he led them into battle."

For a moment Max said nothing. Then he shrugged. "I saw no point in humiliating the chief. He's a good man, but he's old and tired. His people are poor. He does the best he can for them." He looked shrewdly at Owl. "I won't have to embellish what I see in you. I can paint the truth."

"That would please me." Owl liked Max, and he believed the painter would keep his word.

Daniel Dupree came out of the building and cast a glance at the painting, but he did not seem impressed by it. Owl had already figured out that if something was not related to trading, Dupree had no interest in it. Dupree said to Max, "We will head out tomorrow, Captain Standard says, and it cannot be soon enough to suit me. I want to have that trading post set up at the mouth of the Platte before the summer is over."

"I'm sure you will, Mr. Dupree." Max turned his head and for some unaccountable reason closed one eye and quickly opened it again so that Owl could see but Dupree could not. "I'm told that a Scotsman lets nothing deter him where business is concerned."

"We cannot control everything, laddie . . . but it does not hurt to try." Dupree gestured toward the portrait. "Good paintin'. Looks just like the chief."

"Thank you," Max said dryly, and once more exchanged a glance with Owl. It was obvious what he was thinking.

A man could have keen eyesight in some areas and be almost blind in others.

* * *

The wagons left the fort early the next morning. The party's supplies had been replenished, and the horses and mules were much fresher for their few days' rest. The same could be said of the men. The journey from the east had been a tiring one, but now everybody was ready to push on.

Max's gear was stowed in the wagon on which he rode. Brother Owl walked alongside, easily matching the pace of the mules. Max remembered the way the young man had run across the prairie, a marvel of strength and stamina. That had been bred into him over generations, Max supposed.

The day's travel might not have been a strain on Owl, but Max was tired by the time Captain Standard called a halt that night. Long hours of rocking and jolting on a wagon seat had taken its toll. Yet once camp had been set up and a good-sized fire was blazing, he felt an undeniable surge of excitement as he set up his easel and canvas and unpacked his paints, palette, and brushes. When his preparations were complete, he went in search of Owl, who seemed to have vanished.

Max's concern grew as he looked all around the camp without finding any sign of the young man. He was about to go to Captain Standard and raise an alarm when he spotted a figure several hundred yards from the camp. The sun had not quite set, and Max had not seen Owl at first because the young man was west of the camp, hidden by the glare. As Max walked out toward him the sun dipped behind a rolling hill, leaving Owl outlined in stark silhouette against the red sky. His arms were uplifted, and he held a pipe in his hands. He stood very still.

Max stopped before he reached Owl, suddenly sensing that he was about to intrude on something private. He stood at a distance, waiting, until Owl finally lowered his arms and turned toward the camp. "Max," he said, looking surprised.

"I'm sorry, Owl," he said. "I didn't mean to interrupt anything."

Owl shook his head. "It is all right. I was praying to the Creator, to Wakon-tah. Do you know of him?"

"I'm afraid not. But I would like to."

"He is the source of all things. He is the Giver of Breath. He brings us joy in life, and he brings us tears. Look around you."

Owl swept his hand in a broad circle. "He is there. He is every-where. I pray to him with this pipe. The prayer is called *niniba-ha*. I ask for guidance on my journey."

"And does Wakon-tah answer?"

"The wind blows. The rain falls. The grass grows. Is that not answer enough?"

Max could not argue with that. He was glad he had not inter-rupted Owl's prayer. Obviously the young man had a strong spiritual side to his nature. Max changed the subject by asking, "Are you ready for me to start painting your portrait?"

"You can work by the light of the campfire?"

"It's not as good as sunlight," Max said, "but we must make do with what we have."

"I will come with you. Tell me what to do."

"Gladly. Come along."

Together, the two young men walked back to camp. Before they got there, they were met by Captain Standard, who rode out on his horse to meet them. Even in the fading light Max could tell that the officer was not happy.

"Begging your pardon, Mr. Adolphus, but what the hell are you doing out here this far from camp? You need to stay inside the circle of wagons. I can't protect you if you start wandering off." Standard's tone was angry and impatient.

Max gestured at the boundless prairie, the seemingly endless sea of gently waving grass. "Protect me from what? There is nothing out there."

"There might be a lot more than you think. I'm told the natives can hide where you least expect to see them." Standard glanced at Owl, but that was his only acknowledgment of the young Indian's presence.

"I don't think there was anything to be afraid of," Max said. "I was with Owl, and he would have told me if there was danger."

"This is true," Owl said, forcing Standard to look at him again. "Max is my friend. I would not allow him to be harmed."

The captain controlled his temper with a visible effort, then snapped at Max, "Just don't go wandering off again. You're not under my orders, Mr. Adolphus, but I'd appreciate it if you'd consider that a very strong request."

"Of course, Captain. I didn't mean to cause trouble."

Standard wheeled his horse around and rode alongside them as they walked back to the camp. Max led Owl to the spot where he had his easel and canvas set up and showed Owl where to stand.

"Move as little as possible," he said. "I'll sketch out your figure first." He picked up a piece of charcoal and got to work.

As always when he was caught up in what he was doing, time flew by unheeded. He was surprised when Dupree came up to him and said, "You've been at that for more than an hour, lad. Aren't you going to stop and eat some supper?"

Max looked around. Most of the men had already finished their bowls of stew. "Yes, I suppose that's enough for tonight," he murmured. To Owl he said, "You can move again now. You did very well for the first time."

"It is not difficult to stand still," Owl said as he came over to look at the canvas.

Max moved quickly to shield it from his gaze. "It's bad luck for the subject to look at the portrait before it's finished," he explained. "Give me a few days, perhaps a week or so. Then it will be done."

Owl said, "We will eat now."

Max put his equipment away, then joined Owl. They sat cross-legged near the fire with their food. As they ate, Owl said without looking at Max, "The soldier chief was right."

"What? Oh, you mean Captain Standard?"

"You should not leave the camp alone, as you did tonight."

"Why not? You were out there. Besides, it's so peaceful here."

"You see a land of peace. You see people who are in harmony with themselves and the land around them." Owl shook his head. "But it is not always so. There is sometimes danger, even where none can be seen."

Max said, "But from everything I've seen and read, the way of life of your people is as close to paradise as can be found anywhere."

"It is not for nothing that the time you call February is called in our tongue the Moon of Starvation. Every year, some of the old ones die from hunger, and so do little ones. There are other dangers. Always there is a war somewhere on the prairie between the bands of the people. There are those who would enslave their enemies, and others who try to destroy them. We live short lives, hard lives, Max." Once again, Owl shook his head. "There is much good in the way we live, but it is not what you call paradise. Such a thing does not exist in this world."

"Perhaps not," Max said, chastened.

The days became a blur for Max. He sketched almost constantly as the group traveled up the Missouri toward the Platte. Prince Otto wanted drawings of every new kind of plant life they encountered, and whenever they saw deer or sage hens or rabbits or prairie dogs, the prince had to have sketches of them, too. There were also geographic features to document: an occasional cathedral-like bluff reared up against the sky, and they crossed tree-lined creeks from time to time. But much of the terrain was flat and monotonous to the European eye. Max was anxious to see mountains again. He missed the peaks of his native Austria.

Despite his almost continuous sketching during the day, Max still had enough energy left in the evenings to work on the portrait of Brother Owl. The painting rapidly took shape, and Max was pleased with the way it developed. Back at the fort he had boasted that it would be his best portrait, and he was beginning to think he could make good on that boast. He hoped Owl would be pleased.

Then, after a week of following the river, the wagon train encountered something else that Max had been eagerly awaiting. He saw the Osage scouts who had been hired at the fort ride back in from a foray ahead and talk excitedly with Captain Standard. Wondering what was going on, Max leaned toward Dupree, who was seated beside him on the wagon seat, and asked, "What do you think that is all about?"

"I don't know. I hope 'tis not some sort of trouble."

"I think I know," Owl said.

Max looked at him. "Well, what is it?"

Owl smiled, and his voice was uncharacteristically playful as he replied, "You will soon see."

Half an hour later, after the wagons had rolled up a long, gentle hill, they reached the crest, and Max's breath caught in his throat as he saw the scene spread out before them.

All along the western bank of the river, the carpet of lush green was hidden by a multitude of shaggy brown bodies. The sea of grass had been replaced by a sea of hides and horns. There were thousands, scores of thousands, perhaps even millions of the beasts. Max looked at them in openmouthed awe.

"Te," Owl said. "You call them . . . buffalo."

Chapter Forty-one

"Mein Gott, look at them!" Otto said excitedly as he leaned forward in his saddle. "I've never seen anything so magnificent in my life!"

Standard had reined in beside the prince. As he studied the huge herd of buffalo spread out alongside the river, his face grew pale under the tan, as if he was frightened as well as impressed. "I'd heard stories about the creatures," he muttered, "but I wasn't sure I believed them."

"There must be . . . I don't think I can even count that high, Captain!" Otto glanced over at Standard. "I must have a trophy."

"Of course, Your Excellency." Standard's tone was more brisk and businesslike again; a hunt was something he understood. It was the middle of the afternoon, late enough to justify making camp. He turned in the saddle and gestured for the wagons to form a circle. "We'll camp here, Lieutenant!" he called to his aide.

Otto's pulse pounded with anticipation. Ever since the scouts had ridden in and reported the herd of buffalo up ahead, he had been waiting for this moment. So far, just the sight of the creatures had exceeded his expectations. This was undoubtedly the most exciting thing that had happened since he left Saxe-Coburg.

The prince turned his horse and trotted over to the wagon Max had been riding. The young painter had already climbed down from the seat and was sketching furiously. "Very good, Max!

We mustn't miss an opportunity such as this one." Otto noticed the Indian standing nearby and asked, "What do you think of this, Brother Owl?"

Owl looked only mildly interested in the buffalo, but of course they were not a novelty to him. "It is a good-sized herd," he said. "I have seen much larger."

Otto could not imagine any herd being larger than this gargantuan gathering. "I want you to tell me tonight all about how your people hunt the buffalo."

Owl replied, "I can do this. I have been on many of the big hunts in the spring and fall."

"And tomorrow . . . we will have a hunt of our own!"

Both Owl and Max looked at him in surprise, but in his excitement Otto did not even notice.

It was all Daniel Dupree could do not to rub his hands together and lick his lips. It had never bothered him much that some considered him a greedy, tightfisted Scotsman. After all, that was what he was. But he did not want to be too obvious about it.

Buffalo hides were already in demand back east as lap robes, rugs, even coats. The herd Dupree was looking at now could warm many a rich man traveling in his carriage, could cushion countless feet in the parlors of mansions in Boston, Philadelphia, and New York. It was a fortune on the hoof, a bloody fortune! And the buffalo were only part of it; there were beaver, elk, antelope, all sorts of creatures out here in the west . . . and they would all fatten his purse and the purses of the men who employed him, the owners of the Columbia-American Fur Trading Company.

That evening, while the prince and young Adolphus were talking to the Indian lad, Brother Owl, Dupree sought out Captain Standard. He found him in the shadow of one of the wagons, and as he approached he thought he saw Standard hastily shoving something under his coat. Not knowing or caring what the officer might have to hide, Dupree said, "Ah, good evening, Captain. Might I have a word with ye?"

"Of course, Mr. Dupree," Standard replied, and the Scotsman smelled the liquor on his breath. So it had been a flask the captain was stashing away, a bit of fortification for a civilized man who found himself far from civilization. Standard went on, "What can I do for you?"

"I'm told that we're going to be having a buffalo hunt tomorrow."

"That's right. Prince Otto has requested a chance to take a trophy."

"Will you and your men be shooting any of the creatures?"

Standard shrugged. "I don't know. I hadn't really thought about it."

" 'Tis just that I was thinking . . . we have some extra room in some of the wagons, and with a bit of moving around, I think we could make even more. If we filled that room with buffalo hides, there would be a pretty penny to be made once you got back to St. Louis with them."

In the shadows Dupree saw Standard scowl. "I'm not in the fur-trading business," Standard said. "That's your line, not mine."

"Yes, but it never hurts to make a wee bit extra to go with your service pay, now does it?"

"The army isn't overly generous with its wages," Standard said slowly, considering the possibilities.

"I thought not. I could give you a letter to take back to my superiors in the company, stating the price we agree on for the hides. All you would have to do would be to present that letter and the hides at the offices of the Columbia-American Fur Trading Company, and you'd be paid straightaway, no questions asked."

"An intriguing idea. How many buffalo skins do you think we could carry in the wagons?"

Dupree considered. "Dried, stacked, an' bundled . . . perhaps as many as fifty. Not a great number, considering how many of the beasts there be just in this one herd, but—'twould be a start."

"Yes. A start," Standard repeated. "I like the way you think, Mr. Dupree. I'll speak to some of my men. We'll see that you get some hides to send back to your bosses."

Dupree stuck out his hand, and after a second of hesitation Standard took it. "What do you say we seal the agreement with a wee nip of whatever's in that flask of yours?" the Scotsman suggested.

Standard grinned and slipped the silver flask from his coat. He uncapped and lifted it. "To success in business."

Dupree chuckled. "Is there any other kind that matters?"

"The buffalo are our friends," Owl said to Max and Prince Otto, "and have been ever since they first came up into our world through a hole in the ground. The Creator put them on this earth to provide my people with food and shelter and clothing. We must approach them carefully. Countless moons ago, when our ancestors first hunted them, the buffalo had no fear of man. Now enough of them have died that they are more cautious. But if we come upon them slowly, they will often allow us to surround them, and then we can fire our arrows and throw our lances before they even know they are being killed."

Prince Otto leaned forward eagerly. "I want to use a bow and arrow. Can I do that?"

"Have you ever fired a bow?"

The prince shook his head.

"It is much more difficult than it looks. But you can try. One of the Osage scouts will probably let you borrow his bow. If not, you can use mine."

"Thank you, Brother Owl. This is very exciting."

These white men were easily entertained, Owl thought. True, a buffalo hunt could be exciting, and he always enjoyed them because he was with his friends. The hunts were of vital importance to his people because so much of their precarious existence depended on the buffalo. In a way Owl felt sorry that some of the animals would die tomorrow for what he did not consider a very good reason: to provide trophies for this prince from a faraway land. But Otto and Max had been friendly toward him, and besides, only a few of the buffalo would perish. Owl would give thanks and praise to their departed spirits after the hunt.

"I must get up early in the morning, before the hunt begins, and do some sketches," Max said. He was almost as excited by the prospect of a buffalo hunt as Otto was, and he seemed to have forgotten about working on Owl's portrait this evening. Owl decided not to remind him. While he looked forward to seeing the picture when it was finished, standing still and trying to look like a gallant warrior was more difficult than he had thought it would be.

"We should all get some sleep," Otto said. "Tomorrow will be a busy day."

Owl hoped Wakon-tah would look kindly on them and not be angered by what was going to happen to the buffalo. Owl was worried enough about completing his quest without having to be concerned about the disapproval of the Creator.

The day broke with overcast skies and a light wind. Max would have preferred sunshine for his sketching, but the soft gray light had its own appeal. He had been up since before dawn, and by the time the prince rolled out of his blankets, Max already had charcoal and pad in hand as he stood atop the rise and drew the scene before him. Quick strokes with the charcoal outlined the general shape of the buffalo herd. He drew in the river, then added more details, flicking his eyes up and down as he checked his shaggy subjects.

The herd had drifted a little farther north along the river, which Owl had told them might happen. Barring a stampede, though, the herd's movement would be slow. The hunters would have no trouble catching up to it.

Otto came to the top of the hill and stood beside Max, drawing a deep breath. "Ah, it is a glorious morning, is it not, Max? A good day for a hunt, I hope. Will you be joining us?"

Max hesitated before answering. He had been asking himself the same question since Otto had suggested the hunt. He doubted that he would be able to use a bow very effectively, and he had never been a particularly good shot with a flintlock. He might frighten the buffalo without killing any and ruin the hunt for everyone else. And, truth to tell, he could not muster up any great enthusiasm for killing them. No one could call the buffalo beautiful, but they had an undeniable majesty and power about them.

"I think our purposes would be better served if I stayed here and sketched the hunt," he said. "That way we will have an accurate record of what occurs."

Otto said, "An excellent idea, if you are certain you will not be disappointed."

"No, not at all." Max tried to hide his relief.

Otto went to find Brother Owl, and they returned a short while later, accompanied by Captain Standard, Daniel Dupree, and several soldiers. Standard, Dupree, and the others were on horseback. Otto, Brother Owl, and some of the Osage scouts would approach the herd on foot first, but Standard had insisted that riders stand by to rush in and pick up the hunters in case of trouble. "I can't allow you to be trampled by buffalo, Your Excellency," he had explained to Otto. "My superiors would never forgive me."

Holding a borrowed bow, Otto stood still long enough for Max to sketch him. He had a quiver of arrows slung on his back and had stripped to his breeches and boots. Owl had painted his face and torso in the manner of the Crane band. Max thought Otto looked rather ridiculous with his pale skin, which seemed even whiter with the bright hues daubed on it. Otto was very excited, however.

"I am ready, Brother Owl," he said huskily. "Let us go slay the mighty buffalo."

For the briefest moment Max thought he saw a smile playing around the corners of Owl's mouth. Then Owl indicated for Otto and the Osage scouts to follow him.

They advanced quickly but quietly, the scouts following Owl's gestured directions to spread out around the herd. Max drew them into his sketch. Captain Standard took off his cap, wiped sweat from his forehead. "I'm not sure I like this. Those buffalo are farther off than I thought they were."

Dupree shifted in his saddle and hefted the long-barreled flintlock he held. "If there be any problems, we can pull the prince out of there before the beasts have any chance to hurt him."

Max hoped the Scotsman was right; if anything happened to Otto, the expedition would be ruined. They would probably have to turn around and return to St. Louis, and from there he would go on to Boston and eventually to Vienna. He had already completed a significant body of work, but he wanted to carry on with the journey as it had been planned.

As Otto, Owl, and the other hunters drew nearer to the herd,

Max's heart was pounding heavily, almost as if *he* were down there about to test his prowess against the beasts. He stopped working, his eyes following Otto and Owl, who stayed together instead of spreading out as the other hunters did. That was a good idea; Owl could look out for the prince if anything happened.

"Get on with it," Captain Standard said softly.

Finally, everyone was in position. Owl gestured once again to the scouts, then straightened and took an arrow from his quiver. He nocked the shaft and drew back the bowstring. Otto followed his example, watching Owl closely. Both men aimed carefully, then let fly.

Owl's aim was true, and his arrow lodged deeply in the side of a massive buffalo, just behind the foreleg. Otto's shot was not as good. His shaft struck another buffalo in the side, but farther back, toward the rump. That buffalo let out a bellow of pain and surprise. Meanwhile, the animal Owl had shot lurched forward, running some distance before collapsing onto its forelegs. It rolled onto its side, dying without a sound.

Otto's buffalo cow swung around, still bellowing as it searched for the source of the pain in its flank. Otto reached for a second arrow and fumbled it out of the quiver. By the time he had it nocked, the buffalo's dim eyes had fastened on him, and it charged.

"Damn!" Captain Standard grated as he lifted his flintlock. He grimaced as he realized that the prince was likely to be struck if he and his men started shooting. "Hold your fire!"

Max felt fear race through him and knew that what Otto was experiencing had to be far worse. Otto stood his ground bravely and loosed his second arrow, miraculously striking the charging buffalo between the horns. The tip of the arrow merely glanced off the beast's thick skull.

Owl darted to one side as he readied another arrow. He fired, and from his position he was able to send the shaft into the buffalo's side. But it entered at too much of an angle to find the animal's heart, and that was the only way to stop the charging cow quickly.

One of the Osage scouts had seen what was happening and fired from the other side. His arrow struck the beast perfectly.

The animal's momentum carried it forward for several strides before its forelegs folded beneath it. Its snout plowed a furrow in the ground a few feet from where Otto stood.

Max realized he had stopped breathing. He drew in a lungful of air with a gasp and watched as Owl seized Otto's arm and hustled him away from the herd. The other hunters were firing into the mass of buffalo as fast as they could. The great beasts had begun to mill about as the knowledge that something was wrong began to dawn on them. Several had slumped to the ground, arrows protruding from their thick hides.

Otto and Owl were halfway up the slope now, and Captain Standard raised his arm. Sweeping it forward, he called to his men, "Fire at will!"

Max jerked around in surprise as flintlocks began to roar. The soldiers had dismounted and were shooting into the herd over the heads of Otto and Owl. Dupree had also left his saddle and was firing. More buffalo dropped to the ground as the men began to reload.

"What are you doing?" Max asked Standard, who yanked cruelly on the reins as his horse danced back and forth, made skittish by the gunfire.

"Protecting the prince," Standard snapped.

"But the prince is safe! Owl got him away from the herd."

"I'll thank you not to question my orders, Mr. Adolphus." Standard's tone was cold and angry. He looked away from Max.

But Max was in no mood to be so easily dismissed. He reached up and caught hold of the harness on Standard's horse. "This was supposed to be a hunt as the Indians carry them out! That was what the prince wanted!"

"The prince got his trophy," Standard snarled. "Now I'm doing what needs to be done. Get your hand off my horse, sir!"

Max fell back from the unmistakable threat in the captain's voice. Standard's men, along with Dupree, continued shooting into the milling herd as fast as they could load and fire. His eyes filled with growing horror, Max tried to count the buffalo that had already fallen. It was impossible; there were too many.

Otto reached the top of the rise, gasping for breath. Both he and Brother Owl looked shocked and dismayed by what was happening. "What are you doing, Captain?" Otto demanded.

"There is no need for this slaughter! I want you to stop immediately."

"I'm just taking measures to make sure that you're safe, Your Excellency," Standard said. "That buffalo almost killed you."

"But I am safe now! Tell your men to stop shooting!"

"I have to do what I think is best," Standard said over the roar of the guns.

Max looked down at the herd again. The Osage scouts had all fled when the shooting started, and now they regrouped a safe distance from the herd. The buffalo were moving to the north along the river. As Max watched, the surge of hairy bodies in that direction became a full-fledged stampede. A sound like thunder rolled over the prairie, and clouds of dust billowed upward into the overcast sky. Left behind were dozens of carcasses.

"My God," Otto said, his voice little more than a whisper. "Why? Why was this necessary?"

Because you wanted a trophy, Max thought, catching himself before the words left his mouth. He did not want to upset the prince even more. Besides, the sentiment was not entirely fair. Otto had planned to kill only a few of the beasts, enough to provide a trophy for himself and fresh meat for the group for several days. Max was sure the prospect of such wholesale destruction had never entered the prince's mind.

"Hold your fire!" Standard finally ordered. "That's enough, men. Now I want a detail to get down there and skin as many of those beasts as you can. Mr. Dupree will go with you and show you what to do."

Max's mouth tightened grimly. So that was it. The whole ghastly spectacle had been arranged so that Dupree could collect some buffalo hides to ship back to his employers in St. Louis. Max watched angrily as the Scotsman led several soldiers down the hill and got them started on their grisly work.

Otto reached out and put a hand on Owl's arm. "I am sorry, my friend," he said. "I promise you, I knew nothing of this."

But Owl pulled away, a look of suspicion and fury in his eyes. Max could not blame him for being angry.

After this betrayal, Max was not sure that Owl would ever

trust any white man again—not even the one who had been painting his portrait.

Chapter Forty-two

Owl said nothing to anyone the rest of that day. He was filled with a roiling mass of emotions: sorrow for the unnecessary deaths of the buffalo, anger at the men who had killed them—and guilt because of his own part in the slaughter, inadvertent though it had been.

He knew that Max and Prince Otto had had nothing to do with what had happened. The killing had been the idea of Captain Standard and the man Dupree; Owl's instincts told him that much. Dupree cared for nothing except the strange thing white men called money, and Standard was easily led, thinking himself a strong man when actually he was filled with fear and weakness. But Max and Otto both had pale skin like Standard and Dupree and the soldiers who had done the killing with their guns, and right now all white men seemed alike to Owl. They all shared the blame.

The party camped overnight again in the same place. It took most of the day to skin the buffalo carcasses. After a hide had been ripped from one of the violated bodies, it was stretched out on the ground and pegged down. Dupree had been well prepared, Owl realized. The man must have been planning all along to take advantage of the first opportunity that presented itself. Some of the meat was harvested, too, and the soldiers ate well that night. Owl and the Osage scouts held themselves apart from the others, preferring not to take part in the "feast." Owl noticed that Max and Otto did not eat the buffalo meat, either, and he felt a grudging respect for them.

The rest of the meat was left for the scavengers of the plains.

The next day, Dupree was still not ready to move on, because the hides were not yet dry. The clouds had blown away on a breeze that sprang up during the night, and the sun shone brightly. Standard agreed without hesitation to remain camped there another night, confirming Owl's suspicion that the officer was under the thumb of the Scotsman.

Owl considered leaving the group and pushing on by himself, but he had given his word to accompany them as far as the place where the Nibthaska-ke joined the river they called the Missouri. That promise bound him, despite his anger and revulsion.

On the second day, as the sun was drying the staked-out buffalo hides, Max went in search of Owl and found him sitting under a tree near the river. Owl recognized Max by his footsteps but did not look up to greet him. Max's movement stopped, and after a moment Owl heard a sigh. Max sat down beside him.

"I don't blame you for being angry," Max said. "I would be, too."

"I am filled with sorrow," Owl said without looking at him. He kept his gaze focused on the slow, ponderous current of the river.

"So am I. I am sorry the buffalo were killed."

"It was none of your doing," Owl conceded. "If I had known white men better, I would have known not to trust any of them."

"You can trust me," Max said. "You have my word, Owl. I have never lied to you, and I never will. Neither has the prince. He is very upset about this whole matter."

"Did he take his trophy?" Owl asked coldly. "Did he take the horns of the buffalo he shot? Did he eat its heart?"

"He did none of those things. He did not want a trophy after what happened. It was all Mr. Dupree's idea, I think, and Captain Standard went along with him."

"I have thought the same thing." Owl finally turned to look at Max and saw the pain in his eyes. "I know you are sorry, Max. And that gladdens me. It tells me you have a good heart."

"Prince Otto plans to lodge a formal protest with the United States government when we return to Washington City."

"I know nothing of such things," Owl said. "The ones called Standard and Dupree should ask forgiveness of Wakon-tah the Creator for what they have done—but I think that they will not."

"You're right. They do not believe they have done anything wrong. To them, the buffalo are here to kill."

"The buffalo are here so that the people may live," Owl whispered. "This is the will of the Creator."

"I agree. But there is nothing we can do now except move on." Max took a deep breath. "I'll understand if you don't want me to finish your portrait, Owl. But I am asking for your forgiveness for what happened."

After a moment Owl replied, "There is nothing to forgive. You are not to blame, Max. But tell the prince that I forgive him for his part in the killing."

Max smiled.

"And you can finish the picture of me. It would not be right to deny you after you have done so much work on it."

Max heaved a sigh of relief. "Thank you, Owl. You are most kind."

Owl did not feel kind; he was still filled with remorse. But at least he had settled in his mind what he was going to do.

He would keep his word. Until they reached the place where their paths would part, he would remain with the white demons.

The next day, Dupree decided that the buffalo hides were dry enough and had them stacked and bundled. If any of the soldiers thought it odd that Captain Standard had ordered them to do whatever the Scots fur trader told them to, none of them said anything about it. It could be, Max decided, that they hoped Standard would share with them the profits he made from the hides. Max thought that unlikely; Standard and Dupree would no doubt split between themselves whatever they realized from the sale.

The hides were bundled and loaded on the wagons by midday, and the party was ready to pull out once more. Otto rode alongside Max's wagon rather than joining Standard at the head of the column. Dupree rode horseback now and had taken over Otto's former position.

"I despise that man," Otto said in a low voice to Max as they got under way.

"Which one?" Max asked, looking at Standard and Dupree.

"Well, both of them, I suppose. I think it was Dupree's idea to slaughter all those bison and take their hides. But Captain Standard is the one who made it possible."

Max agreed. "You're right, Your Excellency."

The prince snorted. "We've been through enough together that you can stop calling me that, Max. My name is Otto."

"Very well . . . Otto. And I share your opinion of the captain and Mr. Dupree. I'm surprised any of the Indians even stayed with us after what the soldiers did to that buffalo herd."

Otto looked around. "Speaking of the natives, where is Brother Owl? I don't believe I have seen him today."

"He said he was going to ride with the scouts. I don't think he particularly enjoys the company of whites any longer."

"I cannot say that I blame him," Otto said. "I'm pleased he has forgiven me for the hunt, but I'm sure he's still resentful."

"He'll come around," Max predicted. Already Owl had allowed him to continue working on the portrait. Their relationship might never be exactly the same as it was before the buffalo hunt, but Max had hopes that it would improve.

"We should all be ashamed of ourselves," Otto muttered, as much to himself as to Max. "What have we brought to the Indians, after all? Nothing but death and disease and treachery."

Max remembered what Owl had told him about the lives of the people who made their home here on the prairie. It was not an idyllic existence, he knew, and much of what the Europeans and Americans had brought with them had made life even harder for the Indians. But not all of it had been bad.

"From time to time we have extended the hand of friendship to them," Max said. "That ought to be worth something."

"I hope so, my friend. I hope so."

Owl made a habit of riding with the scouts who had come from the Little Osage band near the Fiery Prairie Fort. Though he missed talking with Max Adolphus, he found that being around Captain Standard and Daniel Dupree angered him almost to the point of losing control. He would have liked to take his bow and put arrows through both men.

But he knew that was no way for a holy man of the people to feel, and since it was easier to turn his mind away from such thoughts when he was not with the soldiers, he continued to ride with the scouts for the week after the buffalo hunt. Every night, however, he came back into camp and sat for Max as he worked on the portrait. Max had assured him that another night or two would see the picture finished. Owl recalled how Max had transformed Chief Birds Fly Against the Sun, and he was curious what his own portrait would look like. He hoped Max had painted him truthfully.

He was thinking about that when the Osage scout with him, a man named Flooded Creek, touched his arm. Owl pulled back on the light reins of the pony he had borrowed. As he brought his mount to a stop he looked in the direction Flooded Creek indicated.

Dust was rising from behind a distant hill—more dust than a few animals would make but less than a herd of buffalo would kick up. More than likely that meant riders.

Owl and Creek exchanged a worried glance. The presence of a large group of men on horseback meant the potential for trouble. Owl knew little of the bands who roamed through this area, but he took it for granted that some of them would not be friendly toward the white intruders.

"We must go and look," he said.

Flooded Creek and Owl dug their moccasined heels into the flanks of their mounts, urging the ponies into a run toward the hill.

The slope was long and gradual, but the two scouts covered the distance quickly. When they neared the crest of the rise, they brought their mounts to a halt and slid from their backs. After tying the reins to small bushes, they started forward again on foot.

The top of the hill was covered with tufts of grass. Owl and Creek bellied down behind the scant cover and edged their heads up to peer over the crest. Both men grunted in surprise at what they saw, but Owl's breath caught in his throat, and his blood froze.

Riding toward them was a group of at least forty warriors, the roaches of hair on their heads daubed with mud and red paint so that they stood up like horns. The upper half of the men's faces had also been painted red. It was clear they were riding to war.

"Horned Heads," Owl breathed. "Pawnee." He had heard much about the traditional enemies of his people but had never seen them. He remembered the legend in the story skins of the

Red Horns' raid on the town of the Crane band and their abduction of many prisoners. The great warrior and mystic Storm Seeker had led the effort to rescue the captives and avenge the raid, and he had killed the huge Pawnee warrior called Fallen Tree. Though hundreds of years had passed since then, the epic battle was still the most celebrated in the history of the Crane band.

Creek touched Owl's arm. "They come this way. We must go."

Together they scuttled backward down the hill, came to their feet when it was safe, and ran back to their horses. Owl swung up, hauled the pony's head around, and kicked it into a run. Flooded Creek was right behind him.

In his mind's eye Owl still saw the large war party of Horned Heads. He recalled that in the distance, beyond the Pawnee party, he had seen a line of trees intersecting the growth along the Missouri River. That was probably the spot where the Nibthaska-ke flowed into the Missouri. The Pawnees stood squarely between him and his objective.

More importantly, perhaps, the Pawnees were heading downstream along the Missouri, which meant they were on a direct course to encounter the party of white men. Though he felt nothing but contempt for Standard and Dupree, Owl did not want any harm to come to Max and Prince Otto. They had to be warned about the approaching war party.

He leaned forward over the neck of his pony and rode even faster, urging all the speed he could from the racing animal.

Chapter Forty-three

The group of wagons and riders had paused for the midday meal, and while they were stopped, Max took advantage of the opportunity to sketch a small, rodentlike creature that emerged from its burrow some twenty feet away to watch the strange invaders of its territory. The little animal seemed unafraid of them; its eyes shone brightly, and its nose twitched with curiosity. Whenever anyone came too near, it darted back into its hole, but after a few minutes the little brown head always reappeared, poking tentatively out of the ground. Max knew these creatures were called prairie dogs, because of the barking sounds they sometimes made, and he found them delightful. As he looked out over the plains he saw small mounds marking other burrows and realized he had come upon an entire prairie-dog town.

Otto came up to him and looked over his shoulder as he was finishing the sketch. "That's very good, my boy," he said. "Asking you to accompany me was perhaps the best decision I made before I left Vienna."

"Thank you sir. I'm glad I've lived up to your faith in me."

Captain Standard strode by, and the prairie dog ducked back into its hole. The captain glanced toward the spot where the little animal had been, frowned as if he was not quite sure what he had seen, and said to Max and Otto, "We'll be pulling out soon."

Otto responded curtly. After the buffalo hunt there had been a palpable coolness between the Prussian nobleman and the American officer.

Perhaps he and Otto should both be watching their backs, Max thought. It would be a black mark on Standard's record should any unfortunate "accident" befall them, but the captain might consider it even worse to have a foreign dignitary accuse him of conduct unbecoming an officer. More importantly, Standard would not want his business arrangement with Dupree exposed.

Yes, Max decided, he and the prince would definitely have to be more careful in the future. He decided to have a talk with Otto about the matter as soon as possible.

He was back in the wagon and ready to leave when Standard gave the order to move out. The half-dozen vehicles and score of riders got under way again. They had not gone far, however, when Standard held up his hand and called out for them to stop. Otto brought his horse to a halt next to Max's wagon and leaned forward in the saddle. "There is dust up ahead," the prince said after a moment. "Someone is coming. And quickly, from the looks of it."

Max stood up on the wagon seat to see the tendril of dust pluming into the air in the distance. It drew closer as he watched, and finally two riders came into view. They were little more than dark dots on the prairie at first but quickly drew close enough for Max to make them out.

"Two of our scouts, I believe," Otto said.

"I think one of them is Owl," Max said. "They seem to be in a hurry."

The two men looked at each other, both thinking the same thing. Whatever had prompted Owl and the Osage scout to ride so fast could not be good.

The riders would reach Captain Standard and Daniel Dupree at the head of the column in a matter of minutes. "I'm going to see what this is all about," Otto said, then heeled his horse forward. Max hesitated for a moment, then dropped to the ground beside the wagon and followed the prince on foot.

Owl and the Osage reached Standard, Dupree, and Otto about the same time Max did. "What is it?" Standard demanded harshly. "What's got the two of you so spooked?"

The scouts were breathless from their hard ride, though not as winded as their ponies. "There is . . . a war party . . . coming this way," Owl said. He took a deep breath. "About forty Horned Head warriors. What you call Pawnee."

Max's heart lurched. He knew nothing about the Pawnee, but if Owl was this worried about their approach, they had to be fearsome warriors. Glancing at Standard and Dupree, he saw that both men had paled.

"What do you think we should do?" Standard said after a moment.

In a voice cold with contempt Owl said, "You are the chief of these soldiers. You decide."

"Can we avoid them?"

Owl did not answer. The other scout, the Osage called Flooded Creek, Max recalled, said, "Pawnee follow the river, like white-eyes men."

"Then we'll leave the river and head west," Standard said.

Flooded Creek shook his head. "Not enough time. Pawnee

have scouts out, too. Scouts see you, lead war party to you. Better wait here."

"And prepare ourselves defensively." Standard appeared a bit less rattled, Max thought; his military training was no doubt taking over as he considered his options. He turned and called, "Draw the wagons into a circle! Assume defensive positions inside the circle!"

His men hurried to follow his orders. As they did Otto asked, "Why do you assume that these Indians approaching us are hostile, Captain? Have they attacked travelers before?"

"I don't know, but I'm not going to take any chances."

"Horned Heads are enemies of the Osage," Flooded Creek said. "Raid our towns, steal our horses and women."

"That's enough for me," Standard snapped.

Max left the prince discussing the situation with Standard and Dupree. He saw Owl walking his horse toward the rear of the column and followed.

"What do you think of the Pawnee, Owl?" Max asked as he came alongside the young warrior.

"They are the enemies of my people as well," Owl replied. "There has always been bad blood between us. The biggest battle in the history of my people took place when the Red Horns raided the town of the Crane band many generations ago."

"Red Horns?" Max repeated. "I thought you called them the Horned Heads before."

"They have more than one name, but they are still the same: evil."

"You think we're in danger from them."

"When they see Osage with you, they will attack. Friends of the Osage are enemies of the Pawnee."

Such was the way of the world, Max thought. In European alliances the friend of one nation was often considered the enemy of another. That obviously held true here in the wilderness of the new land called America.

"So all we can do is wait and see what will happen."

Owl stopped and smiled gravely at him. "You are an artist, not a warrior. Keep your head down, and you will be safe."

Max wondered if Owl really believed that. He knew *he* certainly did not.

*   *   *

The soldiers pulled the wagons into a circle as Captain Standard had ordered, but with only six wagons the circle was a small one. The soldiers, civilians, and scouts crowded into it and waited for the Pawnee war party to approach.

As he knelt beside a wagon wheel Owl thought about what Max had asked him earlier. Perhaps the Pawnee would *not* assume the whites were their enemies simply because the party had Osage scouts with them. Was it possible the Pawnee might turn aside without attacking them?

Every instinct cried out otherwise. The Horned Heads were raiders and killers, and this group outnumbered the white party almost two to one. Owl could not imagine them passing up such a tempting target.

Max came over to him, a rifled flintlock in his hands despite Owl's warning to stay out of the fight. He held it awkwardly, and it was clear from his demeanor that he had no real hope of using the weapon effectively.

"You look more comfortable holding a paintbrush, my friend," Owl said.

"I am. Much more comfortable. But I've got to do my part. If there *is* a battle, you'll be in the thick of it, won't you?"

"Can I do less than my ancestor Storm Seeker? The tale is written in the story skins of how he fought the Red Horns and defeated their greatest warrior."

"I never got to see those story skins," Max mused.

Owl reached for the large parfleche that hung on his back beside his quiver of arrows. "I can show them to you now."

Max's eyes widened in surprise as Owl drew the sheaf of buffalo hide from the pouch. "You had them with you all along?"

"I am their keeper. I would have shown them to you sooner, but to reveal these things to an outsider is not easy for my people." Carefully, almost reverently, Owl unrolled the scrolls. He put a finger on the pictures that told the story of his people. "These were painted by my great-grandmother Hummingbird, daughter of Black Robe and Bright Water. She could read the writings of her father and change them into the picture writing used by our people. She was the only one who could."

Max stared with intense interest at the bold, simple, yet

powerfully evocative pictures on the skins. "Your great-grand-mother was an artist of great skill. But what do you mean, she was the only one who could read her father's writings?"

"They are here," Owl said, moving aside several pieces of hide. "I will show you."

"My God!" Max exclaimed as he caught sight of the faded writing. "That's French!"

"Black Robe was a Frenchman who came to live with us. He was a . . ." Owl searched for the word. "A missionary, my great-grandmother called him. He came to teach my people what the French believed about the Creator. He wanted to make them believe as he did. But he failed, and in the end he shared more of our beliefs than we did his."

"What an incredible story! That means you are part white."

"It is not something I boast about," Owl said dryly.

"No, I suppose not. Especially after everything you've seen on this trip."

Owl looked up, distracted by movement to the northwest. "The Pawnees come."

A haze of dust hung above the horizon. Soon it resolved into a cloud, and figures on horseback came into view. Max gasped. The size of the Pawnee war party was indeed impressive.

As Owl quickly returned the story skins to the pouch, he assessed the situation. He and Max were in as good a place as any, shielded by the heavy body of the wagon as well as the two water barrels tied to its side. The Pawnees outnumbered the sol-diers and their group, but the soldiers had guns that could kill at a much greater range than bows and lances.

"Hold your fire until I give the word, men!" Standard called out from his position behind the next wagon. He gripped a flint-lock pistol tightly in one hand, a saber in the other. Dupree and Otto stood next to him, each holding a gun. Owl heard the prince ask, "Shouldn't you at least attempt to talk to them, Captain? Perhaps they will let us go on our way without any trouble."

"That's not very likely. I'm not going to chance being overrun. If they ride around us, fine. If not, they'll find a blis-tering reception waiting for them."

Owl had to admit that the captain's caution was probably wise. He did not trust the Pawnee either.

Prince Otto tried again to convince Standard not to initiate the hostilities but finally gave up. The Pawnee were closing in.

Owl could see them clearly, and suddenly something about the whole situation struck him as wrong. After a moment's thought he realized what it was. In his vision the Pawnee had ridden as *allies* of the white men rather than enemies. Did that mean the events of the vision were yet to come in the future—or that they would never come to pass?

Owl could not say. All he knew was that at this moment the Horned Heads were the enemy, and he—unlikely though it seemed—had allied himself with those who might one day be his destroyer.

"Steady, men," Standard called to the soldiers, who had taken position in three ranks. There was no fear in his voice now, Owl noted. The captain was a greedy, ambitious, brutal man—the slaughter of the buffalo had proven that—but he was not a coward.

The war party's horses never broke stride but came faster and faster. The sound of distant whoops and yips punctuated the low roar of hoofbeats.

"A little closer, a little closer," Standard said. Owl could not tell if he was cautioning his men or imploring the Pawnee. Another few moments passed; then Standard shouted, "Fire!"

Black powder thundered with plumes of smoke. The kneeling men in the front rank stood up and moved behind their companions to reload. The next rank took their position and fired a second salvo, followed by the third. By that time the first group of men were ready to fire again. Owl admired the tactics, which resulted in a withering curtain of fire.

The volleys found their mark. Warriors tumbled from their horses wailing death cries, their bodies sprawled unmoving on the earth seconds later. Their comrades still on horseback grew louder and angrier.

Owl noticed, however, that some of the Pawnees peeled off to the sides and circled back, fleeing from the deadly hail of lead. After two more volleys, all the surviving Pawnees retreated. Their attack had been disastrous. They had lost many men without getting close enough to release a single arrow.

As the breeze carried away some of the smoke, Standard's

men saw what was happening and let out triumphant cheers. Standard had to bellow, "Cease fire! Cease fire! Save your powder and shot, men! The redskins are on the run!" He waved his cap above his head. "Hurrah! Hurrah!"

The soldiers echoed his cheer, clapping each other on the back. These men, most of whom were from places Owl had never heard of, had faced the worst the frontier had to offer and sent the Pawnee scurrying away in shame. At least that was the prevailing attitude, Owl sensed.

Not everyone felt that way, however. He looked over at Max and saw that he was still holding the long-barreled flintlock tightly—so tightly that his fingers had turned white. Max gestured toward the cloud of dust that marked the retreating Pawnees. "Are they gone for good?"

"You mean, will they come back?"

"Exactly."

"I cannot say," Owl replied honestly. "They lost warriors at the hands of their enemies. The Pawnee will want to avenge those deaths. But they will also consider the ease with which those warriors were killed. They may decide the wisest thing would be to avoid your party in the future."

"But what do *you* think they will do?"

Owl was silent for a moment, then said, "The fires of vengeance will burn too brightly to ignore. Captain Standard should not let down his guard. Sooner or later the Pawnee will be back."

"Will you tell him this?"

Owl looked at the other men. Prince Otto appeared as vastly relieved as the soldiers that the Pawnees had not pressed their attack. If Owl had no one to consider but Standard and Dupree, he would slip away from the group at nightfall and urge the Osage scouts to leave with him. But that would mean abandoning his newfound friends as well.

"I do not know what good it will do," he said at last, "but I will talk to Captain Standard."

Chapter Forty-four

After the Pawnee retreat some soldiers wanted to push on immediately, convinced that the Indians had been too frightened to stop running, but cooler heads prevailed, much to the relief of Max and Prince Otto. Captain Standard decided it would be better to stay where they were until the next morning.

Max was also pleased because it meant he could resume work on Owl's portrait that evening. The painting was practically finished, but Max still wanted to make a few small changes. He took out his canvas and easel and had Owl strike the now-familiar pose.

The work went well, and after a couple of hours Max stood back from the canvas and studied it for several moments. No matter how he scrutinized the painting, he could see nothing else that needed to be done. Any further tinkering might make it worse instead of better.

Prince Otto came up to him and regarded the painting. "It's magnificent, my friend. Are you done?"

"I think so," Max said. "I don't see anything I need to do."

"Nor do I. Owl, come look at this."

Owl gave Max a questioning glance.

"It's finished," Max said.

Owl looked a little nervous, as if he were approaching a wild animal rather than a painting. He leaned to one side as he drew even with the easel, craning his neck for a glimpse.

"It will not bite you." Otto smiled regally. "Look, Owl—it is the very likeness of you."

Owl stepped cautiously around the easel and peered at the portrait. After a moment he said to Max, "You have painted me truthfully."

"I tried to. I'm glad you think I succeeded."

Max was relieved. Indeed, the portrait *was* true to life, not idealized as that of Chief Birds Fly Against the Sun had been. Owl stood straight and tall in his buckskin leggings, and his robe was thrown over his left shoulder, signifying youth and speed, according to what he had told Max. His eyes stared out at the viewer, his expression neither challenging nor submissive, but alert and intelligent. His right hand gripped his bow. His face was unadorned. He was not looking for war—but he was prepared for trouble if it came. On his right hip was the parfleche that held the story skins; if Max had known about them earlier, he would have tried to convince Owl to unroll them so that he could incorporate them into the portrait. But Owl might have refused, which would have put them both in an awkward position. The matter had probably worked out for the best, Max thought.

"You have captured my image, but it is a good thing. You have not stolen my soul."

"That was never my intention, as I told you from the first."

Otto clapped Max on the back. "When the people in Vienna see this, your fame as an artist will be assured, my young friend. Your work will make you the toast of the town."

"That will be fine—if it occurs," Max said, "but I am less interested in that now. I simply want to capture these . . . images of truth, I suppose you could say."

Otto laughed. "I am glad to be a simple scientist and scholar. We have only to worry about hard facts, not images."

Owl pointed at the painting. "I will be proud for your people to see this, Max. You should also be proud."

"I am. I promise you, I am."

Max let the finishing touches he had put on the portrait dry, then carefully wrapped it and put it in the wagon with his other canvases. A part of him wished there were some way to ship them back to Austria so that he could avoid the risk of damage or loss here on this wild frontier. At the same time he did not want them out of his sight. There would be time enough to deal with the paintings when he and Otto returned east.

That night Captain Standard doubled the guard, but there was no trouble, no sign of the Pawnee party returning. The next morning, however, the bodies of the slain warriors that had been lying on the ground in the distance were gone. The Pawnee had recovered the bodies during the night, Owl explained to Max, so that they could be buried properly. "To do otherwise would doom the departed spirits to wandering between the worlds forever."

Not long after everyone had eaten, Daniel Dupree approached Standard. "We *are* pushing on today, aren't we? I want to get to where I'll be setting up that trading post as soon as possible."

"I see no reason to linger here," Standard said. "Those Pawnee will not risk their lives attacking us again."

Max overheard the statement. He wished he could be as confident of that as the captain. A glance at Owl told him how dubious *he* was, and Max put more faith in Owl's instincts than in Standard's. Much more.

Over the next couple of days, however, he had to admit that the captain appeared to be correct. They saw no sign of the hostile Pawnee.

The trees Owl had seen in the distance when he and Flooded Creek first spotted the war party lined the banks of a small stream instead of the Platte as he had thought. "I will be with you awhile longer," he told Max, "but soon we will reach the Nibthaska-ke, and our paths must diverge."

"You have been a good friend, Owl," Max said, his emotion sincere. "I will be sad to see you go."

When two days and nights had passed without threat from the Pawnee, Captain Standard relieved the extra men of guard duty. Though still alert, the party no longer traveled in constant fear.

They reached the Platte late the next afternoon, and this time there was no mistaking the broad, flat expanse branching westward from the Missouri. They made camp at the confluence of the rivers.

"I will spend this night here," Owl told Max and Otto. "In the morning, we will go our separate ways."

Otto put a hand on the young warrior's shoulder. "It is my fondest hope that someday our paths shall cross again."

"If Wakon-tah the Giver of Breath wills it, it will come to pass."

Max could not accept Owl's impending departure so easily. He was the best friend Max had made on this journey, and without his company the rest of the trip up the Missouri would not be as pleasant.

But Max would do nothing to dissuade Owl from fulfilling his vision. Though Owl had spoken little of the quest that was taking him to the ancient homeland of his people, Max knew how important it was to him. When morning came, Max would wish him all the best on his journey.

Max woke to the sound of harsh, frightened shouts. He struggled out of his bedroll beneath a wagon and saw the gray light of approaching dawn. Guns roared, and an early-morning breeze carried the stench of burned powder. One thought filled his head: the Pawnees had finally come back for their revenge.

As he scrambled out from under the wagon he saw that he was right. A soldier stumbled past him, clutching at the shaft of an arrow embedded in his throat. Blood, black in the dim light, welled over the man's fingers. He fell a few feet from Max, shuddered, and died.

Chaos filled the camp. The Pawnees had penetrated the circle of wagons and were firing arrows, hurling lances, bashing in skulls with their war clubs. It was a slaughter, and as Max pressed against the wagon he felt terrified, sickened. He ducked back under, searching for a weapon, but could find nothing. Thinking that perhaps he could reach Otto, who always had a gun, he was about to emerge into the open again when a hand grasped his collar and practically flung him back under the wagon. Panicking, Max flailed at the bronzed figure who dove after him.

"Stop it, Max!" a voice hissed over the uproar, and Max recognized it at once.

He clutched Owl's arm. "The Pawnee!" he gasped.

Owl crouched with Max. "They have come for revenge. Maybe they will kill only the bluecoats."

It was a feeble strand of hope, but they had nothing else. Owl was armed with bow and arrows and a knife, but that would count for little against such overwhelming odds.

Suddenly another voice called his name from nearby. Using his elbows, Max pulled himself closer to the frenzy of violence. "Otto! We are under here!"

Dropping to all fours, Prince Otto crawled under the wagon with them. There was a dark smear on his cheek that Max took to be blood. His hair was disheveled, and he was clutching a pistol. "Are you all right, Max?"

Owl reached out and snatched the pistol from the prince's hand. He threw it out from under the wagon. "You are not a soldier! The Pawnee must know this if you are to live."

"The gun was empty," Otto said, "but thank you, Owl."

The shouts of the Pawnee and the screams of their victims still filled the air as the sun rose. Huddled beneath the wagon, Max, Otto, and Owl saw soldier after soldier fall, their blood darkening the ground. Finally the ghastly noises began to fade.

A Pawnee warrior neared the wagon and paused. Max felt his heart lurch. The warrior bent and peered under the wagon, the stiff roaches of hair making him look like a demon as he blocked out the sunlight. He let out a yip of surprise at the sight of the three men. Owl spoke to him in a tongue that was unintelligible to Max and Otto, but the Pawnee seemed to understand. He gestured for them to crawl out as he backed away.

"Come," Owl said grimly. "Make no threatening moves."

"I assure you, I do not intend to," Otto said.

Neither did Max. He slid out from under the wagon with Otto and Owl and held his hands in plain sight as he stood. He breathed deeply, trying to calm himself. Within seconds they were surrounded by victorious Pawnees.

One young warrior strode up to them with a haughty look on his painted face. "I am Cries for War," he announced in English, taking Max and Otto by surprise. "Tell me why I should not kill you now."

Otto squared his shoulders. "I am Prince Otto Wilhelm of Saxe-Coburg," he said in a firm voice. "These are my friends, the noted artist Maximilian Adolphus and Brother Owl, holy man of the Crane band of the Prairie People."

Cries for War pointed the short lance he carried at Owl. "You are not Osage?"

"The prince has spoken my true name," Owl said.

"Prince," Cries for War repeated. "This is the same as chief?"

"You could say that," Otto admitted.

"Your land is the same land these bluecoats come from?"

"No, no. My land is far away over the great water. We are visitors in this country."

"You did not give the order to kill my warriors with the sticks that throw fire?"

"I did not. I would have told the soldiers to defend themselves if you attacked, but if you and your men had gone on your way in peace, that would have pleased me."

Cries for War scowled thoughtfully. "Why should I believe you?"

"Because I speak the truth."

Max focused on the painted countenance of the Pawnee leader. Moments before, he had let his gaze wander and had seen the corpses of the soldiers being mutilated. He knew that he was perhaps only minutes away from the same brutal treatment.

Cries for War called out a command, and his warriors brought forward several struggling figures, among them Captain Standard, his face ashen under crimson streaks of blood. The Osage scouts were also held. As Max Adolphus watched they stopped trying to pull loose from the grip of the Pawnees, as if accepting their fate.

Cries for War stepped over to Standard and placed the tip of the lance under his chin, pressing it into the soft flesh of his throat. Standard froze.

"You are the war chief of these bluecoats," Cries for War said. "The markings on your coat tell me this. These men say they are not of your band. Is this true?"

"Of . . . course it is," Standard gasped, and Max tried not to heave an audible sigh. "The two white men are very important dignitaries from another country, and you had better let them go. The Indian is not one of our scouts, is not under my command."

That was stretching the truth, since Owl had indeed ridden as a scout for several days during the journey. Not for the first time Max thought that while Standard might be a pompous fool, he did not lack courage.

Cries for War turned back to Max, Prince Otto, and Owl. "You will all live—for now," he decreed. "So will these others." He glanced at Standard and the Osage scouts, and Max noticed a cruel smile touch the chief's lips for a second. "Their slow deaths will bring us much joy."

*   *   *

Daniel Dupree staggered over the plain, the socks on his feet stained with blood from cuts made by sharp rocks and blisters that had burst. He had not had time to grab his boots before fleeing the Pawnee attack, and now the pain in his feet was bad, but not so bad that it could not be ignored. It was miracle enough that he had escaped with his life; he was not going to complain about this discomfort when his scalp could have been decorating a Pawnee lodge by now. To feel pain meant he was *alive*!

Still, his gratitude was tinged with bitterness. His plans for opening a trading post had been utterly destroyed by the Pawnee raid, and he would have to return to his employers in disgrace and defeat, if indeed he lived to see civilization again. Perhaps they would give him another chance.

He looked back over his shoulder for what seemed like the thousandth time since the attack that morning. Still no sign of pursuit. He had run from the camp to the Missouri River and plunged into the muddy water, letting the slow-moving current carry him away from the shouts and shrieks, which gradually faded away. He had not emerged from the river for what he judged to be several miles. Then he had followed its eastern bank back toward Fort Osage.

He was days from the outpost, he knew, alone with no boots, no food, no weapons. Chances were he would not survive long enough to get there. But he had beaten long odds before, and he intended to do so again. The promise of great wealth was still out there, and it would keep him going, he vowed. Footsore and stubborn, Daniel Dupree would conquer this land and wrest from it the bounty that was his to claim.

Chapter Forty-five

Owl was shocked that he was still alive. The Horned Heads— the Red Horn people—were traditional enemies of his people, and the instinctive hatred he felt for them should have been returned. Was it possible they did not know the history of their own tribe? Did their story skins say nothing about Storm Seeker and the great defeat he and the other warriors of the Crane band had inflicted on their ancestors? Did they even *have* story skins?

A wise man did not complain about good fortune, he told himself as he walked alongside Max and Prince Otto. Their wrists had been bound with strips of rawhide, and a longer strip tied the three of them together. The Osage scouts had been bound likewise. Only Captain Standard was not lashed to another captive. The captain seemed to take that as a sign of respect: to the Pawnee, he was the war chief of the whites. He took that honor as his due.

He would find out just how much of an honor it really was when they made camp tonight, Owl thought.

Prince Otto had identified Owl as the medicine man of the Crane band. That was true enough, Owl supposed. Since he was the only one left, he was shaman, chief, and keeper of the story skins. All the responsibilities of the band fell to him. As it became clear that the Pawnee had indeed forgotten all about the Crane band and the part it played in their own history, Owl became angry. He would almost have preferred a quick death to the idea that his people had truly vanished into the mists of time.

But he was no fool. If the Pawnee had forgotten the old grudges, he would not remind them. Better to live and focus on escape . . . so that one day he could meet the Pawnee again and show them the folly of forgetting about the Crane band.

The Horned Heads pushed the captives at a brutal pace all day, not slowing until evening. Then they made camp in a broad, grassy swale between two long ridges. Cries for War ordered several of his men to climb one of the ridges where some small trees grew and bring back wood. Owl knew what the wood was for. He looked at Standard and the Osage scouts with pity. Standard might not know what faced him, but the Osage did. They all wore expressions of stoic acceptance.

Owl, Otto, and Max were told to sit down. When they had done so, Max leaned closer to Owl and asked in a whisper, "Are they going to kill us now?"

Without moving his head, and barely moving his lips, Owl

said, "I do not think so. I understand some of their barbaric tongue, and I have heard nothing about killing us."

Max stiffened suddenly as he glanced around. Owl looked in the same direction and saw that one of the Pawnee was carrying an armful of Max's canvases. The paintings were still wrapped, and their coverings did not seem to have been disturbed. That they had been taken from the wagons did not surprise Owl; the Pawnee had gone through all the vehicles and plundered everything that might be useful to them as well as anything that struck their fancy. Even now, one of them was carrying Prince Otto's polished, silver-headed walking stick, and another had donned a beaver hat from among the prince's belongings.

"What are they doing with my paintings?" Max hissed.

"The shape must have struck them as odd. They know nothing of what you do." An idea sprang into Owl's mind. "Wait until they see what they have really found."

That did not take long. The Indian who had claimed the paintings and carried them on his horse all day impatiently tore the paper wrapping from one of them. The craggy face of General William Clark, whose portrait Max had painted back in St. Louis, stared out at him. The man let out a yip of surprise, dropped the painting, and, snatching up his war club, slammed the head of the weapon into the canvas, tearing through it. Max winced, almost as pained as if the club had struck him.

The Pawnee approached the painting gingerly now, war club poised for another blow if one was required. After a moment, evidently satisfied that General Clark was not going to leap to life, he nudged the canvas with his foot.

Other Pawnee, watching him, laughed at the warrior for defending himself against the portrait. Cries for War walked over and pointed at the painting. "What is this?" he asked.

"I took it from one of the wagons. There are more like it. Devil images, I would say. Evil magic."

Owl saw his opportunity and spoke up. "They are magic," he said in the tongue of the Pawnee, "but they are not evil. They are very powerful, and this is the man who created them. He is a mighty magician." With his bound hands he indicated Max, who looked confused by the whole conversation. In English Owl said quickly, "I have told them the paintings are magic and that you are a powerful medicine man."

"What?" Max exclaimed. "But I'm not—"

"They don't have to know that, my boy," Otto said as he caught on to what Owl was doing. "If they have a healthy respect for you, perhaps even a bit of fear, we will be more likely to live through this ordeal."

Max muttered reluctantly, "All right. I'm a medicine man. What do I do now?"

"Wait," Owl told him. Turning back to Cries for War, he went on, "This magician can capture the soul of anyone he wishes, but he can either set it free again or destroy it, whatever pleases him."

"Then we should kill him now," one of the Pawnee soldiers suggested, lifting his lance threateningly.

"Those are not his only powers," Owl said quickly. "I am his friend, and even I do not know everything he can do."

Cries for War said, "I would see this magic."

"Look at the other paintings," Owl said. "There is one of me."

"Then the white devil has captured your soul?"

"He returned it to me," Owl said. "Now I am stronger than ever for having been a part of his medicine."

The Pawnee stripped the wrappings from the other portraits and landscapes. They were impressed by the paintings of Owl and Chief Birds, less so by the others. But Owl sensed they had seen enough to be convinced that Max was indeed a magician, a man powerful enough that he should be left alone. With any luck, that respect would extend to Otto and Owl, too.

After looking at the paintings, Cries for War strode over to look down at Max. "Can you do more?" he asked in English.

"Well . . . I don't have my paints and canvases with me now." Max eyed the big pieces of paper and oilcloth that had been wrapped around the paintings. They would do, and he had a piece of charcoal in the pocket of his shirt.

Owl could almost see the workings of Max's mind, so well did he know the young artist by now. He was not surprised when Max said, "If you would untie my hands and bring me that paper, I could make a sketch of you."

Cries for War hesitated. For a moment it looked as if he was going to refuse the request. Then he drew his knife and leaned over. Max paled, but the Pawnee leader merely slashed his bonds. Cries for War signaled to one of the other men, who brought over a good-sized piece of paper that was torn in a ragged, irregular rectangle.

By this time the men who had been sent to fetch wood were returning to the camp with their arms full of branches. The light of day was fading quickly, but it proved sufficient for Max to sketch the returning Pawnees, capturing their figures and the long, tree-topped ridge behind them.

The Pawnee were impressed, even Cries for War. "Truly, this is powerful magic," he muttered.

Owl was relieved. Feeling the way they now did about Max, the Pawnees most likely would not harm him. As the "chief" of a foreign people, Otto was probably safe, as well. And since Owl was not an Osage scout, they might even spare him.

Standard, however, was not so lucky. Cries for War told some of his men to build up a fire so that the flames leaped high. They would need plenty of light for the work they would do this night.

As those men went to work, others walked closer to the prisoners. One sketch was not enough for these childlike Pawnee. They wanted Max to do more. Max complied, drawing feverishly to meet the demand, his very life at stake.

Standard and the Osage captives were being held on the other side of the camp, too far away for Owl to talk to. There was nothing left to say, he reflected. Their fate was sealed.

When the fire was large enough to satisfy Cries for War, he had the first captive brought forward. The chosen scout was cut loose and prodded to his feet, then shoved forward until, his face defiant, he stood before the Pawnee war chief. At another command from Cries for War, a Pawnee warrior staked the captive next to the fire. Cries for War approached, knelt beside the Osage, and reached out with his knife, holding the blade in the edge of the flames until it was glowing.

"What is he doing?" Max asked, the sketches forgotten now. He and Otto stared in horror at what was unfolding before them. They cried out, aghast, as Cries for War suddenly plunged the white-hot tip of the knife into the left eye of the Osage captive.

The man's eyeball sizzled and sputtered. But not a sound came from his lips.

"It begins," Owl whispered.

And it was a long time ending.

Owl had lived his life among the Osage and knew they were a brave, strong people. He was not surprised that all the scouts died in stubborn silence—blinded, mutilated, flayed alive, but defiant to the end. Even some of the Pawnees muttered in appreciation of their courage while taking turns at the torture, performing their bloody tasks with enthusiasm. Max and Otto both had to turn away. Max doubled over and retched.

Owl watched the torture, honoring the Osage as they died.

Standard saw what was happening, too, and he began whimpering and thrashing around long before the Pawnee came to get him. When all the Osage had been killed and it was his turn to be dragged to the fire and stripped naked, he screamed until no more sound would come from his raw throat. His dreams of advancing in the ranks and commanding a post in the east were forgotten now, washed away by the horror of the reality that had befallen him.

Cries for War leaned over him and said with a smile, "We will not blind you, white man. I want you to see what we are doing to you."

Then, with a swift, efficient stroke, he cut off Standard's testicles and shoved them into the captain's mouth as it opened in a silent screech of agony.

The Pawnee war chief was good at what he was doing; Owl had to admit that. Cries for War kept Captain Vincent Standard alive for a very long time. At last even Owl had to turn his eyes away from what was being done to the bloody, quivering thing that had once been a man. By the time Standard finally shuddered for the last time and died, he resembled nothing human. And Cries for War had performed all the torture himself. He stood up and raised his arms—coated with gore to the shoulder—above his head, and an ululating shout of triumph came from his throat.

Max was huddled on the ground, sobbing. Prince Otto's eyes were closed, his face ashen. Cries for War lowered his arms and came to stand in front of them, breathing heavily. "The three of you will live," he said, "but you will remain captives of the Pawnee for now. In time, the two white men will perhaps be returned or traded back to their people. You, Brother Owl of the Crane band, will remain with us as a slave for the rest of your days."

Owl was silent. Cries for War could change his mind and decide to kill them, but that was unlikely after he had made that declaration in front of all the other Pawnee warriors. The prospect of a lifetime of slavery did not appeal to Owl, of course, but it was better than immediate death.

And he did not intend to remain a slave for the rest of his life. Sooner or later there would be a chance to escape. When it came, he intended to seize it with all the strength in his being.

Chapter Forty-Six

A brush made of coarse hairs plucked from a buffalo hide, paints made from plants and clay and crushed rocks mixed with water, hides scraped thin and then stretched and dried in the sun: those were the tools of Max's trade now. An artist made do with what was at hand, and Max had learned much from his Pawnee captors.

Cold air plucked at his long hair and beard as he set up the makeshift easel he had constructed from sticks and branches tied together with strips of rawhide. He lifted into place a piece of hide attached to a crude frame also made of sticks. The painting was a partially completed landscape showing the Pawnee village far upstream on the Platte. It was a winter scene, painted from life, with tendrils of gray rising from the smoke holes in the moundlike earthen lodges. The sky was a lighter gray, filled with jagged, angry clouds that promised a snowfall. Max looked up at the same sky now. According to the old Pawnee woman who cooked for Max Adolphus and Prince Otto and kept the lodge they shared, the first big snow of the winter would soon be here, probably in one or two risings of the sun.

When the snow came, everyone would stay inside for a time. All through the summer and fall, the band had busily stored food for the winter. Max remembered what Owl had told him about the time of year called the Moon of Starvation. The Pawnees had the same concept, though the words were different. No matter how good the autumn hunt was, before spring came again at least a few members of the band would starve to death. It was a foregone conclusion.

Max sighed and kept at his work. He could do nothing about the plight of the Pawnee. And after seeing how Cries for War and the other warriors had slaughtered the troopers and tortured Captain Standard and the Osage scouts to death, Max was not sure he would help them, even if he could.

The women and children could be just as brutal and merciless; Max had seen that with his own eyes when other unlucky captives from different tribes were brought to the Pawnee village. Torture was a way of life with these people. Any prisoners they did not choose to enslave were gleefully put to a slow, agonizing death. Yet it was difficult to think of women and children and old people starving to death, even if they were Horned Heads.

He had picked up that name from Owl, who had told him of the ancient enmity between the Pawnee and the Crane band. The Pawnee had obviously forgotten the old grudges, but Owl had not.

The Pawnee had long since stopped sending a guard with Max when he came up here to paint. The squat hill on which he had set up his "studio" was about two bowshots from the edge of the village. If he fled, where would he go? They were hundreds of miles from anywhere Max would consider civilization, and although he had become accustomed—to a certain extent—to the ways of the Pawnee, he knew that he would have no chance of surviving out here on his own. Cries for War knew that, too, and so did his father, Cloud Shadow, the principal chief of the band. The only one of the three prisoners Cries for War had brought back who was still guarded was Brother Owl, and the vigilance of the Pawnee had begun to slacken even where he was concerned. With winter upon them, the possibility of a successful escape, or even an attempt, diminished with each day that passed.

A figure wrapped in a buffalo robe emerged from one of the lodges and began trudging up the slope. Max recognized Otto's tall, broad-shouldered form and long, fair hair. By the time Otto reached the top of the hill, Max had removed from a hide pouch the small wooden bowls in which he kept his paints.

"Working again, eh?" Otto said as he came up.

"What else is there to do?" Max was seated on a rock that put him at the correct height to reach the square of buffalo hide. "The Pawnee have not invited me to sit and smoke with them in their councils."

"That was Cloud Shadow's idea, my friend," Otto said. "He said that as the chief of a tribe from a faraway land, it was my right to join them. Young Cries for War was not pleased."

"Cries for War wishes he had killed us months ago when he had the chance."

It was true; although Max and Otto had caused no trouble since they had been captured in midsummer, they knew Cries for War regretted his decision to spare them. Otto had been invited to sit in the council of elders, and Max had been befriended by several warriors. The children adored him because he was always willing to draw pictures for them. Some of the women had begun to wonder what sort of match he would make for their daughters of marriageable age. He was widely regarded as a powerful magician.

Cries for War's biggest regret, however, was that he had not killed Owl.

"Have you seen our young friend?" Max asked as he filled in more clouds on the canvas.

"Not this morning," Otto replied. "But there is one thing I would wager: wherever Brother Owl is, Sacred Paint will not be far away."

"Ah, yes, Sacred Paint," Max said with a knowing smile. "I do not think I will take that wager, Otto."

Sacred Paint was one more reason Cries for War no doubt wished he had killed Owl a long time ago.

* * *

The girl was lovely, Owl thought. In a way, it would have been easier if she were not.

He had sensed her interest when he and the others had first been brought to this Pawnee village as prisoners. He had seen the way her eyes followed him as he was forced to do the most contemptible, menial tasks Cries for War could find for him. His ankles were bound together with a length of rawhide so that he could take only short, awkward steps. He burned with shame, his humiliation made more acute by the intensity with which the young woman watched him. Sacred Paint was the daughter of Cloud Shadow and the sister of Cries for War. She had seen seventeen summers, and though several suitors had sought her hand, she still lived in the lodge of her parents, the lodge in which Owl suffered his own existence as the slave of Cries for War.

Sacred Paint had kept her distance at first, as had the younger children in the lodge, and would not even talk to him. Gradually, as they all became more accustomed to his presence, she spoke to him occasionally. By the time summer was over and autumn had arrived, her attitude had become more than one of casual interest. Owl could not deny that he was drawn to her as well.

Unfortunately, Cries for War was all too aware of how his sister and this slave were beginning to feel about each other.

Owl trudged toward the river with a basket of clothing. Soon the Nibthaska-ke would freeze over, and there would be no more washing there until spring. Trembling Leaf, the mother of Cries for War and Sacred Paint, had sent Owl down to the river to assist in the washing, a task she knew he would find humiliating. Leaf doted on her oldest son, and she shared his dislike for Owl. Sacred Paint had quickly volunteered to accompany him and had ignored her mother's suggestions that perhaps she should not.

The young woman walked alongside him now. They were trailed by a warrior whose duty it was to guard Owl. The man was bored and distracted, however, and paid little attention to them. Fettered as he was, Owl would not likely try to escape.

"It will snow soon," Sacred Paint said.

Owl nodded but said nothing.

"When the snow and the cold winds come, the buffalo robes in the lodges will be very warm."

That was bold talk. She might as well have come right out and said that she wanted to share those robes with him, Owl thought. He felt a surge of desire.

How had this happened? he asked himself. How had he come to be attracted to this woman who belonged to a band of his people's mortal enemies? Sacred Paint was beautiful, of course, and she had been kind to him . . . but she was still Pawnee. He was not—could not be—in love with her.

He took a deep breath and said quietly, so that the guard would not overhear, "The warmth of a lodge and a buffalo robe in the winter are good things."

"Good things should be shared," Sacred Paint said.

Nothing could have been plainer. Owl glanced at her, meeting her eyes for a second before they both looked away. He saw a warmth there deeper than any that came from a buffalo robe.

Several women were already at the river. Owl and Sacred Paint joined them, Sacred Paint kneeling beside them on the bank. She took the clothes from the basket and pounded them with rocks to clean them. Her hands turned red from the cold water, and Owl found himself wishing he could take them in his own to warm them.

He looked back over his shoulder at the warrior who was guarding him. The man was not watching Owl but had turned his head to look up at the top of the hill. Owl followed his gaze and saw two figures there, Max Adolphus and Prince Otto. Both Europeans had adapted to life among the Pawnee. They had no ancient hatreds to overcome, as he did, and were well respected among the band. That was good, because Owl did not want them to suffer when he escaped.

During the first weeks of his captivity, Owl had had no chance to flee. He had been watched carefully night and day. After that, even though his captors' vigilance had eased, he made no attempt to leave the village for fear of what the Pawnee might do to Max and Otto. Now he was confident that his friends would be safe. For one thing, Max was still feared somewhat as a magician.

But winter was upon the land, and only a fool would even

consider trying to make a walk of many days across a landscape that would soon be frozen and snow-covered. Owl was no fool.

Spring would come eventually, and by then everyone in the village would be so accustomed to his status as a slave that escape would be easy, he told himself. All he had to do was be patient.

Sacred Paint looked back over her shoulder and said, "Would you help me with this, Owl?"

Without hesitating he knelt beside her, holding the basket so that she could place the wet clothes inside it. Her fingers brushed his hand. Again he longed to hold them. Despite the legacy of violence and hatred between their peoples, he could not deny what he felt for her.

The shaft of a lance cracked across his back, and the unexpected blow drove him forward. He fell into the edge of the river, floundering and choking for a moment in the frigid water and mud. When he twisted around and looked up to see who had struck him, he was not surprised to see Cries for War standing there holding the lance, an expression of smug satisfaction on his face.

"You should be more careful, dog," Cries for War said. "You will sink in the river and drown."

Sacred Paint shot to her feet and berated her brother, but her tirade only made Cries for War angrier. The Pawnee subchief hated the fact that his own sister was defending this captive, this slave. Owl read that plainly on his face.

He came to his feet, spitting cold, muddy water. The warrior assigned to guard him took a step forward, as if to interpose should Owl try to attack Cries for War. With a curt gesture Cries for War motioned him back and moved Sacred Paint aside so that he could face Owl directly. Sacred Paint fell silent, anxiety replacing the anger on her face.

"You wish to attack me, Owl of the Crane band?" Cries for War asked. "You wish to rise from the mud of the river like a turtle and strike me?"

Owl trembled with rage but forced the emotion down. Now was not the time to give in to it.

"I have been given a task to do," he said, struggling to keep his voice calm. "I would do it to the best of my ability." He could not keep from shivering as the cold wind plucked at his wet buckskins.

"Go ahead, slave," Cries for War said with a sneer. "Washer-woman."

Owl turned and picked up the basket he had dropped. He knew he could not control himself if he continued to look at Cries for War's arrogant face. The robes Sacred Paint had washed had fallen in the mud and would have to be cleaned again. She knelt beside Owl, took the garments from him, and began the task without looking again at her brother.

Cries for War snorted contemptuously and said to the guard, "Watch him closely," then turned and walked away. Owl knew that Cries for War had wanted to goad him into a fight so that he could kill him. Owl would not give him that satisfaction.

"It is hard for me to say it," Sacred Paint said, her voice a half whisper, "but my brother is not a good man."

"He is what he is," Owl said.

"I wish I could leave this village."

Owl felt a tiny thrill go through him, a shiver of anticipation. When the time came to escape, he vowed he would take Sacred Paint with him if she wished to go.

And he knew in his heart that she would.

Chapter Forty-seven

The snows came, just as everyone had predicted they would, and for a time the town of the Pawnee band was a quiet, peaceful place. The people spent much time in their lodges. Many long, dark nights were passed in lovemaking while the wind howled down from the north. As always, many babies would be born in late summer.

Owl was sent to live in the lodge shared by Max and Otto. "Cries for War does not want me in the lodge of his parents when there is no work for me to do," he explained to them.

Otto said, "You mean he does not want you near Sacred Paint."

"Sacred Paint has come to be my—friend," Owl admitted grudgingly.

"Despite the fact that she is Pawnee?" Max asked. He knew of the old enmity between the Horned Heads and the Crane band. Owl had shown him the story skins and told him the tale of how Storm Seeker had slain the mighty Pawnee warrior Fallen Tree. Max had read the story for himself on the document written in French by Owl's great-great-grandfather Black Robe. He was thankful the story skins had not been destroyed by the Pawnee.

Owl shrugged now in answer to Max's question. "This time among them has taught me that the Pawnee are people, too—at least some of them."

"I'm not sure about Cries for War," Otto said. "*He* may not be human."

A few days later the three men were sitting around the fire in the center of the lodge, smoking a pipe. Max, admiring the beautifully carved wooden pipestem, suddenly looked at Owl. "What about your quest to fulfill your vision? Will you ever complete it?"

"Only the Creator knows," Owl said solemnly. "This has troubled me much since the Pawnee took us prisoner. But our captivity must have been the will of Wakon-tah, or it would not have happened. We came near the land of my ancestors when the Pawnee were bringing us here. I think we were within a day's walk of the place. If we had followed the river all the time, instead of cutting across country to save time, we would have seen what was left of the town of the Crane band." He tilted his head. "I am made to think it was never my destiny to return to the land of my people."

Otto took the pipe from Max. "Perhaps someday you will, my friend. Perhaps someday."

Finally the sun shone again with genuine warmth in its touch, and the wind came lightly from the south rather than ripping down from the north like a ravenous wolf. The snow was melting, and everywhere on the prairie were puddles and rivulets. The ice that had covered the Nibthaska-ke cracked with sounds like rifle shots and broke up, carried downstream in large chunks. Green shoots of new grass pushed their way up through the muddy earth. Spring had arrived.

And it was time for Brother Owl to be going.

He could feel it in his bones. As he had predicted, after another season of holding him as captive and slave, the Pawnee paid little attention to him now. Even Cries for War ignored him most of the time.

Owl worked in the garden plots with the women, preparing the ground for the spring planting. Often he was not guarded, although there were men nearby who would give chase if he tried to flee. The task gave him a chance to speak with Sacred Paint again, and for that he was grateful. They talked together in low voices, ignoring the dark looks cast in their direction by her mother, Trembling Leaf.

"I missed you during the cold moons," Sacred Paint said. "I wished I could see you and talk with you."

"And I wished I could see you," Owl said. "There was much that could have been spoken between us."

"It still can."

"The nights were very cold."

"They were cold for me, as well."

Owl took a deep breath. "I am going to leave this place."

He watched for a look of surprise or fear or anger on her face. Instead he saw only calm acceptance. She said, "I would go with you, if you would have me."

It was all Owl could do not to drop his stone hoe and pull her into his arms. He wanted to laugh aloud and swing her around so that her feet came up off the ground. He wanted to share his sleeping robes with her and make her truly his.

He could do none of those things here among so many of her people, of course. All he could do was say in a tightly controlled voice, "It is good. We will leave together."

"We must be careful. Cries for War would try to stop us if he knew."

"He must not know." Owl's words were emphatic. He did not want to have to fight Cries for War. It was not that he feared the subchief—he would gladly have slain the man, given the chance—but he did not want anything to keep him and Sacred Paint from leaving this place.

He would return to the land of his people, and she would go with him.

"When the band is preparing for the spring buffalo hunt," Owl said quietly, "that is when we will go."

The days passed more slowly than ever before in his life, although Owl would not have thought that possible. The nights were still chilly, but the last of the truly cold weather was gone. Green shoots grew in the gardens, and the thoughts of the people turned toward fresh meat. The time for the buffalo hunt was upon them.

The spring and autumn hunts were the biggest events in the lives of the band, and the whole town was caught up in the preparations, as Owl had hoped.

Max Adolphus was in the midst of it, as he had been the previous autumn, eagerly covering hide after hide with his artwork. He and Prince Otto had endured the confinement of winter by observing the Pawnee way of life. Max was particularly taken with the women's crafts and spent hours watching them sew dyed porcupine quills and tiny shells acquired from traveling traders in elaborate patterns on garments and robes and pouches. He would have many stories to tell his friends in the salons of Vienna, he thought, stories of "heathen" arts they would find hard to believe.

But now Max and Otto were as eager for winter's end and the spring buffalo hunt as the Pawnees. One evening in the lodge, Prince Otto said, "I know now what a terrible thing Captain Standard did by ordering the slaughter of those beasts we encountered last year. Without the buffalo, these people simply cannot live."

Owl stared into the fire and said nothing, but his mind went back to his vision. Not for the first time he thought that perhaps its true message had been that the way of life of his people would vanish along with the buffalo. It seemed impossible that anyone could ever wipe out the great herds, even the white invaders with their powerful thunder-lances, but if that day ever did come to pass, the people of the prairie were doomed. It was a sad thought, but an inescapable one.

The flap over the entrance to the lodge was pushed aside, and Sacred Paint peered in. Owl came to his feet. "What are you doing here?" he asked.

"I must speak quickly," she said, but then paused and glanced at Max and Otto.

The prince caught on immediately and stood. "Come along, Max," he said heartily. "I feel like taking a walk around the town and getting a breath of this wonderful spring air."

"Of course," Max murmured. He followed Otto, and Sacred Paint moved aside so that they could step out of the lodge.

She dropped the hide flap behind her and stepped into Owl's arms. The embrace surprised him, but he returned it eagerly, enjoying the soft warmth of her body pressed against his. He felt desire quickening in his loins.

"Tomorrow night," she whispered. "Can we leave then?"

"I think it will be good. The next day the hunt begins. That is all anyone will think about."

"I will come to you in the night."

"I will be ready."

A part of him felt as if he should be making these plans rather than simply agreeing to Sacred Paint's proposal. But he had already come to the same conclusion himself, that there would be no better time for their escape.

"I must go now." She slipped out of his arms, and he felt a sense of loss.

But soon she would be with him again, he told himself as she ducked out of the lodge and disappeared into the night, and after that they would never be separated again.

Otto and Max returned a few minutes later. The prince smiled fondly at Owl and said, "You have the look of a man in love, my young friend."

"What are you and Sacred Paint going to do, Owl?" Max asked.

"Do not ask me," Owl said. "I cannot reply."

Max put a hand on Owl's shoulder. "The prince and I don't know a thing. Do we, Otto?"

"Not a thing, lad, not a single blessed thing." One of Otto's eyelids drooped in a gesture Owl now recognized as a wink. "But what we don't know makes me very glad indeed, and I wish you all the luck in the world!"

Owl swallowed. They were good friends, and it would not be easy to leave them. But his destiny, and a life with Sacred Paint, awaited him. There would be no turning back.

"Strange the things that come to pass in this world," he said quietly. "I am of the Crane band, yet the woman I love is Pawnee. I am red, and my best friends are white."

"All the same under the skin, my boy," Otto said. "Perhaps one day when this is all over, far from here, we may all meet again. And if we do, we shall still be friends."

"I hope so," Owl murmured.

But deep inside him was a sliver of doubt, as cold as the snow that fell in the Moon of the Black Bear.

The next day seemed a year long to Owl. Early that morning Trembling Leaf ordered him to help the women pack for the buffalo hunt. Owl followed her commands, even though he was nervous about being around Sacred Paint. He feared that if he looked at her, the others could read on his face what they had planned, so he kept his eyes averted. He noticed that she was doing likewise, perhaps motivated by the same fear.

Soon they would never have to fear again, he told himself. Soon they would be together.

Night finally came. The men gathered to smoke the sacred pipe and pray to the spirits for a successful hunt while the women tended to the children. Owl returned to his lodge with Max and Otto. The prince was honing the head of a lance that Cloud Shadow had given him. He had been denied the opportunity to participate in last autumn's hunt because the Pawnees did not trust him. By now, though, they almost regarded him as one of the band and were willing to let him take part.

"If you would like, Owl, I will give you this lance," Otto offered quietly. "You may need it more than I will."

Owl declined without hesitation. "If Cries for War found out that you gave me the lance, he might kill you despite his father's fondness for you. If I need a weapon, I will find it elsewhere."

"You may well be correct, my friend. I appreciate your concern."

"As I do yours."

Keeping his voice low, Max asked, "When are you leaving?"

"When Sacred Paint comes for me. She will wait for a time when her mother is most occupied."

"We are going to miss you, Owl."

"And I will miss you. You have been good friends to me."

"What do you think the Pawnee will do with us?" Otto asked. "Are we destined to spend the rest of our lives with them?"

"I cannot say. You began as captives, but now the Pawnee think of you more as visitors. If you ask them to take you back to the white men, they might do it. They could take you to within a day's walk of the Fiery Prairie Fort and leave you there."

"Perhaps after the hunt," Otto said.

The entrance flap moved aside, and Sacred Paint whispered Owl's name. He uncoiled lithely from his cross-legged position and, when she stepped into the lodge, embraced her, then turned to Max and Otto.

"I must go, my friends," he said. "May the Creator protect you and guide your steps."

The two men rose, and he clasped wrists with each of them. Max and Otto looked solemn. "Good luck and Godspeed, my boy," Otto said.

"If I ever get back to Vienna with my paintings, you will be famous, Owl," Max said. "The portrait of you is the best I have ever painted."

"You deserve the fame, not I," Owl told him.

"We must go quickly," Sacred Paint urged.

With a last look at his friends, Owl took hold of her arm, and they slipped out of the lodge. They circled it and walked toward the edge of the town, moving at a normal pace so as not to draw attention to themselves. The night was clear, with an abundance of stars shining overhead, but the moon had not yet risen. Owl wanted to be well away from the village before it did.

A dog barked as they passed a lodge, but there was nothing unusual in that. Owl leaned closer to Sacred Paint and asked, "Do you have any weapons?"

"Only a small knife. That was all I could take without arousing suspicion."

They were almost at the edge of the village when a man carrying a lance stepped out of the lodge just ahead of them. There were no fires nearby, and Owl hoped he would pass them in the darkness without realizing who they were. He walked close beside Sacred Paint. With any luck the man would think they were on their way to one of the other lodges to make love.

Just as they were about to pass the man, he stopped and grunted in surprise. "I know you," he said to Owl. "You are the slave of Cries for War! What are you doing here?"

"Cries for War sent me to get him something for the hunt tomorrow." Owl did not care if the man believed him or not; he was simply using conversation to get close enough to slam his fist into the man's jaw. Then Owl lowered his shoulder and rammed it into the chest of the startled warrior. The impact spilled both of them off their feet, with Owl on top, his left hand closed around the man's throat to stifle any outcry. With his right fist he struck again and again, driving it into the man's face until his body went limp.

Sacred Paint touched Owl's shoulder anxiously. "Are you all right?"

"I am unharmed," he told her.

"Did you . . . kill him?"

"He only sleeps." Owl took the war club and knife tucked behind the man's belt and picked up the lance he had been carrying. The smooth wooden shaft felt good against his palm. He came to his feet, caught hold of Sacred Paint's hand, and said, "Come. We must hurry now, before he wakes."

They were close enough to the edge of the town to break into a run. No outcries rose behind them. Even the barking of the dogs died away. Within moments the lodges were behind them and they were running over the open plain.

Owl's fingers tightened on Sacred Paint's hand. He was a slave no more, he was armed for trouble if it came, and the woman he loved was beside him.

The spirits of his ancestors were surely smiling down upon him.

Chapter Forty-eight

Max Adolphus had never seen Cries for War so angry. When he found out not only that Owl was gone but that Sacred Paint had fled with him, he had been ready to kill both Max and Prince Otto. Only his father's stern intervention had prevented bloodshed—so far.

"These men cannot be blamed for what your slave did," Cloud Shadow said. They stood in front of the chief's lodge, where Cries for War and some of the other warriors had dragged Max and Otto. Max's heart was pounding wildly in his chest. He and the prince had been close to death, he realized, and might still be.

"They must have known what the slave was planning!" Cries for War said. "They knew he meant to steal my sister and run away!"

"I have seen the way Sacred Paint looked at the one called Brother Owl," Cloud Shadow said. "He did not have to steal her. She would have gone willingly with him."

Trembling Leaf stepped up beside her husband. "You must send every warrior in the band after them. You will find them and kill the slave and bring my daughter back to me." Her tone made it clear that she would accept no argument.

Cloud Shadow gave her one anyway. "It is the time of the buffalo hunt," he said heavily. "It is more important that the people have meat. The hunt will go on."

"I will have vengeance!" Cries for War shouted. Trembling Leaf opened her mouth to protest, too, but Cloud Shadow silenced them both with an upraised hand.

"You may take three warriors and follow the slave," he said to Cries for War. "The rest of us will leave tomorrow morning on the buffalo hunt, as we have planned." The chief indicated Max and Otto with the flat of his hand. "These men will not be harmed. They have nothing to do with this."

Cries for War looked as if he was about to be stricken with apoplexy, but there was nothing he could do. His father's decision was final. He took a deep breath and said, "When the slave is in my hands again, he will be a long time dying."

Max and Otto glanced at each other. They remembered all too well how Captain Standard and the Osage scouts had been tortured to death. They prayed that Brother Owl was already far from the town of the Pawnees—and getting farther away with each passing moment.

Sacred Paint ran well, but she tired before Owl did. Several times during the night they were forced to stop so that she could rest. Each delay chafed at Owl; he would have preferred to be putting more ground between them and the inevitable pursuit led by Cries for War. He was certain Cries for War would come after them, even if it meant defying Cloud Shadow.

By morning Owl reckoned they were quite a distance southeast of the Pawnee town. They had followed the river, since Owl did not know this country well enough to risk taking shortcuts in the dark. As the sun rose and they stopped for another short rest, he looked behind them, straining his eyes for any sign of pursuit. There was none. But somewhere back there, Cries for War was coming after them. Owl could feel his presence, could sense his thirst for vengeance.

Sacred Paint had brought a parfleche containing some jerked meat and pemmican. They ate sparingly, drank from the river, then moved on, Owl setting the pace in a ground-eating trot. As the day passed he veered away from the river several times, only to come back to it later. Every time they found a stretch of rocky ground, he led Paint over it, hoping the absence of tracks would throw off the pursuers from their trail. At one place, where a rocky ledge ran all the way down to the water's edge, they waded across the broad, shallow stream. Owl turned due south from that point. He knew he had to do something unexpected. Cries for War would follow them on horseback, and they could not hope to outdistance him on foot. They would have to elude him through trickery.

The rest of that day they made their way south, stopping only for a short time when night fell. Then they moved on, Owl guiding them by the stars, until much of the night had passed. Sacred Paint reeled from exhaustion, so Owl finally called a halt and let her curl up to sleep in a hollow he tramped down in the tall grass. He dozed sitting up so that he would remain alert.

When the sun rose, they loped toward it. Owl knew that they would eventually come to the river again by going in this direction. When they did, they would follow it at a distance, he decided, since they would be less likely to encounter Cries for War that way. He hoped, though, that by now Cries for War had completely lost their trail.

Late that afternoon they spotted the line of vegetation in the distance that marked the course of the Platte. They turned again, keeping the river barely visible to their left. Other than buffalo, prairie dogs, and birds, they seemed to have the plains to themselves.

When night fell, they went to the river, slaked their thirst, and moved on, staying close to the water. Owl was fairly certain Cries for War would not try to track them at night. In fact, he was beginning to feel somewhat safe at last. If they could avoid being found for another few days, it was unlikely the pursuers would ever catch up to them.

Again they traveled much of the night, then stopped to sleep. This time Owl found a small tree against which he could lean, and slumber claimed him quickly.

He awoke to Sacred Paint's touch, and when he opened his eyes, he saw that the sky was gray with the approach of dawn. She had moved beside him and rested her head on his shoulder. Both of them were cold, so he slipped his arm around her. As she snuggled against him he felt himself growing aroused.

"You are my woman," he whispered, and she nodded.

"Would you take me?" she asked.

"Here? We have no robes, no lodge."

"We have the soft grass below and the sky above. We have each other. We need nothing else."

She was right. The desire they felt for each other would no longer be denied. They made love there beside the river with dawn breaking to the east, and it was everything Owl had hoped it would be and more. As he stiffened and spilled his seed into her, he was overcome with love. The tight clutch of her arms and the little sobs that came from her throat told him she felt the same way.

Despite the languor that threatened to overwhelm both of them, they forced themselves to dress, eat a small portion of their rations, drink from the river, and keep moving. Owl's worry of being caught had eased somewhat, but he was not ready to declare that they were safe.

After two more days and nights with no sign of pursuers, Owl decided that Cries for War must have abandoned the chase. He turned and for several moments concentrated intently on the way behind them. Though he put no great stock in the idea of magical powers, he knew that he had been able to sense Cries for War before, during the first days of their flight. Now he felt nothing behind them. They were alone.

He took Sacred Paint's hand and smiled at her. Hope lit up her eyes, and she said, "Are we safe now?"

"I believe so. But we must keep moving, and we must be alert. I would not risk our lives on a hope that might turn out to be empty."

They held each other for a few moments before resuming their trek.

Owl lost track of the days. When they had run out of food, they lived on the small game he killed with the lance and caught in snares. Always there was water from the river. The sun grew warmer each day. It was the middle of spring when they finally reached a spot just upstream from a sharp bend in the river. Owl stopped in his tracks and looked across the water at the long, open area beside the Nibthaska-ke. He heard a pounding in his head and thought at first it was the beating of his heart.

But then he realized it was drumming, and in the next moment he heard voices lifted in a chanting song. "Do you hear that?" he asked Sacred Paint.

"Hear what?" she asked with a puzzled frown. "I hear nothing except the sound of the river and the song of birds in those cottonwood trees."

Owl shook his head. The drumming and chanting grew louder

and louder in his ears. It must be a vision of some kind, he realized, because there was nowhere it could be coming from. There was no town across the river. No one lived here to beat the drums and sing the ancient songs.

"This is the place," he said in a hushed voice as the sounds gradually died away. "This is where the town of the Crane band stood. I . . . have come home."

He plunged into the water and waded out into the river, then swam toward the far shore. Sacred Paint followed, worriedly calling his name.

He reached the bank and looked for any sign that his ancestors had lived here once. Their lodges, long since abandoned after the sickness that had ravaged the town, would have collapsed and gone back to the earth by now. Owl searched for mounds that might mark where lodges had been. As his eyes combed the ground he spotted something half-buried in the dirt. Falling to his knees, he dug with his fingers until he brought up what was left of a flint knife. There was no way of knowing how long it had been there: many, many summers, surely, more than he could ever count. He held it tightly in his hand. This knife might have belonged to Storm Seeker or Fire Maker or Black Snake or Cedar That Does Not Bend or any of the other legendary figures from the story skins that told of his people. This bit of flint, worn and weathered by the ages, was a direct link to all who had come before him. He was shaken by the power of the emotions coursing through him.

Then he became aware that Sacred Paint was speaking to him. "Owl," she said nervously, "what is that sound?"

He raised his head. What he heard this time was no mystical chant, no drumming by ghostly hands. It was the squawking of birds and the flapping of wings. The sound grew louder, and Sacred Paint hurried to his side in fright. They lifted their eyes and saw the birds, darkening the sky against the sun—more than ten times the ten fingers of his hands, perhaps as many as the boundless herds of buffalo. They swept up from the south, graceful long-necked birds, their wingspan the height of a man, their feathers white and gray and silver, shining in the sun. One by one they settled in the trees along the banks of the river and on the sandbars in the middle.

Overwhelmed by the sheer numbers of them, Sacred Paint cried out in fear, and some of the birds, startled by the sound, soared back up into the air. Owl stood up and drew her into his arms. He looked around in amazement. The birds all had a small patch of red just above their beaks, between the eyes. He had seen them before, bound for the northern lands, following the springtime as it advanced. They were a bit late this year . . . or perhaps they had waited so that they could meet him here, in this place on this day.

"They are cranes," he said to Sacred Paint in a trembling voice. "They come here every year. They gave my people their name." He had to swallow before he could go on. "They are . . . my brothers."

His voice rose on the last words, and the sandhill cranes cried out as if answering him. With a beating of wings that rolled like thunder over the earth, they rose into the air once more. Owl and Sacred Paint stood together, caught in the shower of sights and sounds. Owl hardly dared breathe as he watched the cranes flying higher and higher, the instincts given to them by the Creator making them turn northward again after this brief stop. Owl's gaze never left them until they had vanished in the distance.

"It is over," he said.

Sacred Paint looked at him, puzzled. "I do not understand."

"We will make our home elsewhere. The Omaha, the Ponca, the Iowa—all have towns within a few days' walk from here. The days of the Crane band have passed. I am the last of the people. The cranes and I—we have said farewell to each other."

Sacred Paint took his hand in hers. "Wherever we go, you and I, we shall be our own people. A new people."

He embraced her. The shard of flint knife fell from his hand, but he did not pick it up. The earth would reclaim the knife and perhaps one day give it up again. The fingers of another young man might grasp it and hold it high above his head, but that young man would never know what it truly meant. By then the Crane band would not even be a memory.

Owl walked along the river with his woman and did not look back.

Chapter Forty-nine

Max was glad that Cries for War had not come along on this journey. The man hated him and Otto and would gladly have seized any excuse to kill them. That was why Cloud Shadow had ordered his son to remain in the town of the Pawnee while the two white men were taken back to Fort Osage.

When the Pawnees had returned to their town after the buffalo hunt, Cloud Shadow had decreed that Max and Otto would be returned to their own people. A few members of the council had objected, Cries for War most strenuously of all, but Cloud Shadow had won them over, with the exception of his son.

Max had presented many members of the band with sketches and paintings he had done of them. He would take back the oils he had done on canvas before being captured, along with the sketchbooks he had filled, but he planned to leave behind much of the work he had done while a captive—or guest, depending on how one looked at it. His canvases, which he had gone to great lengths to protect during his sojourn with the Indians, were lashed onto a travois pulled by the horse Cloud Shadow had given him. The chief had shown uncommon generosity to Max and the prince by giving them each a mount rather than making them walk back to the fort. "We will steal them back from the white men later, after you have returned to your homeland," Cloud Shadow had said confidently.

Now Max and Otto sat on their horses at the top of a small hill and said their farewells to Cloud Shadow and the warriors who had brought them this far. "I wish you did not have to go, my friends," the chief said to them. "But I grow old, and someday Cries for War will be the chief of this band. If you were still among us when that day came, he would kill you. You remind him too much of his defeat."

A defeat was exactly what Cries for War considered Owl's

successful escape. For many days he and three other warriors had searched along both sides of the Nibthaska-ke, but though they had found tracks belonging to the fugitives, they had never seen the fugitives themselves. The trail seemed to vanish at will, and finally the men with him had persuaded Cries for War to give up and return to the town. A bitter rage had filled the war chief, and he had sworn that one day he would have vengeance on Brother Owl, no matter how long it took.

In the distance Max could see Fort Osage on the bluff overlooking the Missouri River. In less than an hour he and Otto would be back among their own kind.

That prospect excited Max, but mixed with the anticipation was an unexpected melancholy. Cloud Shadow and a few others had become his friends, and he knew he would never see them again.

"We will wait here until you have had time to reach the fort," the chief said solemnly. "I do not think my son will disobey me, but our presence here will make sure that does not happen."

"Thank you, Cloud Shadow." Prince Otto was dressed in buckskins and had a Pawnee robe over his shoulder. Despite his clothing, his long fair hair would identify him as white. Neither he nor Max wanted some nervous recruit standing guard inside the fort to fire on them. Max was wearing the same tattered clothes he had been in when he was captured.

Cloud Shadow lifted a hand, palm outward. "Farewell, my friends," he said.

"Good-bye, Chief," Max said. "I shall never forget you and your people."

Otto said, "Farewell, Cloud Shadow. May you have many horses and many grandchildren. May the Pawnee always be strong and favored by the Great Spirit of the Prairie."

"Go in peace, my friend."

Max and Otto urged their horses into a walk, looking back as the Pawnee fell behind them. Cloud Shadow's hand rose again, and they returned the gesture. Max asked quietly, "Will you ever come back here, Your Excellency?"

"I don't know, Max. And even if I do, they probably will not be here. I fear their time draws to an end already, although they will struggle mightily to keep it from going." Otto sighed. "What about you?"

"I will be back," Max said without hesitation. Despite the sadness that gripped him, he had to smile as he gestured at the landscape around them. "There is more to see, more to paint. If there is any way to do it, I will be back."

"I think you will find a way." Otto chuckled. "In fact, I am sure of it."

They rode on to the fort, and as they approached they could hear the excitement behind the stockade walls. The lookouts had surely seen them coming, and a surprising welcome awaited them: the barrels of at least four rifles leveled in their direction over the tops of the pickets.

Otto drew rein and shouted, "Hello, the fort! I am Prince Otto Wilhelm of Saxe-Coburg! This man with me is Maximilian Adolphus! We come in peace! May we enter?"

Max had brought his mount to a halt beside Otto's, and the ludicrous thought suddenly struck him that after surviving the attack by the Pawnees and a long captivity in the wilderness, they might be shot down now that they were finally back on the threshold of civilization. Why anyone would think they presented a threat he did not know, but the irony of the situation was inescapable.

Then the gates swung open, and several men rode out. The man in the lead, wearing the blue coat, peaked cap, and epaulets of an officer, was fairly young, and unfamiliar to both Max and Otto. He brought his horse to a stop and saluted them. "Lieutenant John Brownson, sir," he said to Otto, "at your service." Then, his military discipline slipping a little, he added, "Are you really Prince Otto?"

"Yes, Lieutenant. Where is Captain Clemson?" The other men with Brownson were also young army officers. There was no sign of the captain.

"He's on furlough, sir. I'm the acting officer in command here at Fort Osage." Brownson looked at Max. "You're the artist?"

"Yes. Maximilian Adolphus."

"I heard about the Pawnee attack on your party, though I wasn't here at the time. We all thought you were dead."

Otto frowned. "How did you hear about the attack? There were no survivors except for the few taken prisoner."

"Oh, no, sir," Brownson said. "Mr. Dupree, the fur trader, got back safely. He was mighty footsore, but he was alive, all right."

Max and Otto looked at each other in surprise. They had both assumed Dupree was killed in the battle. "Where is Dupree now?" Otto asked.

"Gone back to St. Louis to try to explain things to the Columbia-American Fur Trading Company." Brownson grinned sheepishly. "I don't imagine he had much luck." More solemnly, he went on, "What about Captain Standard? Dupree didn't know what had become of him."

His expression grim, Otto said, "Captain Standard was killed in the line of duty, Lieutenant. He died bravely, fighting the enemy."

That shading of the truth was more compassion than Standard deserved, Max thought. But it would serve no purpose to reveal that Standard had actually died shrieking and begging for his life.

Brownson said, "Well, this is simply amazing, gentlemen. As I said, we'd given you up for dead. Come into the fort and we'll give you the most comfortable quarters we have. You'll have to tell us all about what happened to you since last summer. Almost a year with the Pawnee . . . *amazing*," the lieutenant said again.

There was nothing amazing about it, Max thought, except their luck. Both of them could easily have died at almost any time during their journey.

But then, a man could get run over by a beer wagon crossing the street in Vienna, he reminded himself. Danger could be found anywhere. And so could beauty and nobility. That was one of the lessons the American West had taught Maximilian Adolphus.

Chapter Fifty

Few things made a man feel more content, Brother Owl thought, than the sight of his wife nursing their child at her breast. Sacred Paint was truly beautiful sitting in the firelight on thick buffalo robes and holding Little Black Bear. The infant suckled greedily; Owl was proud of his appetite. Little Black Bear had been born six moons earlier, in the Moon of the Black Bear, which had given him his name. The white men called it— Owl had to stop and think—December, that was it.

This was the second summer since he and Sacred Paint had escaped from the Pawnee town far to the west. For a time Paint had seemed barren, and it had appeared that they would have no children. But then her belly had swollen with Little Black Bear, and now Owl was a happy father. The child completed the life they had made for themselves here in the small Omaha-Ponca town a short distance from the Platte.

From the first, Owl had been accepted as a holy man by the people here, who numbered approximately fifty. His visit to the ancestral homeland of the Crane band had fulfilled the quest his vision had offered him, and he understood that its purpose had been his farewell to the past. With that behind him, he had been able to look to the future. The Omahas and Poncas had needed spiritual guidance, and Owl had provided it. Now, in a lodge near the one in which he and his family lived, a Sacred Pole stood. The almost forgotten rituals that revolved around it had been revived, symbolizing the unity of the tribe and the spiritual authority of the Creator.

He turned his attention from his wife and child back to the piece of buffalo hide in his lap. With a hair brush he painted on the hide, adding to the story skins he still faithfully kept. Sacred Paint and the others of the town regarded this activity as rather odd. Though rich in oral tradition and storytelling ability, the people did not keep written records. The story skins of the Crane band were the only such documents that Owl was aware of. And, of course, the story skins of old Black Robe, written in the language called French, were unique also.

Perhaps Little Black Bear would one day apprentice as a medicine man, and Owl could pass this legacy on to him. Owl fervently hoped so. The story skins would always need a faithful keeper.

The infant had finished nursing and had fallen asleep at Sacred Paint's breast. She laid him carefully on a robe and draped it over him. He made a noise of contentment in his sleep. Sacred Paint joined Owl at the fire and said, "Our son sleeps."

Laying the story skins aside, Owl took her left hand in both of his. Solemnly he said, "He sleeps very well. Already he has mastered a talent, and this is only his first summer."

Sacred Paint laughed, a sound that Owl never tired of hearing. She lifted her arms and twined them around his neck, and the two of them fell back into the sleeping robes.

The night passed very pleasantly.

The next day, Owl was walking near the lodge of Many Otters, the peace chief of the town, when he heard people talking loudly and excitedly. Owl sought the source of the disturbance and found nearly half the town's population gathered around Gray Sky and Wind from the East, two young men several summers younger than Owl. Sky and Wind . . . they were as inseparable as their names.

Many Otters stood before them. "You are certain about what you claim to have seen?"

"It is not a claim," Sky said. "We saw the white men."

"We are sure," Wind added.

"But they did not see us."

Many Otters nodded. "That is good. What were they doing?"

"They rode their horses along the river. Coming this way."

"How many?"

Sky declared, "Three times the fingers of my hands."

Owl felt a surge of mingled excitement and apprehension at the mere mention of white men in the area. He had not seen any whites since his farewell to Max and Otto at the town of the

Pawnee. White men were most unpredictable creatures. Some might be like Max and Otto, good friends for life, but others were like Captain Standard: greedy and ruthless in their quest for whatever they wanted.

Moving closer to the gathering, Owl asked, "These white men you saw—did they wear buckskins, like us, or blue coats?"

Wind said without hesitation, "They were not like us."

"They were soldiers," Sky said. "They wore the blue coats and carried the thunder-lances we have always heard about."

Owl said, "The weapons are called muskets or flintlocks."

Many Otters turned to him. "You have dealt with white men. Should we fear them as demons?"

"I have never dealt with these. But some I have known were indeed to be feared."

"There is something else," Sky said. "The whites were not alone. Others rode with them."

Many Otters faced the young man. "What do you mean, others?"

"They had scouts with them," Wind replied.

"Pawnee scouts," Sky added.

Owl stiffened. "Horned Heads rode with them?"

The young men nodded, and Wind held up both hands. "This many."

"I have heard of such things," Many Otters said. "Osages have ridden for the white soldiers as scouts, but now others are doing this as well."

Owl frowned in disbelief. It was hard to credit what Sky and Wind had told them. True, the Pawnee had seldom warred with the white men. The attack on Prince Otto's party had been a rare exception and probably would never have occurred had Captain Standard not ordered his men to open fire at long range during the first encounter. Now that he knew more of their ways, Owl felt sure that the warriors led by Cries for War would have charged the wagons of the white men, then circled around and left in peace after the show of force.

The Pawnee had always been such rapacious marauders of the other bands living on the prairie, however, that Owl could hardly imagine them allied with anyone, even white soldiers. Yet Gray

Sky and Wind from the East were known to be truthful men. The Pawnees, with their distinctive roaches, were hard to mistake.

"If the whites and the Pawnee continue in this direction, they will be here late this afternoon," Sky added.

"We must speak in council," Many Otters declared. "We must decide what to do about this matter." He turned to Owl. "You will anoint the Sacred Pole and pray for the Creator to give us wisdom."

Word of the council spread quickly through the town. Due to the urgency of the gathering, dried meat would be used instead of fresh for the ritual meal that preceded the anointing of the Sacred Pole with buffalo fat.

Owl returned to his lodge to fetch his buffalo robe and tell Sacred Paint what had happened.

"There are Pawnee with the white men? My people?" She seemed as surprised as Owl had been.

"They were your people once but no more. Now we are members of this Omaha-Ponca band."

She bent her head and murmured, "Of course."

Owl understood her reaction. A part of her was still Pawnee, just as a part of him still belonged to the Crane band. Most of the time they kept the old allegiances deeply buried, but sometimes, as now, they rose again, unbidden.

"I go now to anoint the Sacred Pole and sit in council," he told her. "I will return when we reach a decision."

"Will there be trouble because of this?"

Owl considered for a moment, then said, "There is no reason for trouble. We are not at war with these white men."

"What of the Pawnee?"

Owl could only shake his head. "I do not know what they will do."

He embraced her and left, walking quickly to the lodge of the Sacred Pole. Inside, the members of the council, all wearing buffalo robes, were gathered around the revered relic.

The mood was solemn. Few words were spoken as the men ate the dried buffalo meat. Afterward they smoked a pipe, and the young son of a warrior chosen by lots brought them a piece of buffalo fat. As the keeper of the Sacred Pole, Owl took the fat and rubbed it along the smooth wood. He tossed what was left into the fire in the center of the lodge, then chanted a song of prayer and supplication.

When the ritual was completed, Many Otters said, "We have come here to talk of the white soldiers who ride toward our town. Who will speak first?"

"Brother Owl knows white men," one elder said. "He should tell us of his knowledge. Will these white men make war on us, Brother Owl?"

Owl stood, draping his robe over his left shoulder. "I can speak only of those with whom I traveled. Some were good, some were evil. Most of the soldiers were neither; their actions for good or ill depended on their leaders. I cannot say what these white intruders will do."

"If you spoke to them," Many Otters said, "would they tell you of their intentions?"

Owl considered the question. "It is possible."

One of the councilmen said, "Many Otters should choose men to meet the whites before they come to our town. To find out whether they mean to harm us."

"And Brother Owl should lead the party," another added. "He speaks the tongue of the whites, and he is a powerful medicine man. He will be able to tell if they speak the truth."

Owl inclined his head in acknowledgment of the compliment. He was not as certain as the speaker, however, that he could tell whether the white men spoke the truth. In his experience, determining that could be difficult.

"I will lead a party to meet them if that is the wish of this council," he said without hesitation. The people of the town had given him a home, had made him feel that he and his family belonged here. He owed them a debt, and he would pay it any way he could.

"Take as many warriors as you have fingers," Many Otters said. "The bluecoat soldiers and the Pawnees must know that we are a strong people. Ask them what they want of us. If they come in peace, we will greet them in peace." The chief's voice hardened. "If they come in war, we will meet them with death."

Owl prayed it would not come to that. From what Sky and Wind had said, he was certain the combined force of soldiers and scouts outnumbered the Omaha-Ponca warriors. They had the added advantage of being armed with rifles. He feared the people could not defend their town successfully if the soldiers attacked.

There was no time to lose. The council ended quickly, and Owl asked several men to go with him. All agreed readily, as did the handful of warriors he spoke to outside the lodge of the Sacred Pole.

When he returned to his lodge for his bow and quiver, Sacred Paint was waiting for him outside the dwelling, Little Black Bear in her arms. The boy smiled up at his father. With a feeling of love so strong it was painful, Owl tickled Little Black Bear's fat chin, then looked into the worried eyes of his wife.

"I am to lead a party that will meet the soldiers and find out why they are here," he told her.

"I will bring your weapons."

She went into the lodge and emerged a moment later no longer holding the baby. Instead she carried Owl's bow and a full quiver. She had spent many days working on the buckskin quiver, decorating it with fringes and porcupine quills as befitted a man of her husband's stature. She also gave him a spiked war club that he had fashioned from buffalo bone, stone, and sinew.

He took the weapons from her and gave her his robe. He pulled her into his arms for a moment, then strode quickly away. He did not look back, for he carried the images of Sacred Paint and Little Black Bear with him wherever he went, inside his mind and his heart.

The rest of the men were waiting for him. They mounted their horses and rode toward the river. When they reached it, they followed it to the east.

Owl judged they had been gone for about an hour, as he had learned the white men reckoned time, when they saw dust from riders coming toward them. If they could see the sign of the whites and the Pawnee, then the other party could see their sign as well. There would be no surprise meetings today.

The two groups gradually drew closer, and when they were about two bowshots apart, Owl lifted his hand in a signal for the men with him to stop. The other riders drew rein as well. Owl could clearly see the blue coats and peaked black caps of the soldiers. He also saw the tall roaches of the Pawnee scouts and knew that Sky and Wind had been correct.

He half turned on his horse and pointed toward two of the warriors with him. "You will come with me," he said. "The others will stay here. Perhaps the whites will do the same."

He and the two companions he had chosen rode forward slowly. As he had hoped, three riders broke off from the larger group and, moving at the same deliberate pace, came toward Owl. Two of them wore the garb of soldiers, and the decorations on their coats told Owl they were officers. The third man wore a broad-brimmed hat and a buckskin jacket. Owl had not noticed him until he separated himself from the others in the party. This third rider was neither a Pawnee nor a soldier. Owl peered intently at him.

He was not prepared for the shock of recognition that went through him as the smaller parties came together. He knew the man in the buckskin jacket. He remembered the angular planes of the face and the sandy, reddish hair.

"For the love of God!" Daniel Dupree exclaimed. " 'Tis Brother Owl himself!"

Chapter Fifty-one

"Dupree," Owl said after a moment, when he had absorbed the shock of seeing a man he had thought to be dead. "Why have you come here?"

"I could ask what you're doin' in these parts, too, laddie," Dupree said. "Last I saw you was durin' that fight at the wagons."

"When our party was attacked by the Pawnee—who are now riding with you."

Dupree shrugged. "Things change."

"Do you know this red savage, Mr. Dupree?" an officer asked.

Dupree raised a hand slightly, a gesture to Owl asking him not to lose his temper at the insult. "Brother Owl's no savage, Lieutenant. He's as civilized an Indian as I've ever run across out here."

"You compliment me less than you think, Dupree," Owl said. He had not forgotten the slaughter of the buffalo, when Dupree had conspired with Captain Standard. Still, Dupree had been a fellow journeyer, although certainly not a friend, of Prince Otto and Max Adolphus, and for that reason Owl was willing to allow him the benefit of the doubt—for now.

After a moment of awkward silence Dupree said, "I don't know if you remember or not, Owl, but I work for the Columbia-American Fur Trading Company. I'm on my way up the Platte with these gentlemen of the military to establish a trading post. I'm to be the factor."

"That was your mission when we met before."

"Aye, 'twas." For a second Dupree's mouth twisted bitterly. "That time was a failure. It's taken a while, but I've convinced the owners to give me another chance. Now the trade goods are comin' behind us. They'll be along in a couple of weeks."

The lieutenant said, "I'm not sure it's a good idea to reveal all our plans to these Indians, Mr. Dupree."

"Like I told you, we don't have to worry about Brother Owl here. He's from peaceful folk." Dupree looked at Owl. "The Crane band, or some such, wasn't it, lad?"

"Now I am of the Omaha-Ponca band," Owl replied coolly. "But they are peaceful people, too . . . so long as they are not threatened."

"We're not here to cause trouble, boy," the lieutenant snapped. "We just came to hunt buffalo."

Owl stiffened, and watching him, his companions did, too. "You will hunt the *buffalo*?"

Dupree started to protest, but the lieutenant continued, "Of course we will. That's the main reason Columbia-American wants to establish an outpost on the Platte. By autumn there should be several hundred hide hunters in these parts."

"I'm sure there won't be that many," Dupree added quickly.

Owl felt a hollow chill inside him. The vision—difficult to believe that only three summers had passed since then—was suddenly as fresh in his mind as if it had just occurred. White spirits . . . bluecoats with rifles . . . accompanied by the Horned Heads . . . all of them coming to wipe the buffalo herds from the face of the earth. Owl had thought his return to the ancestral homeland of the Crane band had fulfilled the vision. Now he saw that his journey had been worthless; the vision was coming to life after all.

"What is it, Owl?" Dupree asked. "You look as though you've seen a ghost. I guess seein' me after all this time—"

Owl could not explain, not to a man like Dupree who thought only of the strange thing called money.

There was nothing he could do, at least not now. The soldiers were too many. Even if all the warriors of the Omaha and Ponca faced them, the white invaders would still be too many and too deadly with their rifles. Owl's adopted people could not turn them back.

Yet the warriors would not allow the slaughter of the buffalo to go unchallenged. For a moment Owl closed his eyes, and what he saw was the prairie covered with blood. The day was coming soon.

But not this day. Not this day. There was time yet, and something might happen to change the plans of the white men. Bloodshed could be avoided for now.

"Are we going to have trouble with you, Indian?" the lieutenant spat.

Owl ignored him and looked instead at Dupree. "The town of the Omaha-Ponca is nearby. Will you leave us in peace?"

"All we want to do is head on up the Platte," Dupree said. "We're not lookin' for trouble."

"Nor are we," Owl said.

He was about to turn away, willing to leave it at that. He had already considered what would happen in the future. If the white soldiers and traders came in great numbers and hunted the buffalo, the buffalo would leave. It was as simple as that. This was good land; it had long been home to the people. But if they had to, they could follow the buffalo wherever they went.

A sudden, shrill war cry interrupted Owl's thoughts. He looked back quickly to see one of the Pawnee scouts charging at him on horseback, yipping loudly. In his hand was a lance decorated with feathers and strips of fur, and he flung it at Owl with all his strength.

Owl slid sideways on the back of his skittish mount, holding his war club with one hand and with the other gripping the horse's mane so that he would not fall off. The lance whipped through the air where he had been an instant earlier. From the corner of his eye he saw his companions nocking arrows and lifting their bows. Their target was the Pawnee who had attacked Owl.

"No!" Owl shouted. He pulled himself upright on the horse's back and stared at the man who had attacked him. The hate-filled eyes of Cries for War glared back at him.

The other warriors started forward, but Owl raised his arm to stop them. Soldiers were readying their rifles. The sense of impending violence was so thick that Owl could barely breathe. He called out, "This is not your fight!"

"Tell your men to hold their fire, Lieutenant!" Dupree said urgently.

The young officer's hand rested upon the butt of the pistol holstered at his waist. "I won't be attacked by savages without fighting back, Mr. Dupree."

"No one's attacked anybody except that hotheaded scout." Dupree wheeled his horse toward Cries for War, who had halted his mount about a bowshot away. "What in the bloody hell do you think you're doin'?" Dupree demanded.

Cries for War pointed straight at Owl, no doubt knowing full well that the gesture was considered an insult among the Prairie People. "He is a thief! He stole my sister from our town! I have sworn vengeance on him."

"I stole no one." Owl's chin lifted defiantly. "Sacred Paint went with me willingly when I escaped from your slavery. Now she is my wife and the mother of my child."

Cries for War let out another howl of outrage. "Lies!"

"It is the truth."

The lieutenant said, "We didn't come out here to get involved in squabbles between savages, Mr. Dupree. I'm thinking the easiest thing to do would be to just kill these Indians and have done with it."

"There'll be no killing today," Dupree snapped. "Your orders are to accommodate my wishes as much as possible, Lieutenant. I expect you to do just that. Owl, I want peace between our people. Why don't I come to your town and speak to your chief? We can work out a treaty."

Owl felt reluctant to be anywhere near Dupree—and even less willing to have Cries for War nearby. But Dupree seemed the most likely of the group to listen to reason. And Owl was determined to do everything he could to convince the white men of the iniquity of their plan to kill the buffalo. He knew the possibility was remote, but anything that might prevent the vision from becoming real, at least for now, was worth attempting.

"Come," he said to Dupree. "You will be welcome." He turned a cold stare toward Cries for War. "Not the soldiers, though, and not the Pawnee scouts."

"Absolutely impossible," the lieutenant snapped.

Dupree nudged his horse over next to Owl's. "Lieutenant, you may follow at a distance, but I don't want you or the scouts coming within a mile of the place I'm going to."

"But, sir, your safety—"

"I'll be safe enough. What about it, Brother Owl? Willing to guarantee that your people won't scalp me?"

"You have my word," Owl said.

He and Dupree, along with the other two warriors, rode away from the soldiers and Cries for War. It was still a shock to Owl that the Pawnee war chief was riding as a scout for the white men. As Dupree had said, much changed.

But as he listened to Cries for War shouting ugly threats after him, Owl knew that some things never did.

"Will you and the men who will come after you kill all of our buffalo?" Many Otters' solemn question hung in the air. The men of the council had gathered as soon as Owl had returned with the white man. Now Daniel Dupree sat across from Many Otters in the lodge. Owl translated the question.

"Of course not, Chief," Dupree replied. "There are too many buffalo for all to be killed. You know that. The buffalo are almost as plentiful as the grains of sand in the bed of the Missouri River. And at any rate, we'll not be hunting in these parts. The trading post will be quite a distance upriver."

Owl put the Scotsman's words into the tongue of the Omaha-Ponca people. Many Otters nodded and in his own language asked, "Does this man tell the truth?"

"He tells the truth as he knows it," Owl said. "He and the soldiers are going farther up the Nibthaska-ke toward the Shining Mountains. They mean us no harm."

"But the buffalo," Many Otters said. "They plan to kill the buffalo only for their hides. This is a bad thing."

"A very bad thing. The ways of the whites are different from our ways. They are ignorant. They know nothing of how the Creator put the buffalo on the earth to meet our needs."

"Can you tell them?"

"I can tell them," Owl said doubtfully, "but they will not listen."

"Tell this one now. He has to listen."

Owl saw that Dupree, although shaken, was eager to appease the council. Perhaps he would hear in his heart the words Owl was about to speak and carry their message to the others. Perhaps the words would, like ripples in a pool, spread to touch the hearts of men in the far reaches of the earth, and once those men saw the way of the buffalo and truly understood its interconnectedness to the people of the prairie, they would let the buffalo live.

Owl chose his words carefully as he spoke to Dupree. "The white man looks at the buffalo and sees a great creature with a large hide that he will trade for other things. He sees a way to become wealthy. Beyond that he sees nothing of value in the beast and leaves its skinned carcass for the birds and scavengers. This is so. I have seen it.

"When the Prairie People look at the buffalo, they also see its ample hide, which will provide them with warm sleeping robes and shelter and many more practical uses than the white men would have for it. But the Prairie People see beyond the skin of the buffalo. They see its abundant meat, which they will cook and dry to nourish them throughout the long Moon of Starvation when snow covers the ground and nothing grows. They see the sinew that they will make into lacings and bowstrings and snares. They see the brain, which will be used to tan the hide, and the horns, which they will make into arrow points and instruments for music. They see the bladder that they will make into waterskins, the hooves they will use for rattles, and the bones they will make into tools and ornaments and handles. When the Prairie People look upon the buffalo, they also see wealth—the wealth of a beast so generous with its life-giving parts, so abundant in its usefulness. The people know that the Great Spirit provided them with the buffalo to keep them alive. The people, in turn, have great reverence for this beast that offers itself up to give them life. The people know they cannot live without it."

Owl was silent for a moment. The firelight danced over the solemn faces of the men seated around him. Though they could not understand the English words he had spoken, they knew their meaning. If only this white trader seated among them could understand as well . . .

"Can you see the buffalo as we do, Daniel Dupree? Have you heard how the way of the buffalo and the way of the Prairie People are one?"

Dupree drew in a long breath and shifted his position. "Yes, I believe I do, Owl."

"Will you tell the others, so that they will know that killing the buffalo just for its hide is wrong?"

Dupree looked down at his clasped hands and blew out a sigh before he spoke. "I will do my best to make them understand. But, Owl, you must know that I hold little hope of changing their minds."

Owl wondered how a man could know the truth but have so little faith in its power. "If you do understand the importance of the buffalo as you say you do, you must find a way to also make them see it."

"These men have come from a great distance to hunt the buffalo for their hides. I doubt that anything I say will keep them from their purpose."

Owl saw concern on the faces of the others, caused by the tone of the conversation. The uneasy silence that followed was broken by the voice of Many Otters, who rose and said, "Do we let them go? Or do we fight?"

Dupree looked nervous, though he could not understand the chief's words.

After a moment of thought Owl said to Many Otters, "Now is not the time to fight. I will talk more to the white man. I will try again to make him understand."

Many Otters was still for a minute before he said, "It is good. We will fight when we must, but not before."

Owl turned to Dupree. "You and the soldiers may go on up the Platte. Our people will not hinder you."

"It's getting late," Dupree said, obviously relieved. "Do you think it would be all right if we were to camp near here tonight?"

Owl put the question to Many Otters, who agreed. "It would be best if the Pawnee Cries for War did not come near the town," Owl said to Dupree.

"Don't worry about him. I'll see that Lieutenant Keegan keeps him away from here."

Dupree started to stand up, but Owl stopped him by saying, "Perhaps it is good you will be staying for a short time. I would talk more with you, Dupree. About the buffalo."

Dupree looked uneasy. "The Columbia-American Fur Trading Company is responsible for deciding what to do. They give me my orders."

"What is ordered is not always right."

"Would you go against your chief, Owl? If Many Otters told you to do something, wouldn't you do it?"

Owl could not dispute that. "We will speak of this later." On impulse he added, "You will stay in my lodge tonight."

Dupree blinked in surprise, then said, "Well, I suppose I could do that. Just let me go back out to our camp for a bit and fetch some of my gear. I'll be back shortly."

Owl followed Dupree out of the chief's lodge. The sun had just set, and soon the shadows of dusk would be gathering. Owl could see the camp on the prairie north of the town. Cries for War was out there somewhere.

"How did Cries for War and the other Pawnee come to ride with you and the white soldiers?" he asked Dupree.

"I don't know for certain. They were at the fort when we were lookin' for scouts. I heard there was some sort of sickness that killed a lot of their people." Dupree shook his head. "A terrible thing, disease."

Terrible indeed, Owl thought, especially since most of the illnesses that now plagued the people of the prairie had been brought here by the European and American invaders. He sighed.

As he had thought long before, during his visit to Fort Osage, there was more than one way to destroy a people and their way of life.

The white men seemed to be intent on finding all of them.

Dupree heard the angry voice even before he rode into the camp. The Pawnees and several soldiers were gathered around someone. Dupree was not surprised that the speaker was Cries for War.

"His people kill children and molest young girls," Cries for War was saying. "They are evil! They rip out the hearts of their enemies and eat them raw!"

Dupree had never heard of any of the Plains Indians committing such atrocities, nor did he believe it of Owl's people. Though he had not learned much about Owl during the journey three years earlier, he knew that Prince Otto and that artist fellow, Maximilian Something-or-Other, had been fond of him. Dupree did not believe a pair of cultured European gentlemen would have extended their friendship to a bloody-handed savage such as Cries for War was describing.

Dupree swung down from his saddle and looked around for Lieutenant Keegan. Several of the Pawnee scouts were shouting agreement with Cries for War's ranting, and one shook a war club in the air. "I would count coup on these evil warriors!"

Dupree knew the concept of counting coup. A fur trapper who had lived with the Indians had explained it to him. To his dismay, some of the soldiers who had been listening joined in the shouting. "We ought to teach the red bastards a lesson!" cried a private named O'Malley, his face florid, his eyes blazing.

"My sister is still the captive of my blood enemy," Cries for War said. "I would go to the town and rescue her from him!"

"We are with you, brother!" one of the scouts shouted.

Dupree did not like the sound of this, did not like it at all. As he turned to find Keegan he almost bumped into the officer.

"Getting pretty stirred up, aren't they?" Keegan asked with a grin.

"You must stop them," Dupree said. "These Indians have promised me they don't want any trouble."

"And you'd take the word of an Injun?" Keegan's tone was contemptuous.

"I trust Brother Owl. I trust him enough to accept his invitation to spend the night in his lodge."

Keegan frowned. "You're going back there?"

"Aye, that I am. I want to hear more of what Owl has to say about the buffalo. We may stand to learn new ways of using the beasts."

"Well, you'd better keep your eyes open if you're going back there."

"What does *that* mean?" Dupree felt alarm course through his body.

"Just what I said. There's bad blood between those Indians and the ones with us. Not only that, but my boys have been itching for a fight. Every good commander knows you've got to give the men what they want every once in a while." Keegan snickered. "Nothing like a victory in battle to catch the attention of the War Department, too."

"My God," Dupree said, his voice hushed. "You're going to attack the village. You and Cries for War have already got it all worked out, haven't you?" Not yet certain of what he was going to do, Dupree started for his horse.

Keegan stopped him with an iron grip on his arm. "You're not going anywhere, Mr. Dupree. In my best military judgment, you need to stay here in camp with us tonight."

Dupree tried to pull away. "You cannot do this!"

"I can do any damn thing I please." Keegan's fist cracked across Dupree's jaw. Dupree's head jerked back as pain shot through him, followed by blackness.

A blackness as deep as the night that soon settled over the plains.

Chapter Fifty-Two

Something was wrong. Daniel Dupree had not returned. Had he changed his mind? Had he decided he did not want Owl to persuade him to change his plans? Had he secretly feared he would come to agree with Owl about not killing the buffalo?

Whatever the reason, Owl was disappointed. He and Dupree would never be friends, but Owl had hoped he was beginning to understand the significance of the buffalo to the Prairie People.

Little Black Bear was cranky and restless, which made Sacred Paint unhappy as well. When everyone went to their sleeping robes, the baby was still crying and fretful. Sacred Paint carried the child around and around the lodge, rocking him in her arms and singing softly to him. Owl could see the weariness on her face. When Little Black Bear finally dropped off to sleep, all Sacred Paint wanted to do was curl up in one of the robes and let slumber claim her.

Owl was not particularly sleepy, however, so he smoked a pipe and watched the fire die to gently glowing embers. It was far into the night before he slept.

His slumber was not restful. Often his ancestors had been visited by dreams; he had read about them in the story skins. Dreams frequently came to him, too, and tonight he was gripped by one that had him stirring and moaning softly in his sleep.

In the dream he lay on his back, looking up into a brilliant sun that blistered him with its heat. Beneath him was the rough surface of a huge rock slab. Although he was not tied down, he could not seem to move. Something held him there, some awesome mystical force. All he could do was twist his head to the side and squint against the terrible glare of the sun.

A soft sound, a scraping sound, caught his attention. He turned his head, straining against whatever held him down and hurting his neck as he did. He opened his eyes a slit and almost

353

cried out when he saw a snake slithering toward him over the hot rock. He tried to scream but could not make a sound. The scraping of scales on stone grew louder, and more snakes appeared, their bodies rippling toward him. Their black skins shone dully in the sun.

Owl expected the snakes to bite him. He tried again to yell at them to frighten them away, but he could not find his voice. Still they came, and when he twisted his head in the other direction, he saw more snakes on that side. He felt one slither onto his thighs, its dry scales rasping against his skin.

He realized he was naked, which only fed his terror. The serpents were all over him now, sliding across his sweat-slicked torso and up and down his arms and legs. One crawled over his throat.

He felt a snake slide between his legs and prod at his buttocks. Owl whimpered as it somehow penetrated the opening there. His head jerked up as he felt another coil around his manhood. To his horror, the creature thinned and elongated somehow and burrowed into the opening at the tip of his shaft.

As his mouth opened wide for another silent scream, a snake slipped into it and down his throat.

They were everywhere now, in his mouth, his nose, his ears, burrowing and slithering. They plucked out his eyes and crawled through the empty cavities into his brain. More and more of them entered his body, filling him until he was bloated and felt as if he were going to explode and shower snakes all over the burning rock on which he was imprisoned. . . .

Shrieking, he threw off the sleeping robes and lunged up, but Sacred Paint's strong arms caught him before he came all the way to his feet.

"Owl!" she cried as she held him tightly. "What is it? What is wrong?"

Relief seeped in around the edges of the terror. It was a dream, he realized, only a dream. He was not filled with evil black snakes.

And yet, dreams always held meaning for those who knew how to interpret them, and Owl was certain what this one signified. Trembling and drenched with sweat, he slipped out of Sacred Paint's arms and forced himself to stand.

"There will be a battle," he said. "Many people will die. That is what my dream meant."

"Tell me about the dream."

He shuddered to the depth of his being. "I cannot talk about it. But I must speak to Many Otters and warn him."

"You can tell your dream to Many Otters, but not to me?"

Owl shook his head, as if to free it from the weird vision. "I will never tell anyone what came to me in my dream. I will speak only of what it means, and this I have already told you. The Pawnee and the white soldiers will come to attack us."

Sacred Paint accepted his explanation. She knew of the visions and dreams that sometimes came to Owl. "Go," she said. "Hurry to the lodge of Many Otters. If there is to be an attack, the town must be ready."

A bit steadier on his feet now, Owl left the lodge. His steps took him quickly toward the lodge of Many Otters. The sky to the east was faintly tinged with gray. Dawn approached but was still an hour or more distant.

Many Otters was not happy about being awakened, but his attitude changed quickly when Owl explained what had brought him there. "I never trusted the Pawnee. We must be ready for the attack."

Together the two men went through the village, waking the warriors and warning them of trouble. Many Otters never questioned the meaning of Owl's dream, and Owl was grateful for his trust. By the time the gray sky was turning red, everyone had been alerted, and warriors, kneeling in the tall grass surrounding the town, watched for any sign of attack.

Owl could see that the fires in the camp of the white men had died down almost to nothing. The camp appeared to be asleep.

What if he was wrong? he asked himself. What if the dream had really held some other meaning? He was well respected among these people, and he knew that none would think ill of him for voicing a fear that turned out to be a false alarm. But he would still have preferred to be wrong. Vindication of his prophecy was not worth a battle in which lives would be lost.

"All is peaceful," Many Otters said to Owl as they stood in front of the chief's lodge. "There have been no cries of warning from our sentries. Do you still think there will be an attack, Brother Owl?"

"I do not know," Owl said with a sigh. "The meaning of the dream seemed so clear—"

A strangled cry from the south broke the early-morning stillness.

Most of the guards had been posted to the north, between the town and the camp of the white men. But someone—Cries for War, no doubt—must have anticipated that. The attack would come from the south, and the death cry of the sentry was the signal for it to begin.

Cries for War and the other Pawnee scouts were in the vanguard. They rose out of the tall grass and charged toward the town, whooping and shooting rifles. Behind them, riding up out of a ravine, came the bluecoats. In the shadowy light of approaching dawn, Owl realized he had made a terrible mistake. Instead of waiting, he and the warriors of the town should have launched their own attack.

But it was too late for that now, and defense was the only possible course. Owl dashed toward his lodge, taking an arrow from the quiver on his back and nocking it as he ran. As he neared the lodge he saw Sacred Paint emerge, Little Black Bear cradled in her arms. She looked frightened.

"Inside!" Owl shouted at her. "Get back inside the lodge!"

At that moment a Pawnee with a lance darted around the lodge from the other side, and Sacred Paint screamed. The Pawnee drew back his arm and poised, ready to throw the lance.

Too far away to reach the man before he released the lance, Owl dropped to one knee and aimed for only an instant before letting fly with the arrow. The shaft whistled through the air and struck the Pawnee in the left side, just below the arm. The man stumbled and fell against the lodge, dropping the lance. He crumpled to his knees and fumbled with the arrow embedded in his body. By that time, however, Owl had reached him and was swinging the war club he had pulled from behind the belt of his leggings. The stone head crushed the Pawnee's skull with an ugly sound.

"Stay inside!" Owl said to Sacred Paint. He caught a glimpse of her frightened face, and then she disappeared, along with the wailing infant.

Owl nocked an arrow and whirled around, spotting Cries for War several lodges away. The Pawnee was holding a rifle, and smoke curled from its barrel. Owl loosed the arrow at him, but it sailed wide of its mark, and in the next instant Owl lost sight of him. Everywhere men were struggling in battle.

Soldiers rode through the village, slashing to right and left with their sabers. Owl saw a running woman go down under a blade and felt a sickness rise in his belly. *This is your fault,* he thought. If he and Sacred Paint had not come to live in this town, Cries for War might not have goaded the other scouts and the soldiers into an attack. Owl had no doubt his vengeful Pawnee brother-in-law had instigated this battle.

But such thoughts of blame served no purpose at the moment. What was important was driving off the invaders. Owl closed in hand-to-hand combat with another Pawnee warrior and soon batted aside the man's war club. Owl's club drove the Pawnee to the ground, then rose and fell in a killing stroke. Owl stumbled past the body and searched for another foe.

There was no shortage of them. Between the lodges were knots of grappling men and billows of smoke. Several lodges were on fire, the blazes set by Pawnee warriors brandishing torches. Despite his evil, Cries for War was a good leader in battle, Owl reluctantly admitted.

If not for Owl's dream and its grim warning, the attackers would have overrun a sleeping village, he knew. This would have been a massacre, and every man, woman, and child in the town would have died. As it was, the resistance put up by the Omaha-Ponca band was much greater than the whites and Pawnees had expected.

Owl caught sight of the lieutenant trying to control his wildly skittish mount. His face was streaked with crimson, and one leg of his uniform trousers was also stained black with blood. "Bugler, sound retreat!" the lieutenant was shouting. "Retreat, damn it!"

Owl's arrows were gone. He snatched up a lance from the ground where a warrior had dropped it and flung it at the officer.

The lieutenant's mount danced to one side, and the lance missed without the lieutenant knowing how close he had come to dying.

All the bluecoat riders were galloping away from the town, followed by the surviving Pawnees. Owl saw Cries for War among them, and a shout of sheer frustration welled up in his throat. The attackers might be fleeing, but pursuit was impossible. Too many townspeople had been killed, and some of the lodges were still burning. The fires had to be beaten out before they spread.

Owl turned toward his own lodge, and terror froze his throat. Smoke billowed and flames licked up around it. Owl broke into a run, shouting the names of his wife and son.

Sacred Paint burst out of the lodge clutching Little Black Bear against her breast. Both seemed unharmed. Owl held out his arms to them as he ran.

Far in the distance, a thunder-lance boomed. Owl saw his son's back arch as a heavy lead ball struck him. Then Sacred Paint was thrown backward as if she had run into a tree. She fell in the entrance of the burning lodge.

"No!" Owl cried. He darted forward and grabbed his wife's legs, pulling her and the baby away from the blaze. He dropped to his knees beside them. The sun was halfway over the horizon by now, and in its slanting, bloody light he saw the wound in Little Black Bear's back. Sacred Paint still held the child tightly. Her eyes were open, but they stared up sightlessly at the lightening sky. Owl sobbed as he pried her hands free and lifted the body of his son. The ball had passed through Little Black Bear and struck Sacred Paint in the chest. Both of them were dead.

Owl threw back his head and wailed to the heavens. He knew that the flintlocks of the white men were not accurate, and he had heard the distant shot that had killed his wife and child. For such a shot to strike them down at that range was almost impossible . . .

Unless some higher power had guided the ball.

Their deaths were a punishment to him, Owl thought. Somehow, in the arrogance of being human, he had offended the spirits, and his family had paid for what he had done.

A weight greater than any he would have thought possible crashed down on him, the weight of guilt. At that moment he would have done anything to bring Sacred Paint and Little Black Bear back to life, would gladly have bartered away his own soul. But there was nothing, nothing he could do.

Through his tears he watched the smoke from the burning lodges rise ever higher into the sky.

Chapter Fifty-three

Four Pawnee scouts and six bluecoats had been killed in the attack on the town of the Omaha-Ponca. The townspeople had suffered far greater losses: nearly half the warriors, and many women and children. The survivors buried their dead and mourned long and loudly.

The bodies of the enemy were thrown into a ravine and burned with piles of brush heaped atop them.

Through the ordeal Owl suffered like one who was dead himself. He thought nothing, felt nothing. Others sang and prayed for the spirits of his departed ones, for he was not capable of performing the rituals himself. Many Otters, who had survived the battle, said to him, "You have brought us the Sacred Pole and made us believe once more in the old ways. You have given us the strength to endure this terrible time, Brother Owl."

But who would give *him* strength? His own lay buried with his wife and son.

The body of Cries for War had not been among the dead, and Owl had no way of knowing if the Pawnee had been wounded. In a way, in his more lucid moments, he hoped that Cries for War was still alive. If he were, then perhaps someday the Creator would give Owl a chance to redeem himself by presenting him once more with the opportunity to kill his hated enemy.

The soldiers were gone; they had broken camp and headed west, taking Daniel Dupree with them. Owl did not know if the fur trader had betrayed what had seemed to be a newfound trust, or if the soldiers and the Pawnee had acted on their own. None of it mattered. Sacred Paint and Little Black Bear were still dead.

How hollow man's boasting! How proud he was of being lord and master of all he surveyed! Those thoughts went through Owl's mind as he stared out at the plains days after the burial. How foolish and ignorant . . . that was the truth. Most people never realized how fragile their happiness and their very lives were. But Owl knew.

As that certainty grew the numbness that had paralyzed him receded. With its departure came the pain of loss. Cries for War had tortured the bodies of Captain Standard and the Osage scouts, yet the torment he had unleashed on Owl was worse—he had not given Owl the blessed release of death.

Owl's lodge had been destroyed by the fire, but even if it had not been, he could not have stayed there, not with all its reminders of what he had lost. He wrapped a robe around himself each night and walked to the edge of the town, then sat cross-legged on the ground until exhaustion claimed him and he toppled on his side.

Five nights after the burial, Many Otters came to Owl and knelt beside him. "We are leaving this place."

"You will abandon the town?" Owl asked dully.

"There is another band of our people two days' walk from here. We will join them. Will you come with us?"

Owl did not have an answer. Leaving was the best thing the Omaha-Ponca could do; he did not doubt that. But where was *his* place now?

A breeze from the prairie brushed his face, and he seemed to hear a voice calling his name. Was it old Storm Seeker summoning him? Because of the visions they had shared, Owl had always felt a special bond with his ancestor. Oblivious to Many Otters, he rose to his feet and let the robe slip from his shoulders. He walked out onto the grass-carpeted plain.

"Brother Owl!" Many Otters called from behind him. "Where are you going?"

Owl did not answer. Instead he followed the call on the wind.

"When you come back, we will not be here," Many Otters cried. "But you can find us. You will always have a home among us!"

No, Owl thought, there would never be a home for him again
. . . except the boundless prairie with its grass that waved in the
silvery moonlight.

He strode on through the night.

Owl did not know how long he had been on the plain, how
long since he had eaten or slaked his thirst. The sun had risen,
gone down, risen again, and still he walked on. He had seen no
people since leaving the town, and even the animals seemed to
have deserted the prairie. He was alone on the rolling, open
grassland.

The sight of something rising from the ground far in front of
him shocked him so much that he stopped in his tracks for several moments and stared at it.

The thing was a tree, a cedar tree, the source of the Sacred
Pole. No cedar trees stood alone in the middle of the prairie.
After a moment he realized that he was experiencing another
vision.

"No! Go away!" he muttered. Visions had never brought him
anything but danger and death. The spirits had betrayed him, and
he had no wish to see anything they might want to show him
now. He closed his eyes and covered his face with his hands.

But when at last he lowered his arms and opened his eyes
again, the tree still stood there, mocking and beckoning to him at
the same time. He let out a sob, then stumbled on toward the
cedar. He was caught in the grip of the spirits, compelled to
cooperate.

When finally he stood before the tree, he looked up at its green
branches and shouted, "What do you want? Have you not asked
enough of me? What would you have me do now?"

He heard a flapping of wings, and a bird flew out of the east,
soaring majestically. Owl threw up his hand to shade his eyes
from the glare of the sun. The bird glided to the top of the cedar
tree and alighted there gracefully, then looked down at him. *A
Thunder Bird, a thing of legend.* Though the sky was clear, Owl
heard the distant rumble that gave the bird its name. He fell to his
knees in awe.

Then the Thunder Bird spoke words to him.

* * *

For four days Brother Owl remained by the cedar tree. Each day, the Thunder Bird flew to the tree and spoke to him. The first day, it had come from the east. The second day, it appeared out of the north; the third day from the south; the fourth day from the west. Brother Owl listened intently as the Thunder Bird spoke, his pain and sorrow slipping away. The memories of Sacred Paint and Little Black Bear would be with him always, but now he turned his eyes toward the future.

Once again the Giver of Breath and others of the spirits had spoken to him, this time through the Thunder Bird, and again he knew what he must do.

Many Otters heard the shouting of the children and went to see what was exciting them. As a chief and a respected man, he had been given a good lodge in this new town where his people had come to make their new lives. Most of the inhabitants in the town were Iowa, but they had welcomed their Omaha and Ponca brothers. Many moons had passed since the attack by the American soldiers and the Pawnee scouts.

A rider was coming into the town, Many Otters saw as he left his new lodge. Children and dogs were running around the man's horse. At first glance Many Otters saw something familiar about the stranger, but he had to look again to recognize Owl. The young man was carrying a lance and wearing a wolfskin war robe, a slit cut in the pelt behind the neck so that he could wear it over his head. The wolf's head rested on Owl's chest, and the rest of the skin hung loosely down his back.

"Brother Owl?" Many Otters said as he came up to the mounted man.

"I am Thunder Bird," the man said. "I have come to find who will ride with me."

People from the town were gathering around him. One man called, "Ride where with you, Thunder Bird?"

The warrior lifted the lance he grasped in his right hand. "To drive the invaders from our land! All invaders, white and red alike! This is the land of the Prairie People! We will not be defeated!"

Shouts and grunts of agreement came from the men clustered

around this strange warrior. Many Otters swallowed and said, "You are talking about war."

Thunder Bird looked at him, and all traces of Brother Owl vanished. "Then war it will be."

When he rode away from the town later that day, a score of warriors went with him. Many Otters watched them go, and although he was not a man given to visions, for a moment he thought he saw the rich, tall green grass of the prairie turn red.

Chapter Fifty-four

September 1848

I am getting too old for this, Maximilian Adolphus thought as he brushed aside the canvas flap over the entrance of his tent and stepped outside. The morning air had a chill in it, although it was barely autumn. On the northern plains just a few hundred miles east of the great mountains, summer was sweet but fleeting.

Somewhat like life itself, Max mused as he stretched stiff muscles. It was almost impossible to believe that forty years had passed since he had first come to the American West. Forty years . . . more: a long time, yet it seemed like yesterday when he had first gazed out upon the prairie.

Since then he had visited the west so many times he had lost track of the number. His sketches and paintings of this land were known the world over, as were the books Prince Otto Wilhelm had written about their journeys together.

Otto was gone now, of course, and had been for over a decade. But Max kept returning to this land anyway, answering its sweet, dangerous siren call. He had painted portraits of the crowned heads of Europe, and his work had made him wealthy. He had a fine home in Vienna, a loving—and patient—wife, children, and grandchildren. Any sane man would have simply sat back and enjoyed the time he had left upon this earth.

Yet here he was, standing on a chilly, windswept hillside, breathing in the aromas of coffee and bacon and distant evergreens and finding them the most exquisite perfume in the world.

"The chief ought to be here soon," the buckskin-clad man kneeling beside the campfire said. "He said he'd come see you this morning."

"Thank you, Nate," Max said. He moved over to the fire and took the cup of coffee the man handed up to him. Its warmth felt good on his fingers. *Have to keep the fingers from stiffening up,* he told himself. They were still the tools of an artist.

Several other men in buckskins bustled around the camp. Max had hired them in St. Louis. All had worked for him on previous expeditions. They handled the wagons, hunted for fresh meat, and provided protection when the party encountered hostiles. That was rare; Max was widely known among the Plains tribes, and highly regarded. His paintings showed the truth of the people's lives, and they appreciated that.

Of course, just because they would not harm him and his companions did not mean all the Indians he encountered were peaceful. The man he was to meet today, in fact, was a war chief who had fought a long and bloody war against the army.

"Here he comes," Nate said, breaking into Max's thoughts.

Max looked up and saw a lone figure riding over the rolling hills toward the camp. As the rider drew nearer Max could make out the many-feathered war hat. "He's alone," Max said, surprised.

Nate Stanton spat into the fire. "I wouldn't reckon on that. There's probably a hundred or more Indians watching us right now. It's just that we can't see them."

"Well, we're not here to cause trouble. They'll have no reason to molest us."

"Reckon you're right. I never saw anybody the redskins get along with better than you, Mr. Adolphus."

Max stood by the fire and watched the chief ride up to the camp. The warrior pulled his paint horse to a halt and sat for a moment solemnly regarding Max's party. Then he threw a leg over the back of the horse and slid easily to the ground.

My God, he's an impressive figure! Max thought. Though not overly tall, the chief was heavily muscled and imbued with an air of vigor despite his age. He was almost as old as Max. A buffalo robe was thrown over his shoulder, but his chest was bare. Max saw the battle scars there, and on the chief's face. His arms were covered with tattoos, which Max knew to be marks of distinction. This man was one of the most revered—and feared—warriors of the plains.

"I am Thunder Bird," the chief said, his voice deep and resonant. "I have come to speak with the one who paints true pictures." His English was surprisingly good.

"I am Maximilian Adolphus," Max said, "and it is an honor to meet you, Thunder Bird."

For a second he thought he saw a smile flicker across Thunder Bird's face, although such an expression would have been out of place on the stern, forbidding countenance. But there was no mistaking the lighter tone in the chief's voice as he said, "We meet—for the second time, Max."

Max's eyes widened, and he stared in shock at Thunder Bird. His mouth opened, but for a long moment his lips and tongue refused to work. Finally, as the years peeled away in his memory and he saw for an instant the young man within the elder who stood before him, he whispered, "Brother Owl?"

"No one has called me by that name for nearly forty summers." Thunder Bird stepped forward and extended his hand. Instinctively Max clasped wrists with him. "It is good to see you again, old friend."

"I can hardly believe it. Brother Owl . . . is the infamous Thunder Bird? But how—?"

"We will sit and talk, and I will tell you the story."

"I have carried the memory of Sacred Paint and Little Black Bear in my heart since that day," Thunder Bird said, "but I have taken two more wives and fathered four children."

Max looked directly into the eyes of his old friend. "I believed you to be dead. I spoke to Daniel Dupree several years after the attack, at his trading post on the upper Missouri, and he thought you had been killed in the fighting. For whatever it may be worth, Dupree tried to stop Cries for War and that eager young lieutenant from attacking your town."

"Where is Dupree now?"

"Gone. Taken off by a fever, or so I heard." Max sighed. "Life is difficult out here on the frontier, as you probably know much better than I."

"Difficult, yes," Thunder Bird said. "But it is my home, and I will never leave it."

"In a way, neither will I."

Max's assistants had withdrawn a short distance so that he and Thunder Bird could sit by the fire and speak privately. A few moments of companionable silence passed, then Max said, "Did you ever find Cries for War?"

"He and I met again," Thunder Bird said slowly. "He continued to scout for the American army, and he was with the bluecoats when we fought them on the high bluffs. I was unhorsed in the battle, and he thought to dash out my brains with his war club as he rode past me. But I caught his arm and threw him off his horse. Then we fought, hand to hand."

Max leaned forward, caught up in the story. "Did he know you?"

"Not at first, though I knew him as soon as I saw his face. He put his lance here"—Thunder Bird touched a white scar on his upper chest—"and I broke his arm with my club. His knife tore my leg, and I fell. But I took hold of his throat and pulled him down with me. We rolled over and over on the ground, but at last he was beneath me and I was able to keep him there. I put my face close to his and said, 'Before I was Thunder Bird, I was Brother Owl, husband of Sacred Paint and father of Little Black Bear.' Then I broke his neck."

Max shuddered. "He deserved it."

Thunder Bird said, "In truth, he did. Now I would smoke a pipe with you and tell you of my vision, Max."

"I would like that very much."

They smoked, and Thunder Bird spoke of the vision that had given him his name. "From that day until now, I have been a warrior. I have fought to drive from this land anyone foolish enough to try to take it from the Prairie People."

Max hesitated. "But surely you have to know that you cannot win, Owl—I mean, Thunder Bird. There are too many white soldiers, and already the great buffalo herds have begun to grow smaller. I hate to say it, but sooner or later your people's way of life will be gone."

"I know," Thunder Bird said. "I have known this since the vision came to me. In my heart I knew it even before that."

Max asked, "But if you know, why have you done all the things you've done?"

"My people will lose this fight. *This* fight. But my vision showed me other things." Thunder Bird lifted his eyes and looked into the distance. "The people will lose the fight, but they will live on. New generations will come, many summers from now, and they will rise upon the memory of our time and reclaim their place at the breast of Mother Earth. They will fight and win *then* because we fight and lose *now*. They are of a time and a people as yet unborn."

Max sat in silence for a moment, thinking about what Thunder Bird had said and hoping that his old friend was correct. When he spoke again, he said, "I would like to paint your portrait again. We have to leave soon, before winter sets in, but I think I can stay long enough to do that."

Thunder Bird smiled wanly. "I thought you might. I have time, too. The battles will wait. I will pose for you. But before you begin, I would give you something."

He stood up, went to his horse, and took down a parfleche that was slung on the back of the animal. He handed it to Max, who took it and let his fingertips play over the old, cracked buffalo hide. "Is this . . . ?"

"The story skins," Thunder Bird said. "I want you to take the ones written by old Black Robe and keep them. You can sketch the others, so that the story of my true people—the story of the Crane band—can be shared with others as we told it. Will you do this?"

Max was nearly overcome by emotion. He swallowed hard. "I . . . will share it with the whole world."

"Thank you, Max. You are a good friend." Thunder Bird walked to the crest of the hillside and turned to face Max, crossing his arms over his chest and lifting his chin. The sun shone on his face, and the autumn wind lifted his braids and ruffled the feathers of his magnificent war hat. "How is this, old magician friend?"

"Fine," Max said, blinking away the tears that suddenly threatened to blind him. "Just fine, Brother Owl." He went to retrieve his easel, canvas, and paints, but paused and glanced over his shoulder at Thunder Bird, who seemed strong enough to stand there forever. Like the rippling grass and the jutting hills, he was part of the prairie.

And he always would be.